POKÉMON™ ADVENTURES
RUBY & SAPPHIRE

Pokémon ADVENTURES
Ruby and Sapphire
Volume 15
Perfect Square Edition

Story by HIDENORI KUSAKA
Art by SATOSHI YAMAMOTO

English Adaptation/Bryant Turnage
Translation/Tetsuichiro Miyaki
Touch-up & Lettering/Annaliese Christman
Design/Shawn Carrico
Editor/Annette Roman

Printed in the U.S.A.

Published by VIZ Media, LLC
P.O. Box 77010
San Francisco, CA 94107

10 9 8 7 6 5 4 3
First printing, March 2013
Third printing, August 2016

PERFECT SQUARE
www.perfectsquare.com

VIZ media
www.viz.com

RATED A FOR ALL AGES
PARENTAL ADVISORY
POKÉMON ADVENTURES is rated A and is suitable for readers of all ages.
ratings.viz.com

POKÉMON™ ADVENTURES
RUBY & SAPPHIRE

Story by
Hidenori Kusaka
Art by
Satoshi Yamamoto

15
VOLUME FIFTEEN

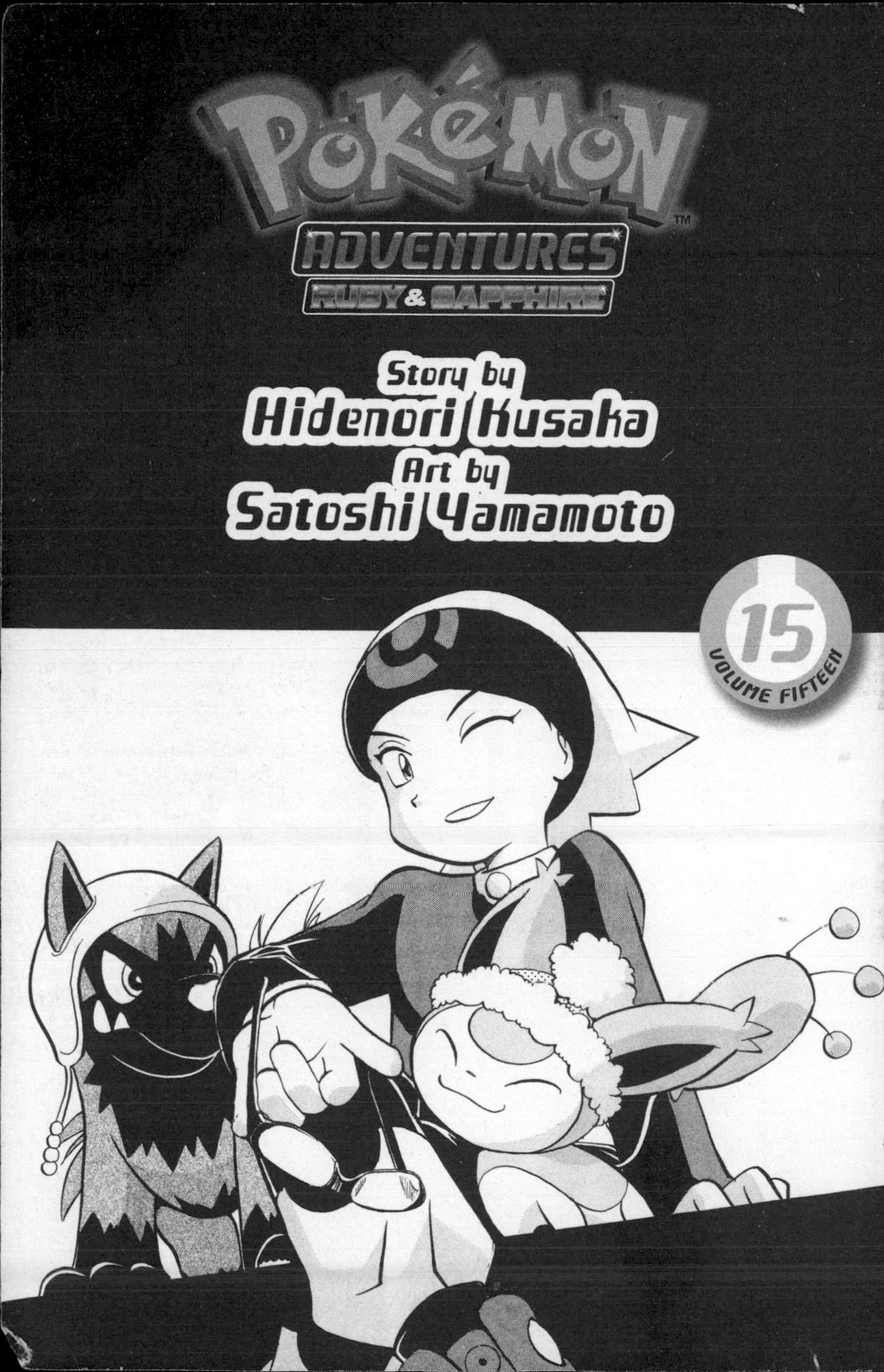

Chapter

Sapphire

Professor Birch

A Hoenn region Pokémon researcher.

Our Story So Far...

Some place in some time... in the Hoenn region. A young boy named Ruby moves to Hoenn from Johto. His dream? To be a Pokémon Contest champion, winning competitions in which Pokémon are compared in five categories: coolness, beauty, cuteness, smartness and toughness!

Ruby

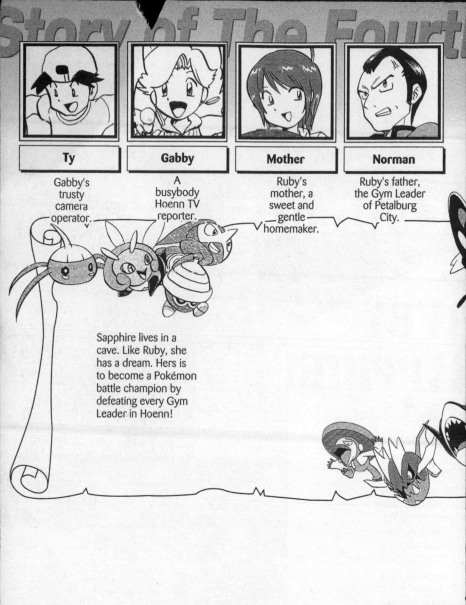

Ty	Gabby	Mother	Norman

Gabby's trusty camera operator.

A busybody Hoenn TV reporter.

Ruby's mother, a sweet and gentle homemaker.

Ruby's father, the Gym Leader of Petalburg City.

Sapphire lives in a cave. Like Ruby, she has a dream. Hers is to become a Pokémon battle champion by defeating every Gym Leader in Hoenn!

POKÉMON
ADVENTURES
RUBY & SAPPHIRE

CONTENTS

15
VOLUME FIFTEEN

RUBY SAPPHIRE

ADVENTURE 181
Creeping Past Cacnea...........................8

ADVENTURE 182
Making Mirth with Mightyena...........19

ADVENTURE 183
Trying to Trounce Torchic.................38

ADVENTURE 184
Distracting Dustox 52

ADVENTURE 185
Nixing Nuzleaf.................................71

ADVENTURE 186
Brushing Past Breloom......................79

ADVENTURE 187
Tongue-Tied Kecleon.........................87

ADVENTURE 188
Lombre Larceny 103

ADVENTURE 189
Mowing Down Ludicolo.................. 112

ADVENTURE 190
Blowing Past Nosepass I 125

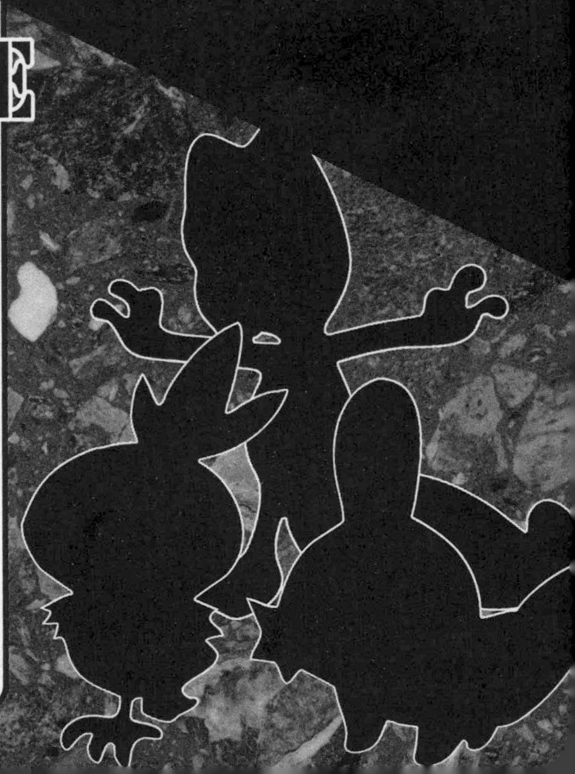

The Fourth Chapter

Pokémon Adventures

The Fourth Chapter

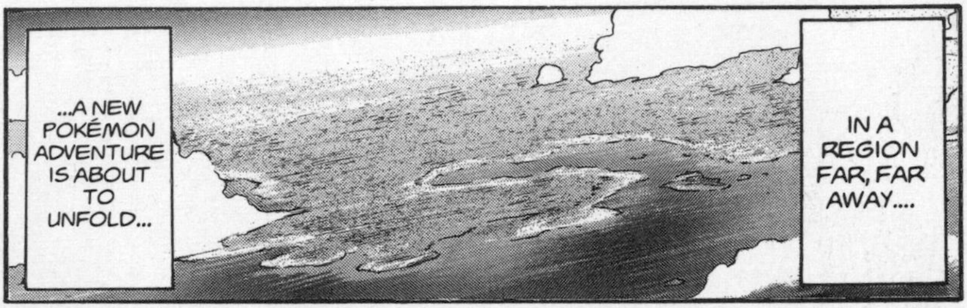
IN A REGION FAR, FAR AWAY....
...A NEW POKÉMON ADVENTURE IS ABOUT TO UNFOLD...

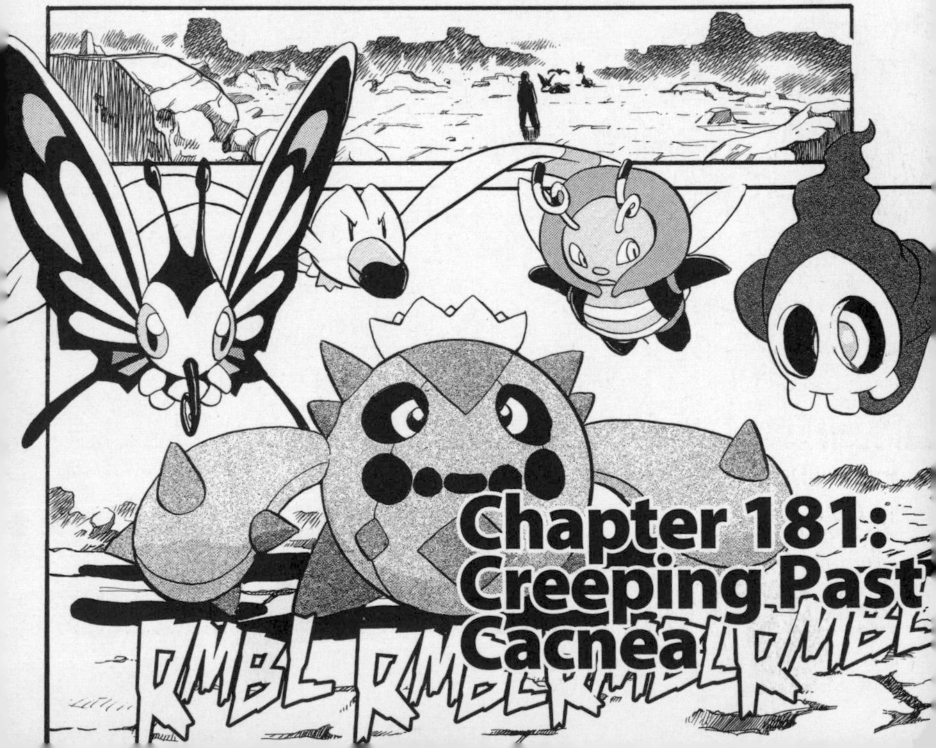
RMBL RMBL RMBL RMBL

Chapter 181: Creeping Past Cacnea

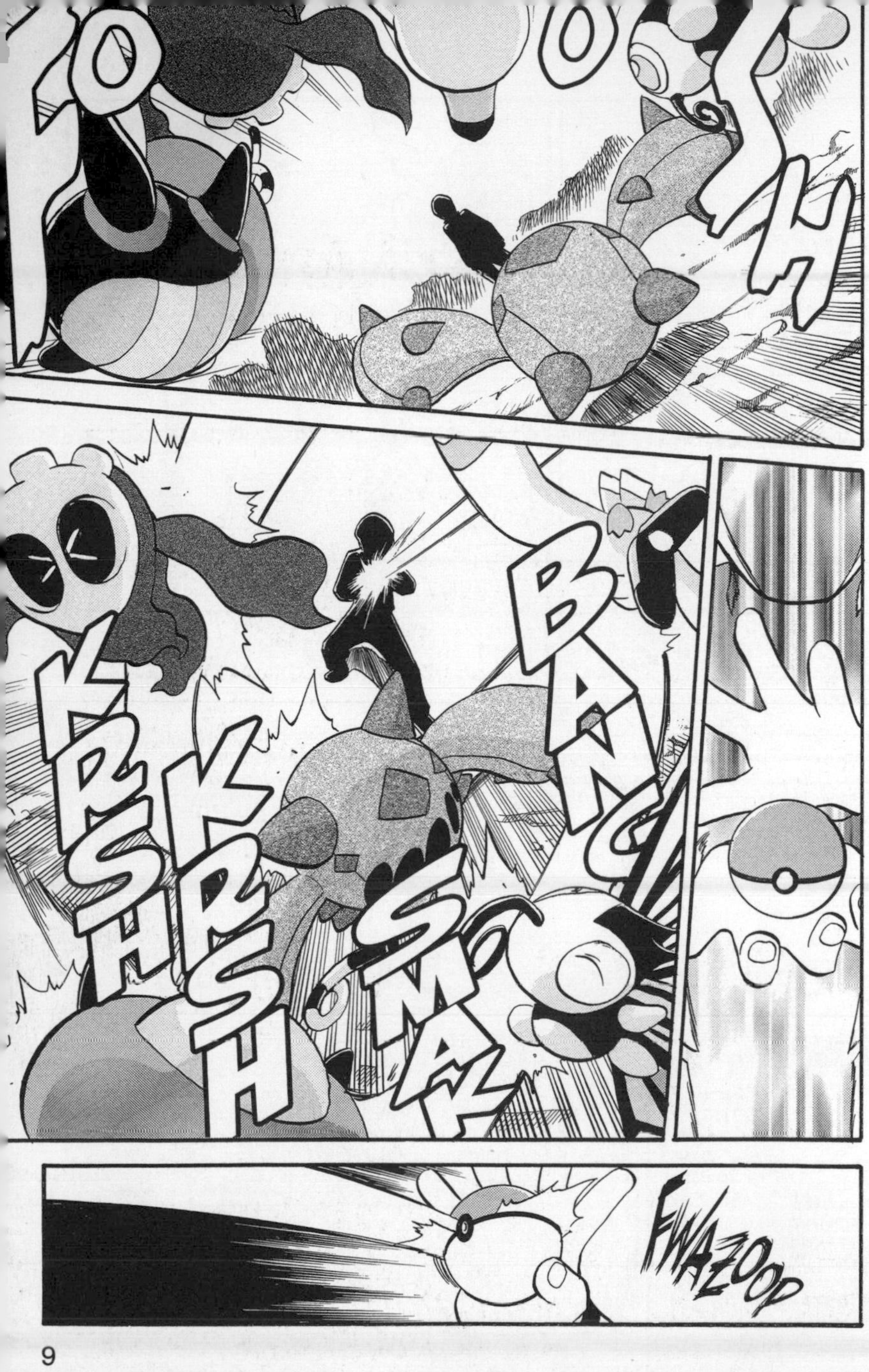
BANG
SMAK
KRSH
KRSH
FWAZOOOP

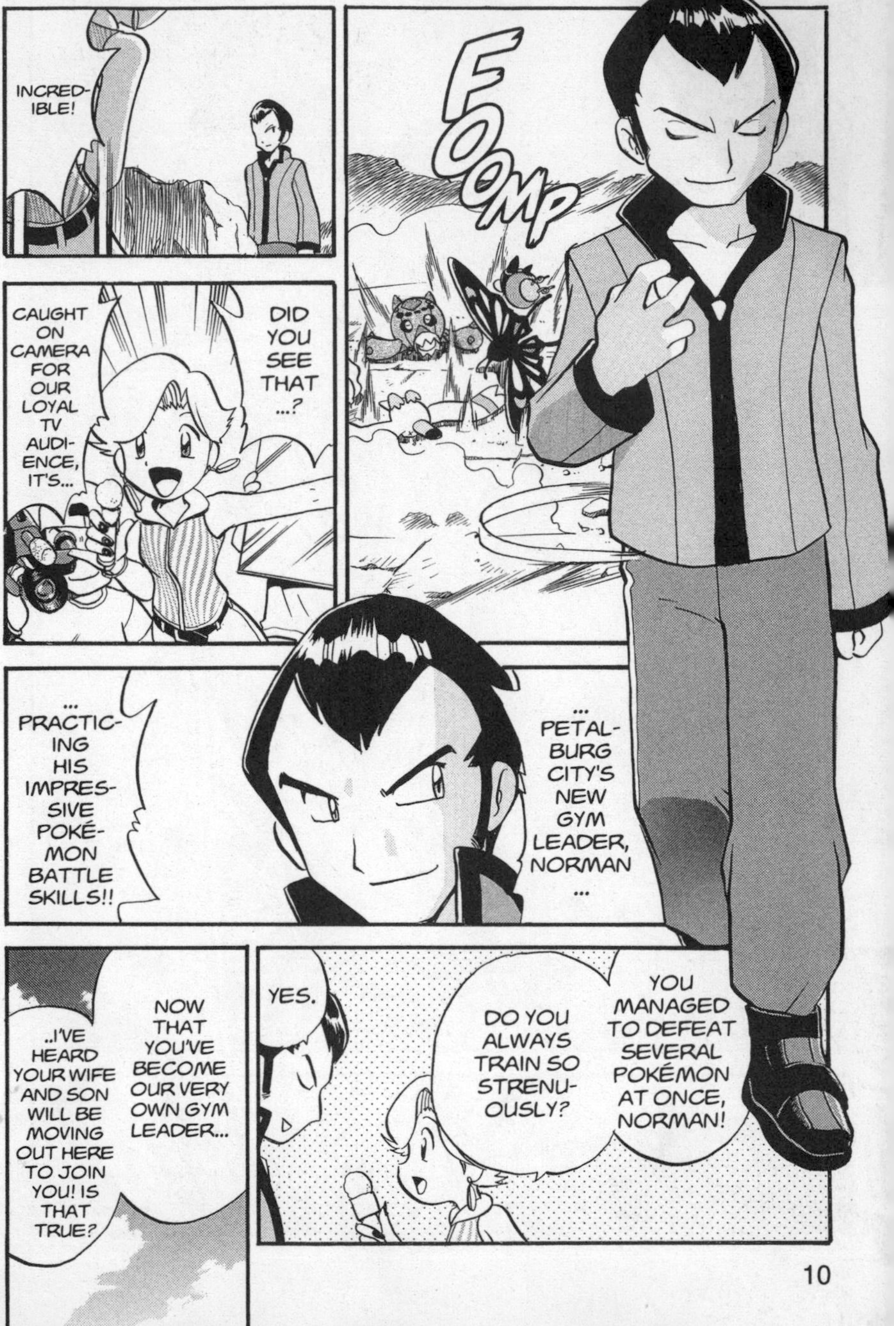
FOOMP
INCREDIBLE!
DID YOU SEE THAT ...?
CAUGHT ON CAMERA FOR OUR LOYAL TV AUDIENCE, IT'S...
... PETALBURG CITY'S NEW GYM LEADER, NORMAN ...
... PRACTICING HIS IMPRESSIVE POKÉMON BATTLE SKILLS!!
YOU MANAGED TO DEFEAT SEVERAL POKÉMON AT ONCE, NORMAN!
DO YOU ALWAYS TRAIN SO STRENUOUSLY?
YES.
NOW THAT YOU'VE BECOME OUR VERY OWN GYM LEADER...
..I'VE HEARD YOUR WIFE AND SON WILL BE MOVING OUT HERE TO JOIN YOU! IS THAT TRUE?

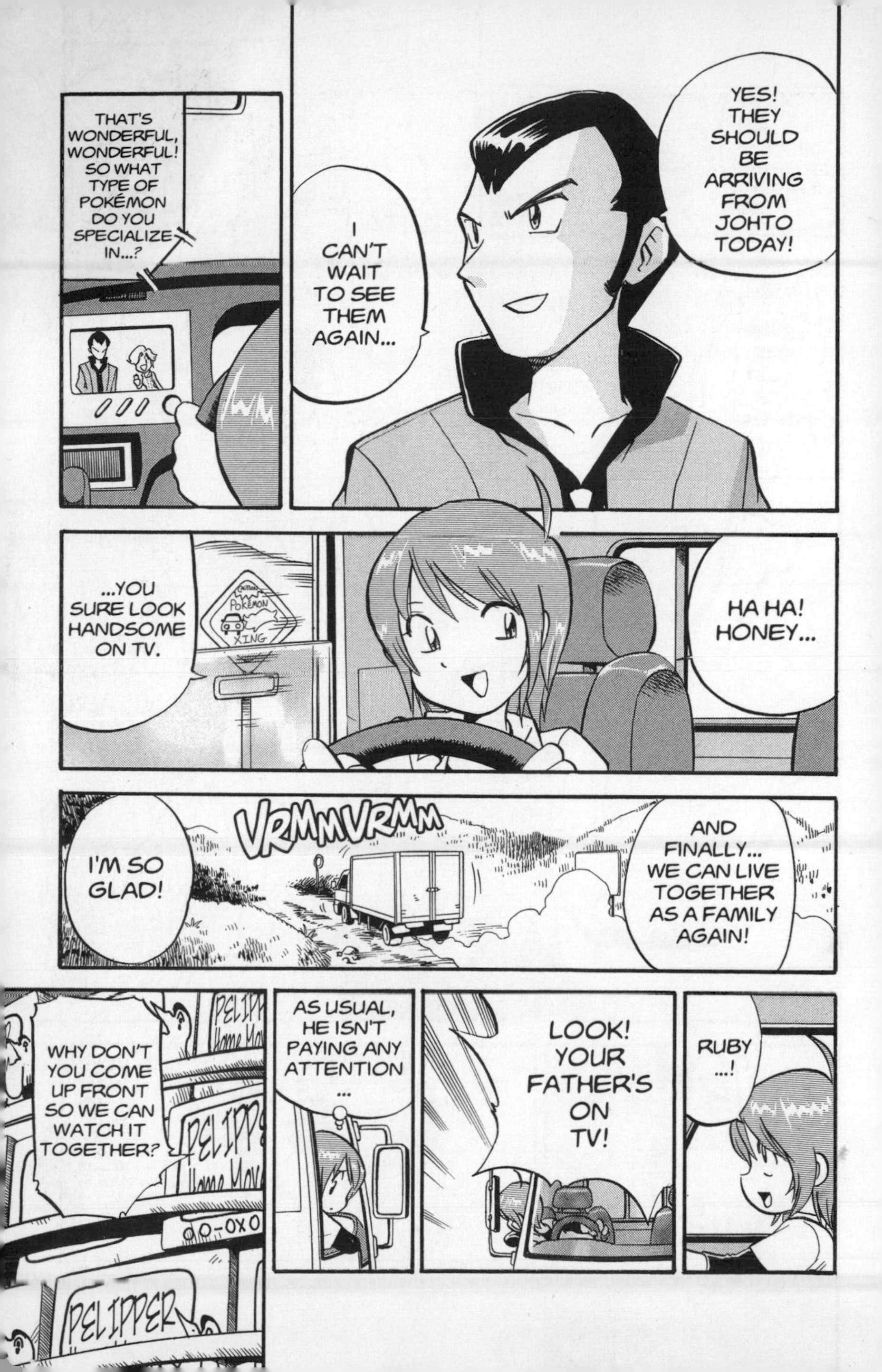
YES! THEY SHOULD BE ARRIVING FROM JOHTO TODAY!
I CAN'T WAIT TO SEE THEM AGAIN...
THAT'S WONDERFUL, WONDERFUL! SO WHAT TYPE OF POKÉMON DO YOU SPECIALIZE IN...?
HA HA! HONEY...
...YOU SURE LOOK HANDSOME ON TV.
POKÉMON XING
AND FINALLY... WE CAN LIVE TOGETHER AS A FAMILY AGAIN!
VRMMVRMM
I'M SO GLAD!
RUBY...!
LOOK! YOUR FATHER'S ON TV!
AS USUAL, HE ISN'T PAYING ANY ATTENTION...
WHY DON'T YOU COME UP FRONT SO WE CAN WATCH IT TOGETHER?
PELIPPER

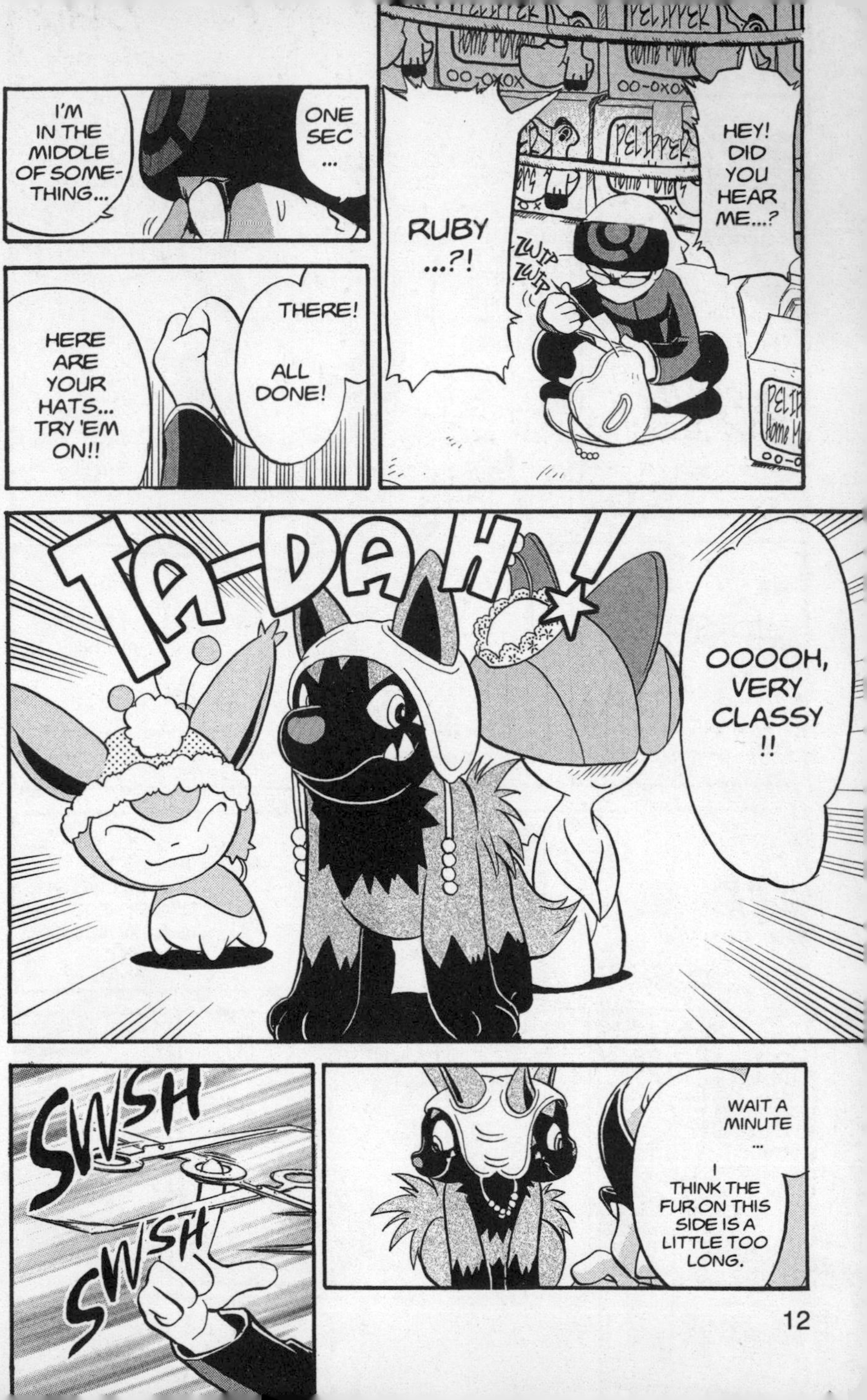
PELIPPER
OO-OXOX
HEY! DID YOU HEAR ME...?
RUBY ...?!
ZWIP ZWIP
ONE SEC ...
I'M IN THE MIDDLE OF SOME-THING...
THERE!
ALL DONE!
HERE ARE YOUR HATS... TRY 'EM ON!!
TA-DAH!
OOOOH, VERY CLASSY!!
WAIT A MINUTE ...
I THINK THE FUR ON THIS SIDE IS A LITTLE TOO LONG.
SWSH
SWSH

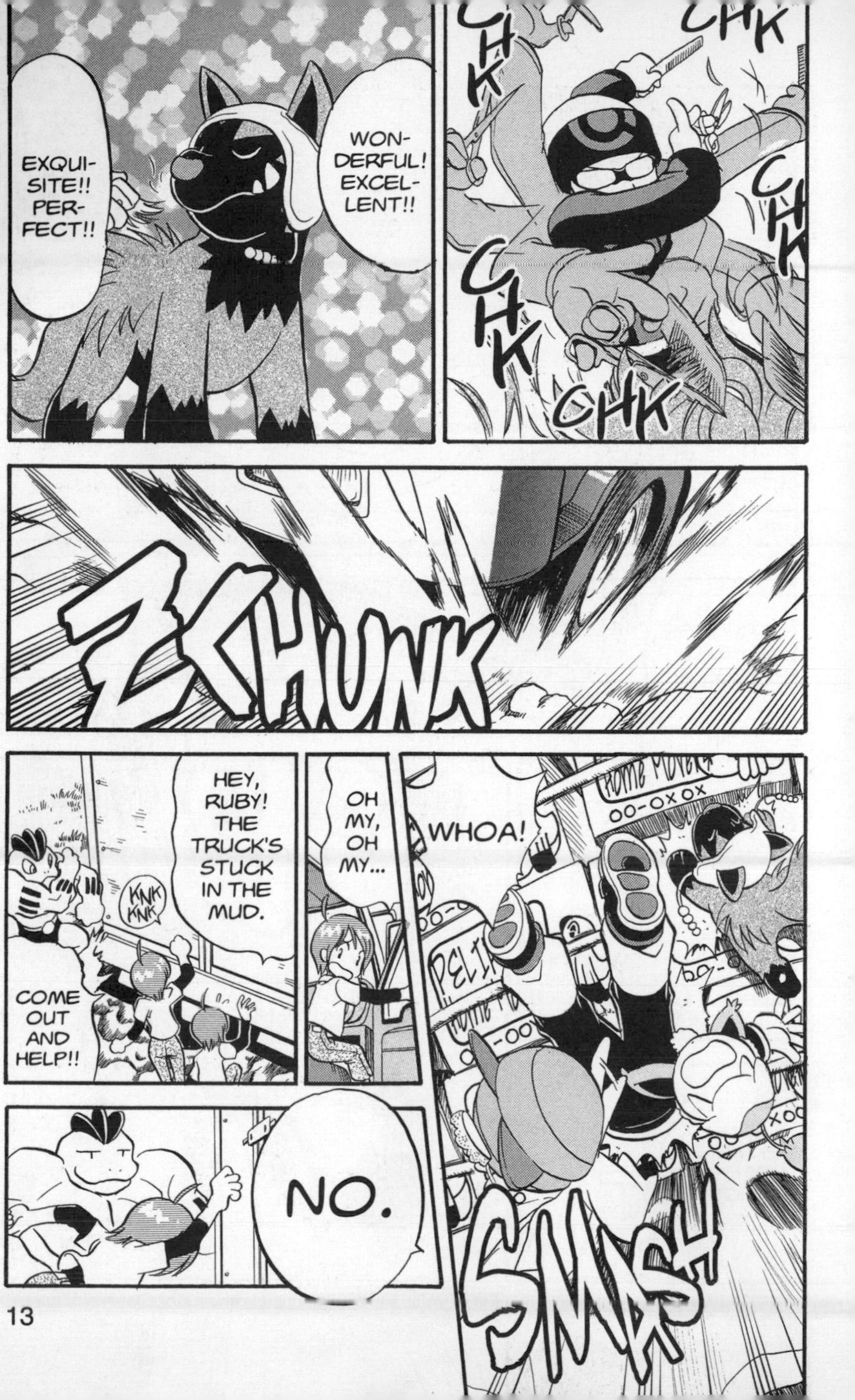
CHK
CHK
CHK
CHK
CHK
WON-DERFUL! EXCEL-LENT!!
EXQUI-SITE!! PER-FECT!!
ZCHUNK
WHOA!
OO-OXOX
SMASH
OH MY, OH MY...
HEY, RUBY! THE TRUCK'S STUCK IN THE MUD.
KNK KNK
COME OUT AND HELP!!
NO.

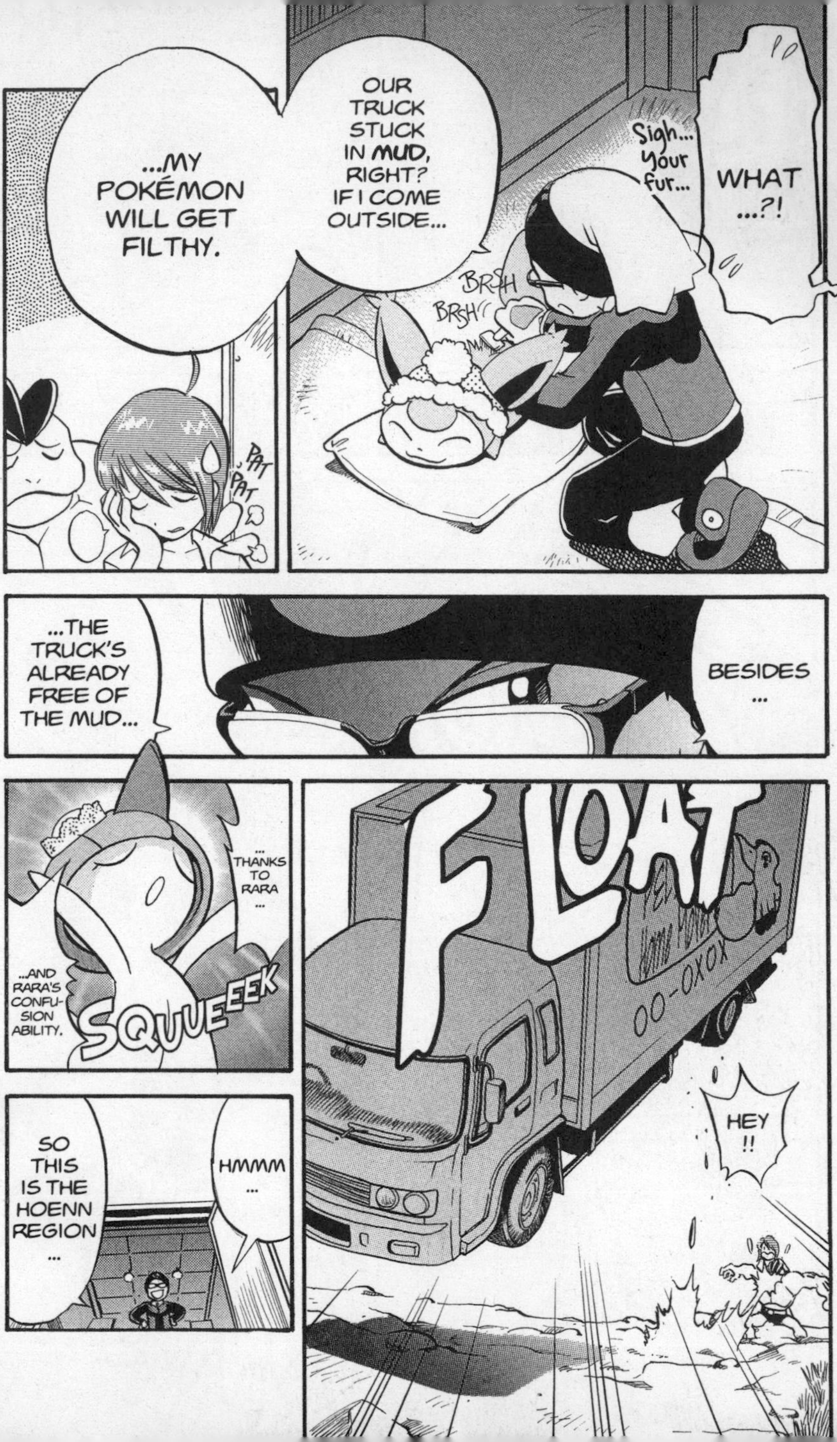

WHAT ...?!
Sigh... your fur...
OUR TRUCK STUCK IN MUD, RIGHT? IF I COME OUTSIDE...
BRSH
BRSH
...MY POKÉMON WILL GET FILTHY.
PAT PAT
BESIDES ...
...THE TRUCK'S ALREADY FREE OF THE MUD...
FLOAT
HEY !!
... THANKS TO RARA ...
...AND RARA'S CONFUSION ABILITY.
SQUUEEEK
HMMM ...
SO THIS IS THE HOENN REGION ...

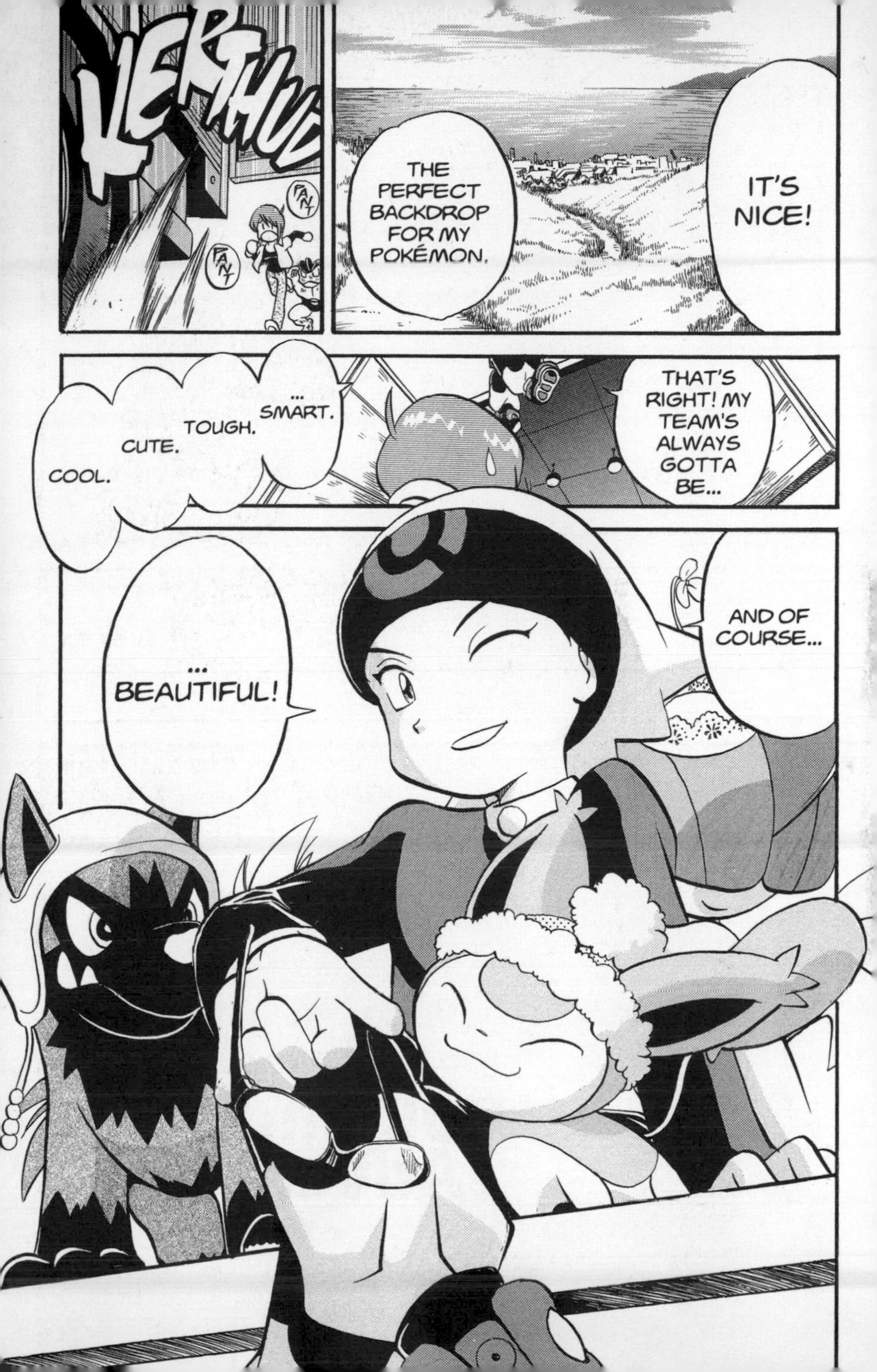

IT'S NICE!
THE PERFECT BACKDROP FOR MY POKÉMON.
KERTHUD
PANT
PANT
THAT'S RIGHT! MY TEAM'S ALWAYS GOTTA BE...
COOL. CUTE. TOUGH. ...SMART.
AND OF COURSE...
...BEAUTIFUL!

Pokémon Adventures
The Fourth Chapter

Chapter 182: Making Mirth with Mightyena

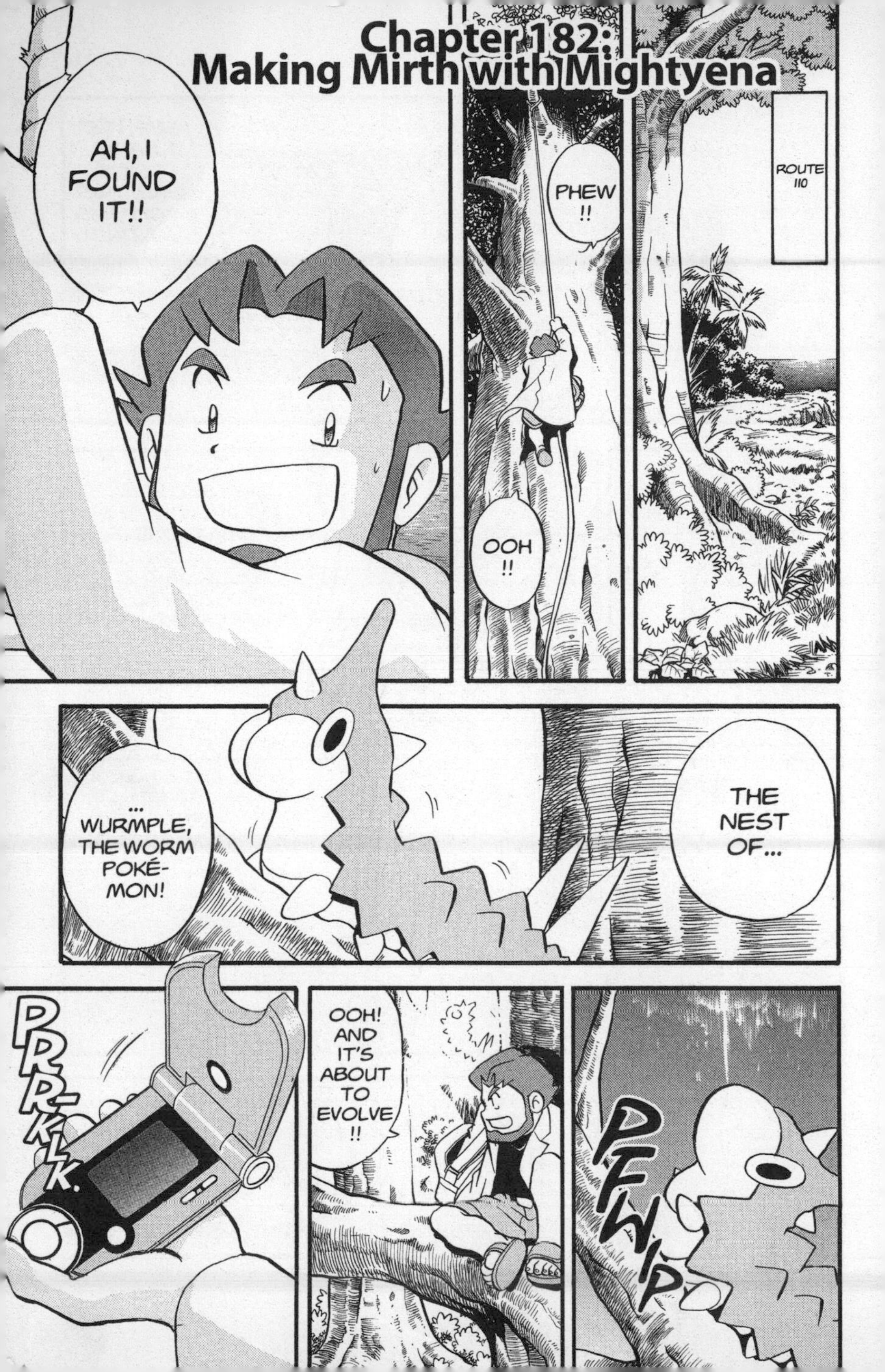

ROUTE 110
PHEW !!
OOH !!
AH, I FOUND IT!!
THE NEST OF...
... WURMPLE, THE WORM POKÉMON!
PEWIP
OOH! AND IT'S ABOUT TO EVOLVE !!
PRR-KLK.

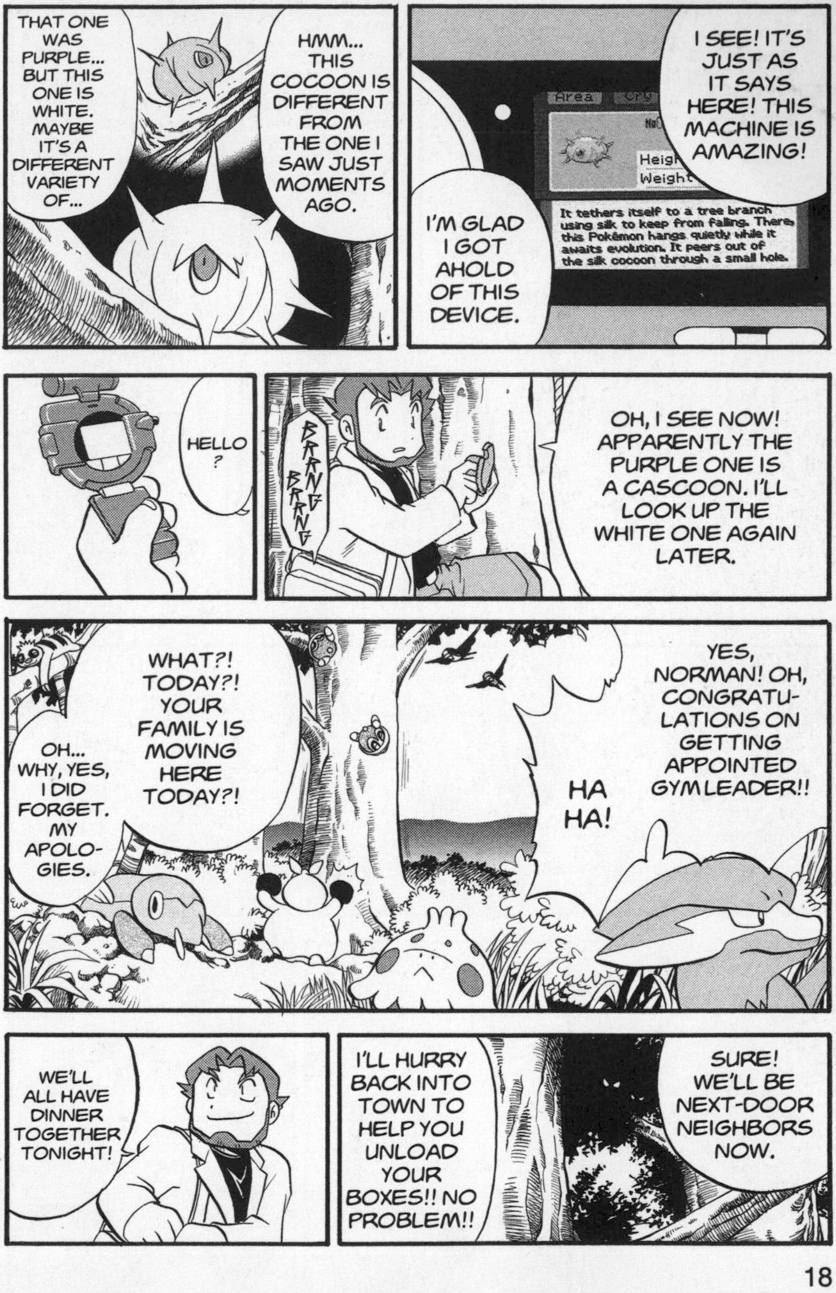
I SEE! IT'S JUST AS IT SAYS HERE! THIS MACHINE IS AMAZING!
Area
Weight
It tethers itself to a tree branch using silk to keep from falling. There, this Pokémon hangs quietly while it awaits evolution. It peers out of the silk cocoon through a small hole.
I'M GLAD I GOT AHOLD OF THIS DEVICE.
HMM... THIS COCOON IS DIFFERENT FROM THE ONE I SAW JUST MOMENTS AGO.
THAT ONE WAS PURPLE... BUT THIS ONE IS WHITE. MAYBE IT'S A DIFFERENT VARIETY OF...
OH, I SEE NOW! APPARENTLY THE PURPLE ONE IS A CASCOON. I'LL LOOK UP THE WHITE ONE AGAIN LATER.
BRRNG BRRNG
HELLO?
YES, NORMAN! OH, CONGRATULATIONS ON GETTING APPOINTED GYM LEADER!!
HA HA!
WHAT?! TODAY?! YOUR FAMILY IS MOVING HERE TODAY?!
OH... WHY, YES, I DID FORGET. MY APOLOGIES.
SURE! WE'LL BE NEXT-DOOR NEIGHBORS NOW.
I'LL HURRY BACK INTO TOWN TO HELP YOU UNLOAD YOUR BOXES!! NO PROBLEM!!
WE'LL ALL HAVE DINNER TOGETHER TONIGHT!

Chapter 182: Making Mirth with Mightyena

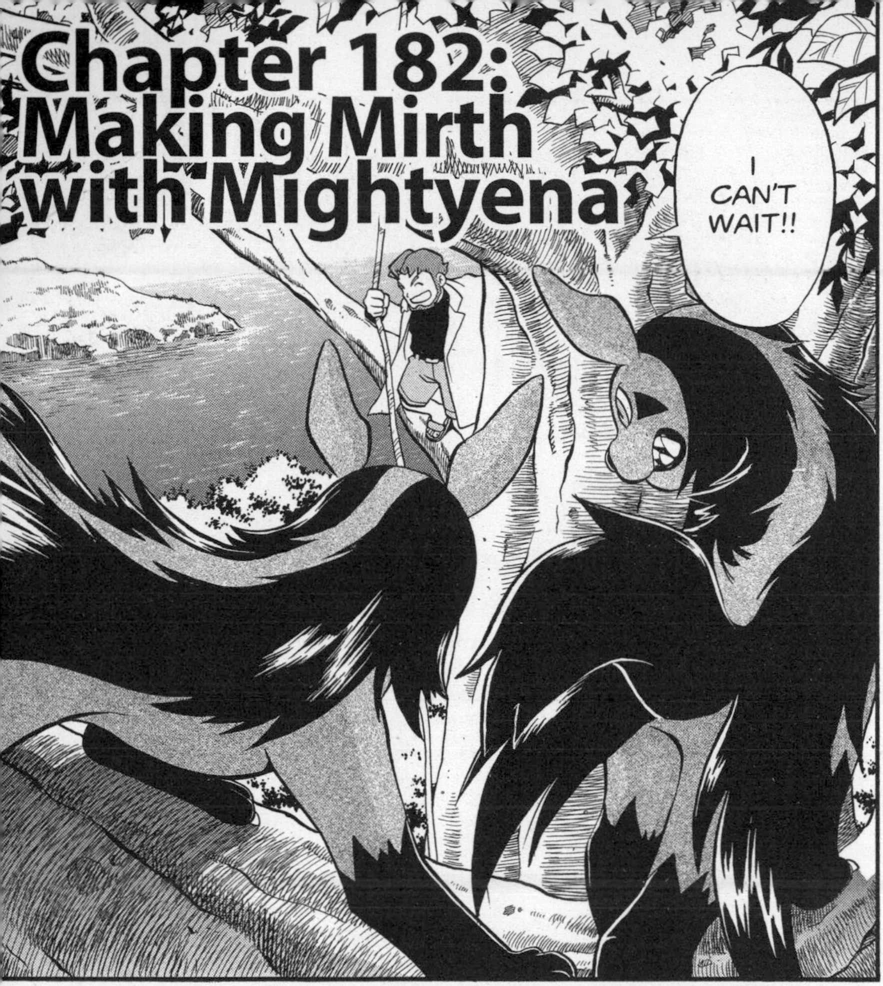
I CAN'T WAIT!!

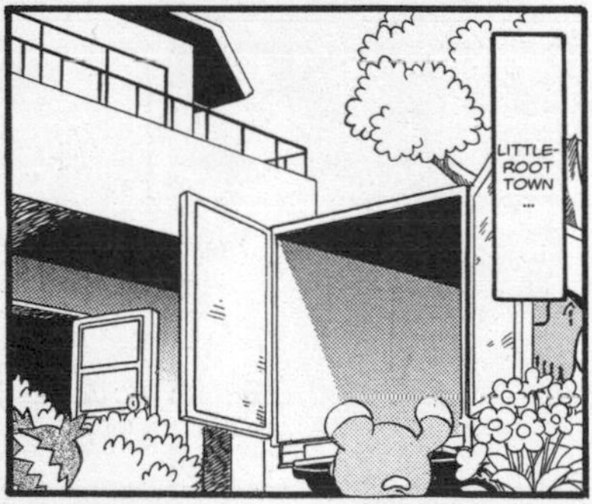
LITTLE-ROOT TOWN ...

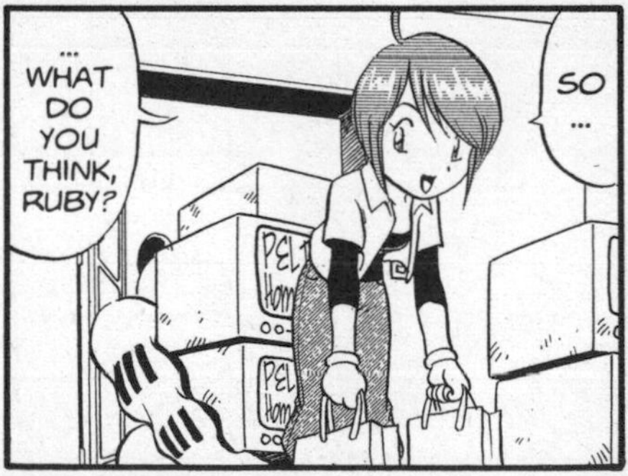
SO ...
... WHAT DO YOU THINK, RUBY?

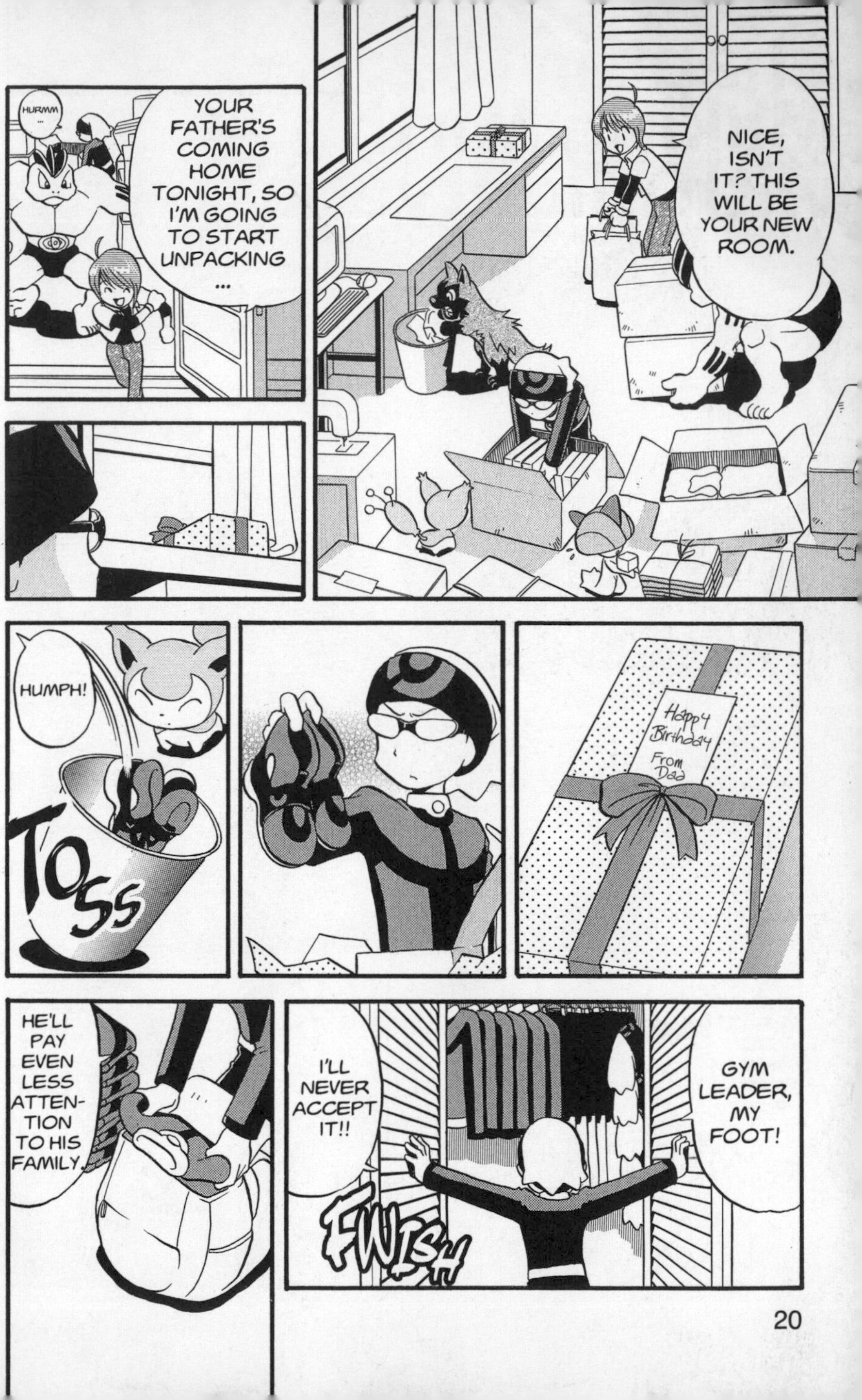
NICE, ISN'T IT? THIS WILL BE YOUR NEW ROOM.
HURMM ...
YOUR FATHER'S COMING HOME TONIGHT, SO I'M GOING TO START UNPACKING ...
Happy Birthday From Dad
HUMPH!
TOSS
GYM LEADER, MY FOOT!
I'LL NEVER ACCEPT IT!!
FWISH
HE'LL PAY EVEN LESS ATTENTION TO HIS FAMILY.

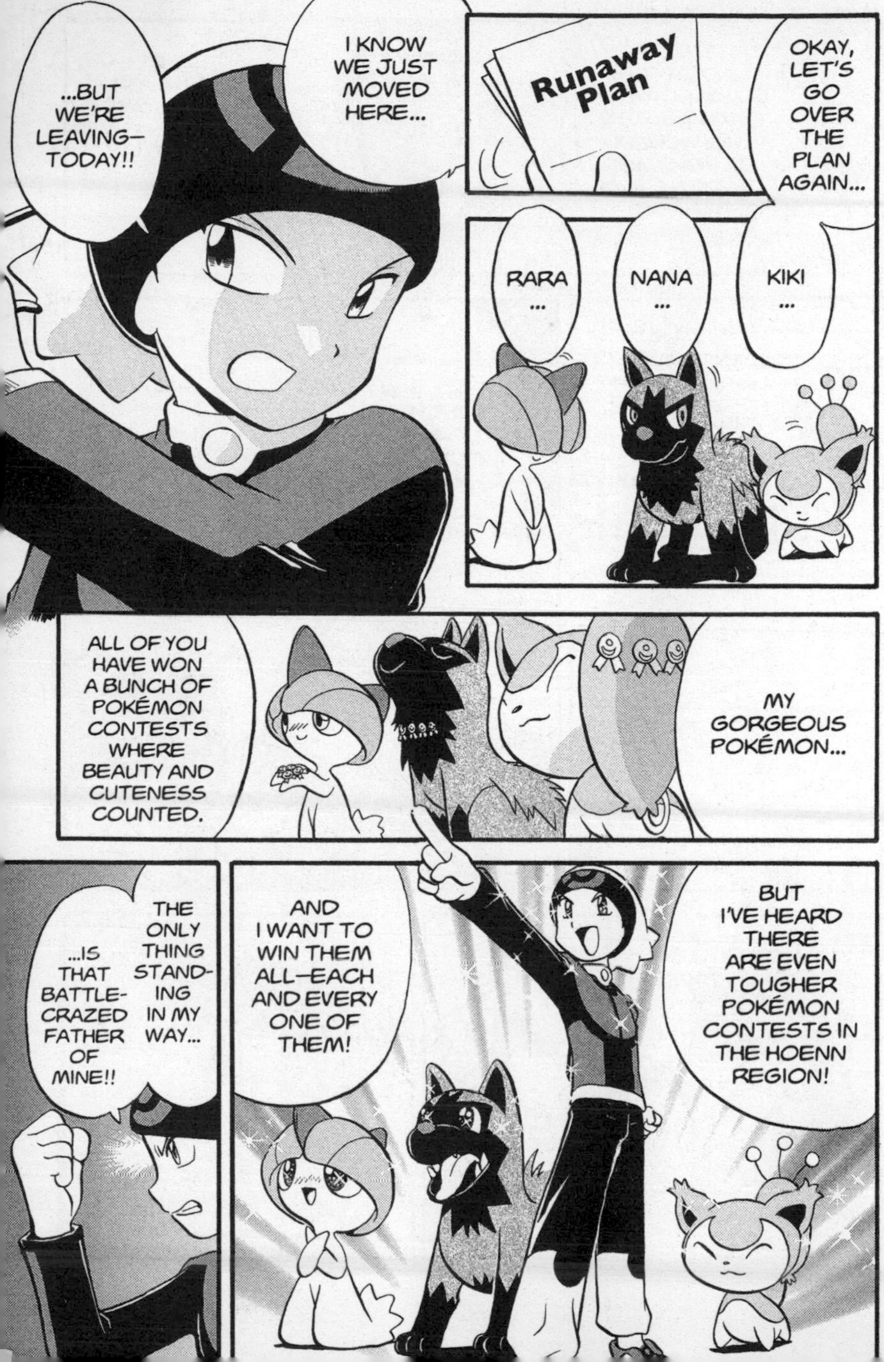
OKAY, LET'S GO OVER THE PLAN AGAIN...
Runaway Plan
KIKI ...
NANA ...
RARA ...
I KNOW WE JUST MOVED HERE...
...BUT WE'RE LEAVING—TODAY!!
MY GORGEOUS POKÉMON...
ALL OF YOU HAVE WON A BUNCH OF POKÉMON CONTESTS WHERE BEAUTY AND CUTENESS COUNTED.
BUT I'VE HEARD THERE ARE EVEN TOUGHER POKÉMON CONTESTS IN THE HOENN REGION!
AND I WANT TO WIN THEM ALL—EACH AND EVERY ONE OF THEM!
THE ONLY THING STANDING IN MY WAY...
...IS THAT BATTLE-CRAZED FATHER OF MINE!!

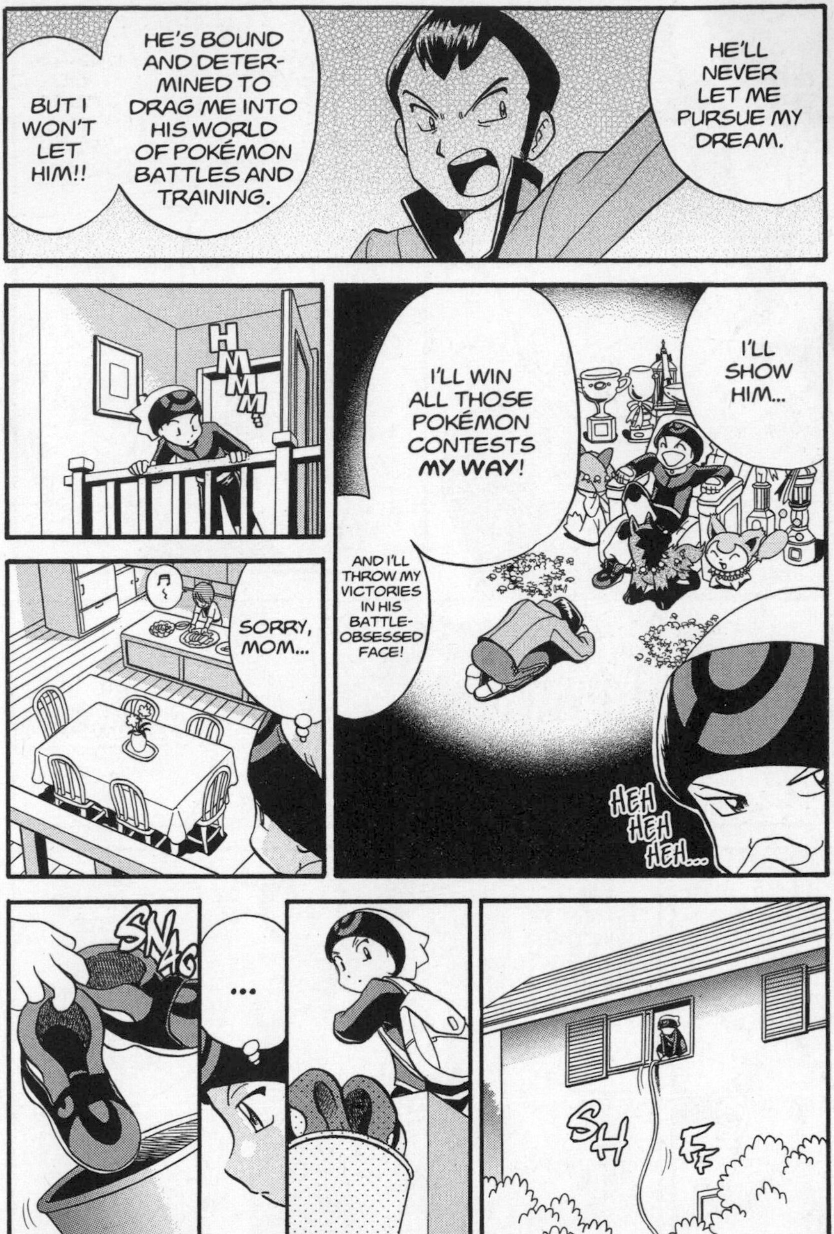
HE'LL NEVER LET ME PURSUE MY DREAM.
HE'S BOUND AND DETERMINED TO DRAG ME INTO HIS WORLD OF POKÉMON BATTLES AND TRAINING.
BUT I WON'T LET HIM!!
I'LL SHOW HIM...
I'LL WIN ALL THOSE POKÉMON CONTESTS MY WAY!
AND I'LL THROW MY VICTORIES IN HIS BATTLE-OBSESSED FACE!
HEH HEH HEH...
HMMM
SORRY, MOM...
SHFF
...
SNAG

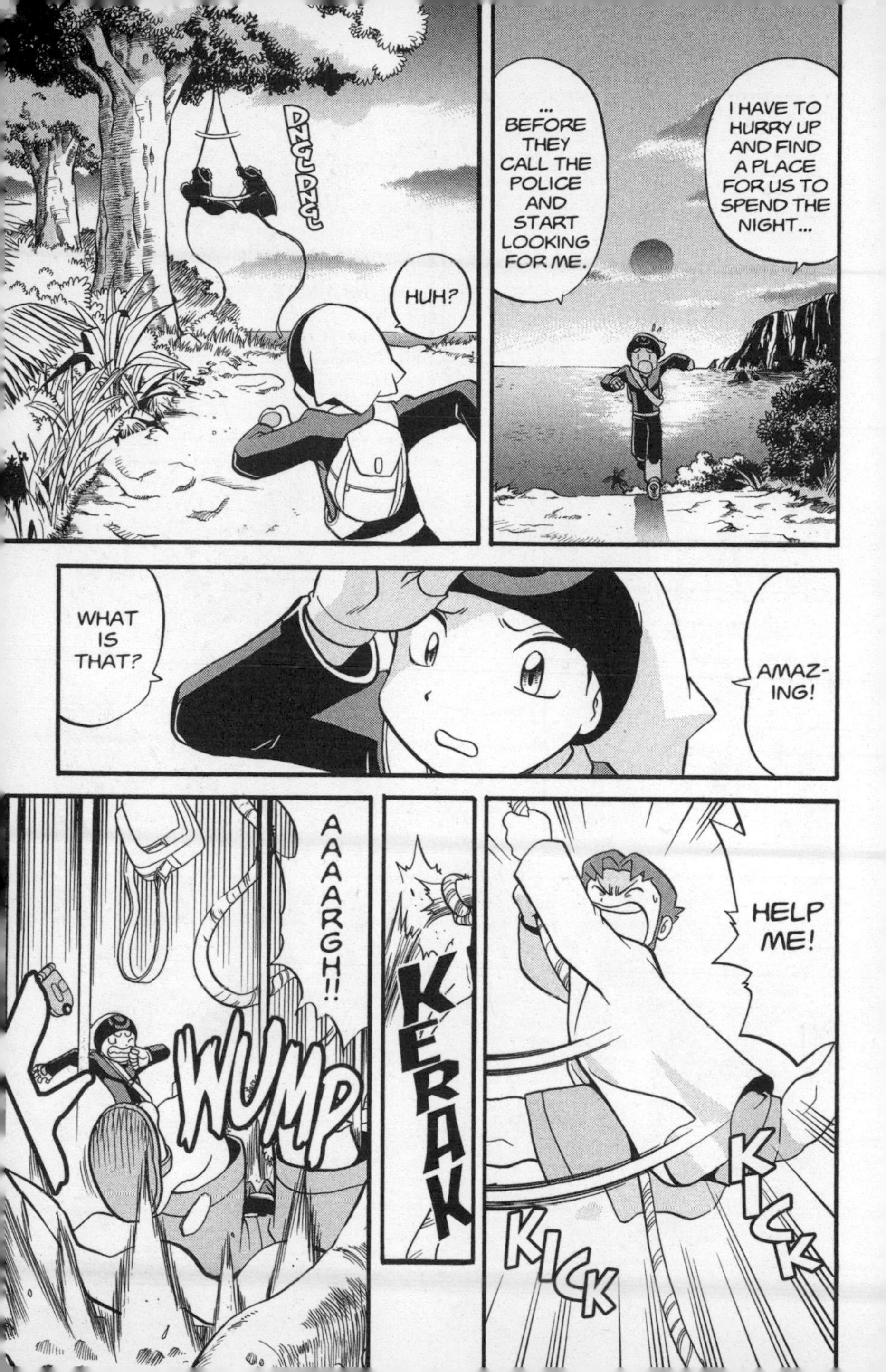
I HAVE TO HURRY UP AND FIND A PLACE FOR US TO SPEND THE NIGHT...
... BEFORE THEY CALL THE POLICE AND START LOOKING FOR ME.
DNGL DNGL
HUH?
AMAZ-ING!
WHAT IS THAT?
HELP ME!
KICK
KICK
KERAK
AAAAARGH!!
WUMP

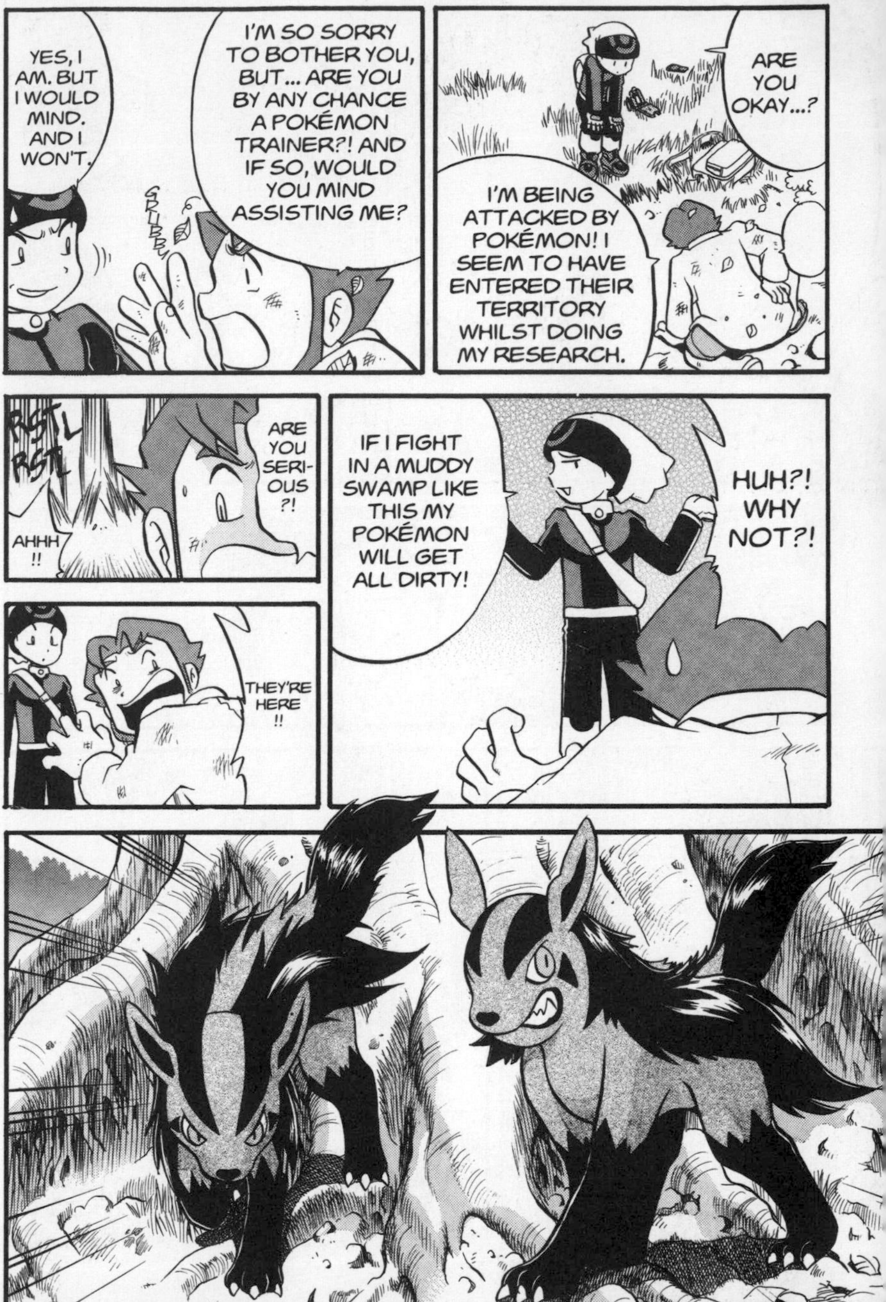
ARE YOU OKAY...?
I'M BEING ATTACKED BY POKÉMON! I SEEM TO HAVE ENTERED THEIR TERRITORY WHILST DOING MY RESEARCH.
I'M SO SORRY TO BOTHER YOU, BUT... ARE YOU BY ANY CHANCE A POKÉMON TRAINER?! AND IF SO, WOULD YOU MIND ASSISTING ME?
YES, I AM. BUT I WOULD MIND. AND I WON'T.
HUH?! WHY NOT?!
IF I FIGHT IN A MUDDY SWAMP LIKE THIS MY POKÉMON WILL GET ALL DIRTY!
ARE YOU SERI-OUS?!
RSTL RSTL
AHHH!!
THEY'RE HERE!!

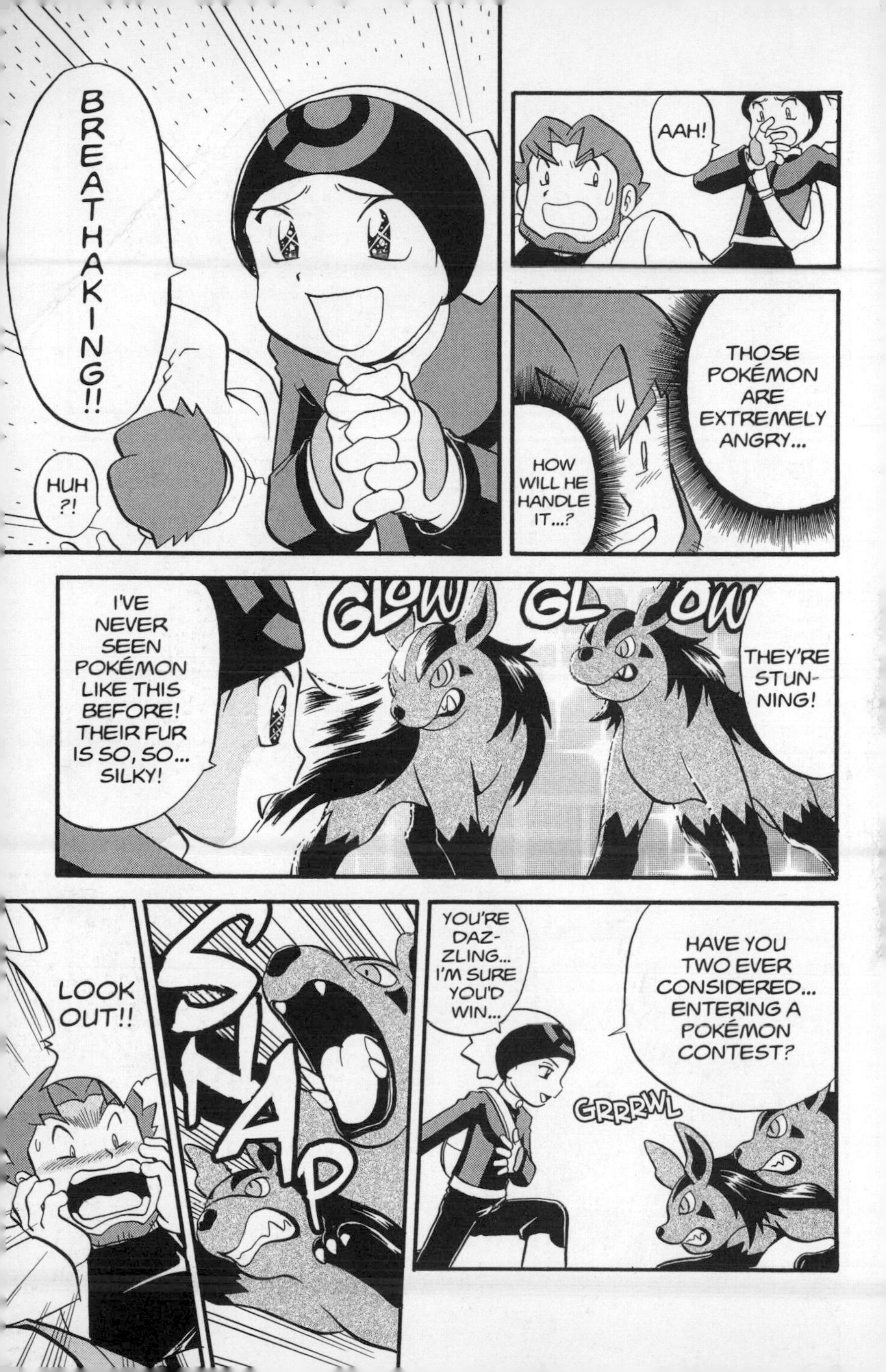
AAH!
THOSE POKÉMON ARE EXTREMELY ANGRY...
HOW WILL HE HANDLE IT...?
BREATHAKING!!
HUH ?!
GLOW GLOW
THEY'RE STUN-NING!
I'VE NEVER SEEN POKÉMON LIKE THIS BEFORE! THEIR FUR IS SO, SO... SILKY!
HAVE YOU TWO EVER CONSIDERED... ENTERING A POKÉMON CONTEST?
YOU'RE DAZ-ZLING... I'M SURE YOU'D WIN...
GRRRWL
SNAP
LOOK OUT!!

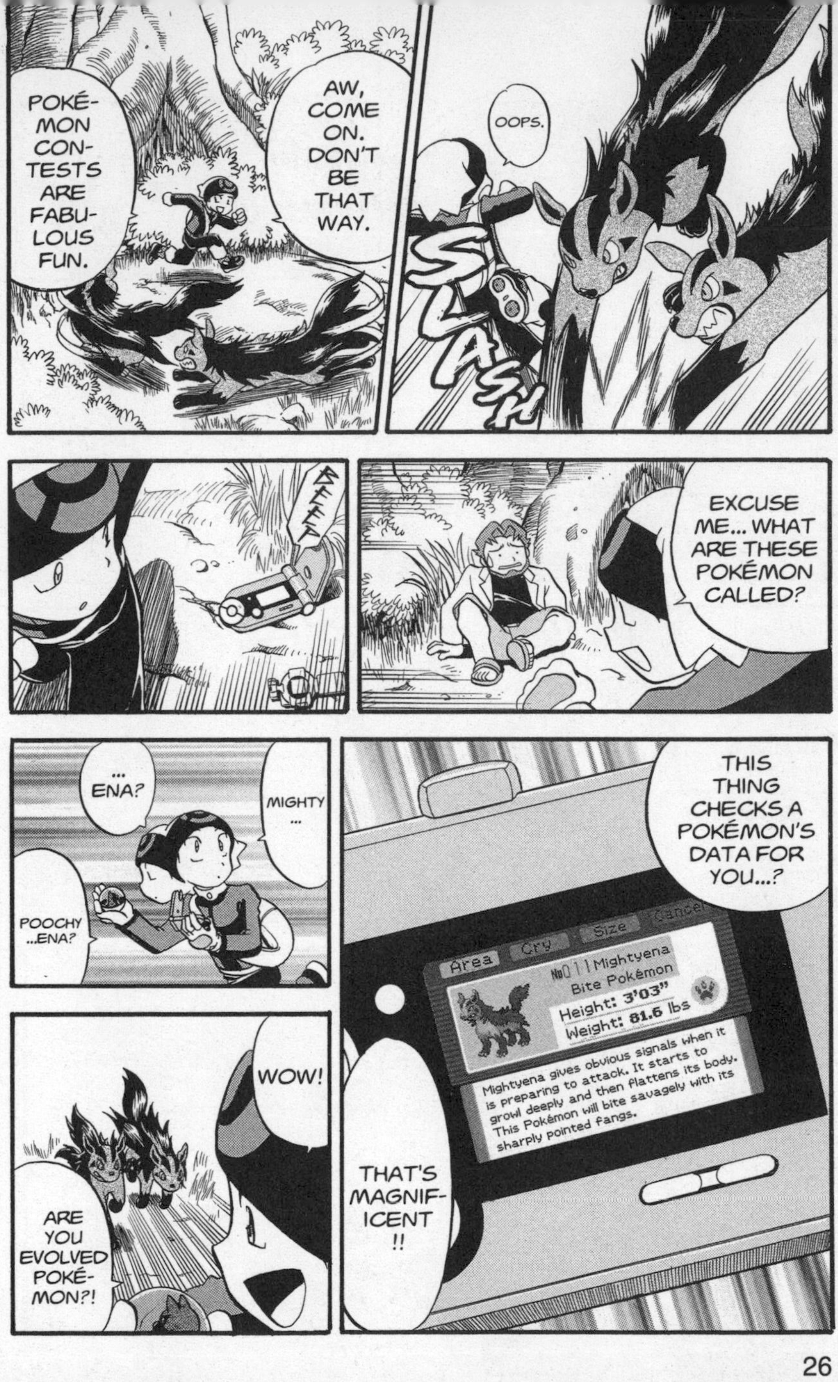
OOPS.
SLASH
AW, COME ON. DON'T BE THAT WAY.
POKÉ-MON CON-TESTS ARE FABU-LOUS FUN.
EXCUSE ME... WHAT ARE THESE POKÉMON CALLED?
BEEEP
THIS THING CHECKS A POKÉMON'S DATA FOR YOU...?
Area
Cry
Size
Cancel
№011 Mightyena
Bite Pokémon
Height: 3'03"
Weight: 81.6 lbs
Mightyena gives obvious signals when it is preparing to attack. It starts to growl deeply and then flattens its body. This Pokémon will bite savagely with its sharply pointed fangs.
THAT'S MAGNIF-ICENT !!
MIGHTY ...
... ENA?
POOCHY ...ENA?
WOW!
ARE YOU EVOLVED POKÉ-MON?!

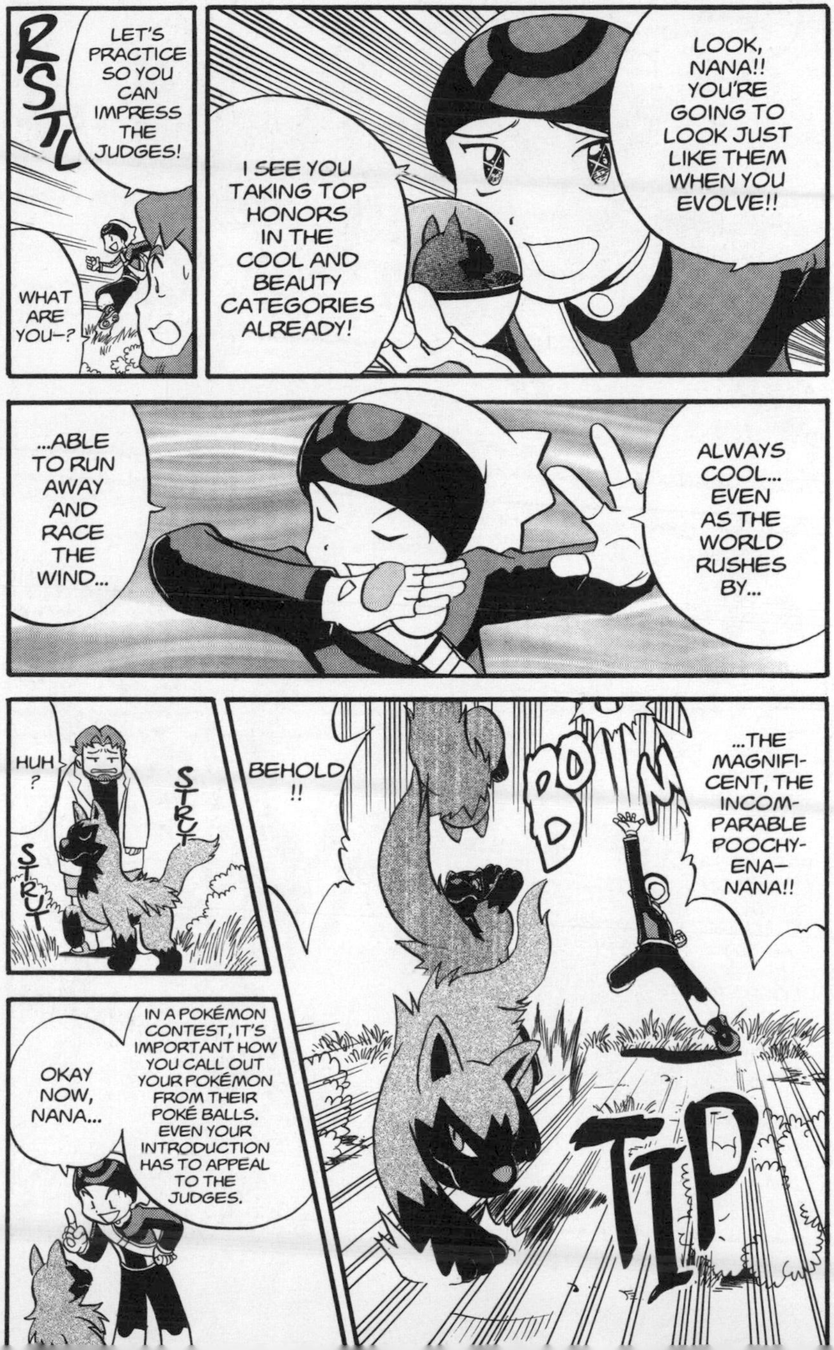
LOOK, NANA!! YOU'RE GOING TO LOOK JUST LIKE THEM WHEN YOU EVOLVE!!
I SEE YOU TAKING TOP HONORS IN THE COOL AND BEAUTY CATEGORIES ALREADY!
LET'S PRACTICE SO YOU CAN IMPRESS THE JUDGES!
RSTL
WHAT ARE YOU—?
ALWAYS COOL... EVEN AS THE WORLD RUSHES BY...
...ABLE TO RUN AWAY AND RACE THE WIND...
...THE MAGNIFI-CENT, THE INCOM-PARABLE POOCHY-ENA—NANA!!
BOOM
BEHOLD!!
TIP
HUH?
STRUT
STRUT
IN A POKÉMON CONTEST, IT'S IMPORTANT HOW YOU CALL OUT YOUR POKÉMON FROM THEIR POKÉ BALLS. EVEN YOUR INTRODUCTION HAS TO APPEAL TO THE JUDGES.
OKAY NOW, NANA...

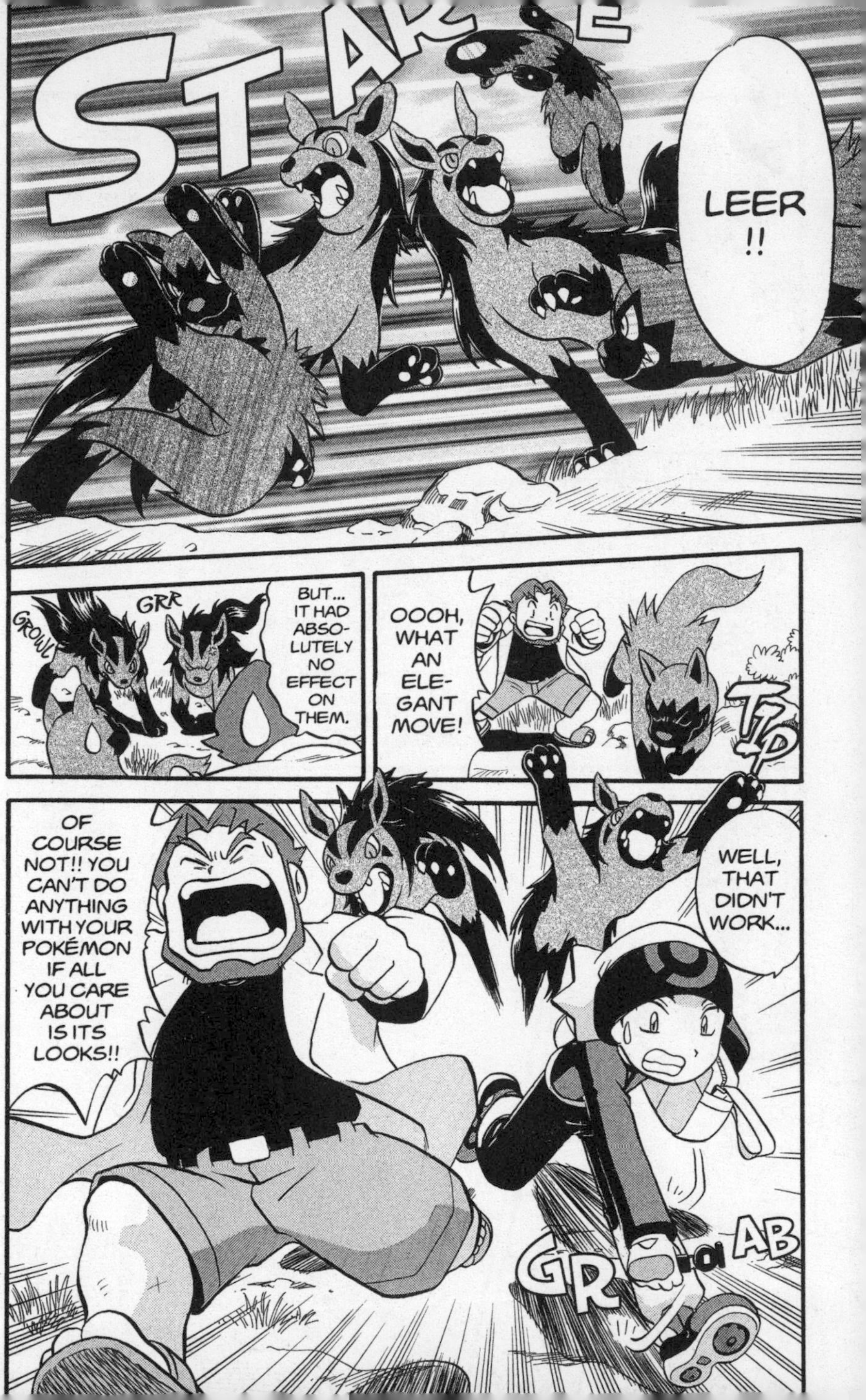
STARE
LEER !!
OOOH, WHAT AN ELEGANT MOVE!
TIP
BUT... IT HAD ABSOLUTELY NO EFFECT ON THEM.
GRR
GROWL
WELL, THAT DIDN'T WORK...
OF COURSE NOT!! YOU CAN'T DO ANYTHING WITH YOUR POKÉMON IF ALL YOU CARE ABOUT IS ITS LOOKS!!
GRAB

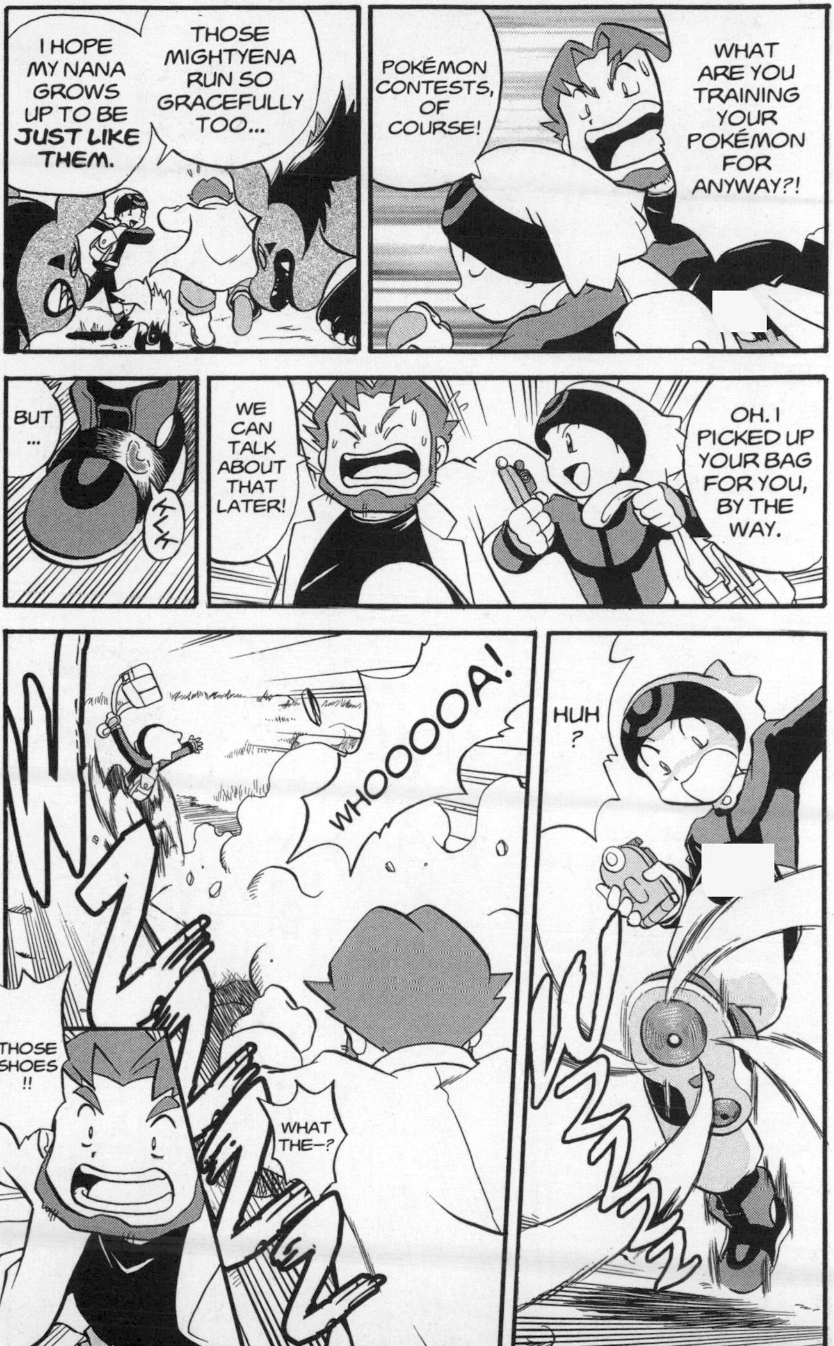

WHAT ARE YOU TRAINING YOUR POKÉMON FOR ANYWAY?!
POKÉMON CONTESTS, OF COURSE!
THOSE MIGHTYENA RUN SO GRACEFULLY TOO...
I HOPE MY NANA GROWS UP TO BE **JUST LIKE THEM.**
OH. I PICKED UP YOUR BAG FOR YOU, BY THE WAY.
WE CAN TALK ABOUT THAT LATER!
BUT ...
HUH ?
WHOOOOOA!
THOSE SHOES !!
WHAT THE--?

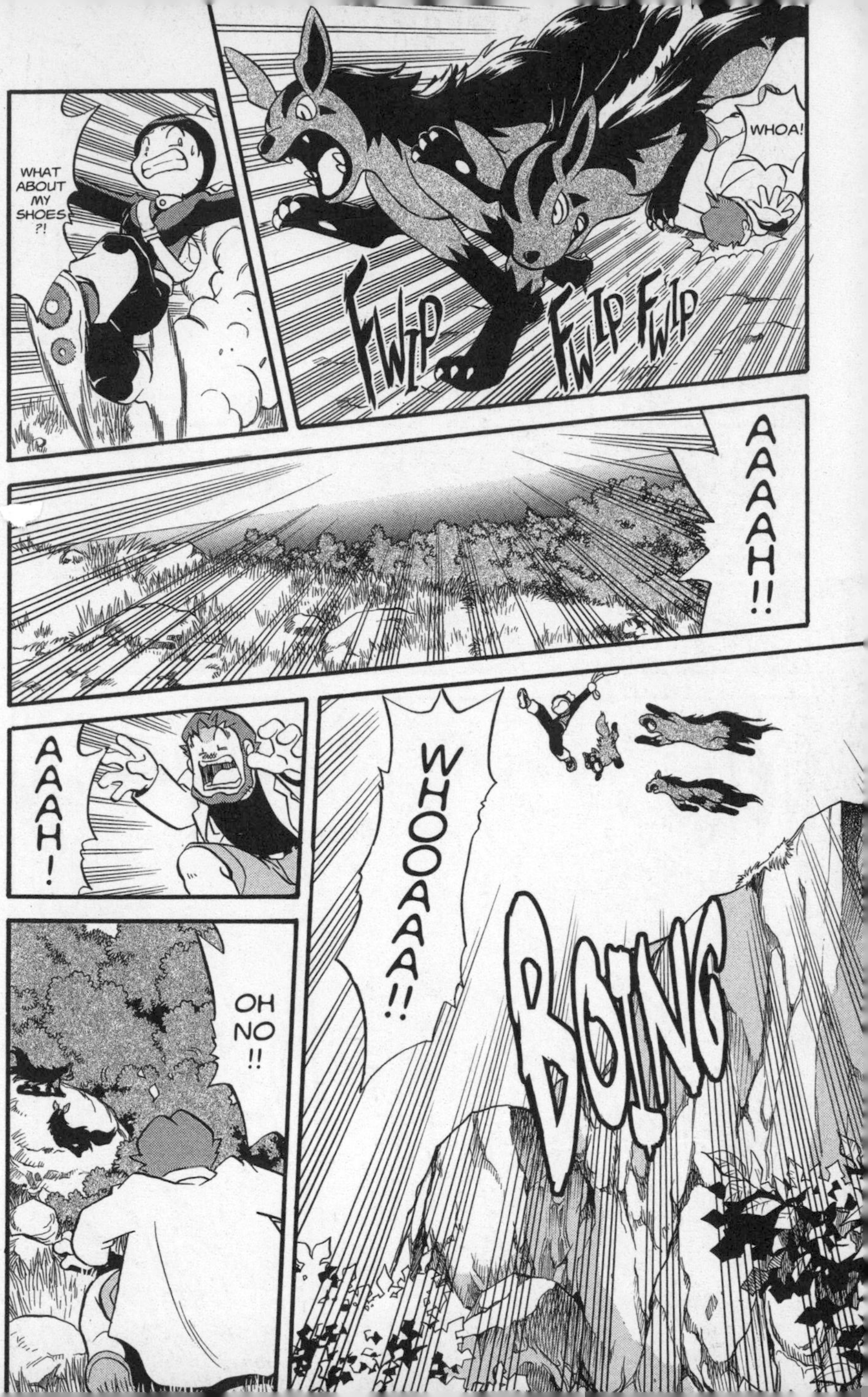
WHOA!
FWIP
FWIP FWIP
WHAT ABOUT MY SHOES ?!
AAAAAH!!
WHOOAAAA!!
BOING
AAAH!
OH NO!!

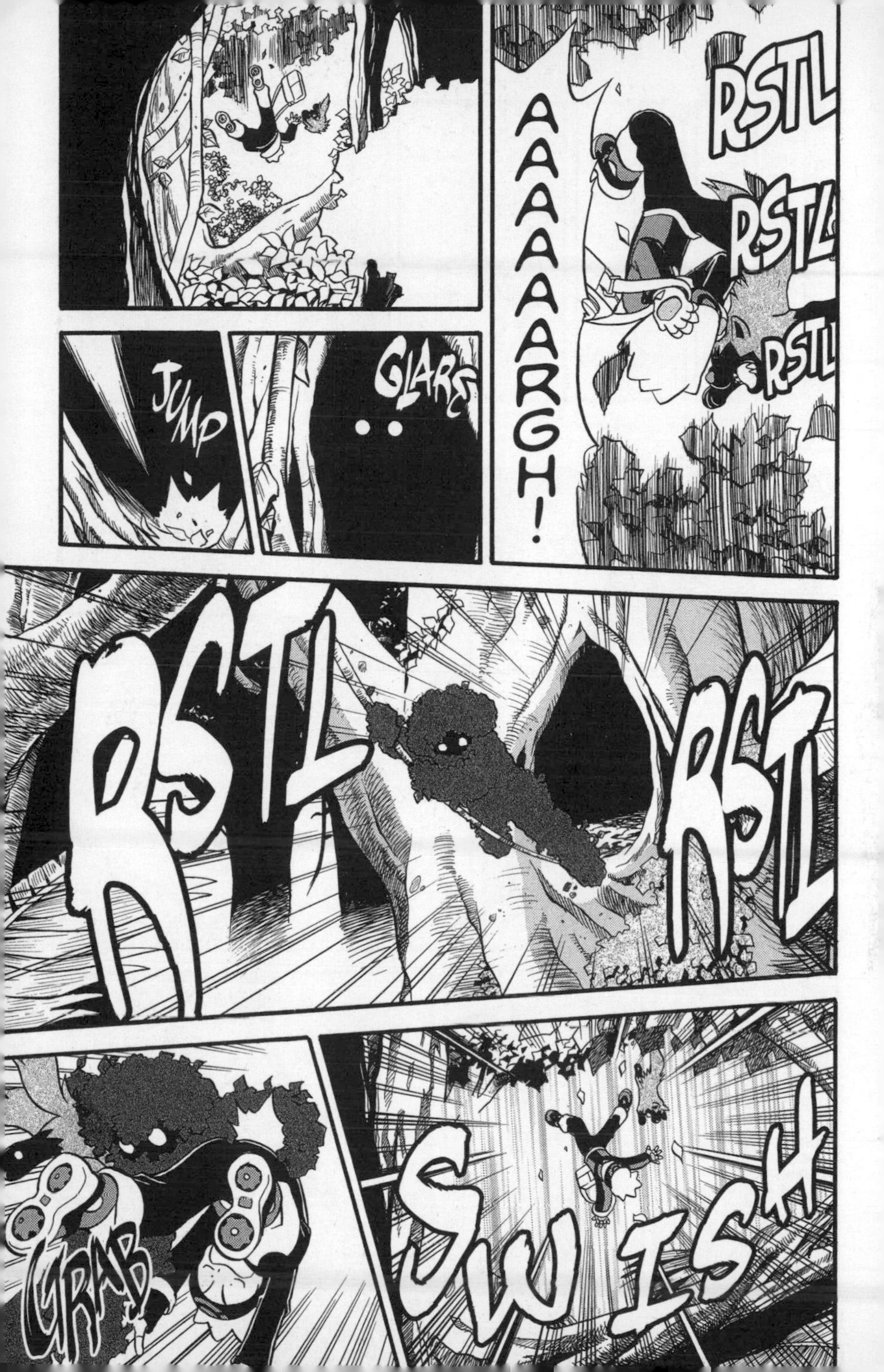
RSTL
RSTL
RSTL
AAAAAAARGH!
GLARE
JUMP
RSTL
RSTL
SWISH
GRAB

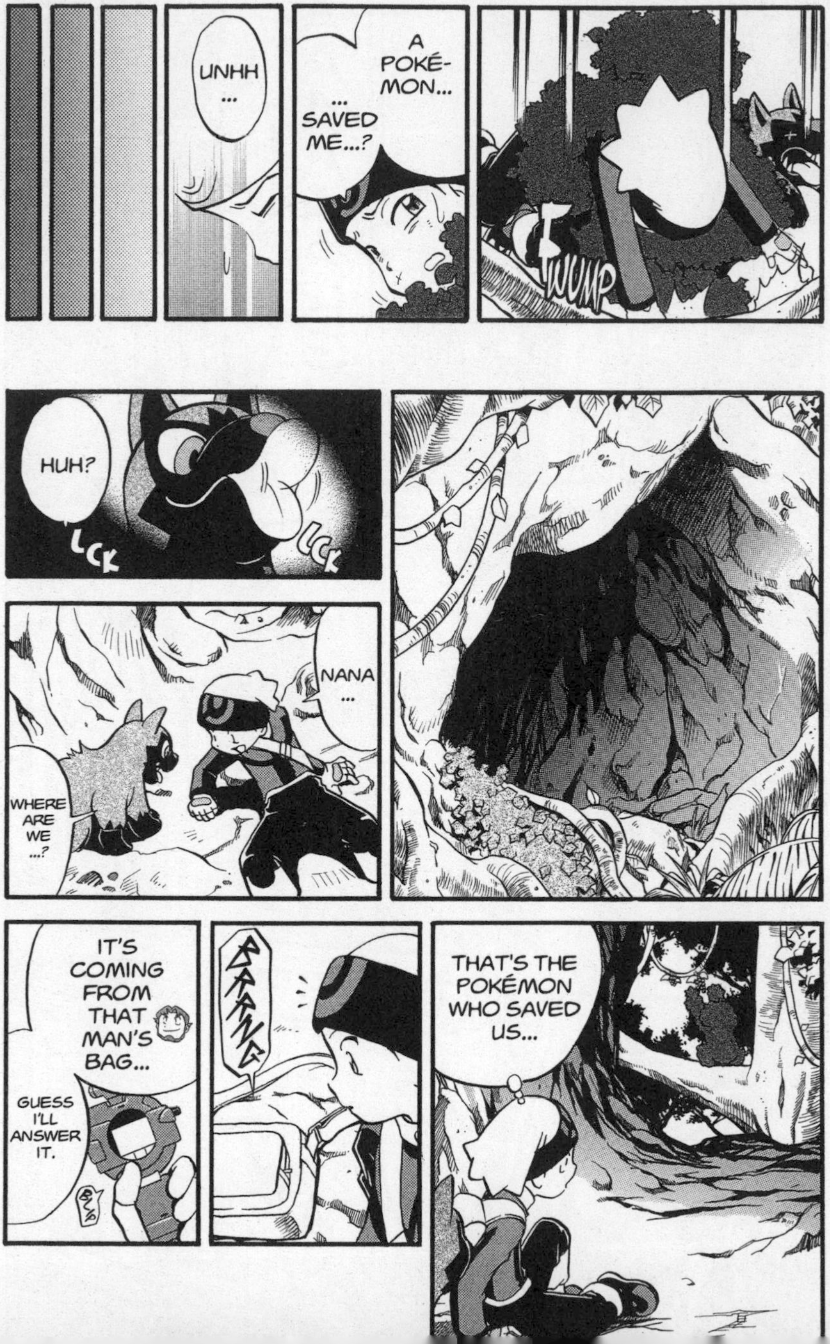
TWUMP
A POKÉMON...
...SAVED ME...?
UNHH ...
HUH?
LCK
LCK
NANA ...
WHERE ARE WE ...?
THAT'S THE POKÉMON WHO SAVED US...
BRRRNG
IT'S COMING FROM THAT MAN'S BAG...
GUESS I'LL ANSWER IT.

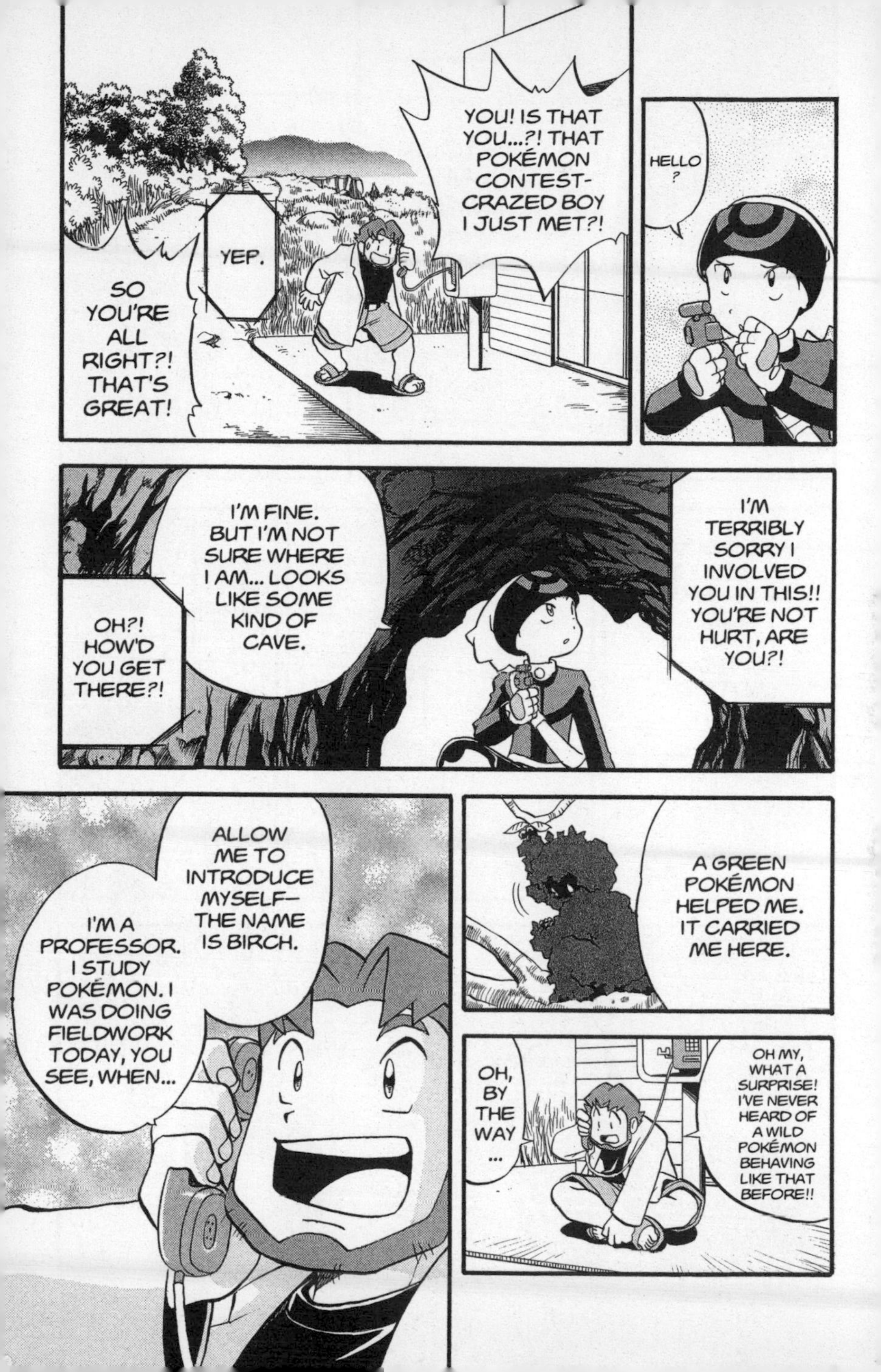
HELLO?
YOU! IS THAT YOU...?! THAT POKÉMON CONTEST-CRAZED BOY I JUST MET?!
YEP.
SO YOU'RE ALL RIGHT?! THAT'S GREAT!
I'M TERRIBLY SORRY I INVOLVED YOU IN THIS!! YOU'RE NOT HURT, ARE YOU?!
I'M FINE. BUT I'M NOT SURE WHERE I AM... LOOKS LIKE SOME KIND OF CAVE.
OH?! HOW'D YOU GET THERE?!
A GREEN POKÉMON HELPED ME. IT CARRIED ME HERE.
OH MY, WHAT A SURPRISE! I'VE NEVER HEARD OF A WILD POKÉMON BEHAVING LIKE THAT BEFORE!!
OH, BY THE WAY ...
ALLOW ME TO INTRODUCE MYSELF— THE NAME IS BIRCH.
I'M A PROFESSOR. I STUDY POKÉMON. I WAS DOING FIELDWORK TODAY, YOU SEE, WHEN...

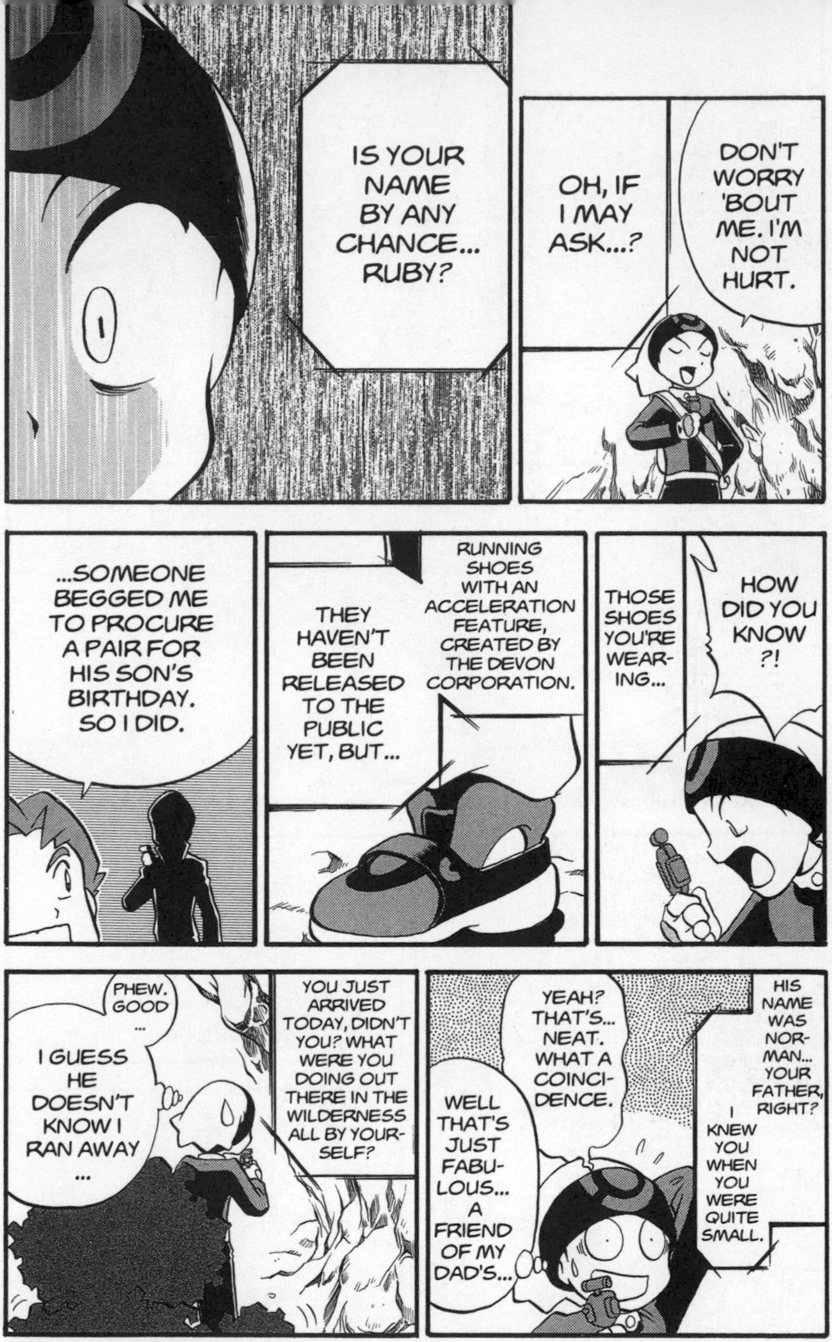
DON'T WORRY 'BOUT ME. I'M NOT HURT.
OH, IF I MAY ASK...?
IS YOUR NAME BY ANY CHANCE... RUBY?
HOW DID YOU KNOW ?!
THOSE SHOES YOU'RE WEAR-ING...
RUNNING SHOES WITH AN ACCELERATION FEATURE, CREATED BY THE DEVON CORPORATION.
THEY HAVEN'T BEEN RELEASED TO THE PUBLIC YET, BUT...
...SOMEONE BEGGED ME TO PROCURE A PAIR FOR HIS SON'S BIRTHDAY. SO I DID.
HIS NAME WAS NOR-MAN... YOUR FATHER, RIGHT?
I KNEW YOU WHEN YOU WERE QUITE SMALL.
YEAH? THAT'S... NEAT. WHAT A COINCI-DENCE.
WELL THAT'S JUST FABU-LOUS... A FRIEND OF MY DAD'S...
YOU JUST ARRIVED TODAY, DIDN'T YOU? WHAT WERE YOU DOING OUT THERE IN THE WILDERNESS ALL BY YOUR-SELF?
PHEW. GOOD ...
I GUESS HE DOESN'T KNOW I RAN AWAY ...

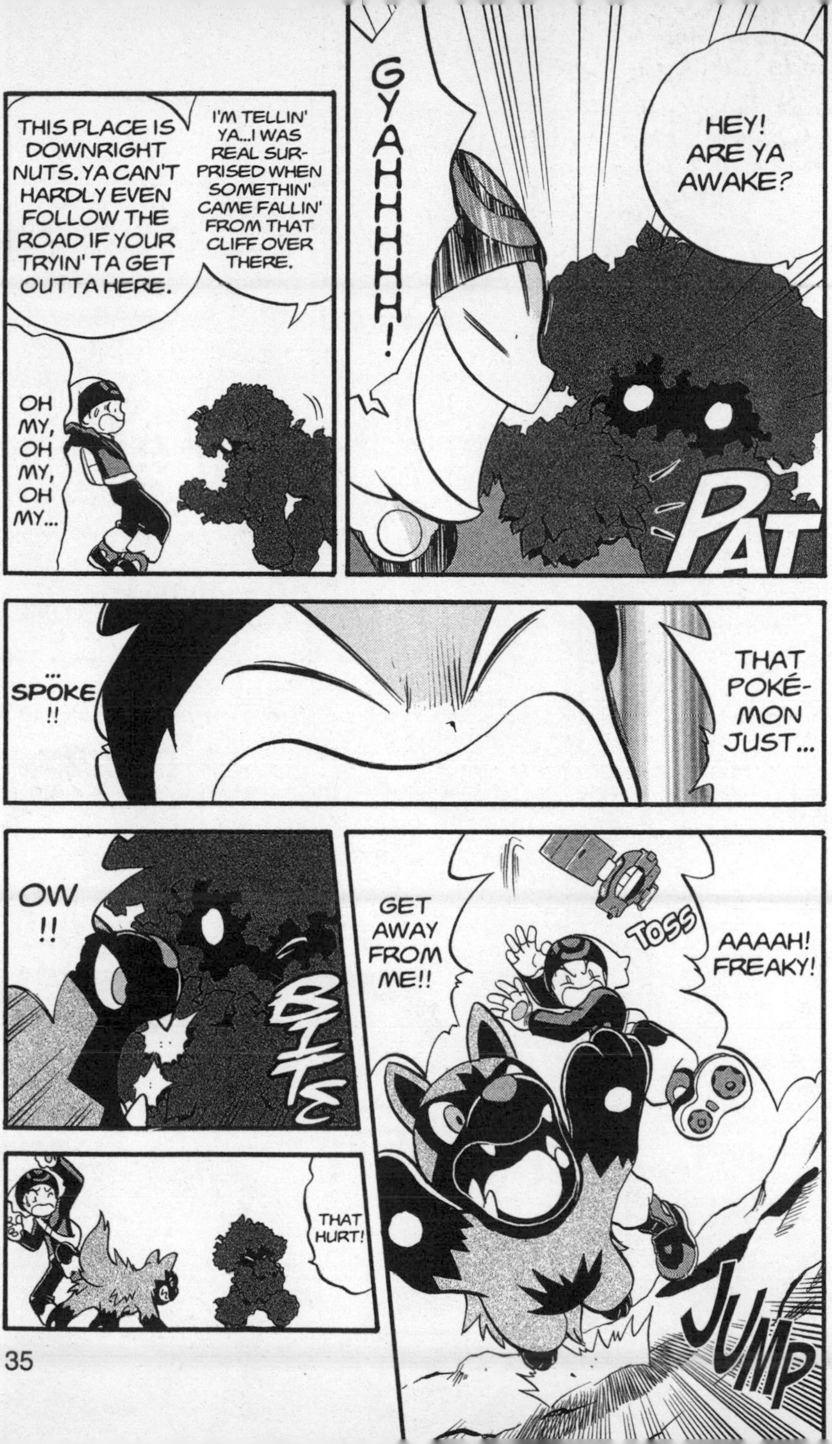
HEY! ARE YA AWAKE?
PAT
GYAHHHHH!
I'M TELLIN' YA...I WAS REAL SUR-PRISED WHEN SOMETHIN' CAME FALLIN' FROM THAT CLIFF OVER THERE.
THIS PLACE IS DOWNRIGHT NUTS. YA CAN'T HARDLY EVEN FOLLOW THE ROAD IF YOUR TRYIN' TA GET OUTTA HERE.
OH MY, OH MY, OH MY...
THAT POKÉ-MON JUST...
...SPOKE!!
AAAAH! FREAKY!
TOSS
GET AWAY FROM ME!!
JUMP
OW!!
BITE
THAT HURT!

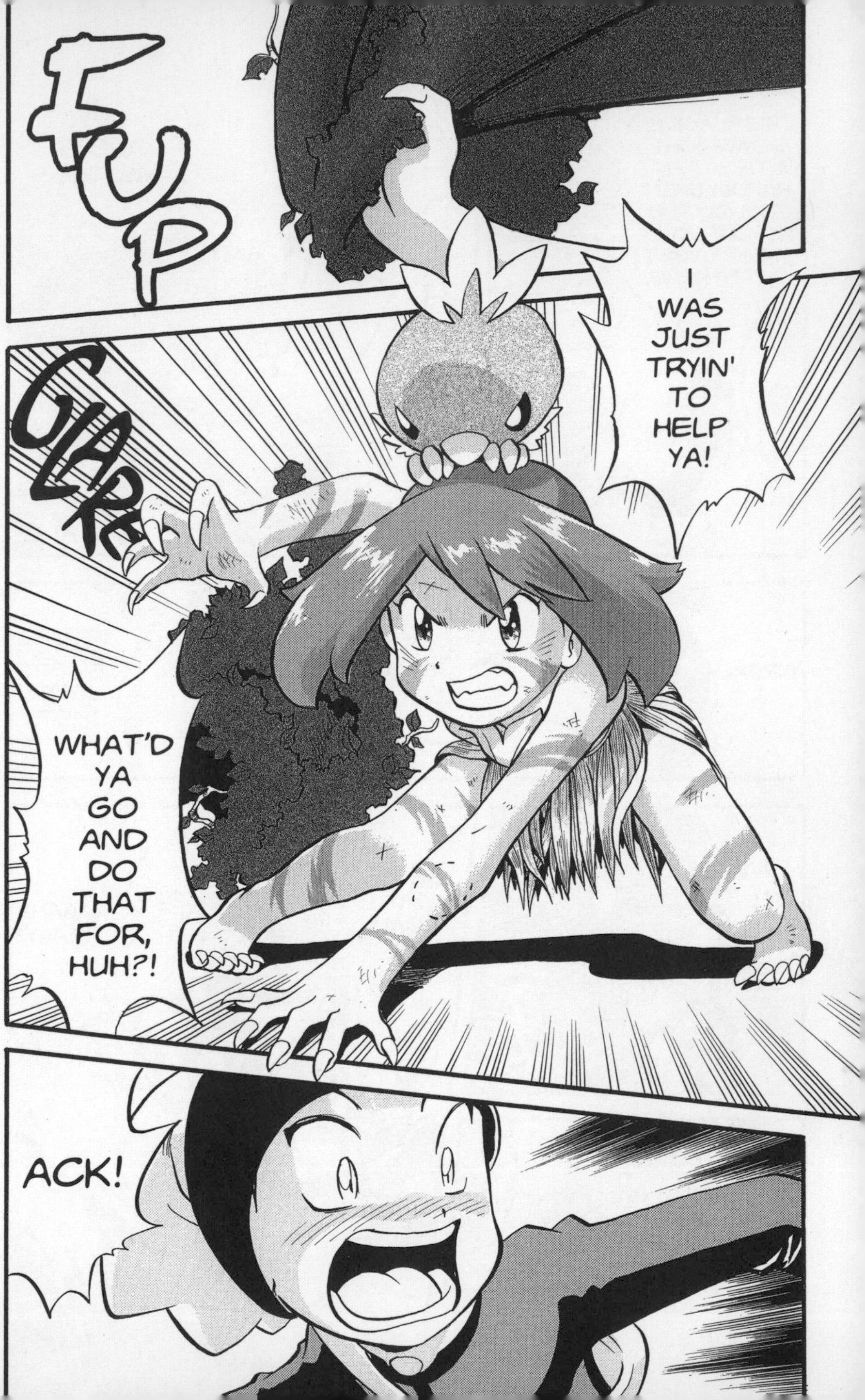
FUP
I WAS JUST TRYIN' TO HELP YA!
GLARE
WHAT'D YA GO AND DO THAT FOR, HUH?!
ACK!

Pokémon Adventures

The Fourth Chapter

Chapter 183: Trying to Trounce Torchic

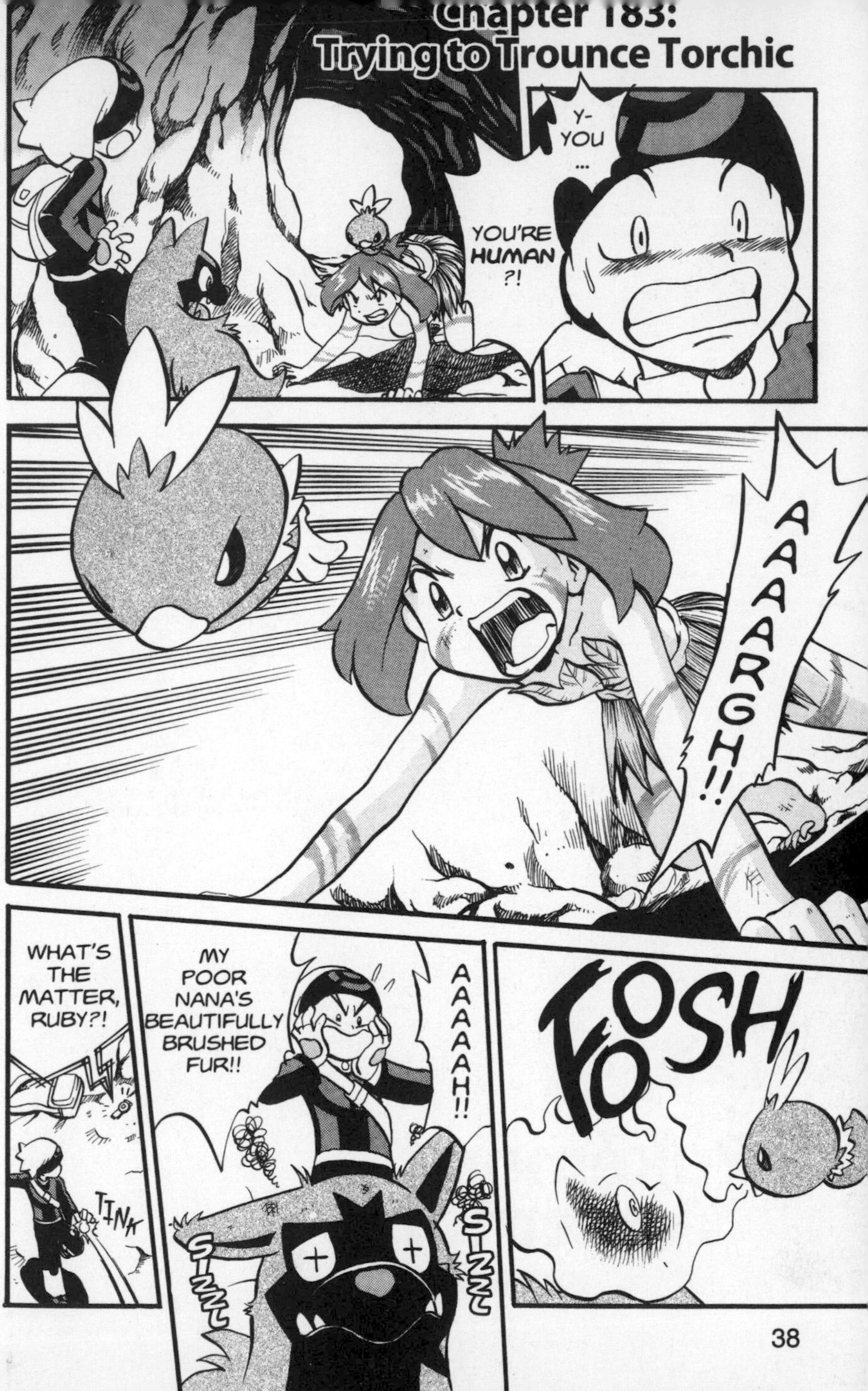
Y- YOU ...
YOU'RE HUMAN ?!
AAAAARGH!!
FOOSH
AAAAAAH!!
MY POOR NANA'S BEAUTIFULLY BRUSHED FUR!!
SIZZL
SIZZL
WHAT'S THE MATTER, RUBY?!
TINK

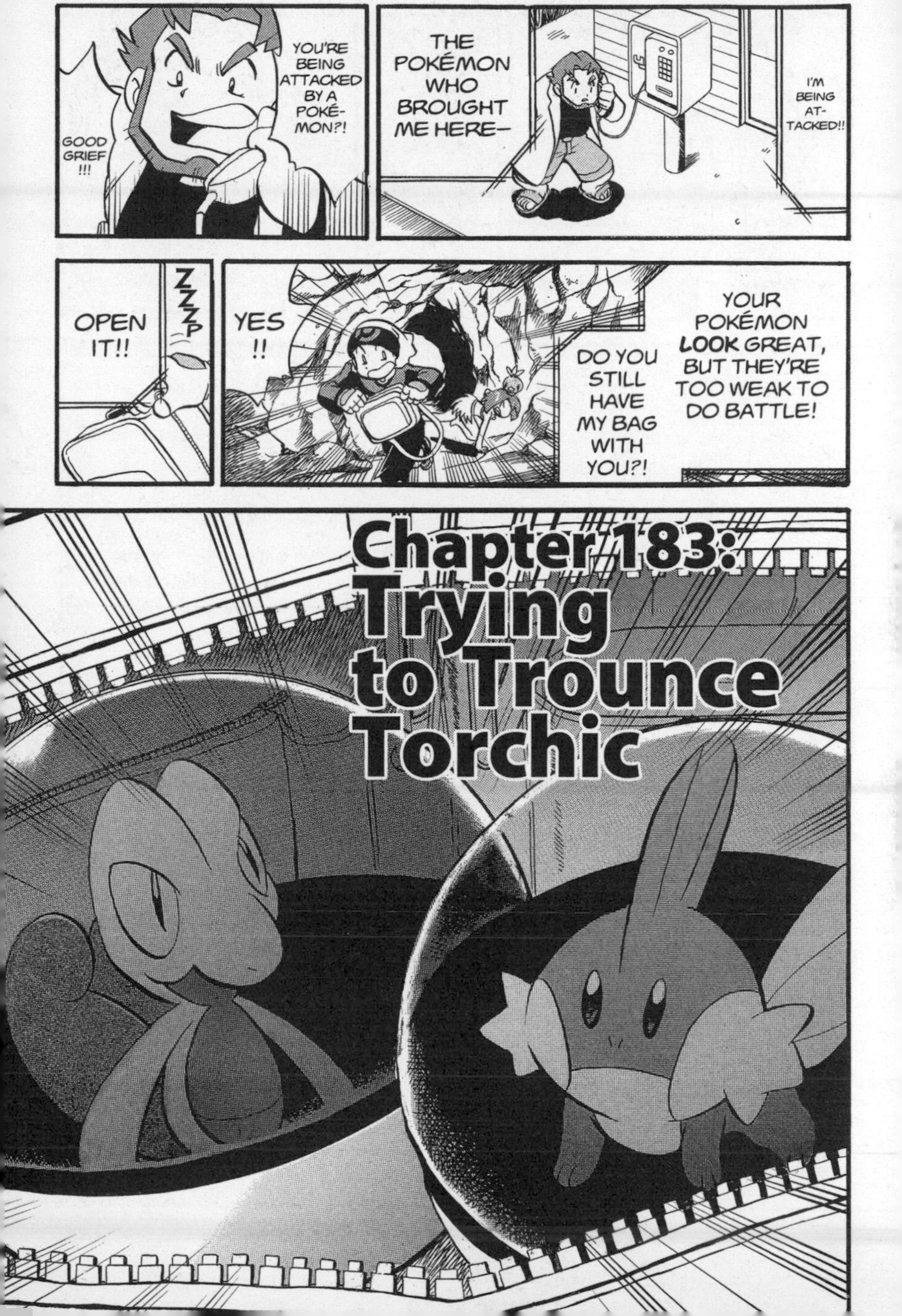
I'M BEING AT-TACKED!!
THE POKÉMON WHO BROUGHT ME HERE—
YOU'RE BEING ATTACKED BY A POKÉ-MON?!
GOOD GRIEF!!!
YOUR POKÉMON LOOK GREAT, BUT THEY'RE TOO WEAK TO DO BATTLE!
DO YOU STILL HAVE MY BAG WITH YOU?!
YES!!
ZZZP
OPEN IT!!
Chapter 183:
Trying to Trounce Torchic

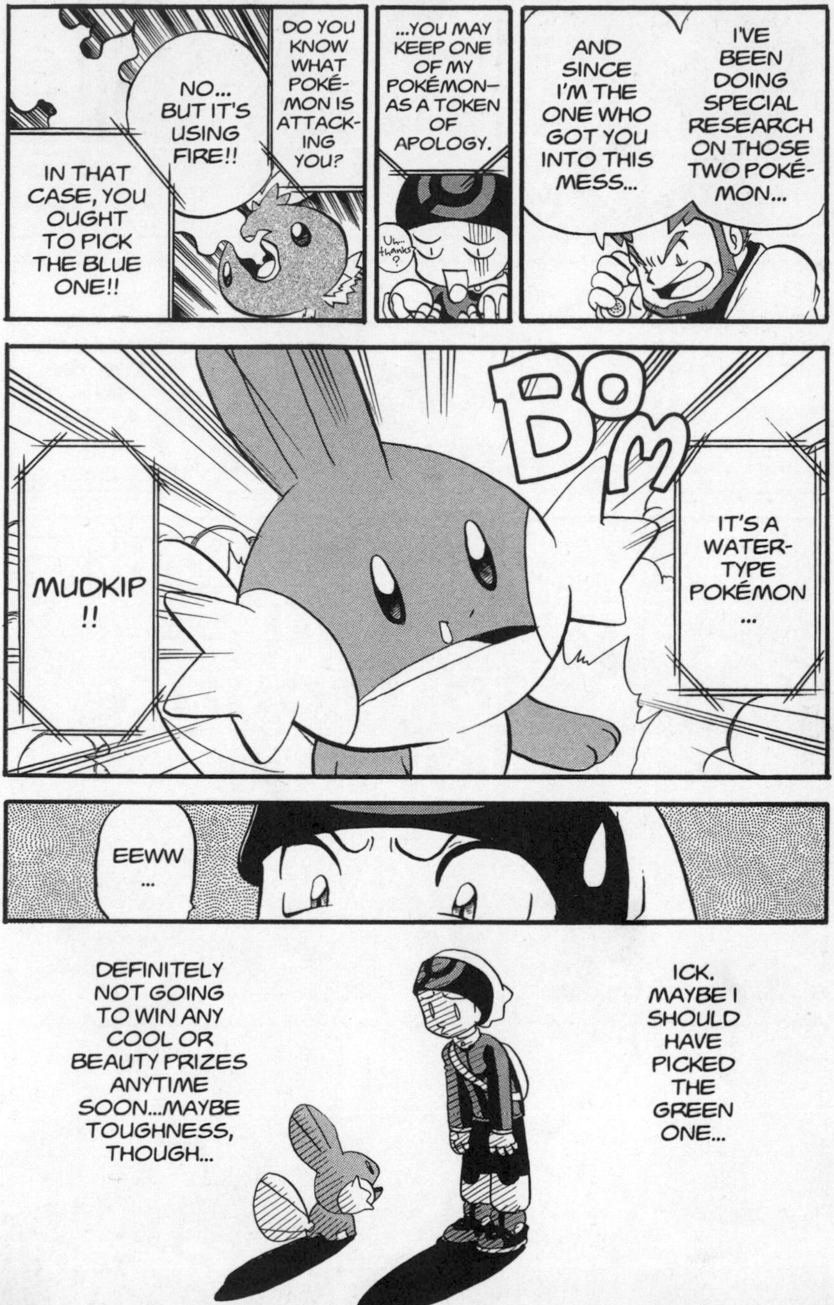
I'VE BEEN DOING SPECIAL RESEARCH ON THOSE TWO POKÉMON...
AND SINCE I'M THE ONE WHO GOT YOU INTO THIS MESS...
...YOU MAY KEEP ONE OF MY POKÉMON—AS A TOKEN OF APOLOGY.
Uh.. thanks?
DO YOU KNOW WHAT POKÉMON IS ATTACKING YOU?
NO... BUT IT'S USING FIRE!!
IN THAT CASE, YOU OUGHT TO PICK THE BLUE ONE!!
IT'S A WATER-TYPE POKÉMON ...
BOOM
MUDKIP !!
EEWW ...
ICK. MAYBE I SHOULD HAVE PICKED THE GREEN ONE...
DEFINITELY NOT GOING TO WIN ANY COOL OR BEAUTY PRIZES ANYTIME SOON...MAYBE TOUGHNESS, THOUGH...

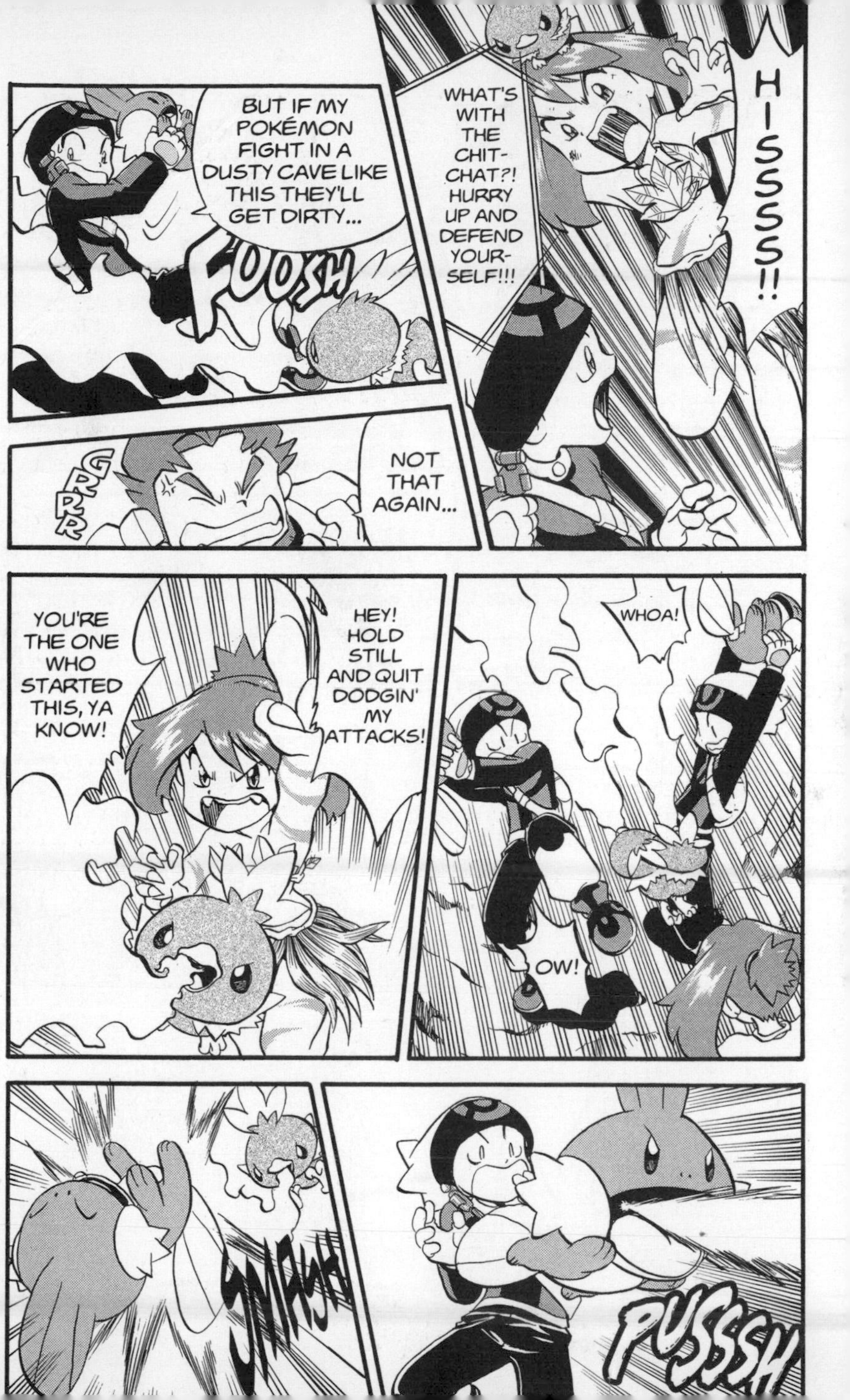
HISSSSS!!
WHAT'S WITH THE CHIT-CHAT?! HURRY UP AND DEFEND YOURSELF!!!
BUT IF MY POKÉMON FIGHT IN A DUSTY CAVE LIKE THIS THEY'LL GET DIRTY...
FOOSH
NOT THAT AGAIN...
GRRR
WHOA!
OW!
HEY! HOLD STILL AND QUIT DODGIN' MY ATTACKS!
YOU'RE THE ONE WHO STARTED THIS, YA KNOW!
PUSSSH
SMASH

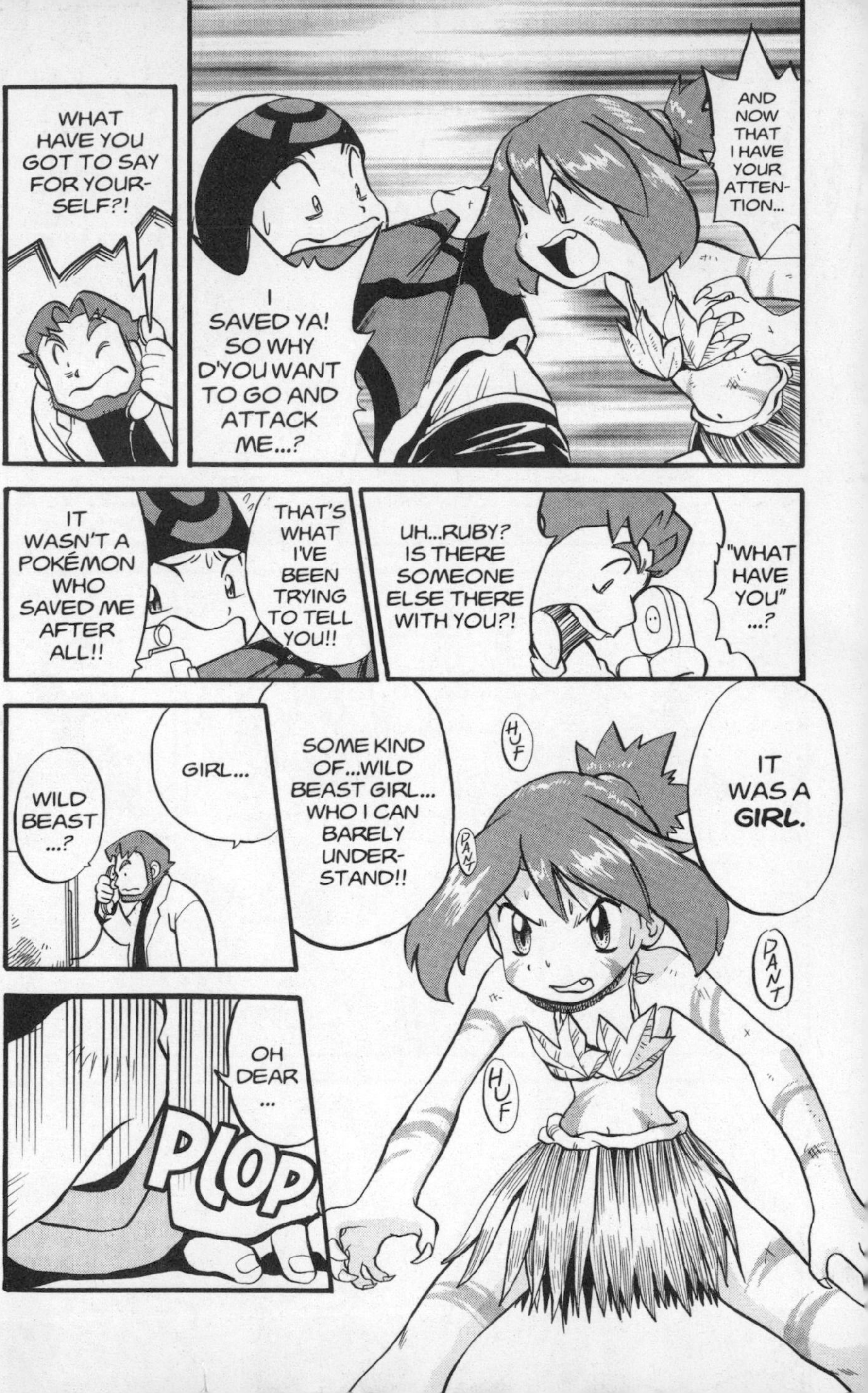
AND NOW THAT I HAVE YOUR ATTENTION...
I SAVED YA! SO WHY D'YOU WANT TO GO AND ATTACK ME...?
WHAT HAVE YOU GOT TO SAY FOR YOUR-SELF?!
"WHAT HAVE YOU"...?
UH...RUBY? IS THERE SOMEONE ELSE THERE WITH YOU?!
THAT'S WHAT I'VE BEEN TRYING TO TELL YOU!!
IT WASN'T A POKÉMON WHO SAVED ME AFTER ALL!!
IT WAS A **GIRL.**
HUF
PANT
SOME KIND OF...WILD BEAST GIRL... WHO I CAN BARELY UNDER-STAND!!
PANT
HUF
GIRL...
WILD BEAST...?
OH DEAR...
PLOP

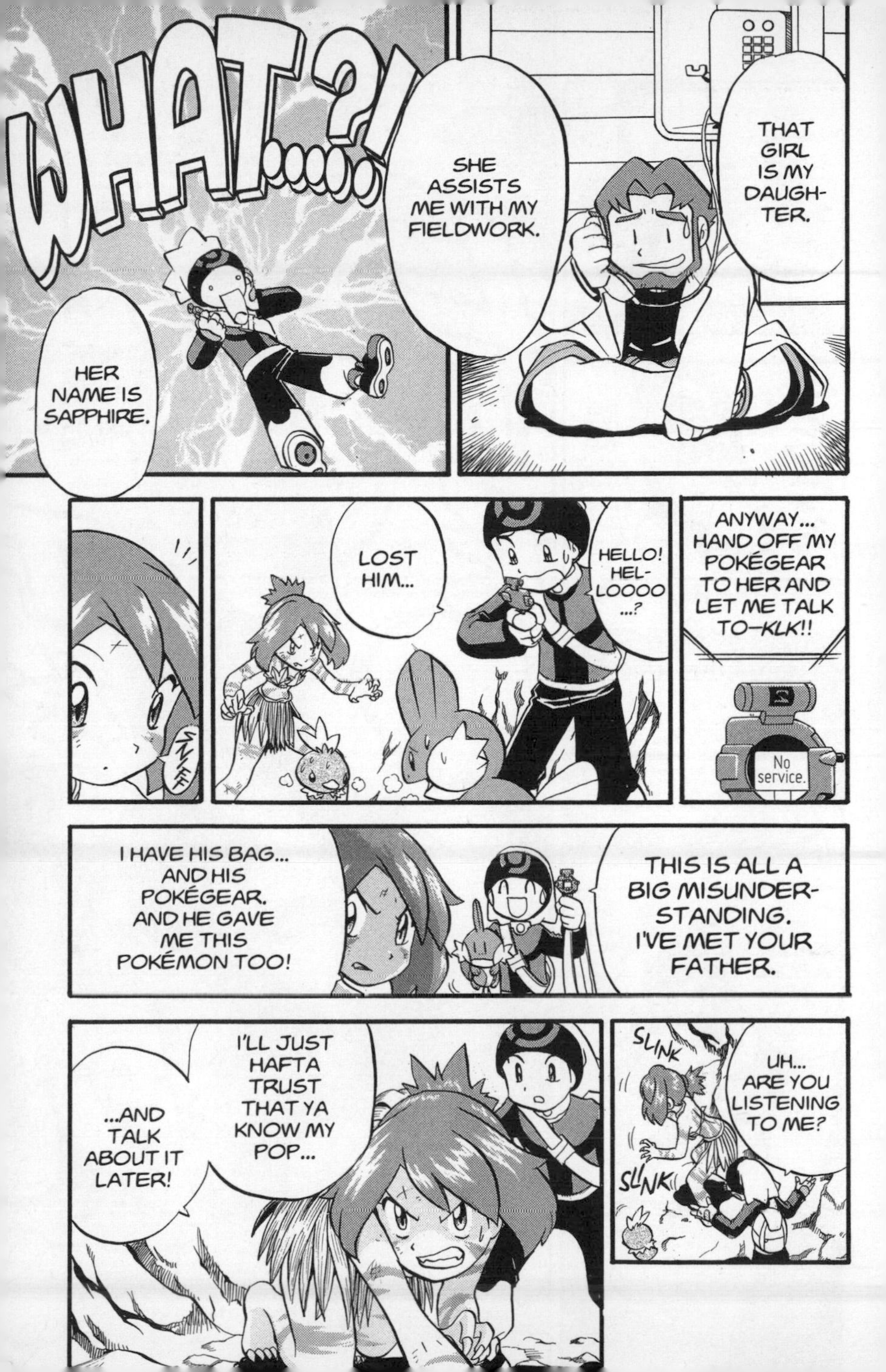
THAT GIRL IS MY DAUGHTER.
SHE ASSISTS ME WITH MY FIELDWORK.
WHAT.....?!
HER NAME IS SAPPHIRE.
ANYWAY... HAND OFF MY POKÉGEAR TO HER AND LET ME TALK TO—KLK!!
No service.
HELLO! HEL-LOOOO ...?
LOST HIM...
SNIFF
THIS IS ALL A BIG MISUNDER-STANDING. I'VE MET YOUR FATHER.
I HAVE HIS BAG... AND HIS POKÉGEAR. AND HE GAVE ME THIS POKÉMON TOO!
SLINK
UH... ARE YOU LISTENING TO ME?
SLINK
I'LL JUST HAFTA TRUST THAT YA KNOW MY POP...
...AND TALK ABOUT IT LATER!

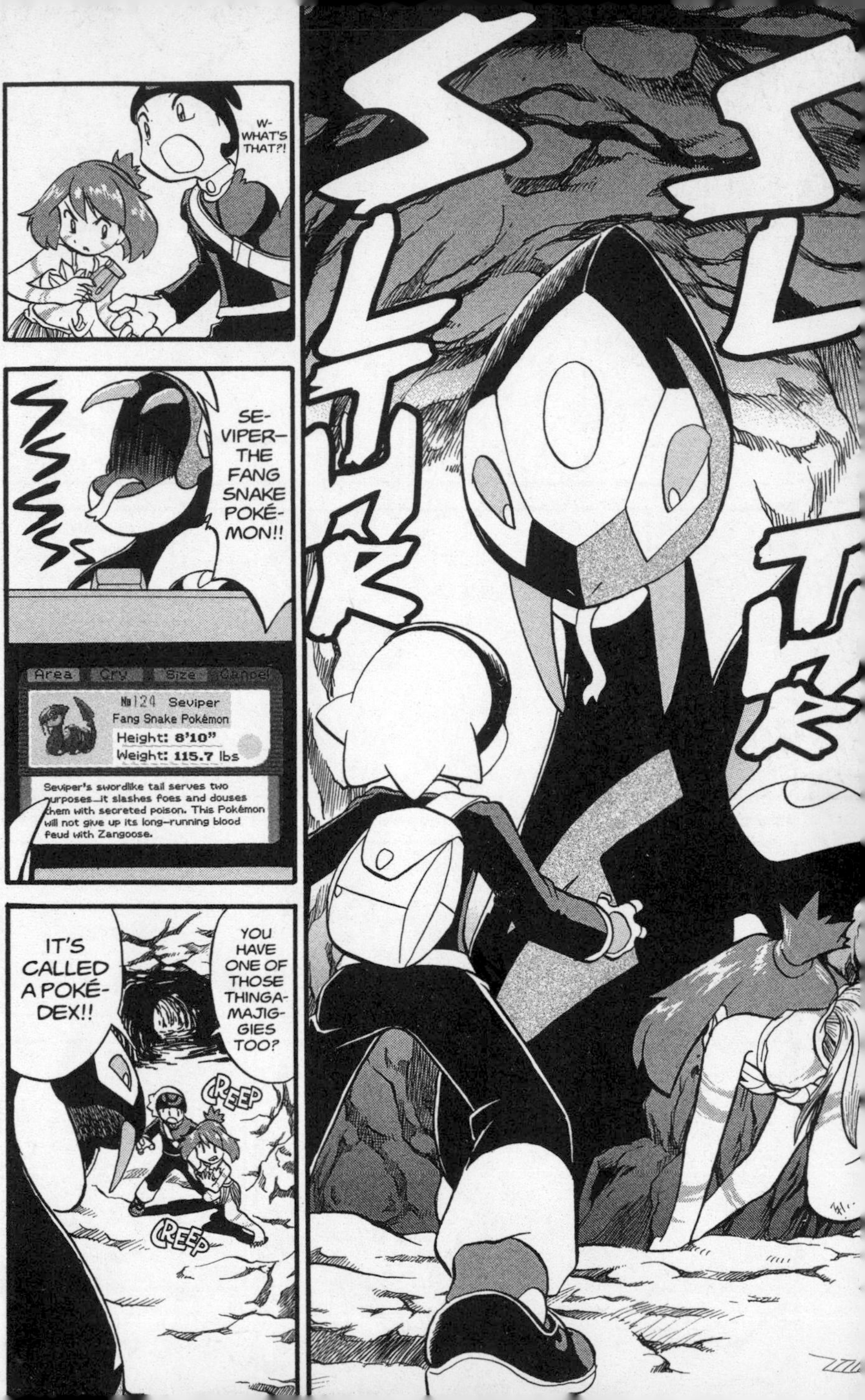
W-WHAT'S THAT?!
SE-VIPER—THE FANG SNAKE POKÉ-MON!!
Area Cry Size Cancel
№124 Seviper
Fang Snake Pokémon
Height: 8'10"
Weight: 115.7 lbs
Seviper's swordlike tail serves two purposes...it slashes foes and douses them with secreted poison. This Pokémon will not give up its long-running blood feud with Zangoose.
YOU HAVE ONE OF THOSE THINGA-MAJIG-GIES TOO?
IT'S CALLED A POKÉ-DEX!!
CREEP
CREEP

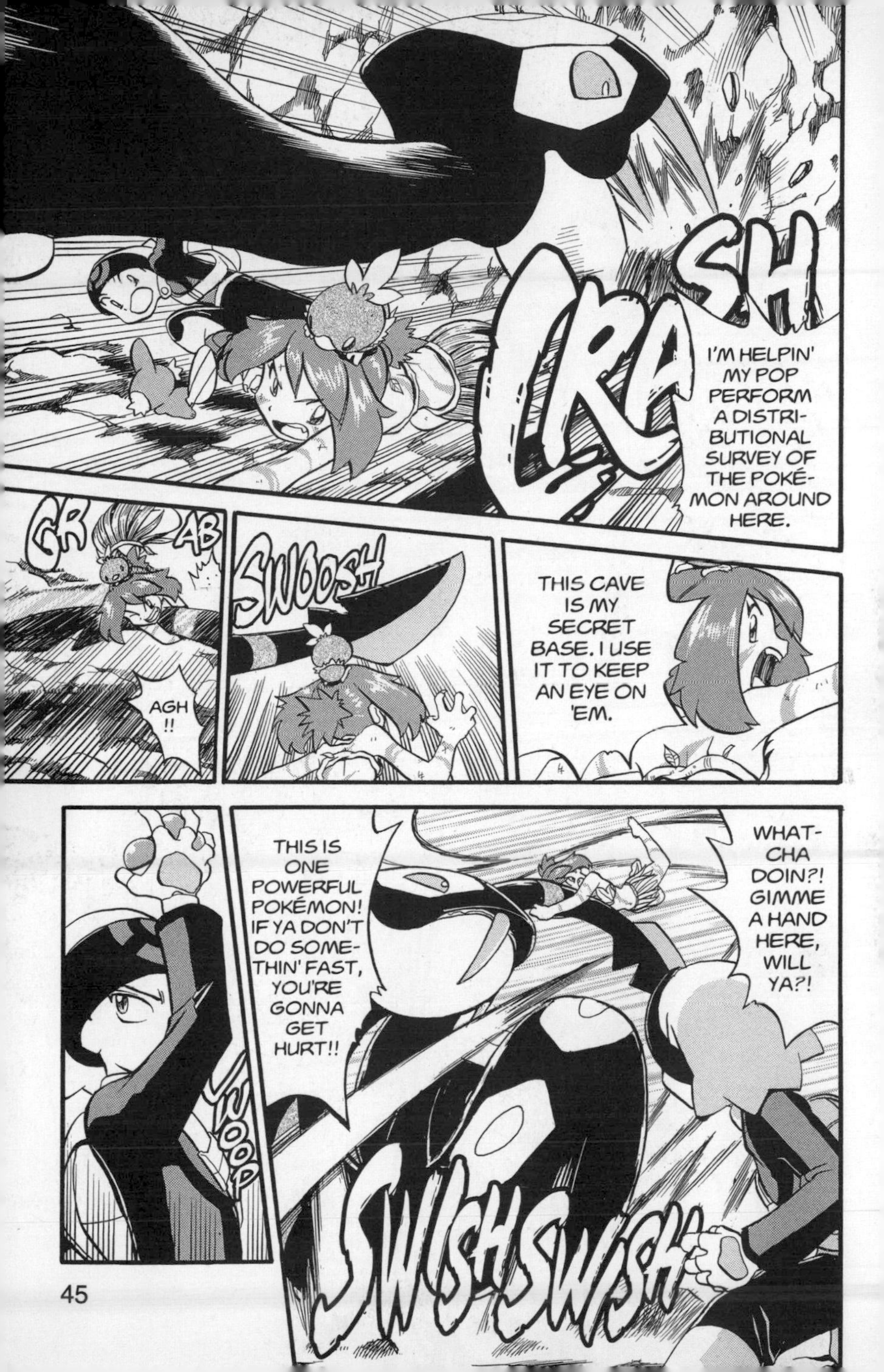
CRASH
I'M HELPIN' MY POP PERFORM A DISTRI-BUTIONAL SURVEY OF THE POKÉ-MON AROUND HERE.
THIS CAVE IS MY SECRET BASE. I USE IT TO KEEP AN EYE ON 'EM.
SWOOSH
GR AB
AGH !!
WHAT-CHA DOIN?! GIMME A HAND HERE, WILL YA?!
THIS IS ONE POWERFUL POKÉMON! IF YA DON'T DO SOME-THIN' FAST, YOU'RE GONNA GET HURT!!
SWISH SWISH
VWOOP

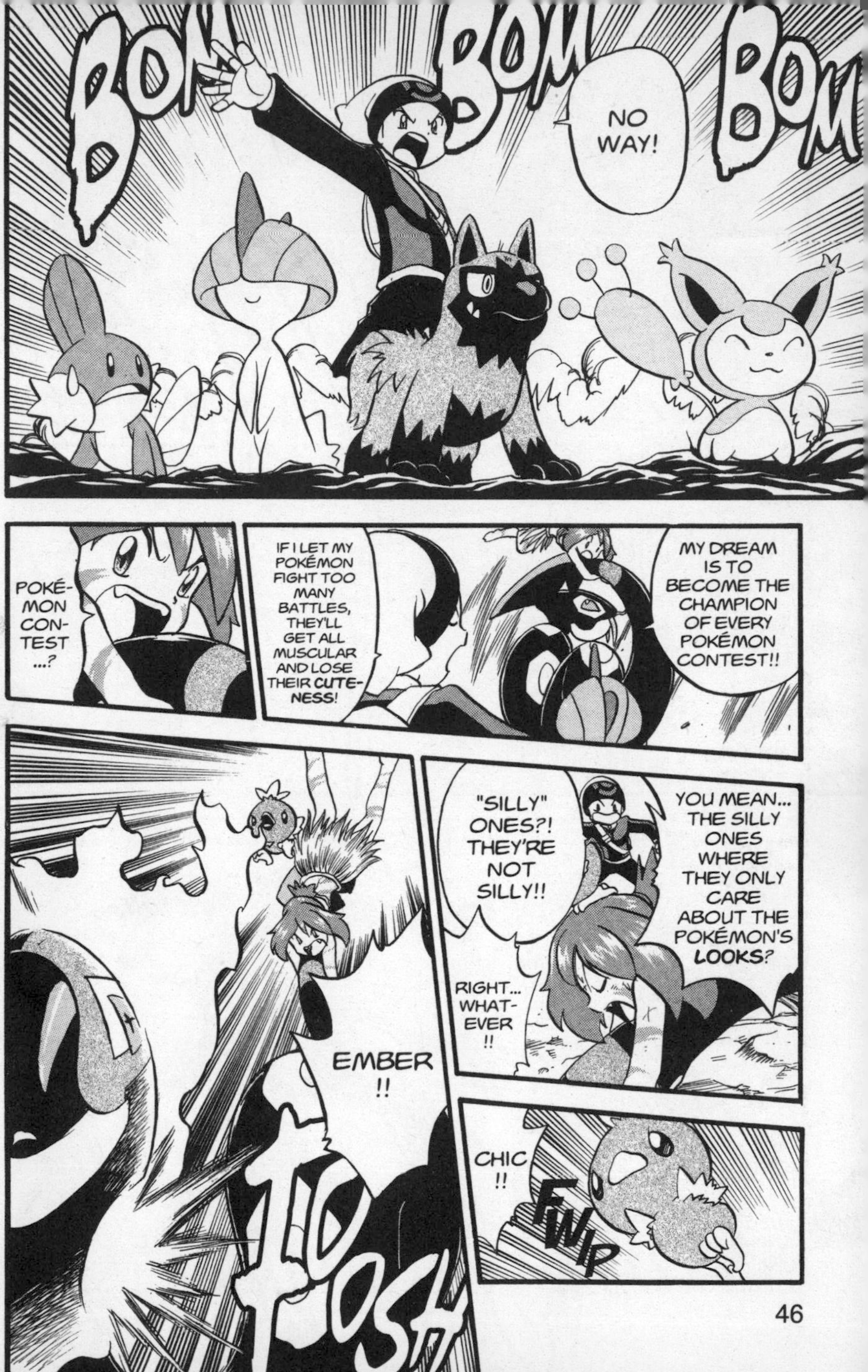
BOM BOM BOM
NO WAY!
MY DREAM IS TO BECOME THE CHAMPION OF EVERY POKÉMON CONTEST!!
IF I LET MY POKÉMON FIGHT TOO MANY BATTLES, THEY'LL GET ALL MUSCULAR AND LOSE THEIR **CUTENESS**!
POKÉ-MON CON-TEST ...?
YOU MEAN... THE SILLY ONES WHERE THEY ONLY CARE ABOUT THE POKÉMON'S **LOOKS**?
"SILLY" ONES?! THEY'RE NOT SILLY!!
RIGHT... WHAT-EVER !!
CHIC !!
FWIP
EMBER !!
FLOOSH

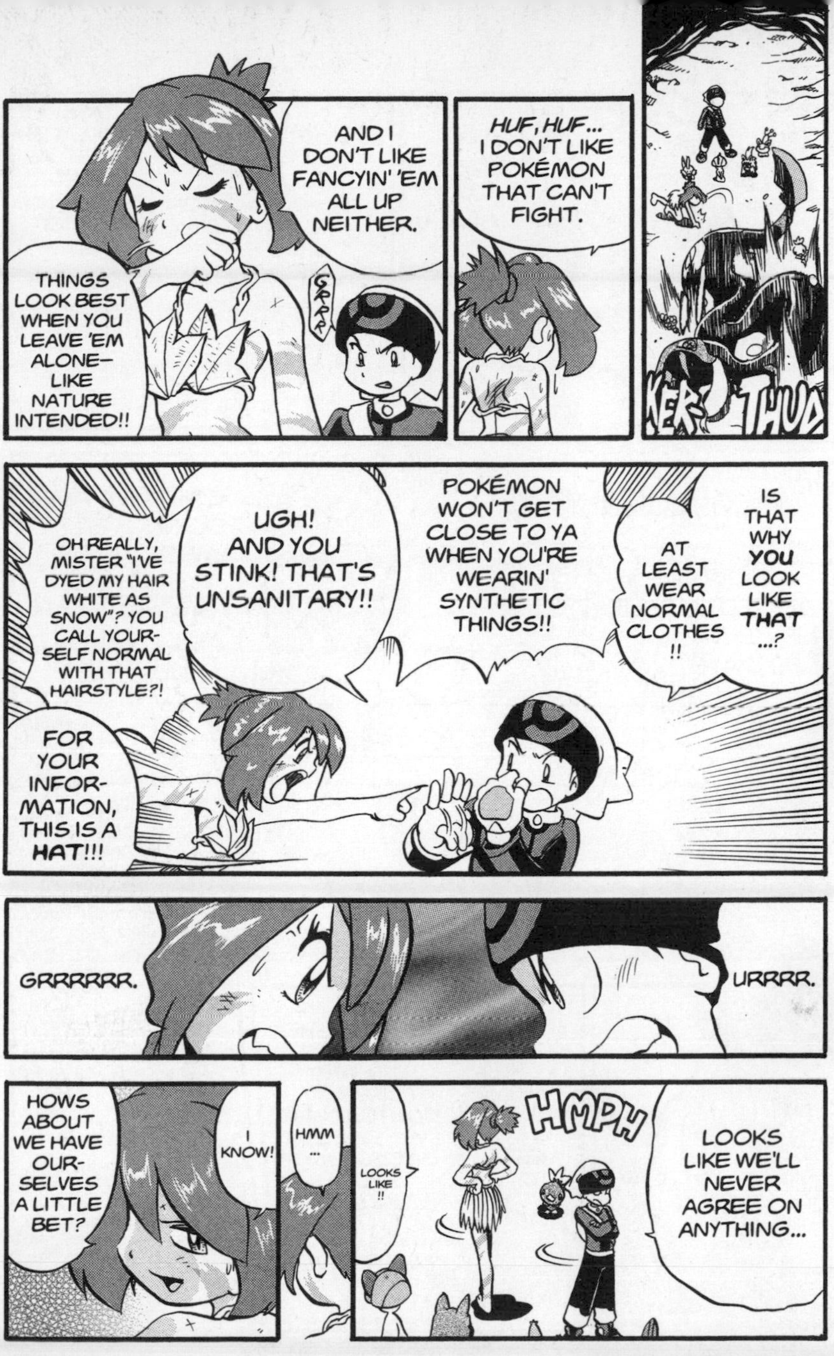
KER-THUD
HUF, HUF... I DON'T LIKE POKÉMON THAT CAN'T FIGHT.
AND I DON'T LIKE FANCYIN' 'EM ALL UP NEITHER.
GRRR
THINGS LOOK BEST WHEN YOU LEAVE 'EM ALONE— LIKE NATURE INTENDED!!
IS THAT WHY YOU LOOK LIKE THAT ...?
AT LEAST WEAR NORMAL CLOTHES !!
POKÉMON WON'T GET CLOSE TO YA WHEN YOU'RE WEARIN' SYNTHETIC THINGS!!
UGH! AND YOU STINK! THAT'S UNSANITARY!!
OH REALLY, MISTER "I'VE DYED MY HAIR WHITE AS SNOW"? YOU CALL YOURSELF NORMAL WITH THAT HAIRSTYLE?!
FOR YOUR INFORMATION, THIS IS A HAT!!!
URRRR.
GRRRRRR.
LOOKS LIKE WE'LL NEVER AGREE ON ANYTHING...
HMPH
LOOKS LIKE !!
HMM ...
I KNOW!
HOWS ABOUT WE HAVE OURSELVES A LITTLE BET?

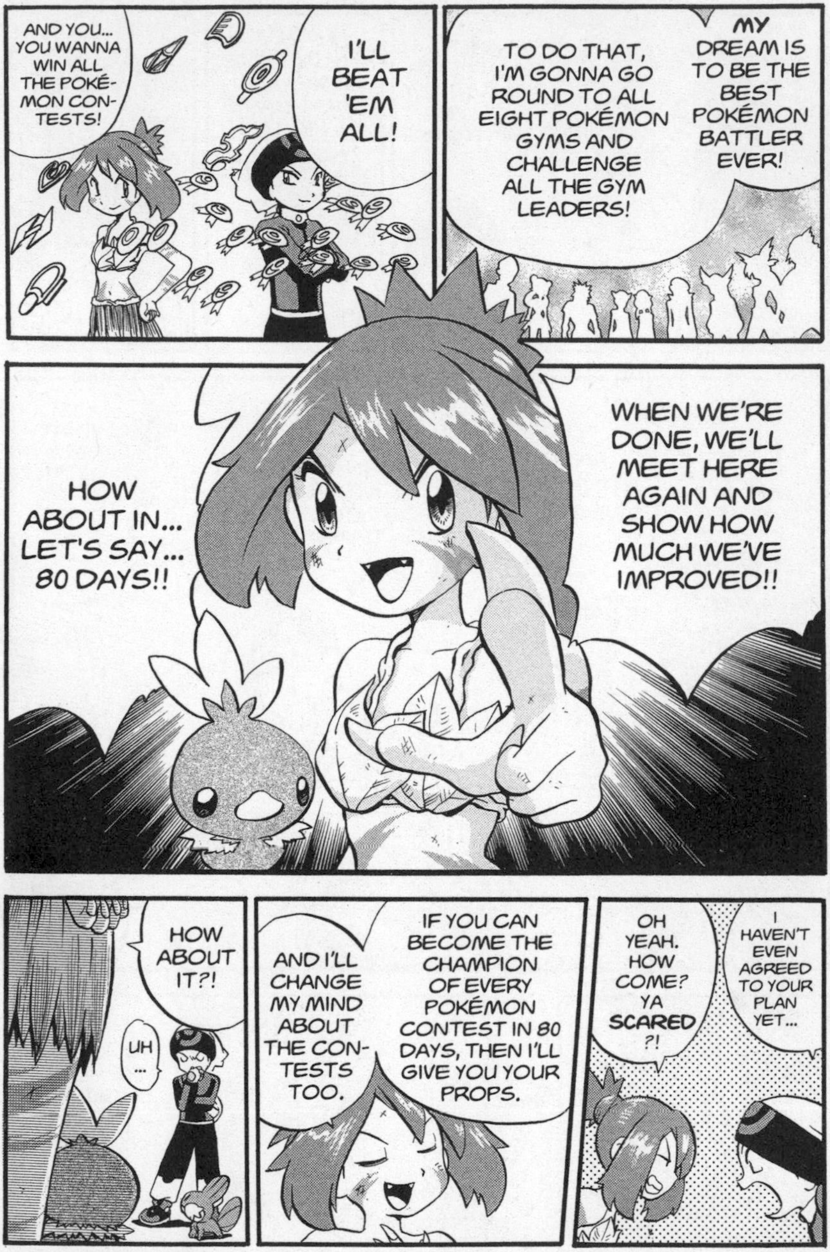
MY DREAM IS TO BE THE BEST POKÉMON BATTLER EVER!
TO DO THAT, I'M GONNA GO ROUND TO ALL EIGHT POKÉMON GYMS AND CHALLENGE ALL THE GYM LEADERS!
AND YOU... YOU WANNA WIN ALL THE POKÉ-MON CON-TESTS!
I'LL BEAT 'EM ALL!
WHEN WE'RE DONE, WE'LL MEET HERE AGAIN AND SHOW HOW MUCH WE'VE IMPROVED!!
HOW ABOUT IN... LET'S SAY... 80 DAYS!!
I HAVEN'T EVEN AGREED TO YOUR PLAN YET...
OH YEAH. HOW COME? YA SCARED?!
IF YOU CAN BECOME THE CHAMPION OF EVERY POKÉMON CONTEST IN 80 DAYS, THEN I'LL GIVE YOU YOUR PROPS.
AND I'LL CHANGE MY MIND ABOUT THE CON-TESTS TOO.
HOW ABOUT IT?!
UH ...

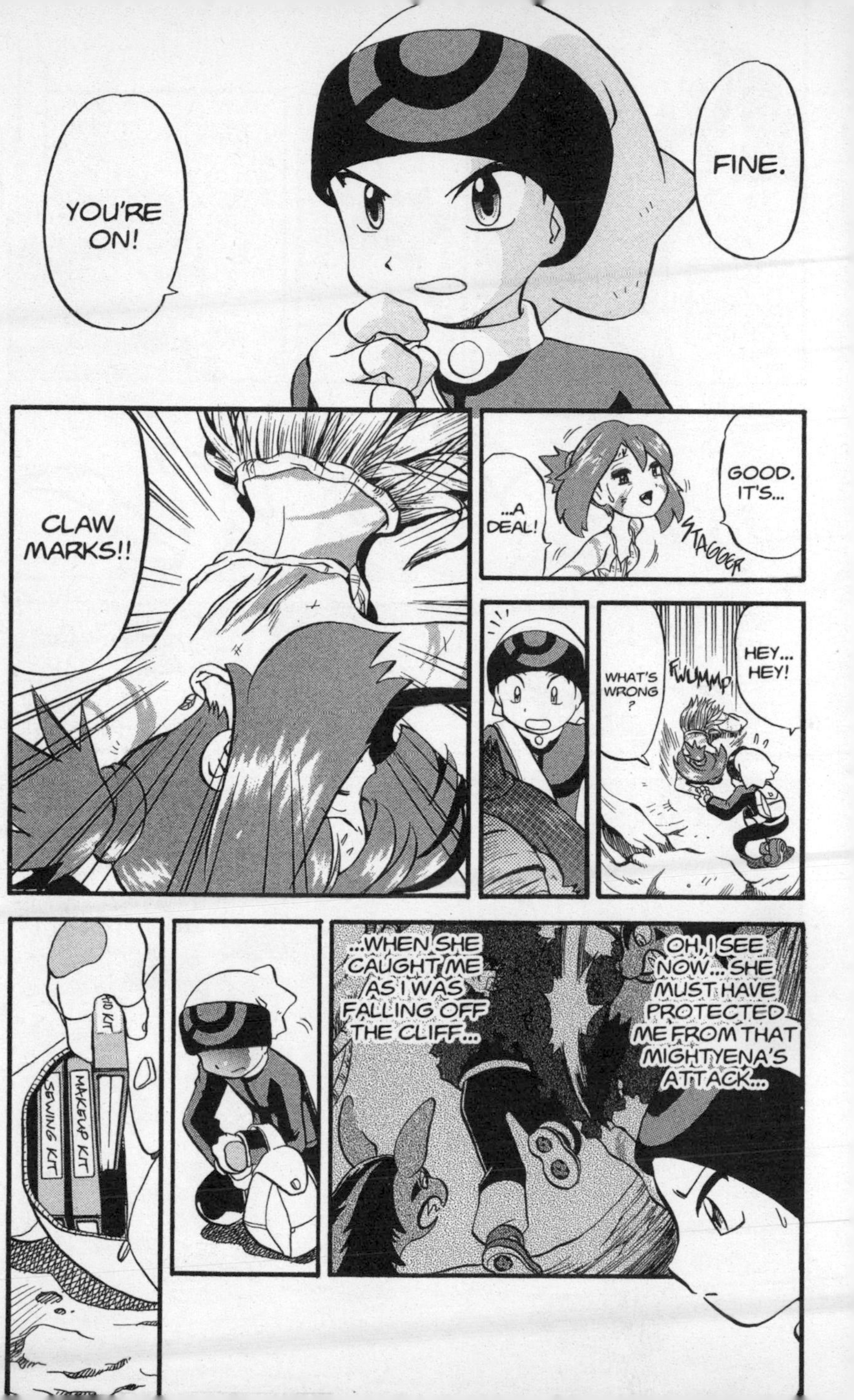
FINE.
YOU'RE ON!
GOOD. IT'S...
...A DEAL!
STAGGER
HEY... HEY!
FWUMMP
WHAT'S WRONG?
CLAW MARKS!!
OH, I SEE NOW... SHE MUST HAVE PROTECTED ME FROM THAT MIGHTYENA'S ATTACK...
...WHEN SHE CAUGHT ME AS I WAS FALLING OFF THE CLIFF...
AID KIT
MAKEUP KIT
SEWING KIT

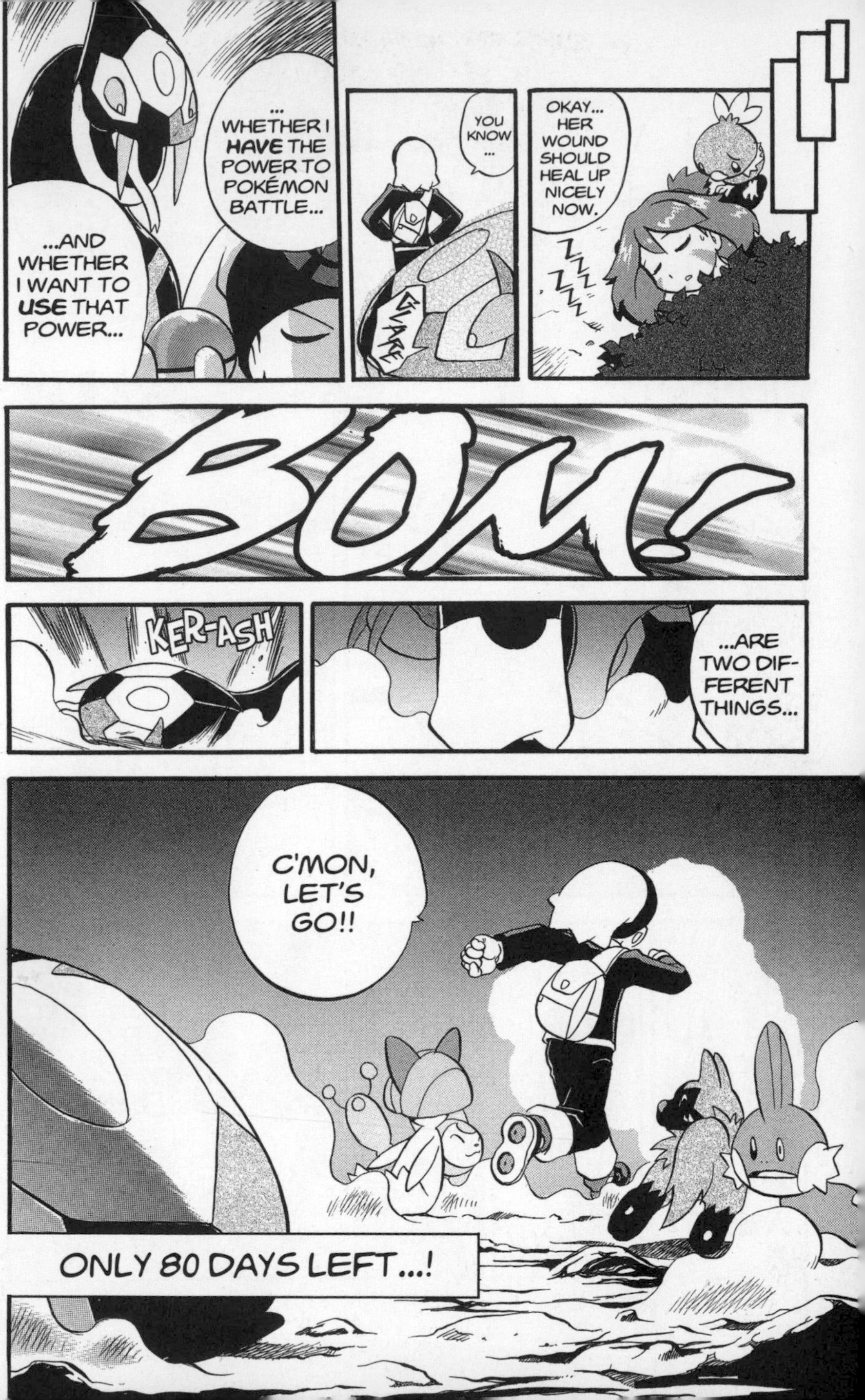

OKAY... HER WOUND SHOULD HEAL UP NICELY NOW.
ZZZ
YOU KNOW...
GLARE
...WHETHER I HAVE THE POWER TO POKÉMON BATTLE...
...AND WHETHER I WANT TO USE THAT POWER...
BOM!
...ARE TWO DIF-FERENT THINGS...
KER-ASH
C'MON, LET'S GO!!
ONLY 80 DAYS LEFT...!

ADVENTURE MAP

SAPPHIRE

RUBY

- Littleroot Town
- ▼
- Route 101
- ▼
- Oldale Town

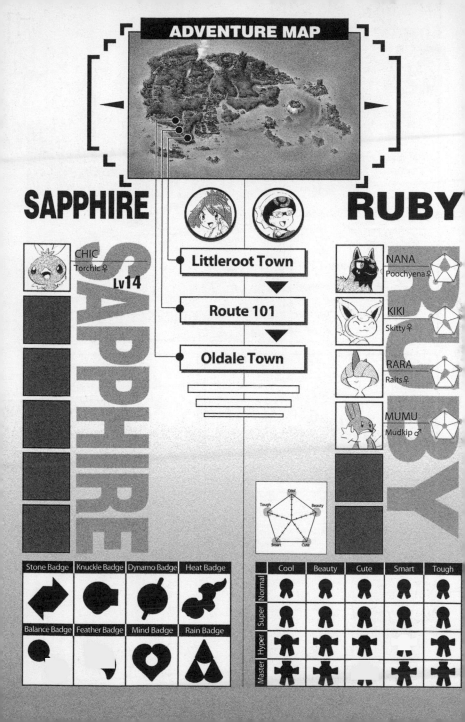

SAPPHIRE

CHIC
Torchic♀
Lv14

RUBY

NANA
Poochyena♀

KIKI
Skitty♀

RARA
Ralts♀

MUMU
Mudkip♂

Cool
Beauty
Cute
Smart
Tough

Stone Badge	Knuckle Badge	Dynamo Badge	Heat Badge
Balance Badge	Feather Badge	Mind Badge	Rain Badge

	Cool	Beauty	Cute	Smart	Tough
Normal					
Super					
Hyper					
Master					

Chapter 184: Distracting Dustox

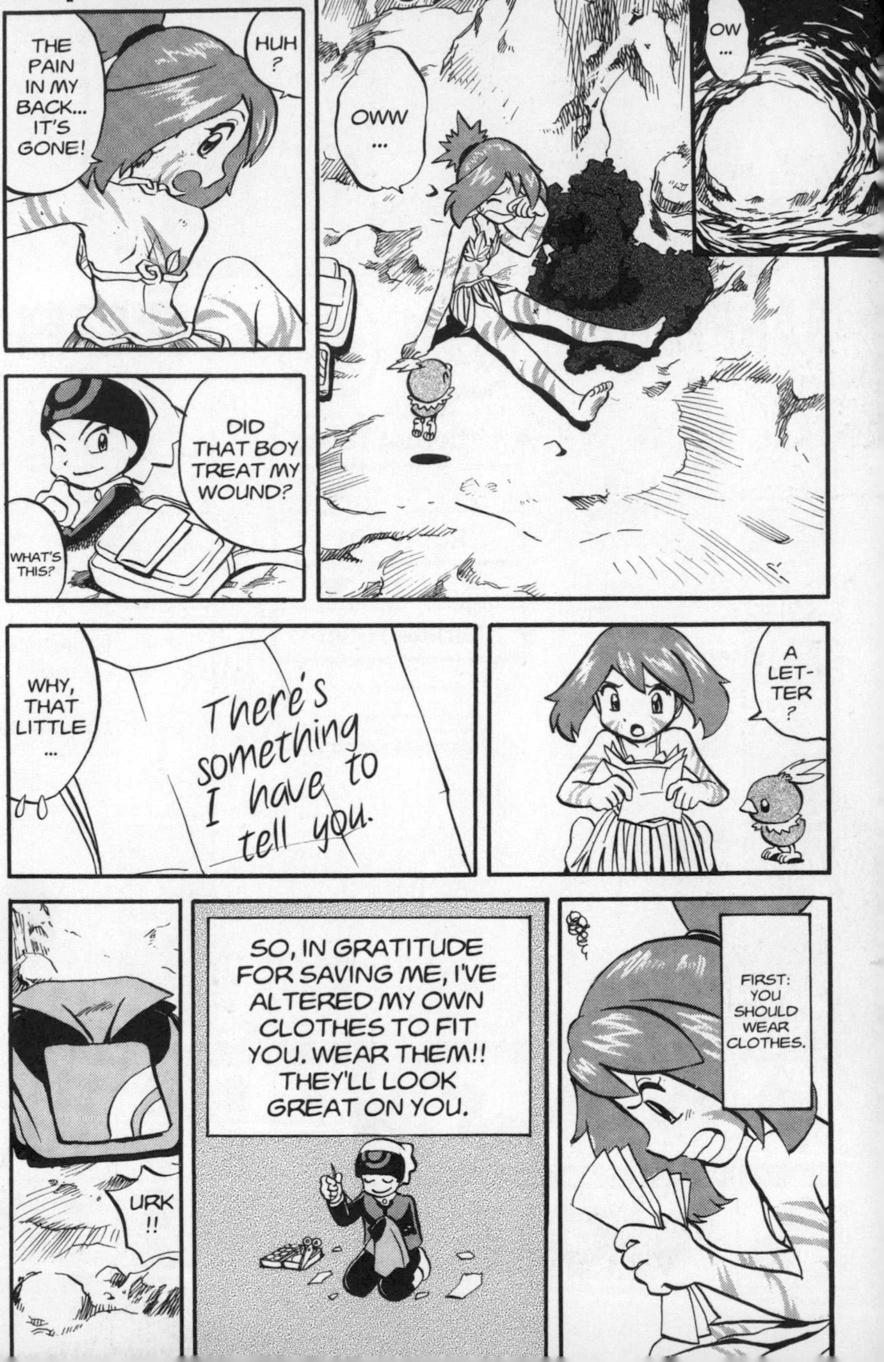
OW ...
OWW ...
HUH ?
THE PAIN IN MY BACK... IT'S GONE!
DID THAT BOY TREAT MY WOUND?
WHAT'S THIS?
A LET-TER ?
There's something I have to tell you.
WHY, THAT LITTLE ...
FIRST: YOU SHOULD WEAR CLOTHES.
SO, IN GRATITUDE FOR SAVING ME, I'VE ALTERED MY OWN CLOTHES TO FIT YOU. WEAR THEM!! THEY'LL LOOK GREAT ON YOU.
URK !!

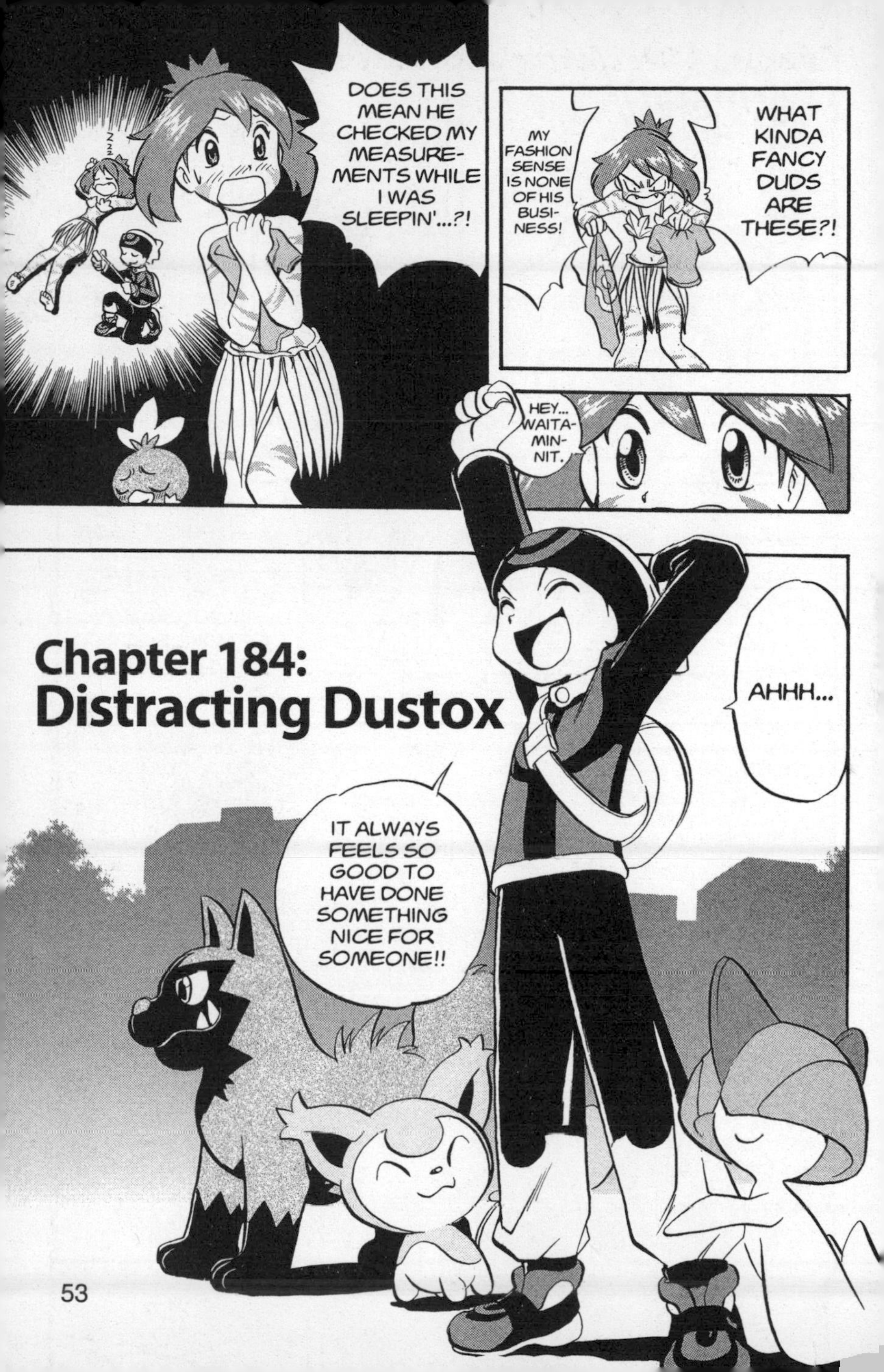
WHAT KINDA FANCY DUDS ARE THESE?!
MY FASHION SENSE IS NONE OF HIS BUSINESS!
HEY... WAITAMINNIT.
DOES THIS MEAN HE CHECKED MY MEASUREMENTS WHILE I WAS SLEEPIN'...?!
Z Z Z
AHHH...
IT ALWAYS FEELS SO GOOD TO HAVE DONE SOMETHING NICE FOR SOMEONE!!

Chapter 184: Distracting Dustox

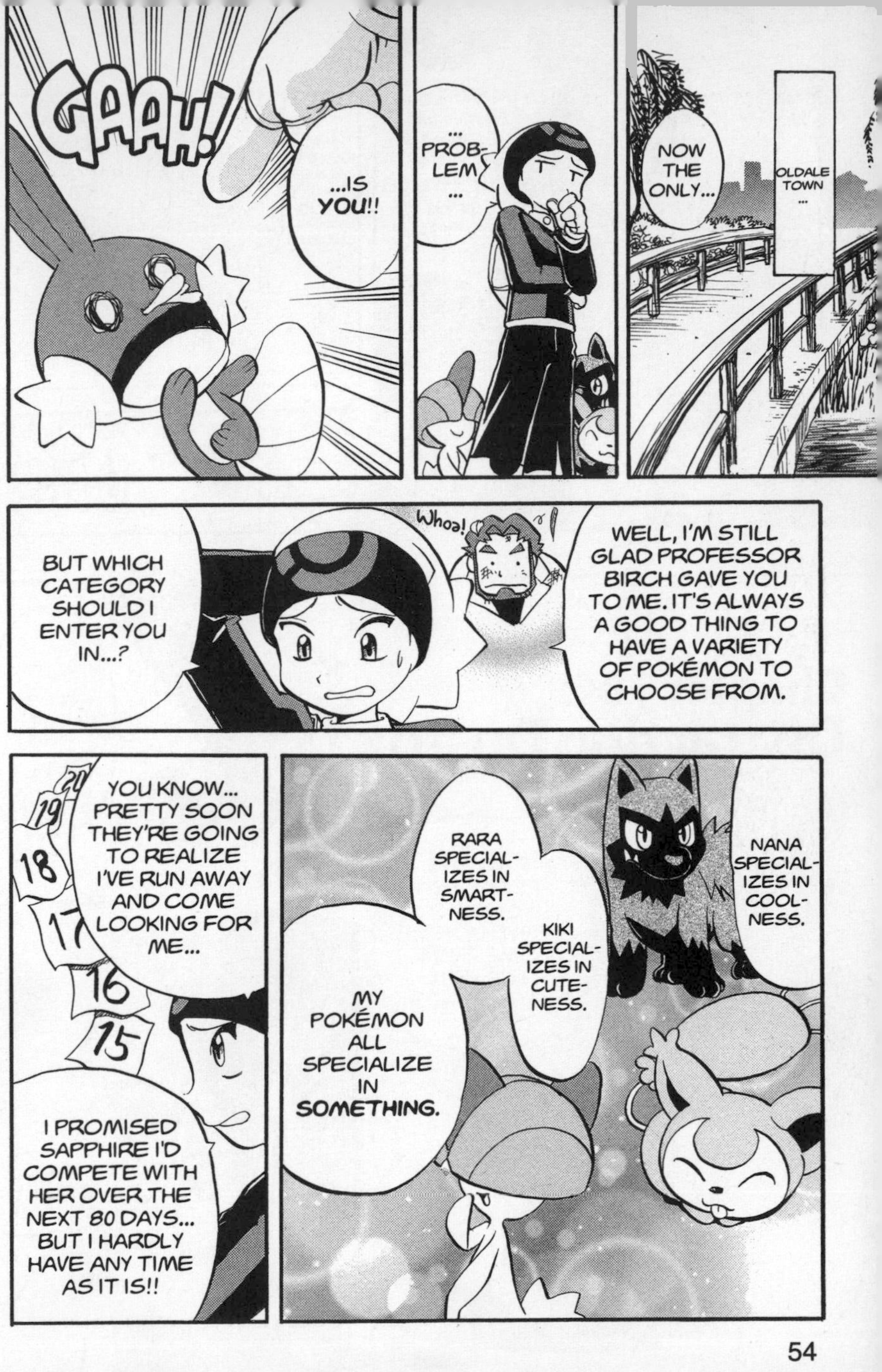
OLDALE TOWN ...
NOW THE ONLY...
... PROBLEM ...
GAAH!
...IS YOU!!
WELL, I'M STILL GLAD PROFESSOR BIRCH GAVE YOU TO ME. IT'S ALWAYS A GOOD THING TO HAVE A VARIETY OF POKÉMON TO CHOOSE FROM.
Whoa!
BUT WHICH CATEGORY SHOULD I ENTER YOU IN...?
NANA SPECIALIZES IN COOLNESS.
RARA SPECIALIZES IN SMARTNESS.
KIKI SPECIALIZES IN CUTENESS.
MY POKÉMON ALL SPECIALIZE IN SOMETHING.
20 19 18 17 16 15
YOU KNOW... PRETTY SOON THEY'RE GOING TO REALIZE I'VE RUN AWAY AND COME LOOKING FOR ME...
I PROMISED SAPPHIRE I'D COMPETE WITH HER OVER THE NEXT 80 DAYS... BUT I HARDLY HAVE ANY TIME AS IT IS!!

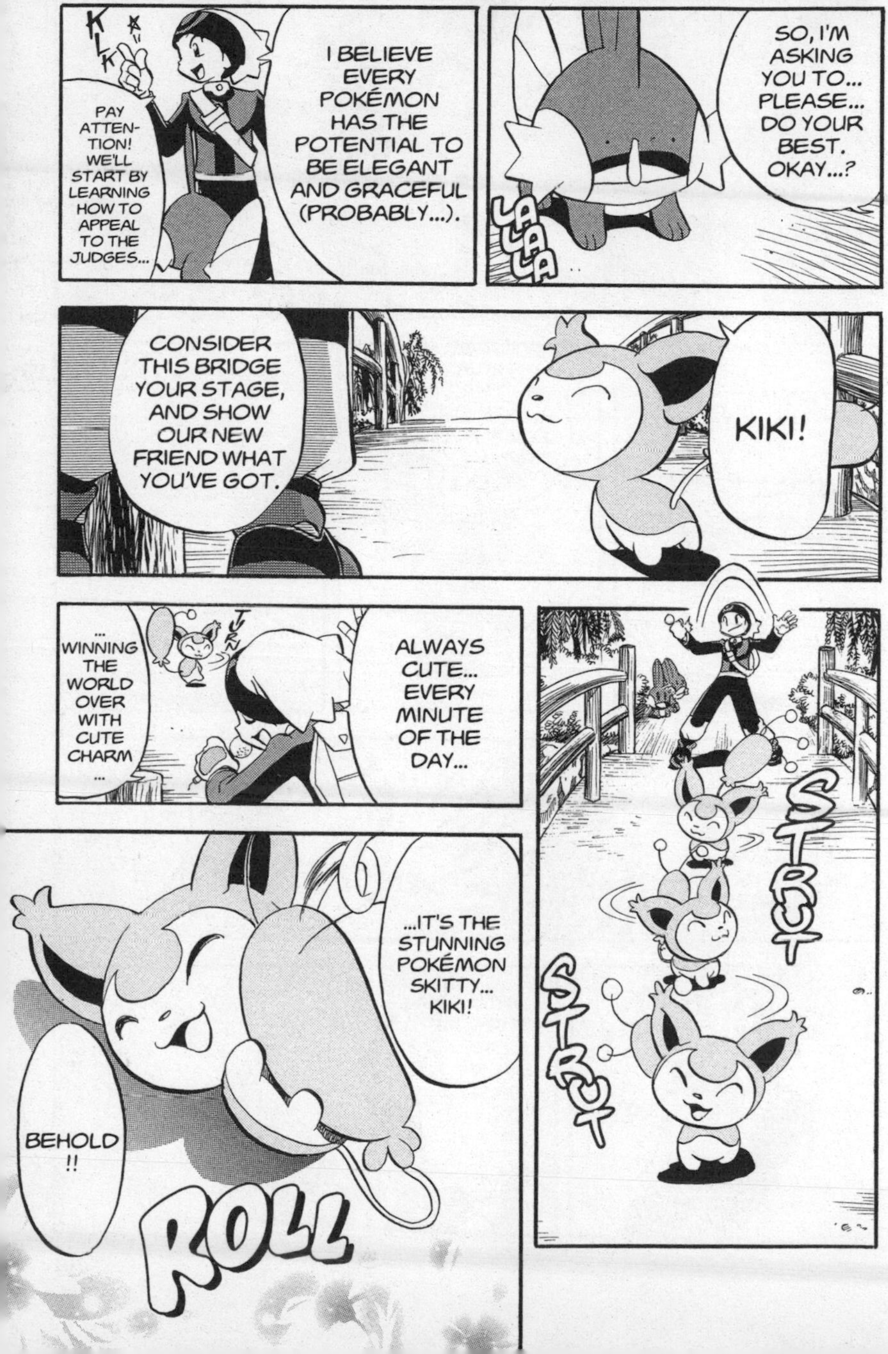
SO, I'M ASKING YOU TO... PLEASE... DO YOUR BEST. OKAY...?
LALALA
I BELIEVE EVERY POKÉMON HAS THE POTENTIAL TO BE ELEGANT AND GRACEFUL (PROBABLY...).
KLK
PAY ATTENTION! WE'LL START BY LEARNING HOW TO APPEAL TO THE JUDGES...
KIKI!
CONSIDER THIS BRIDGE YOUR STAGE, AND SHOW OUR NEW FRIEND WHAT YOU'VE GOT.
STRUT
STRUT
ALWAYS CUTE... EVERY MINUTE OF THE DAY...
TURN
... WINNING THE WORLD OVER WITH CUTE CHARM ...
...IT'S THE STUNNING POKÉMON SKITTY... KIKI!
BEHOLD !!
ROLL

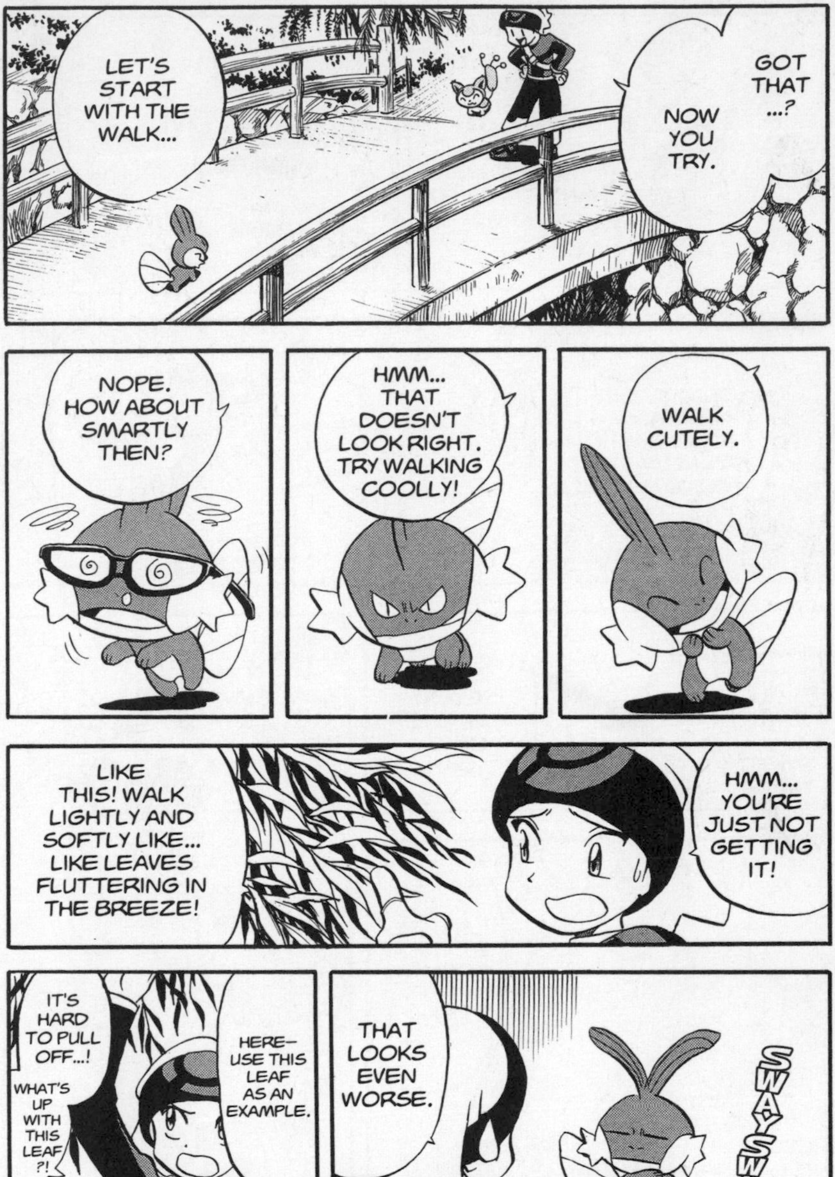
GOT THAT ...?
NOW YOU TRY.
LET'S START WITH THE WALK...
WALK CUTELY.
HMM... THAT DOESN'T LOOK RIGHT. TRY WALKING COOLLY!
NOPE. HOW ABOUT SMARTLY THEN?
HMM... YOU'RE JUST NOT GETTING IT!
LIKE THIS! WALK LIGHTLY AND SOFTLY LIKE... LIKE LEAVES FLUTTERING IN THE BREEZE!
SWAY SWAY
THAT LOOKS EVEN WORSE.
HERE— USE THIS LEAF AS AN EXAMPLE.
IT'S HARD TO PULL OFF...!
WHAT'S UP WITH THIS LEAF ?!

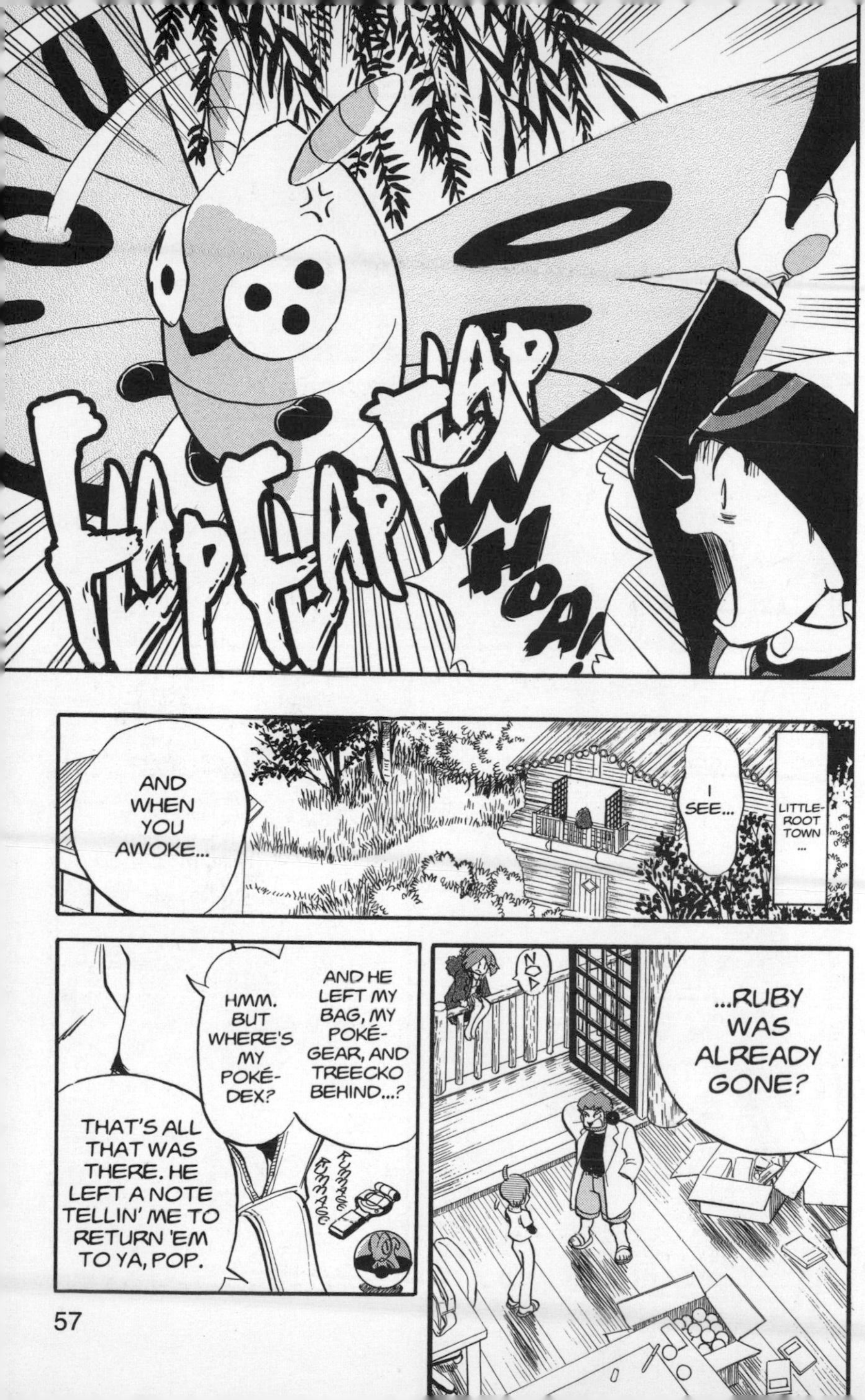
FLAP FLAP FLAP
WHOA!!
LITTLE-ROOT TOWN ...
I SEE...
AND WHEN YOU AWOKE...
...RUBY WAS ALREADY GONE?
NOD
AND HE LEFT MY BAG, MY POKÉ-GEAR, AND TREECKO BEHIND...?
HMM. BUT WHERE'S MY POKÉ-DEX?
THAT'S ALL THAT WAS THERE. HE LEFT A NOTE TELLIN' ME TO RETURN 'EM TO YA, POP.
RUMMAGE RUMMAGE

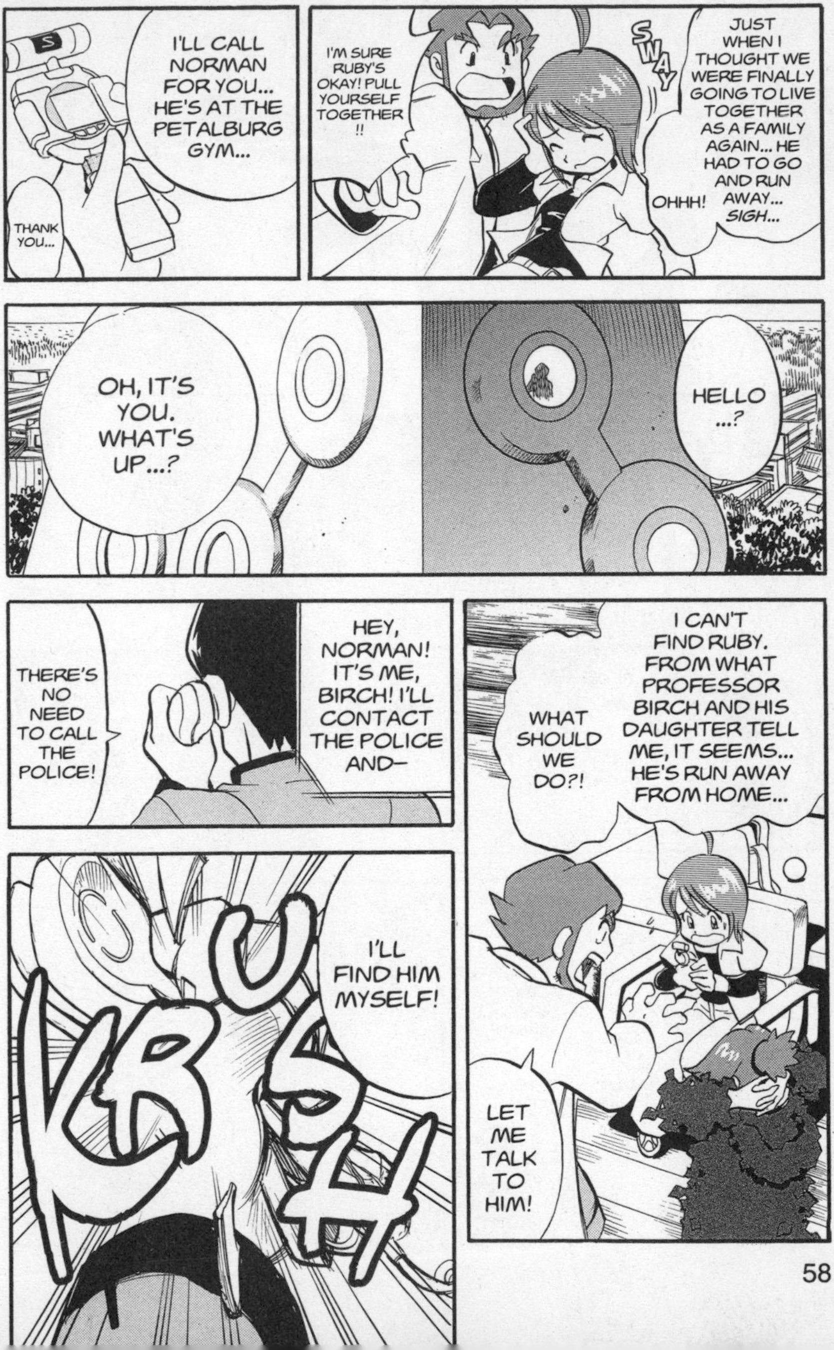
JUST WHEN I THOUGHT WE WERE FINALLY GOING TO LIVE TOGETHER AS A FAMILY AGAIN... HE HAD TO GO AND RUN AWAY... SIGH...
SWAY
OHHH!
I'M SURE RUBY'S OKAY! PULL YOURSELF TOGETHER !!
I'LL CALL NORMAN FOR YOU... HE'S AT THE PETALBURG GYM...
THANK YOU...
HELLO ...?
OH, IT'S YOU. WHAT'S UP...?
I CAN'T FIND RUBY. FROM WHAT PROFESSOR BIRCH AND HIS DAUGHTER TELL ME, IT SEEMS... HE'S RUN AWAY FROM HOME...
WHAT SHOULD WE DO?!
LET ME TALK TO HIM!
HEY, NORMAN! IT'S ME, BIRCH! I'LL CONTACT THE POLICE AND—
THERE'S NO NEED TO CALL THE POLICE!
I'LL FIND HIM MYSELF!
KRUSH

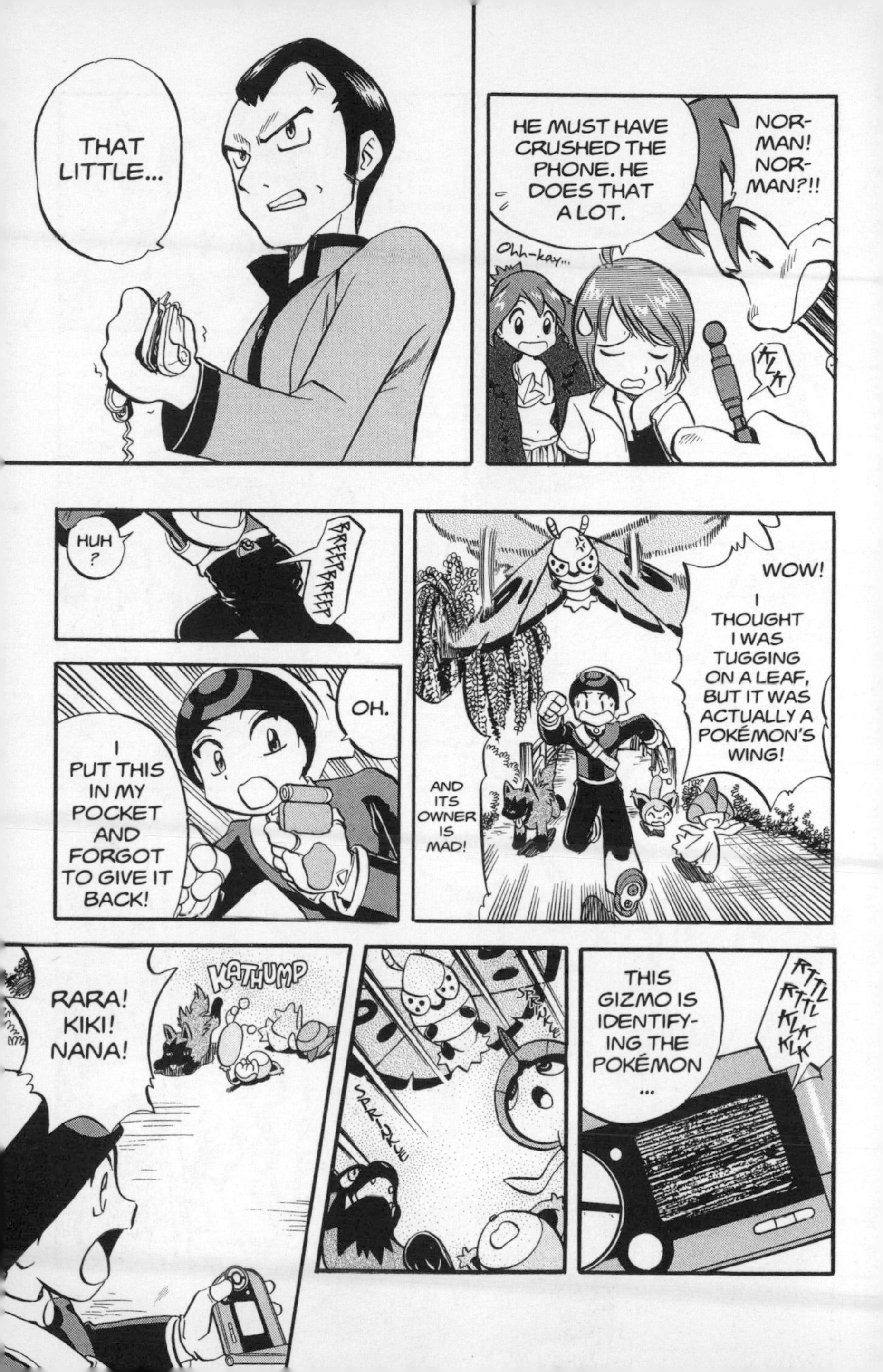
NOR-MAN! NOR-MAN?!!
HE MUST HAVE CRUSHED THE PHONE. HE DOES THAT A LOT.
Ohh-kay...
KLK
THAT LITTLE...
WOW! I THOUGHT I WAS TUGGING ON A LEAF, BUT IT WAS ACTUALLY A POKÉMON'S WING!
AND ITS OWNER IS MAD!
BREEP BREEP
HUH?
OH.
I PUT THIS IN MY POCKET AND FORGOT TO GIVE IT BACK!
RTTTL RTTTL KLK KLK
THIS GIZMO IS IDENTIFYING THE POKÉMON ...
SPRINKLE
SPRINKLE
KATHUMP
RARA! KIKI! NANA!

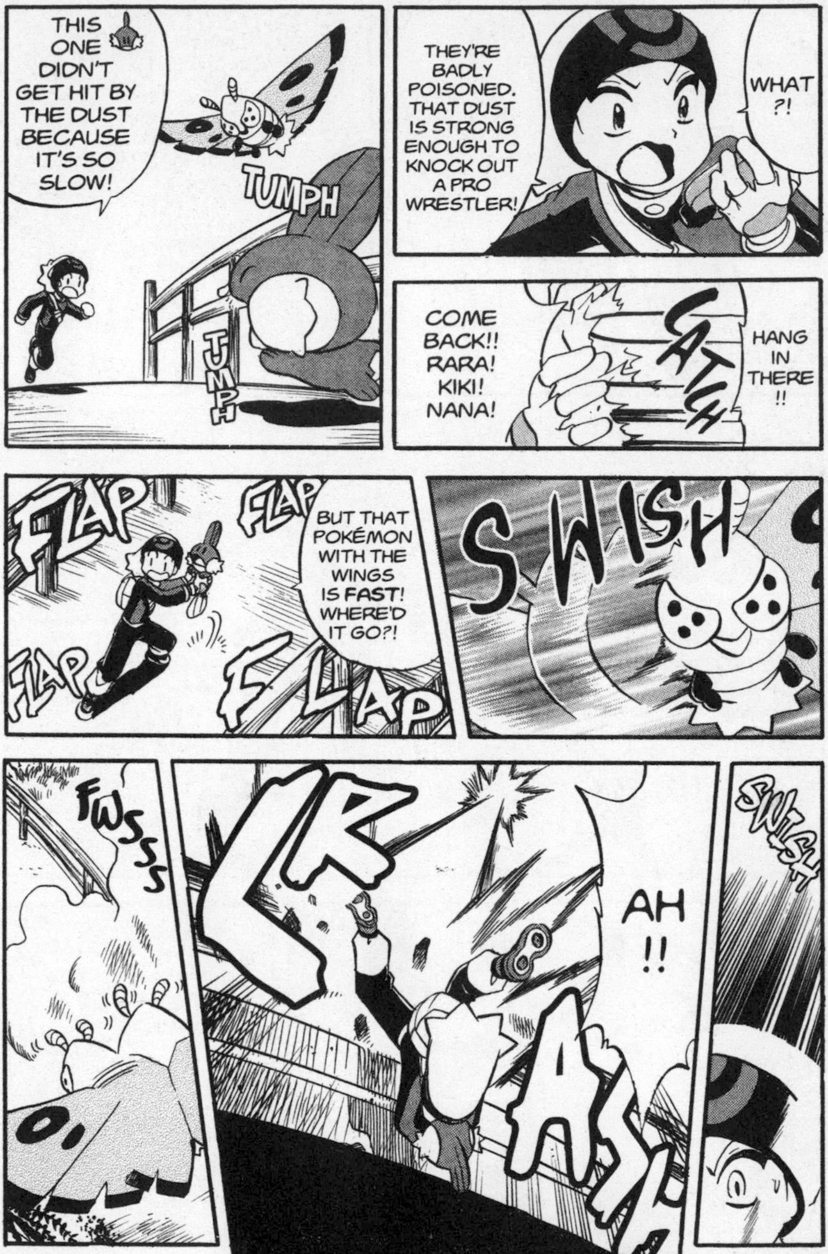
THIS ONE DIDN'T GET HIT BY THE DUST BECAUSE IT'S SO SLOW!
TUMPH
TUMPH
THEY'RE BADLY POISONED. THAT DUST IS STRONG ENOUGH TO KNOCK OUT A PRO WRESTLER!
WHAT?!
COME BACK!! RARA! KIKI! NANA!
CATCH
HANG IN THERE!!
FLAP
FLAP
FLAP
F LAP
BUT THAT POKÉMON WITH THE WINGS IS FAST! WHERE'D IT GO?!
SWISH
FWSSS
AH!!
SWISH

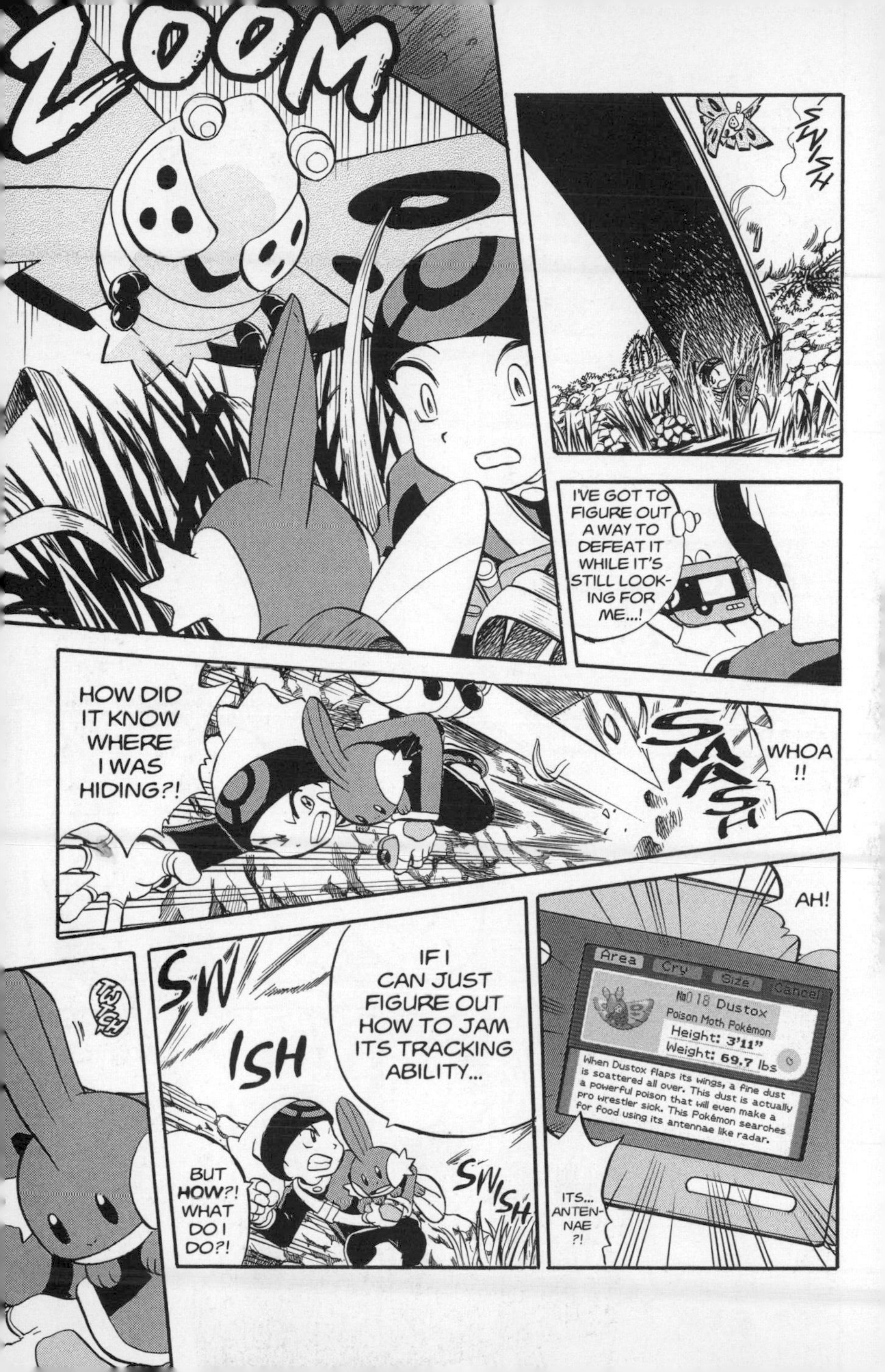
SWISH
I'VE GOT TO FIGURE OUT A WAY TO DEFEAT IT WHILE IT'S STILL LOOKING FOR ME...!
ZOOM
WHOA!!
SMASH
HOW DID IT KNOW WHERE I WAS HIDING?!
AH!
Area
Cry
Size
Cancel
No018 Dustox
Poison Moth Pokémon
Height: 3'11"
Weight: 69.7 lbs
When Dustox flaps its wings, a fine dust is scattered all over. This dust is actually a powerful poison that will even make a pro wrestler sick. This Pokémon searches for food using its antennae like radar.
ITS... ANTENNAE?!
IF I CAN JUST FIGURE OUT HOW TO JAM ITS TRACKING ABILITY...
SW ISH
SWISH
BUT HOW?! WHAT DO I DO?!
TWITCH

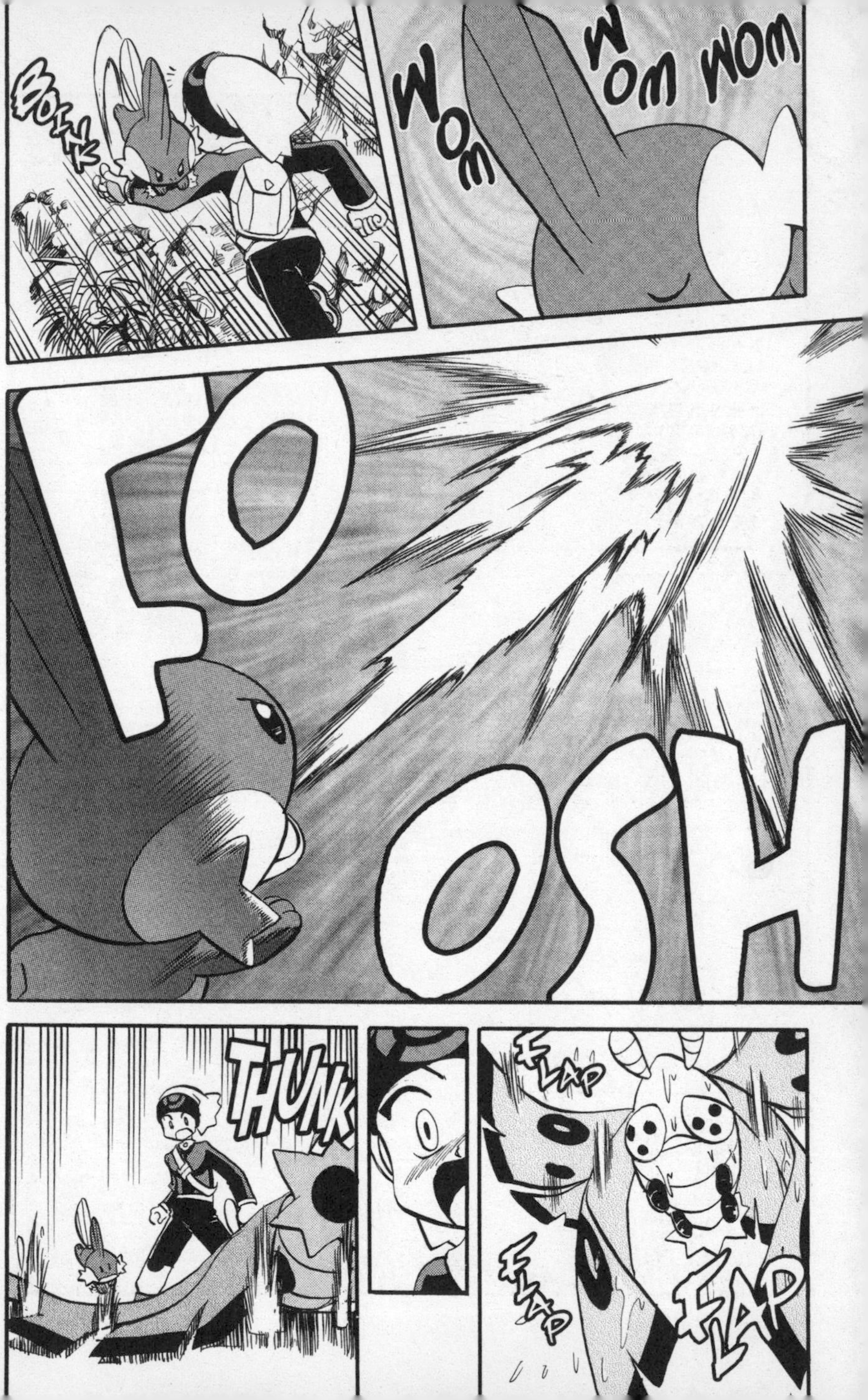
WOM WOM
WOM
BONK
FOOSH
FLAP
FLAP
FLAP
THUNK

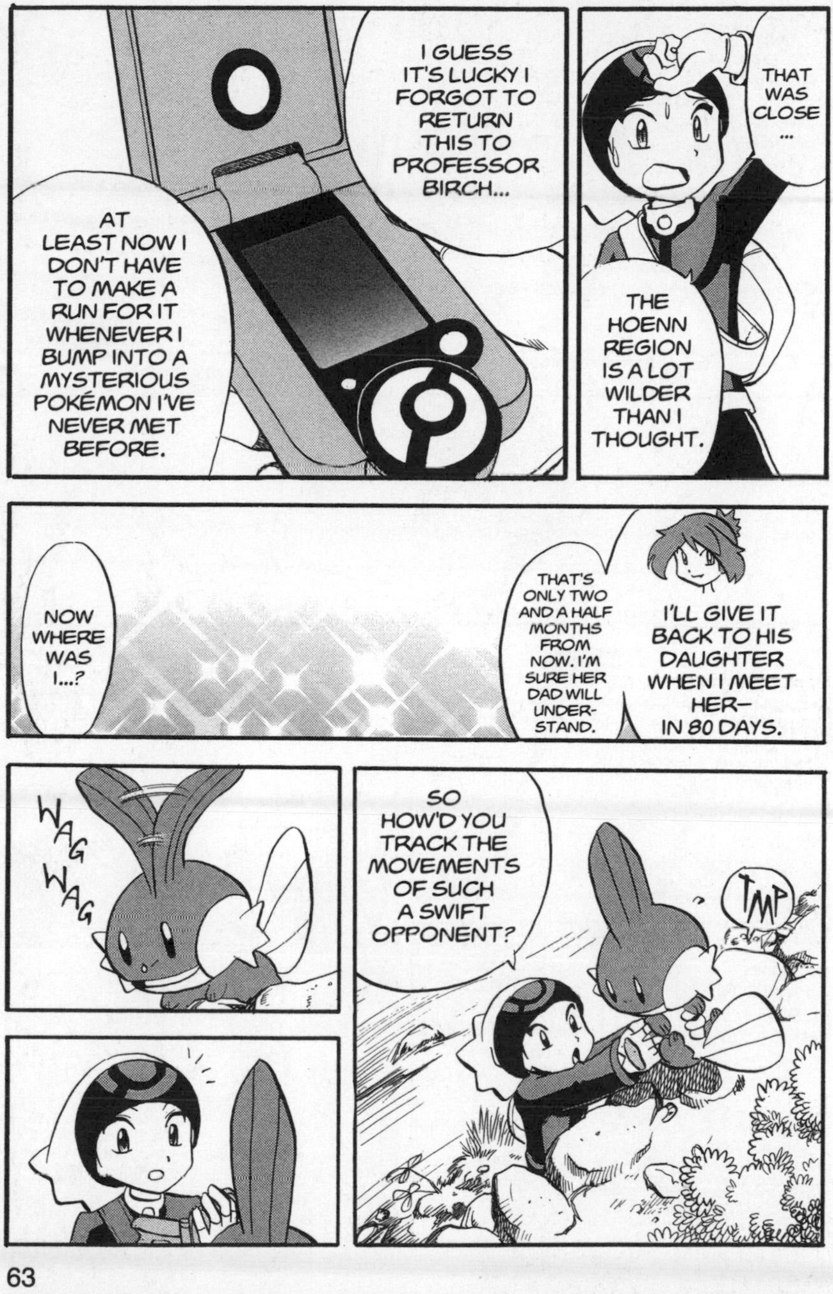
THAT WAS CLOSE ...
THE HOENN REGION IS A LOT WILDER THAN I THOUGHT.
I GUESS IT'S LUCKY I FORGOT TO RETURN THIS TO PROFESSOR BIRCH...
AT LEAST NOW I DON'T HAVE TO MAKE A RUN FOR IT WHENEVER I BUMP INTO A MYSTERIOUS POKÉMON I'VE NEVER MET BEFORE.
I'LL GIVE IT BACK TO HIS DAUGHTER WHEN I MEET HER— IN 80 DAYS.
THAT'S ONLY TWO AND A HALF MONTHS FROM NOW. I'M SURE HER DAD WILL UNDER-STAND.
NOW WHERE WAS I...?
SO HOW'D YOU TRACK THE MOVEMENTS OF SUCH A SWIFT OPPONENT?
TMP
WAG WAG

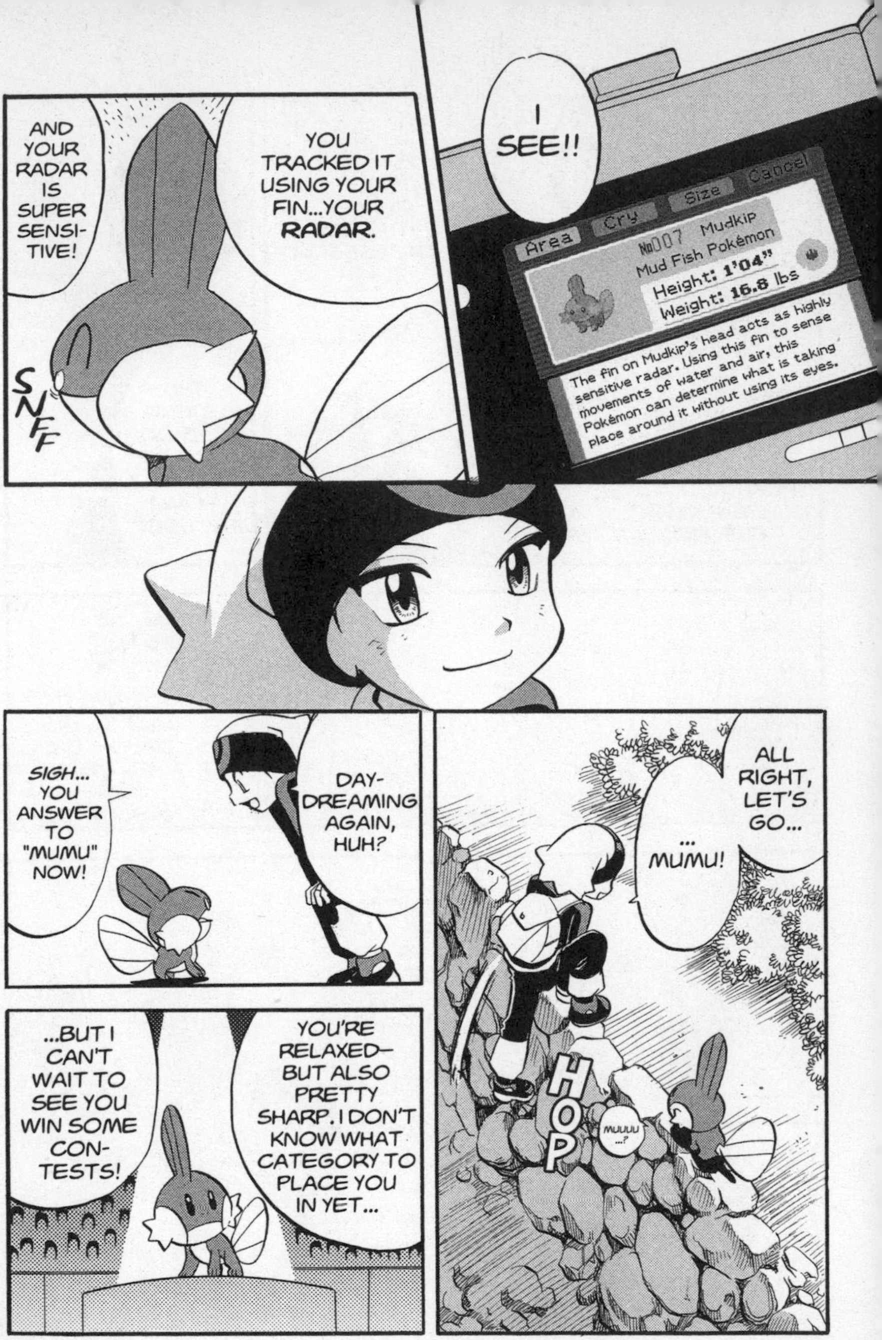
I SEE!!
Area
Cry
Size
Cancel
No007 Mudkip
Mud Fish Pokémon
Height: 1'04"
Weight: 16.8 lbs
The fin on Mudkip's head acts as highly sensitive radar. Using this fin to sense movements of water and air, this Pokémon can determine what is taking place around it without using its eyes.
YOU TRACKED IT USING YOUR FIN...YOUR RADAR.
AND YOUR RADAR IS SUPER SENSI-TIVE!
SNFF
ALL RIGHT, LET'S GO...
... MUMU!
HOP
MUUUU ...?
DAY-DREAMING AGAIN, HUH?
SIGH... YOU ANSWER TO "MUMU" NOW!
YOU'RE RELAXED—BUT ALSO PRETTY SHARP. I DON'T KNOW WHAT CATEGORY TO PLACE YOU IN YET...
...BUT I CAN'T WAIT TO SEE YOU WIN SOME CON-TESTS!

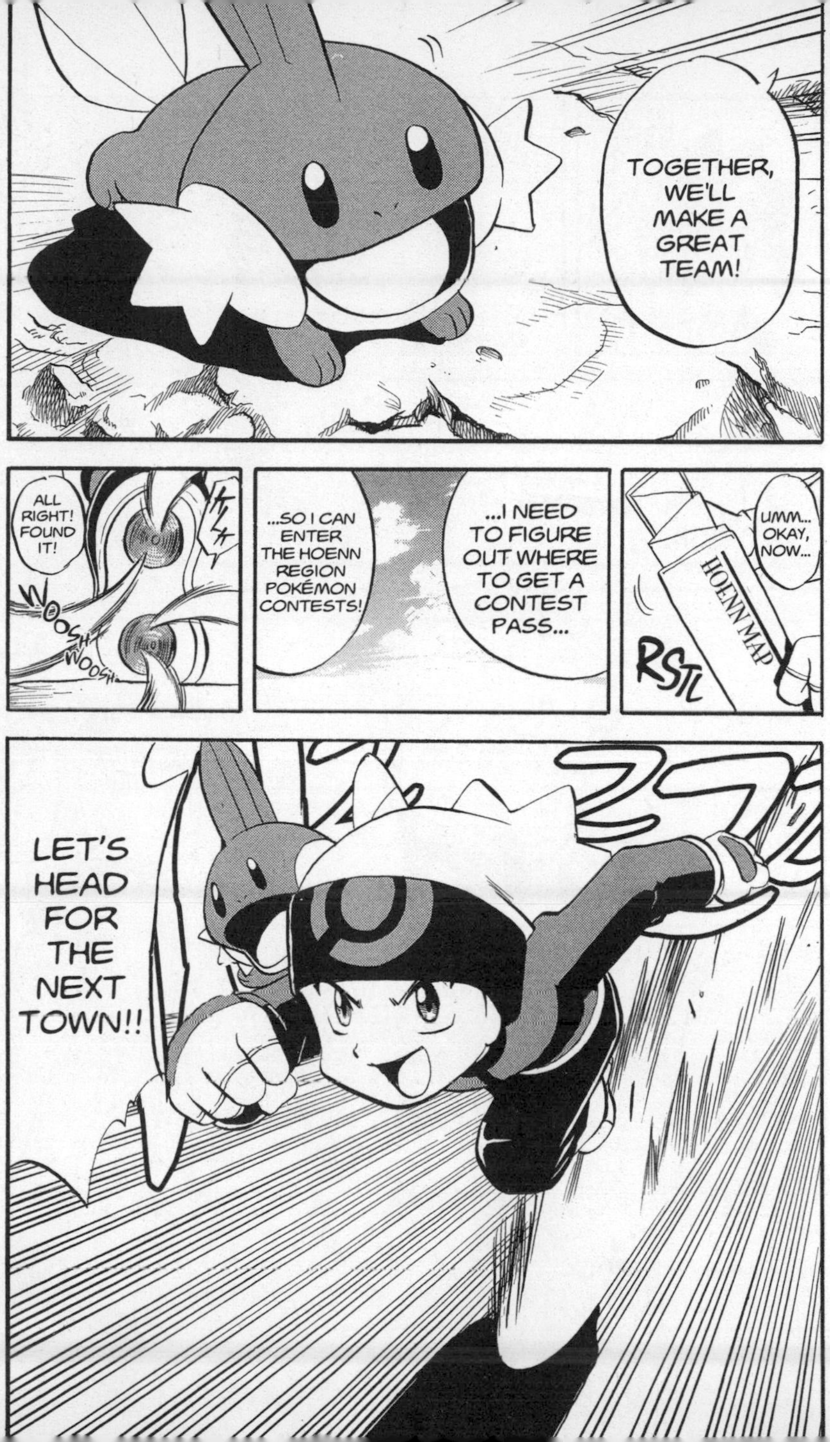
TOGETHER, WE'LL MAKE A GREAT TEAM!
UMM... OKAY, NOW...
HOENN MAP
RSTL
...I NEED TO FIGURE OUT WHERE TO GET A CONTEST PASS...
...SO I CAN ENTER THE HOENN REGION POKÉMON CONTESTS!
ALL RIGHT! FOUND IT!
WOOSH
WOOSH
LET'S HEAD FOR THE NEXT TOWN!!

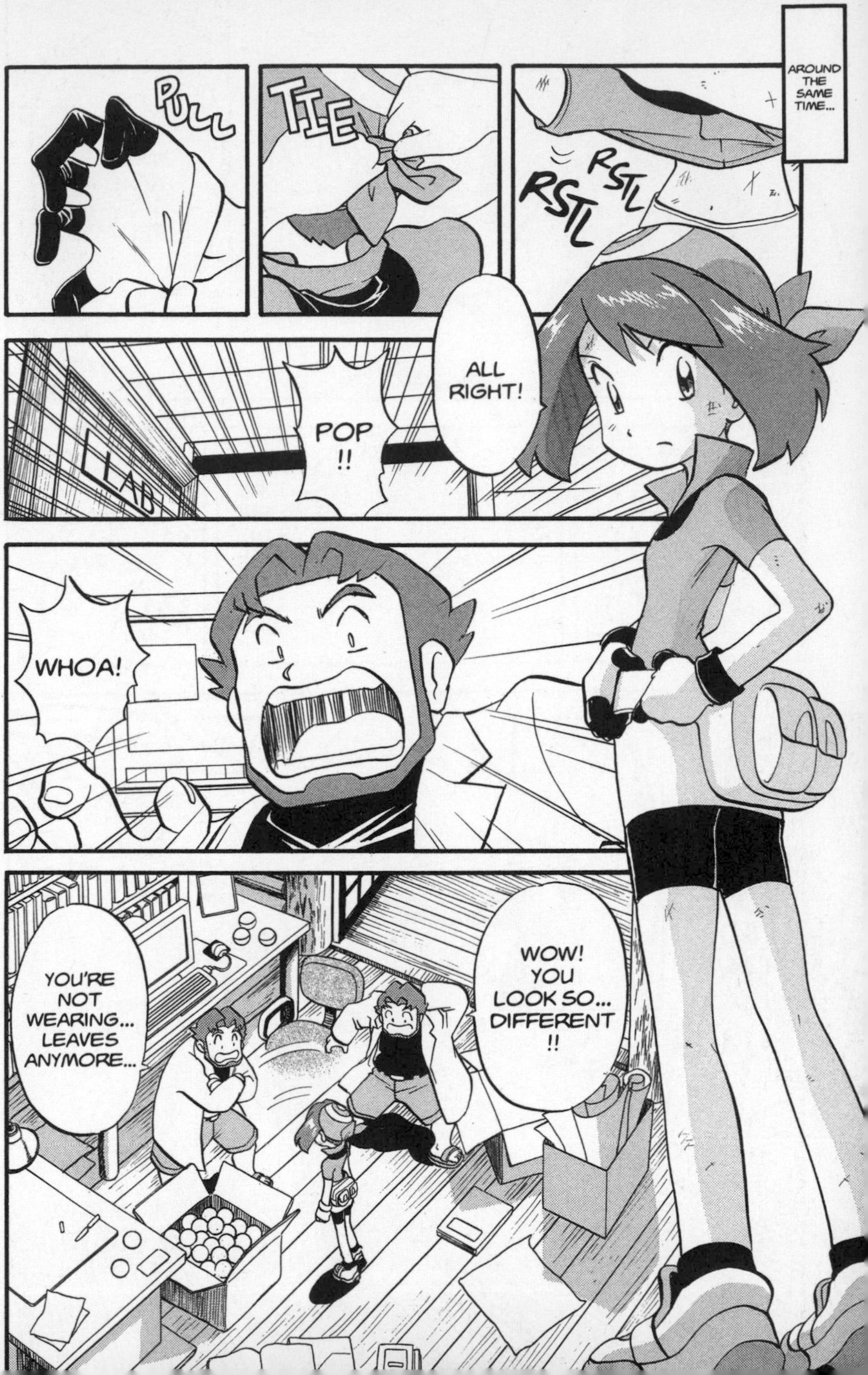
AROUND THE SAME TIME...
RSTL RSTL
TIE
PULL
ALL RIGHT!
POP !!
LAB
WHOA!
WOW! YOU LOOK SO... DIFFERENT !!
YOU'RE NOT WEARING... LEAVES ANYMORE...

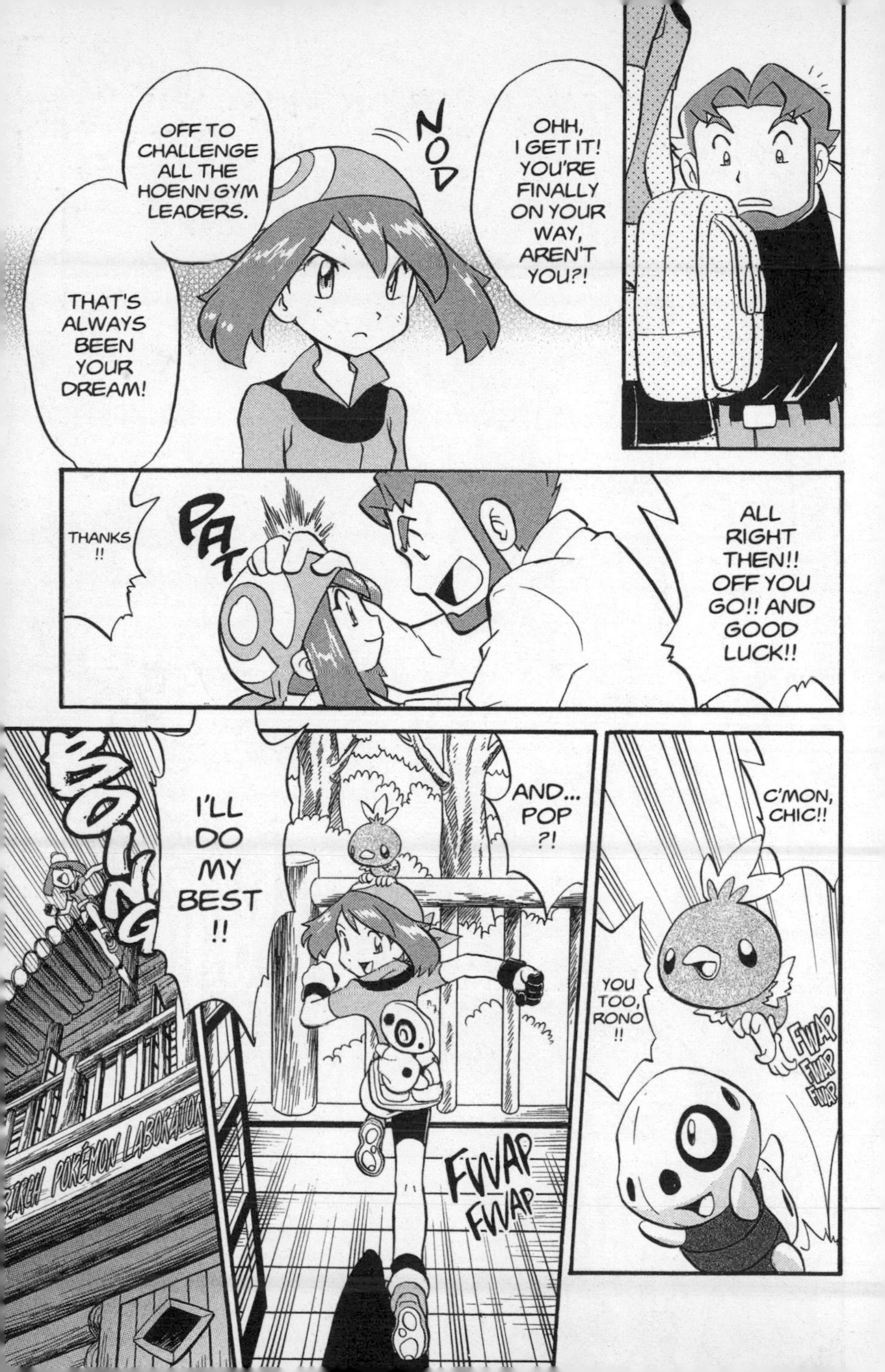
OHH, I GET IT! YOU'RE FINALLY ON YOUR WAY, AREN'T YOU?!
NOD
OFF TO CHALLENGE ALL THE HOENN GYM LEADERS.
THAT'S ALWAYS BEEN YOUR DREAM!
ALL RIGHT THEN!! OFF YOU GO!! AND GOOD LUCK!!
PAT
THANKS !!
C'MON, CHIC!!
YOU TOO, RONO !!
FWAP FWAP FWAP
AND... POP ?!
I'LL DO MY BEST !!
BOING
FWAP FWAP
IRCH POKéMON LABORATOR

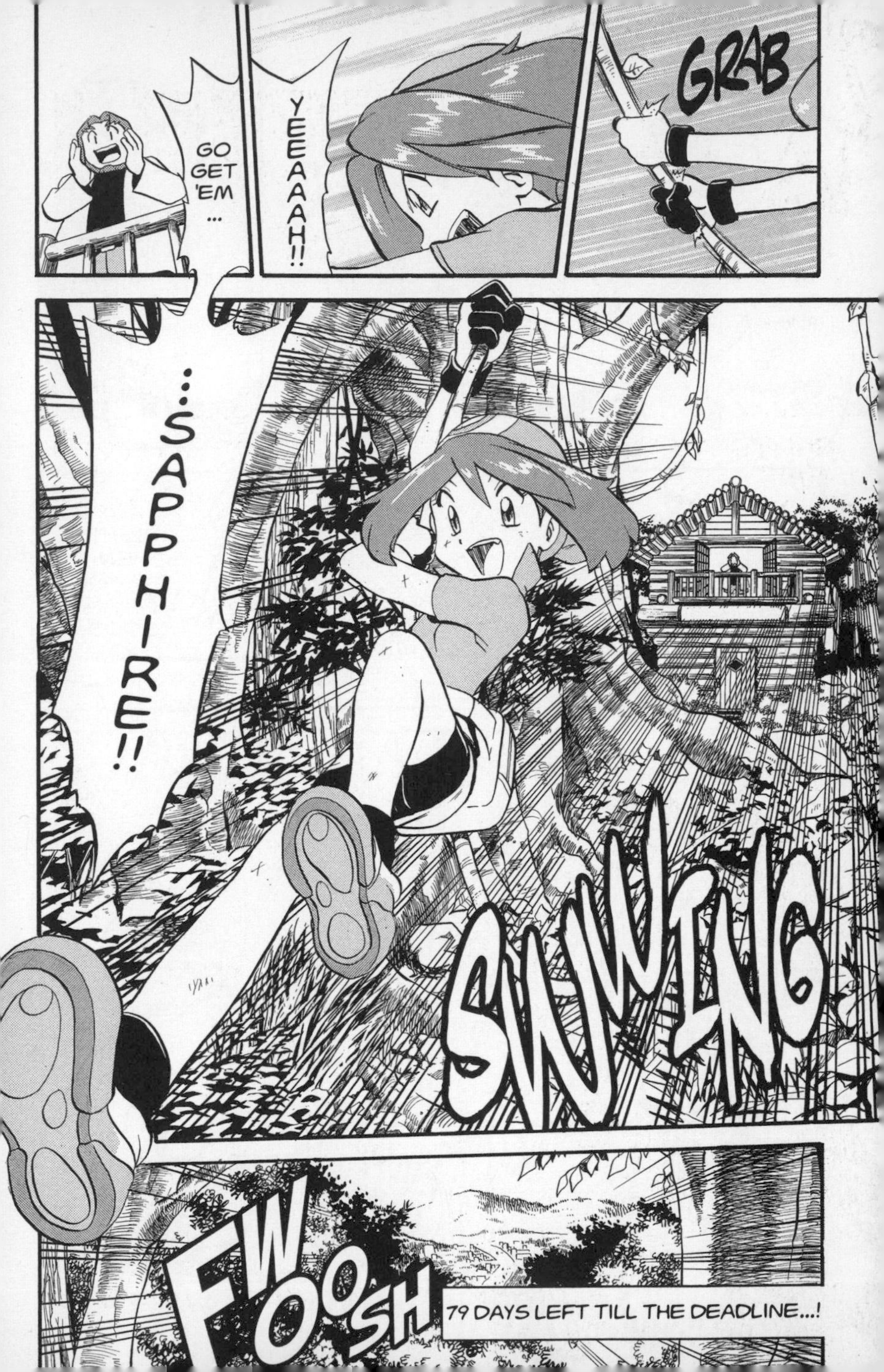
GRAB
YEEAAAAH!!
GO GET 'EM ...
...SAPPHIRE!!
SWWING
79 DAYS LEFT TILL THE DEADLINE...!
FWOOOSH

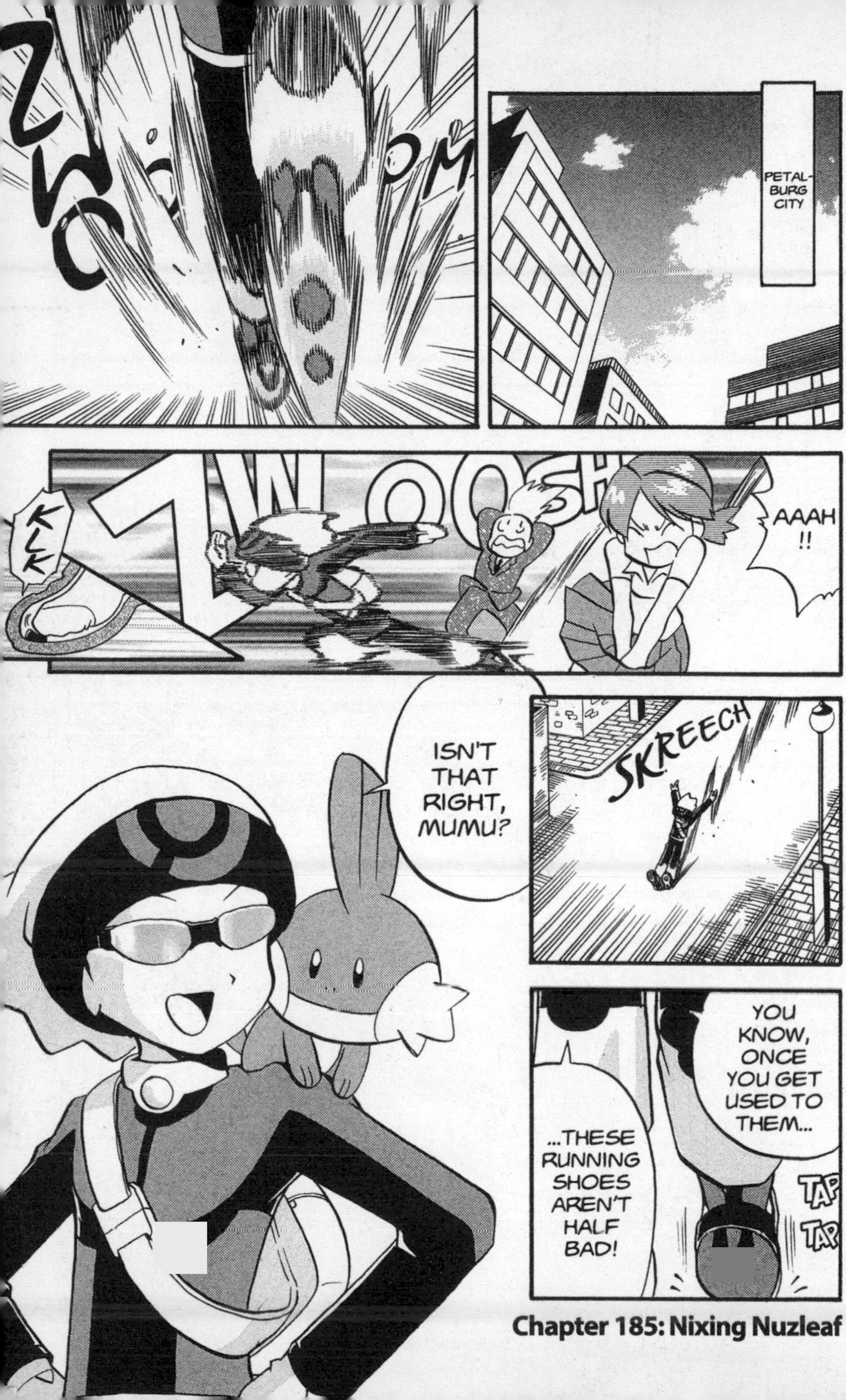
PETAL-BURG CITY
AAAH!!
WHOOSH
KLK
SKREECH
YOU KNOW, ONCE YOU GET USED TO THEM...
...THESE RUNNING SHOES AREN'T HALF BAD!
TAP
TAP
ISN'T THAT RIGHT, MUMU?

Chapter 185: Nixing Nuzleaf

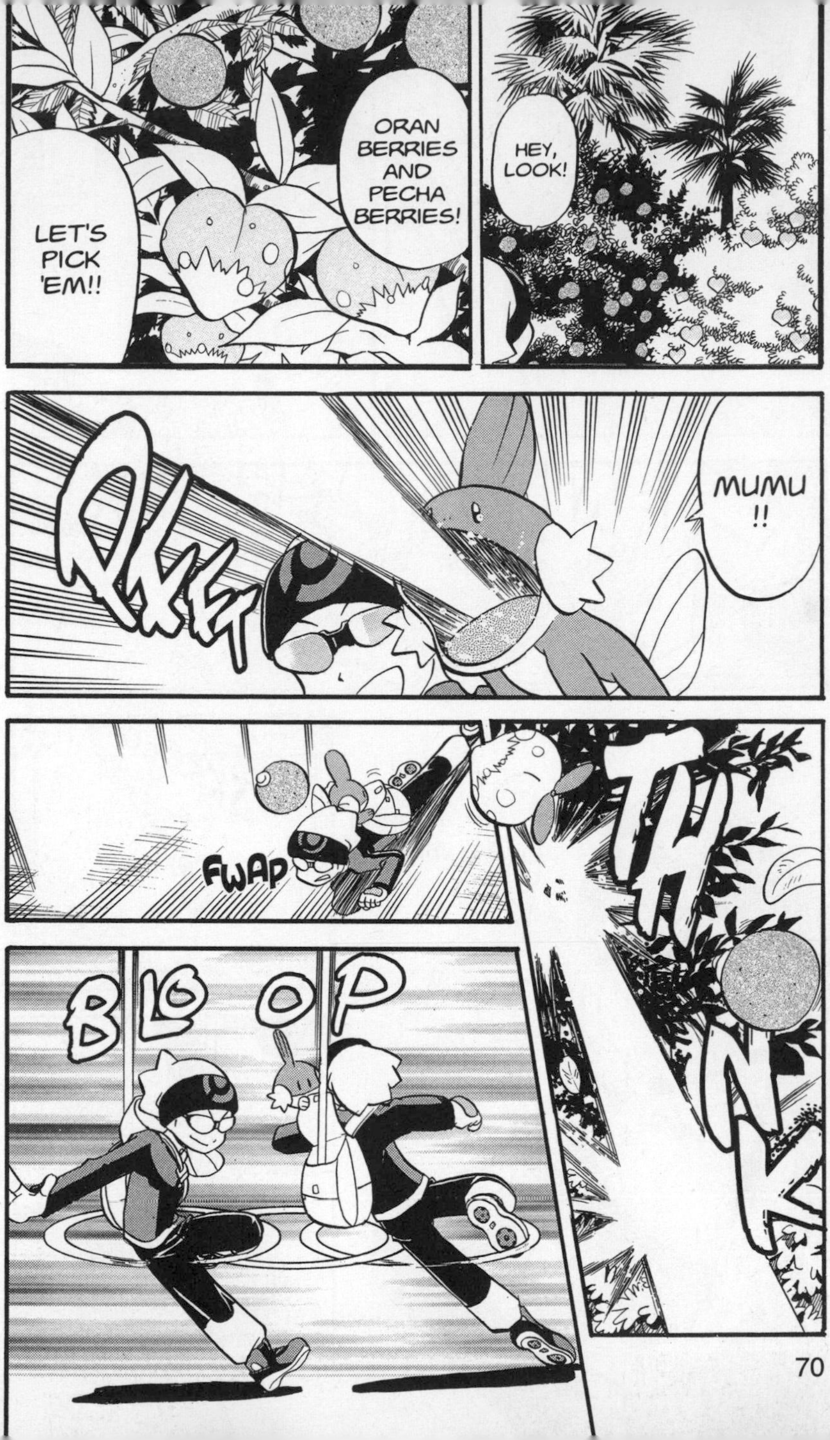
HEY, LOOK!
ORAN BERRIES AND PECHA BERRIES!
LET'S PICK 'EM!!
MUMU !!
THUNK
FWAP
BLOOP

Chapter 185: Nixing Nuzleaf

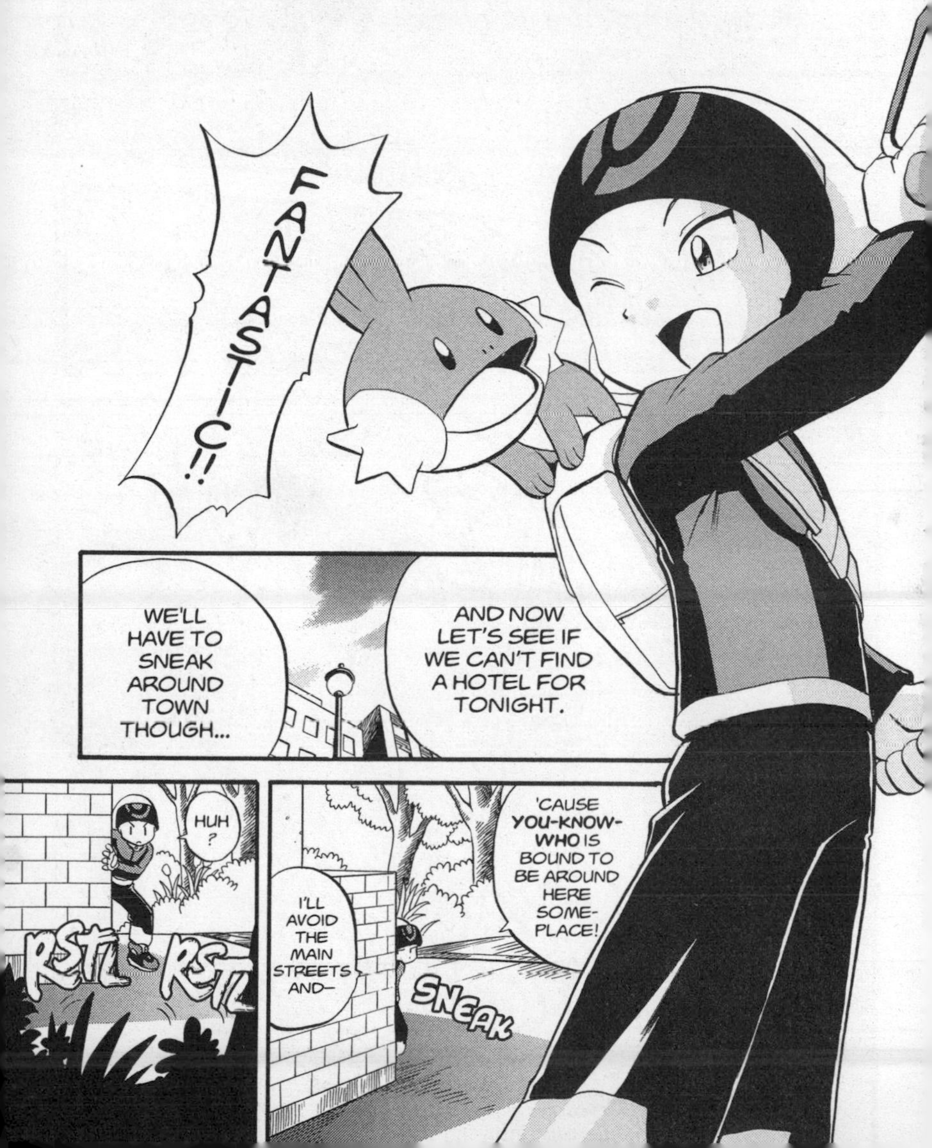
FANTASTIC!!
AND NOW LET'S SEE IF WE CAN'T FIND A HOTEL FOR TONIGHT.
WE'LL HAVE TO SNEAK AROUND TOWN THOUGH...
'CAUSE YOU-KNOW-WHO IS BOUND TO BE AROUND HERE SOME-PLACE!
I'LL AVOID THE MAIN STREETS AND—
SNEAK
HUH?
RSTL RSTL

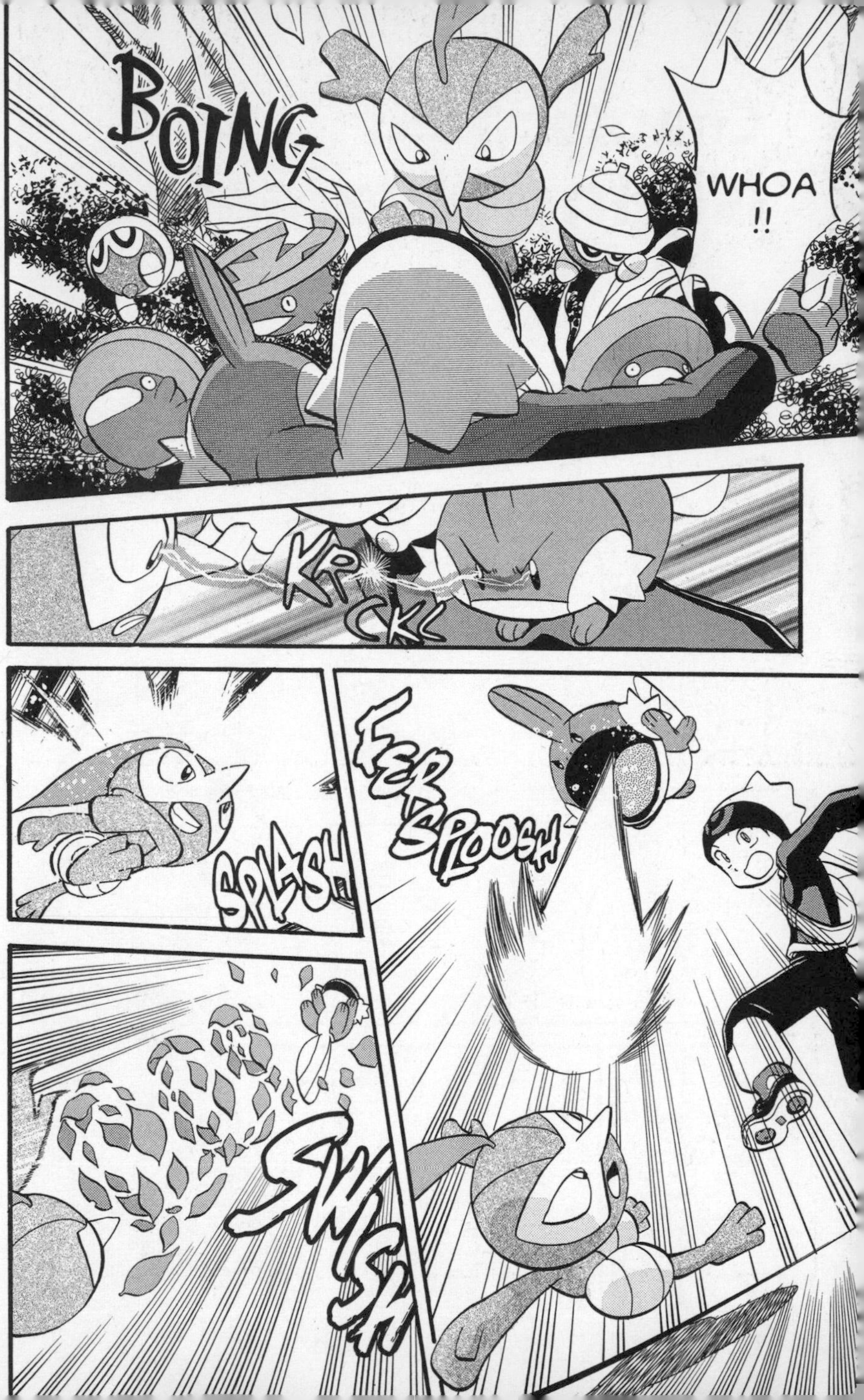
WHOA
!!
BOING
KRPCKL
FER SPLOOSH
SPLASH
SWISH

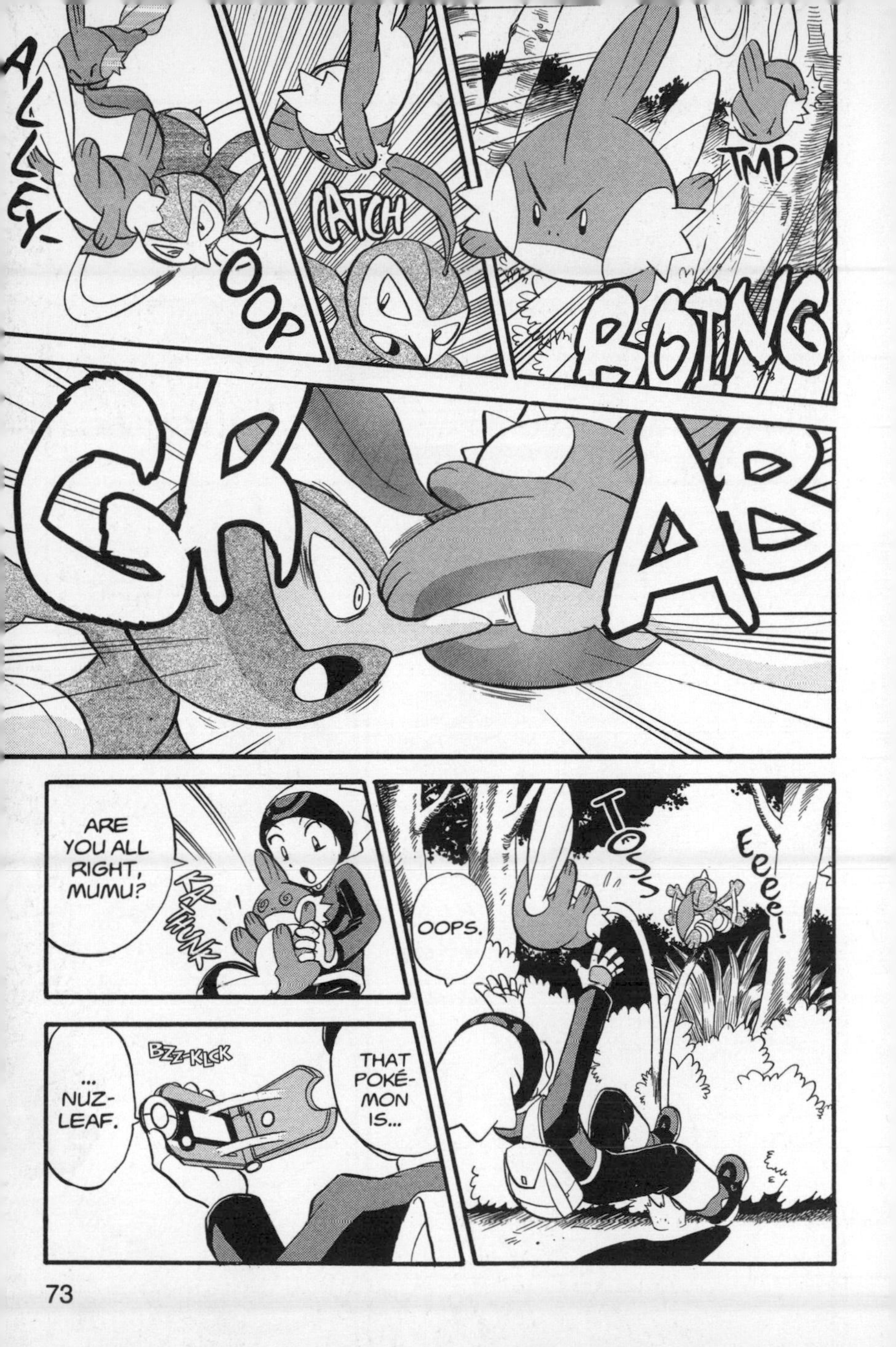
TMP
BOING
CATCH
ALLEY-
OOP
GRAB
TOSS
Eeeee!
OOPS.
ARE YOU ALL RIGHT, MUMU?
KA-THUNK
THAT POKÉ-MON IS...
BZZ-KLCK
... NUZ-LEAF.

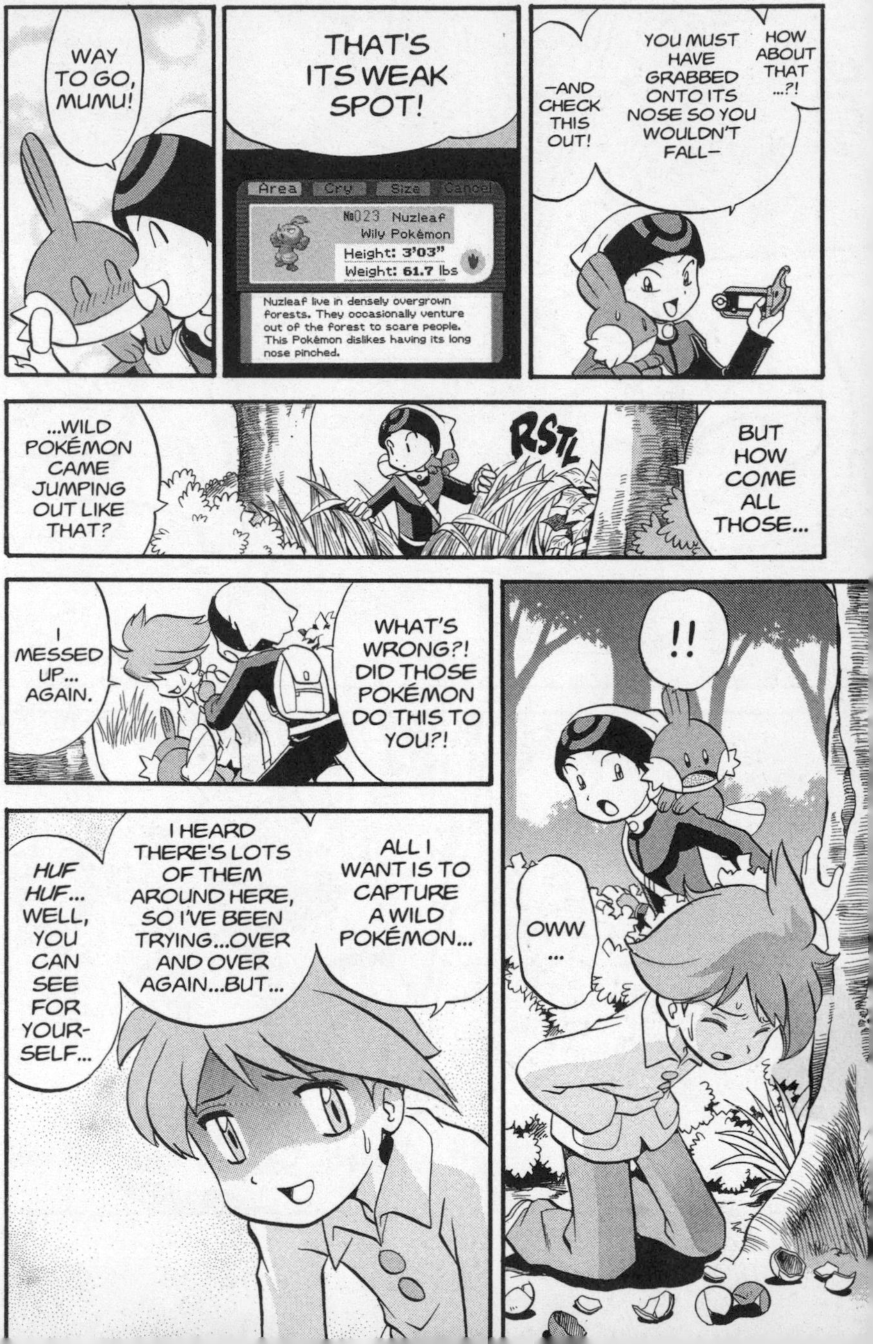
HOW ABOUT THAT ...?!
YOU MUST HAVE GRABBED ONTO ITS NOSE SO YOU WOULDN'T FALL—
—AND CHECK THIS OUT!
THAT'S ITS WEAK SPOT!
Area Cry Size Cancel
No023 Nuzleaf
Wily Pokémon
Height: 3'03"
Weight: 61.7 lbs
Nuzleaf live in densely overgrown forests. They occasionally venture out of the forest to scare people. This Pokémon dislikes having its long nose pinched.
WAY TO GO, MUMU!
BUT HOW COME ALL THOSE...
RSTL
...WILD POKÉMON CAME JUMPING OUT LIKE THAT?
!!
OWW ...
WHAT'S WRONG?! DID THOSE POKÉMON DO THIS TO YOU?!
I MESSED UP... AGAIN.
ALL I WANT IS TO CAPTURE A WILD POKÉMON...
I HEARD THERE'S LOTS OF THEM AROUND HERE, SO I'VE BEEN TRYING...OVER AND OVER AGAIN...BUT...
HUF HUF... WELL, YOU CAN SEE FOR YOUR-SELF...

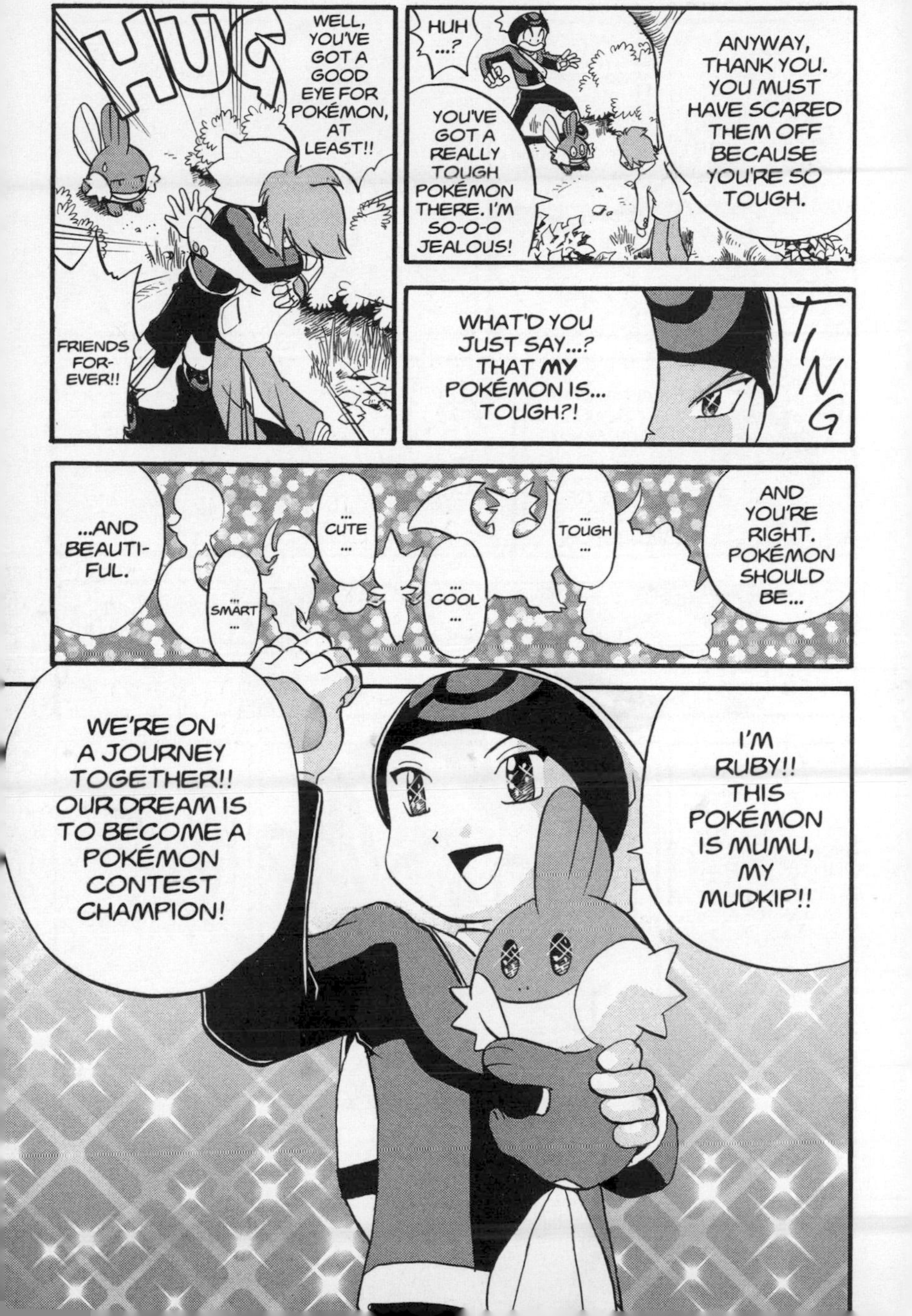
ANYWAY, THANK YOU. YOU MUST HAVE SCARED THEM OFF BECAUSE YOU'RE SO TOUGH.
HUH ...?
YOU'VE GOT A REALLY TOUGH POKÉMON THERE. I'M SO-O-O JEALOUS!
TING
WHAT'D YOU JUST SAY...? THAT MY POKÉMON IS... TOUGH?!
WELL, YOU'VE GOT A GOOD EYE FOR POKÉMON, AT LEAST!!
HUG
FRIENDS FOR-EVER!!
AND YOU'RE RIGHT. POKÉMON SHOULD BE...
... TOUGH ...
... COOL ...
... CUTE ...
... SMART ...
...AND BEAUTI-FUL.
I'M RUBY!! THIS POKÉMON IS MUMU, MY MUDKIP!!
WE'RE ON A JOURNEY TOGETHER!! OUR DREAM IS TO BECOME A POKÉMON CONTEST CHAMPION!

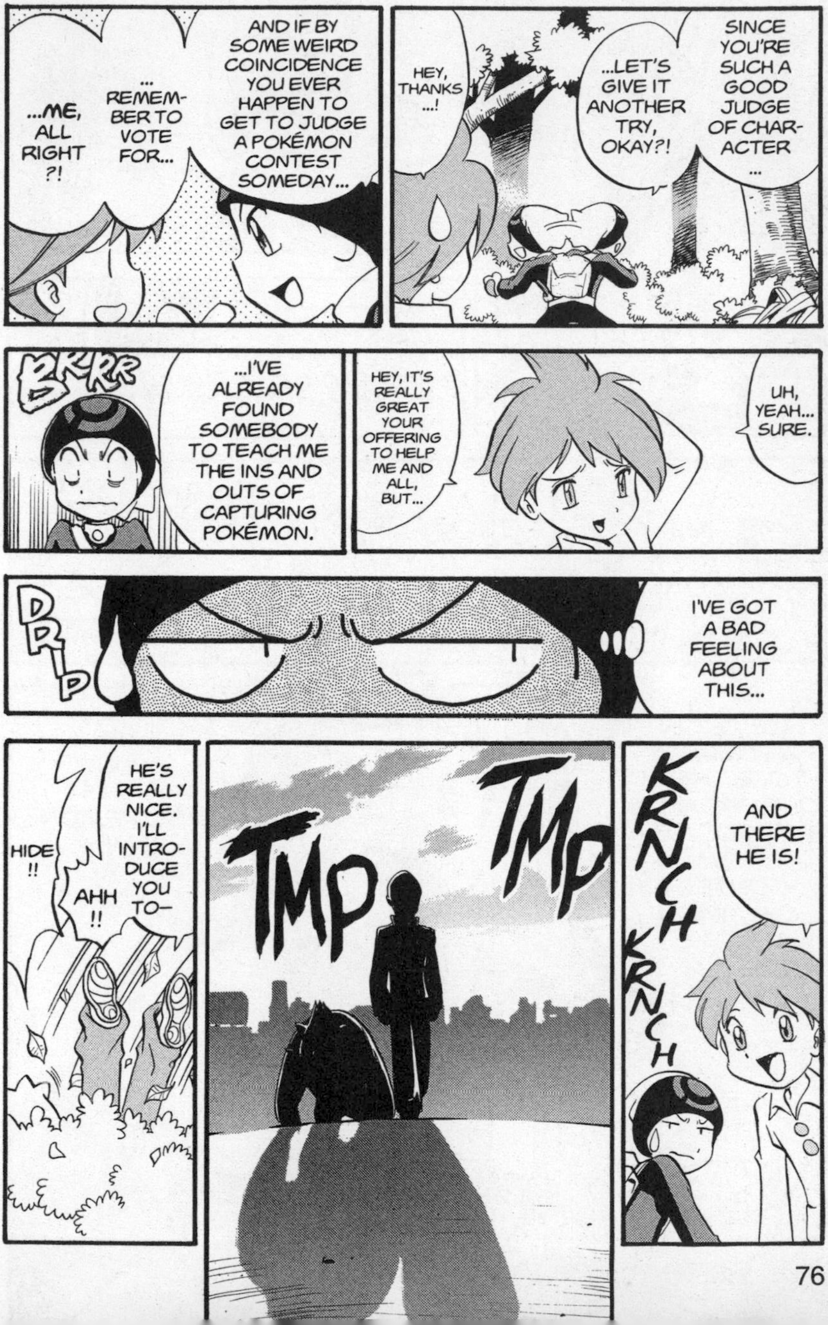
SINCE YOU'RE SUCH A GOOD JUDGE OF CHAR-ACTER...
...LET'S GIVE IT ANOTHER TRY, OKAY?!
HEY, THANKS...!
AND IF BY SOME WEIRD COINCIDENCE YOU EVER HAPPEN TO GET TO JUDGE A POKÉMON CONTEST SOMEDAY...
...REMEM-BER TO VOTE FOR...
...ME, ALL RIGHT?!
UH, YEAH... SURE.
HEY, IT'S REALLY GREAT YOUR OFFERING TO HELP ME AND ALL, BUT...
...I'VE ALREADY FOUND SOMEBODY TO TEACH ME THE INS AND OUTS OF CAPTURING POKÉMON.
BRRR
I'VE GOT A BAD FEELING ABOUT THIS...
DRIP
AND THERE HE IS!
KRNCH
KRNCH
TMP
TMP
HE'S REALLY NICE. I'LL INTRO-DUCE YOU TO—
AHH!!
HIDE!!

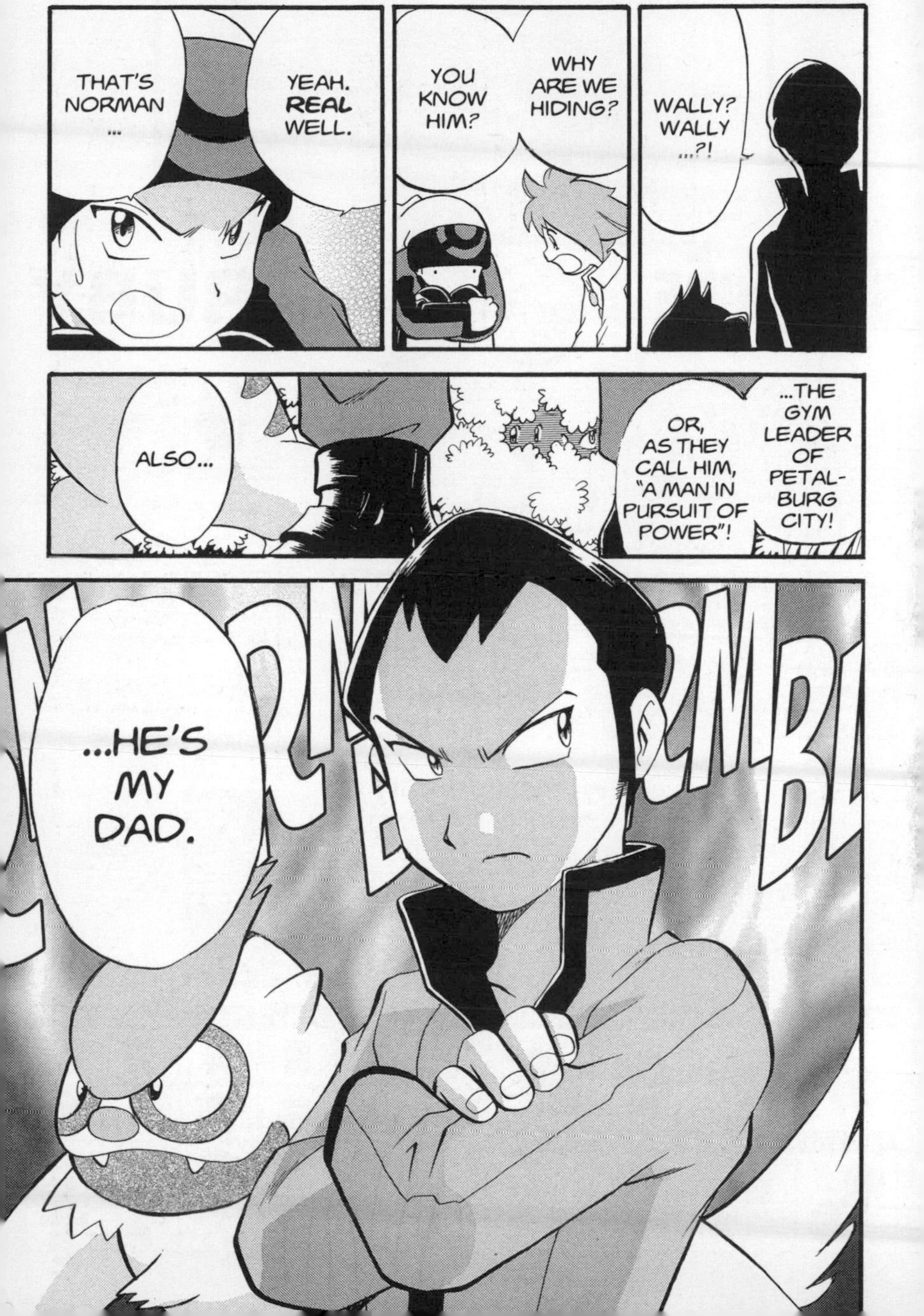
WALLY? WALLY ...?!
WHY ARE WE HIDING?
YOU KNOW HIM?
YEAH. **REAL** WELL.
THAT'S NORMAN ...
...THE GYM LEADER OF PETAL-BURG CITY!
OR, AS THEY CALL HIM, "A MAN IN PURSUIT OF POWER"!
ALSO...
...HE'S MY DAD.

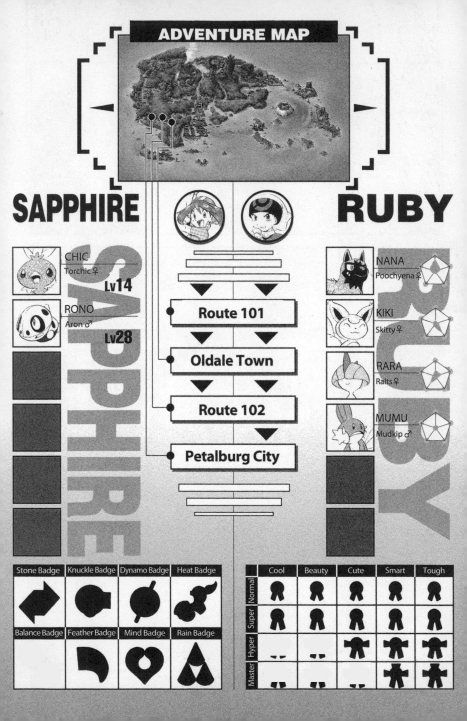

ADVENTURE MAP

SAPPHIRE

CHIC
Torchic ♀
Lv14

RONO
Aron ♂
Lv28

RUBY

NANA
Poochyena ♀

KIKI
Skitty ♀

RARA
Ralts ♀

MUMU
Mudkip ♂

Route 101

Oldale Town

Route 102

Petalburg City

Stone Badge	Knuckle Badge	Dynamo Badge	Heat Badge
Balance Badge	Feather Badge	Mind Badge	Rain Badge

		Cool	Beauty	Cute	Smart	Tough
Super	Normal	R	R	R	R	R
		R	R	R	R	R
Master	Hyper			R	R	R
					R	R

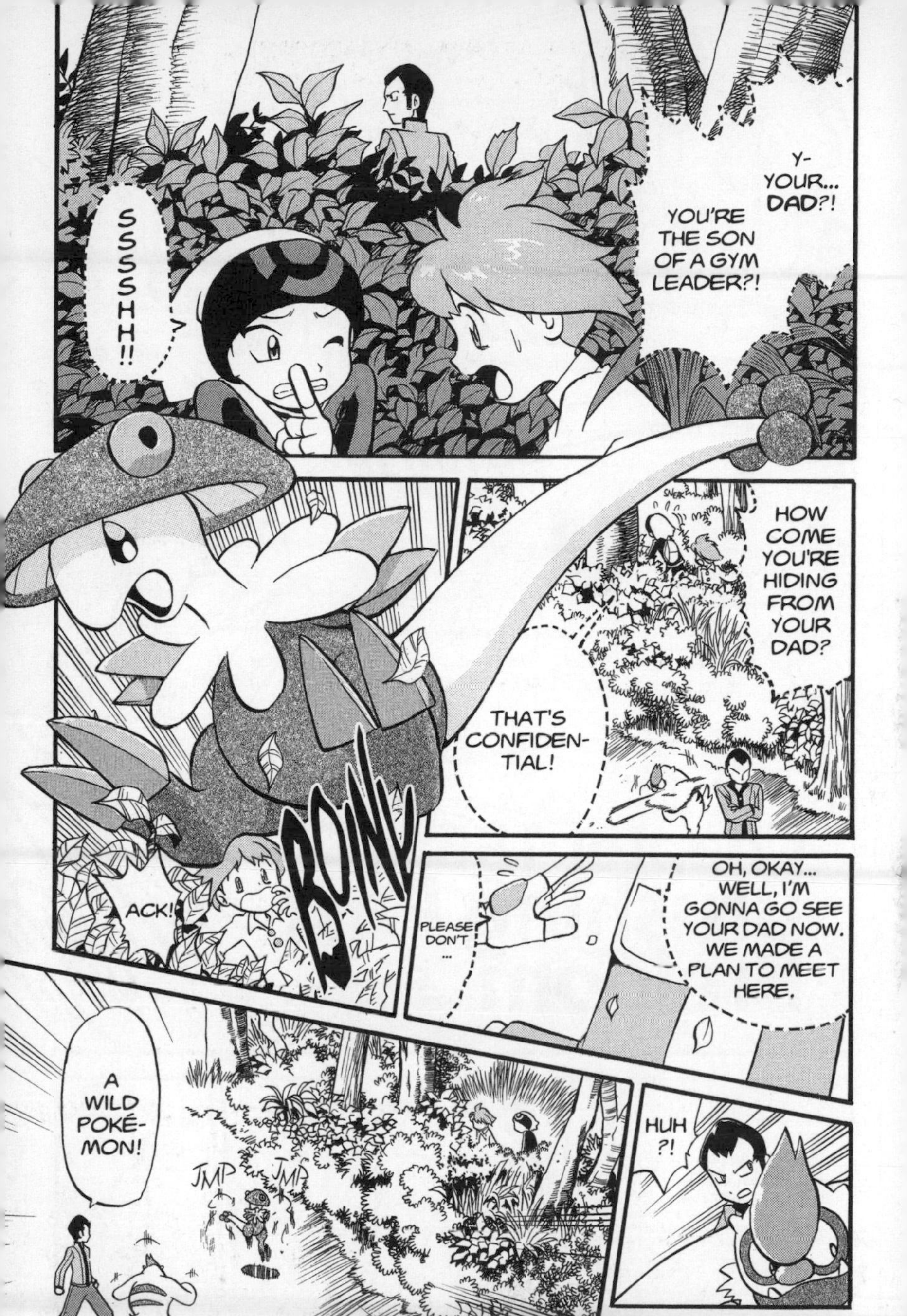
Y-
YOUR... DAD?!
YOU'RE THE SON OF A GYM LEADER?!
SSSSHH!!
SNEAK
HOW COME YOU'RE HIDING FROM YOUR DAD?
THAT'S CONFIDENTIAL!
OH, OKAY... WELL, I'M GONNA GO SEE YOUR DAD NOW. WE MADE A PLAN TO MEET HERE.
PLEASE DON'T ...
BOIN
ACK!
HUH?!
A WILD POKÉMON!
JMP JMP

Chapter 186: Brushing Past Breloom

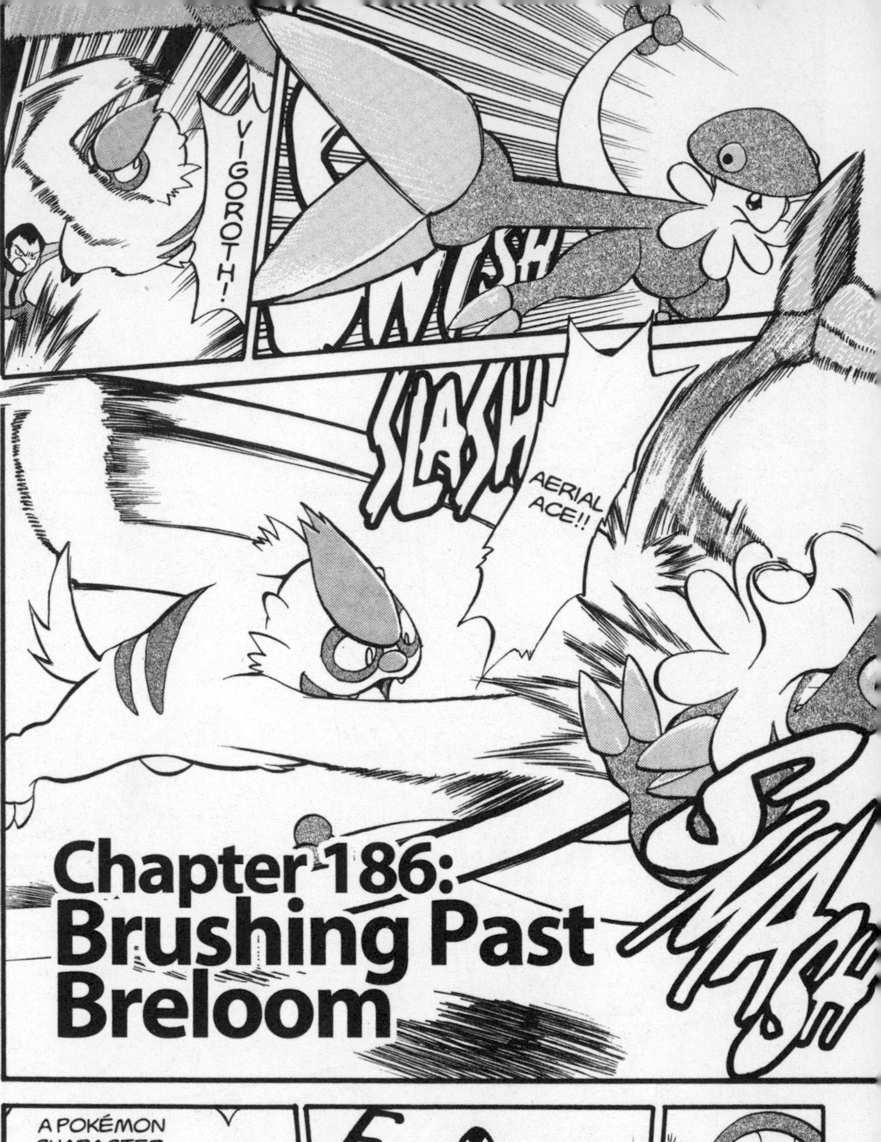
VIGOROTH!
SLASH
AERIAL ACE!!

Chapter 186: Brushing Past Breloom

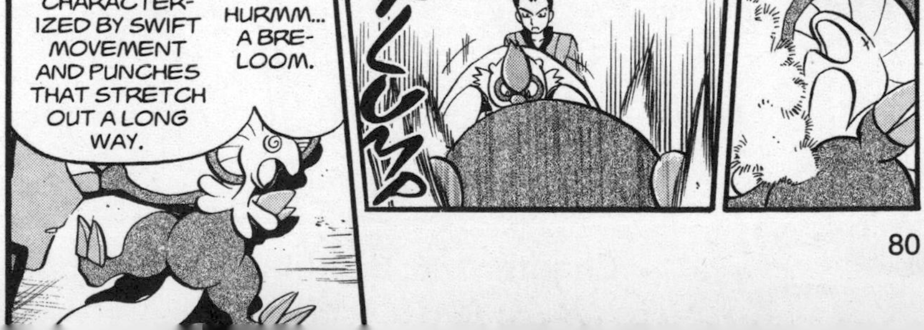
FLUMP
HURMM... A BRELOOM.
A POKÉMON CHARACTERIZED BY SWIFT MOVEMENT AND PUNCHES THAT STRETCH OUT A LONG WAY.

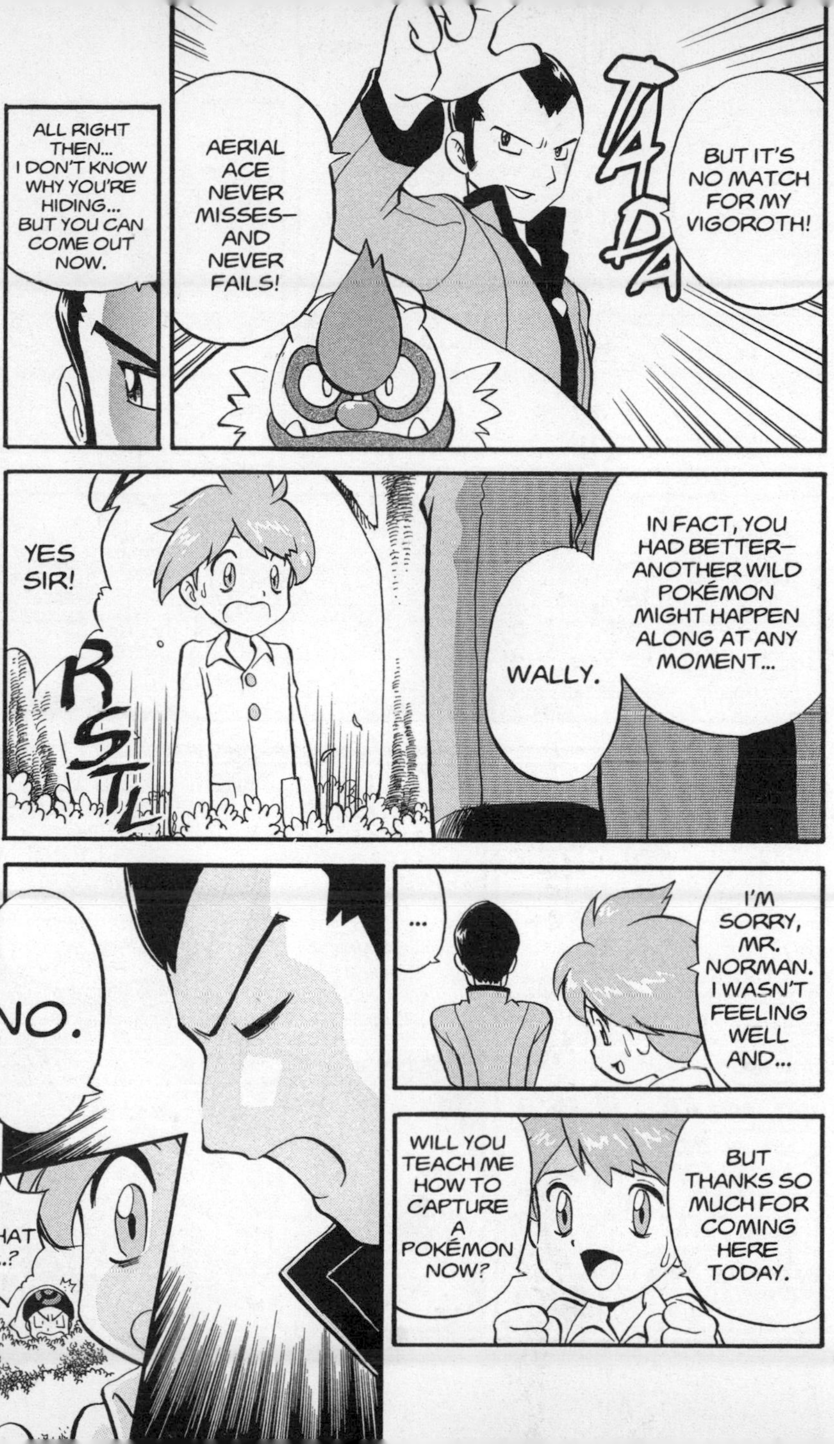
BUT IT'S NO MATCH FOR MY VIGOROTH!
TADA
AERIAL ACE NEVER MISSES—AND NEVER FAILS!
ALL RIGHT THEN... I DON'T KNOW WHY YOU'RE HIDING... BUT YOU CAN COME OUT NOW.
IN FACT, YOU HAD BETTER—ANOTHER WILD POKÉMON MIGHT HAPPEN ALONG AT ANY MOMENT...
WALLY.
YES SIR!
RSTL
I'M SORRY, MR. NORMAN. I WASN'T FEELING WELL AND...
...
BUT THANKS SO MUCH FOR COMING HERE TODAY.
WILL YOU TEACH ME HOW TO CAPTURE A POKÉMON NOW?
NO.
WHAT ...?

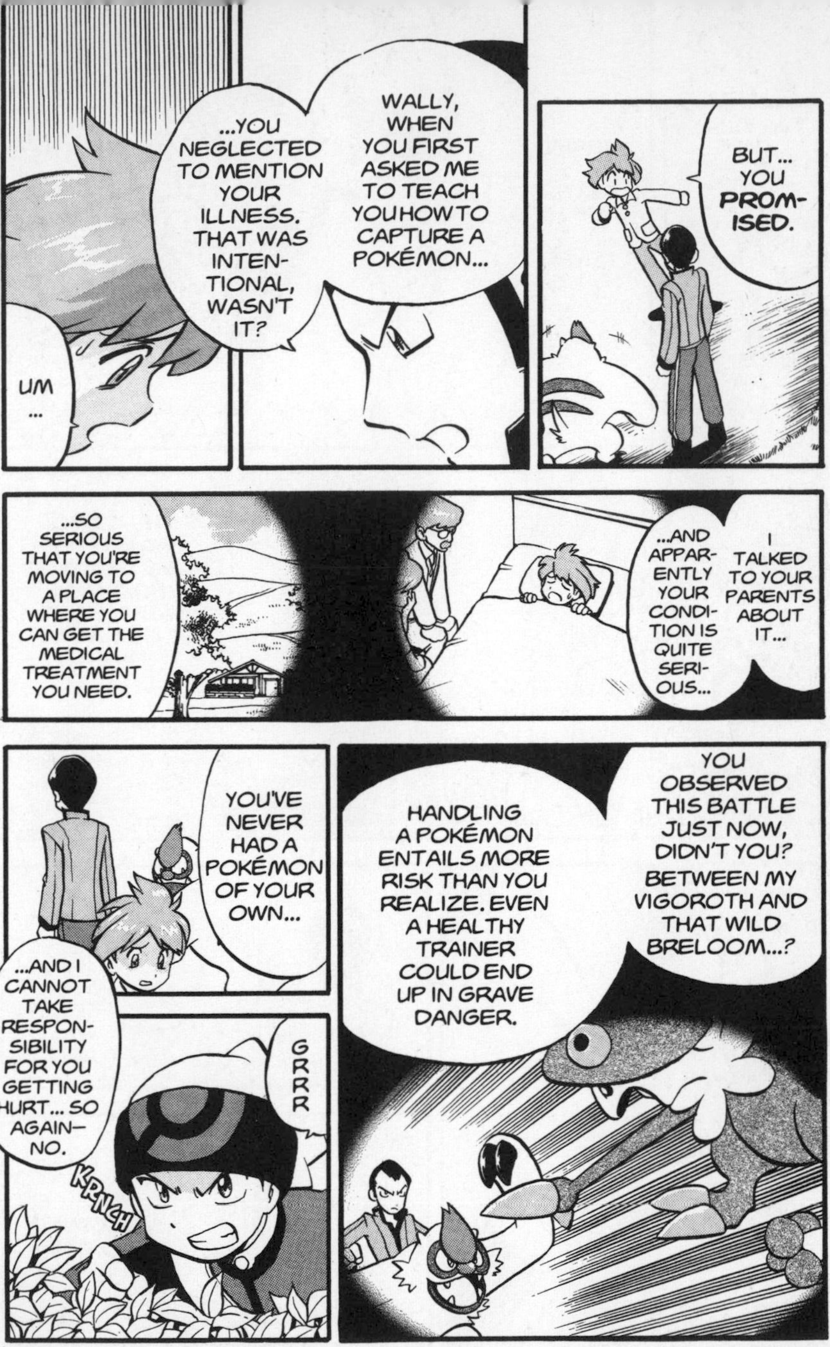
BUT... YOU PROMISED.
WALLY, WHEN YOU FIRST ASKED ME TO TEACH YOU HOW TO CAPTURE A POKÉMON...
...YOU NEGLECTED TO MENTION YOUR ILLNESS. THAT WAS INTENTIONAL, WASN'T IT?
UM ...
I TALKED TO YOUR PARENTS ABOUT IT...
...AND APPARENTLY YOUR CONDITION IS QUITE SERIOUS...
...SO SERIOUS THAT YOU'RE MOVING TO A PLACE WHERE YOU CAN GET THE MEDICAL TREATMENT YOU NEED.
YOU OBSERVED THIS BATTLE JUST NOW, DIDN'T YOU? BETWEEN MY VIGOROTH AND THAT WILD BRELOOM...?
HANDLING A POKÉMON ENTAILS MORE RISK THAN YOU REALIZE. EVEN A HEALTHY TRAINER COULD END UP IN GRAVE DANGER.
YOU'VE NEVER HAD A POKÉMON OF YOUR OWN...
...AND I CANNOT TAKE RESPONSIBILITY FOR YOU GETTING HURT... SO AGAIN—NO.
GRRR
KRNCH

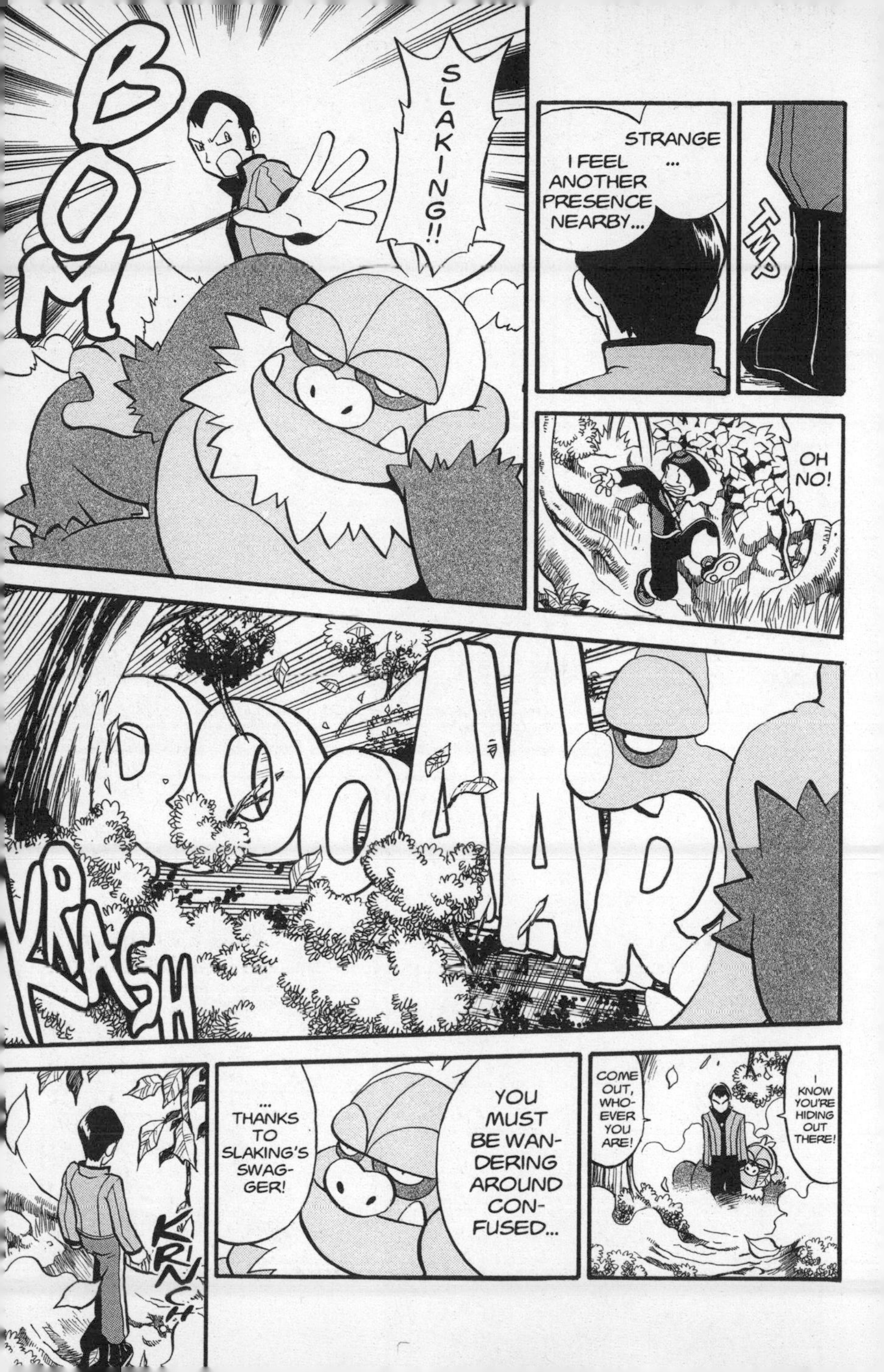
TMP
STRANGE ... I FEEL ANOTHER PRESENCE NEARBY...
OH NO!
SLAKING!!
BOOM
ROOOAR
KRASH
I KNOW YOU'RE HIDING OUT THERE!
COME OUT, WHO-EVER YOU ARE!
YOU MUST BE WAN-DERING AROUND CON-FUSED...
... THANKS TO SLAKING'S SWAG-GER!
KRUNCH

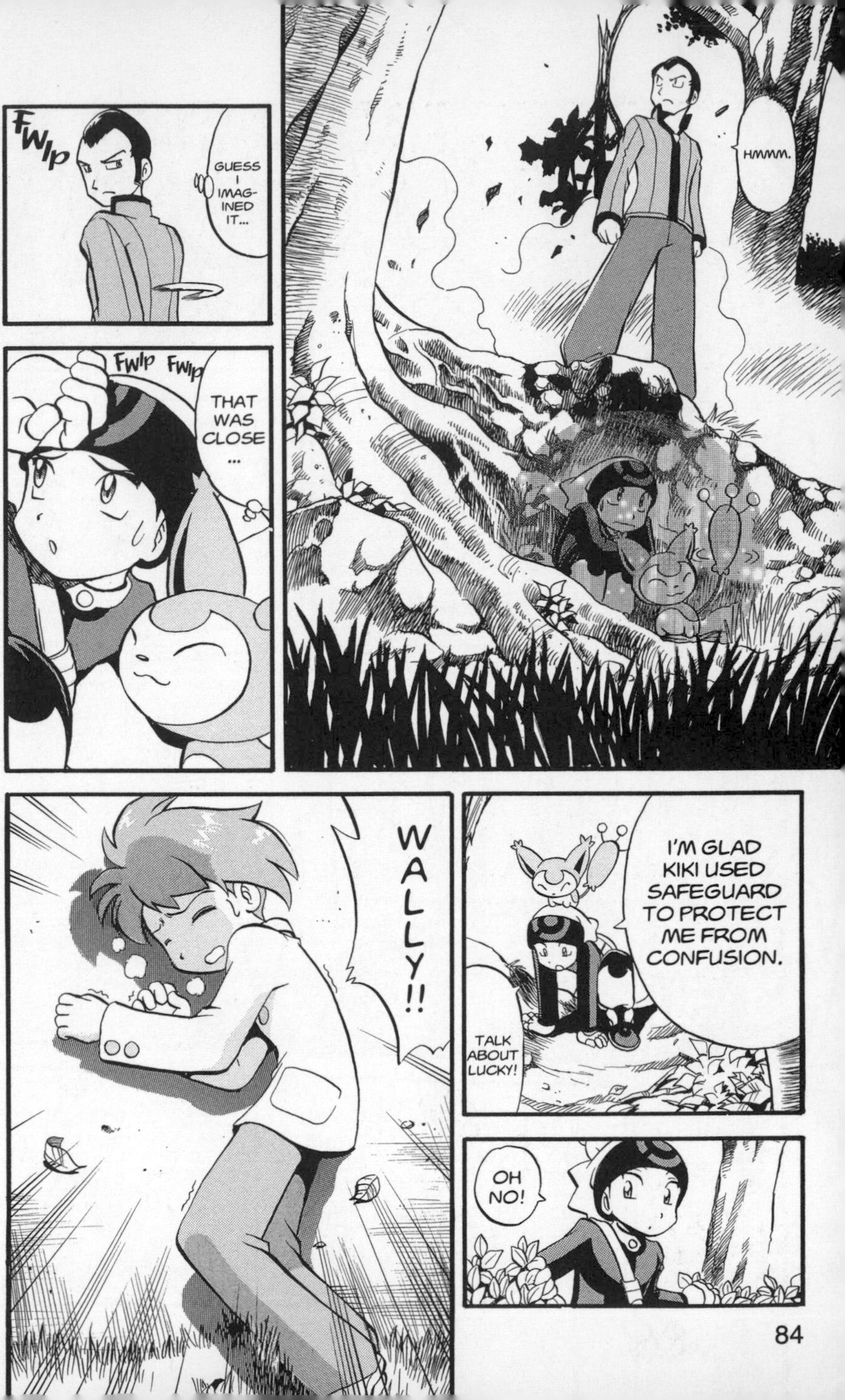
HMMM.
FWIP
GUESS I IMAG-INED IT...
FWIP FWIP
THAT WAS CLOSE...
I'M GLAD KIKI USED SAFEGUARD TO PROTECT ME FROM CONFUSION.
TALK ABOUT LUCKY!
OH NO!
WALLY!!

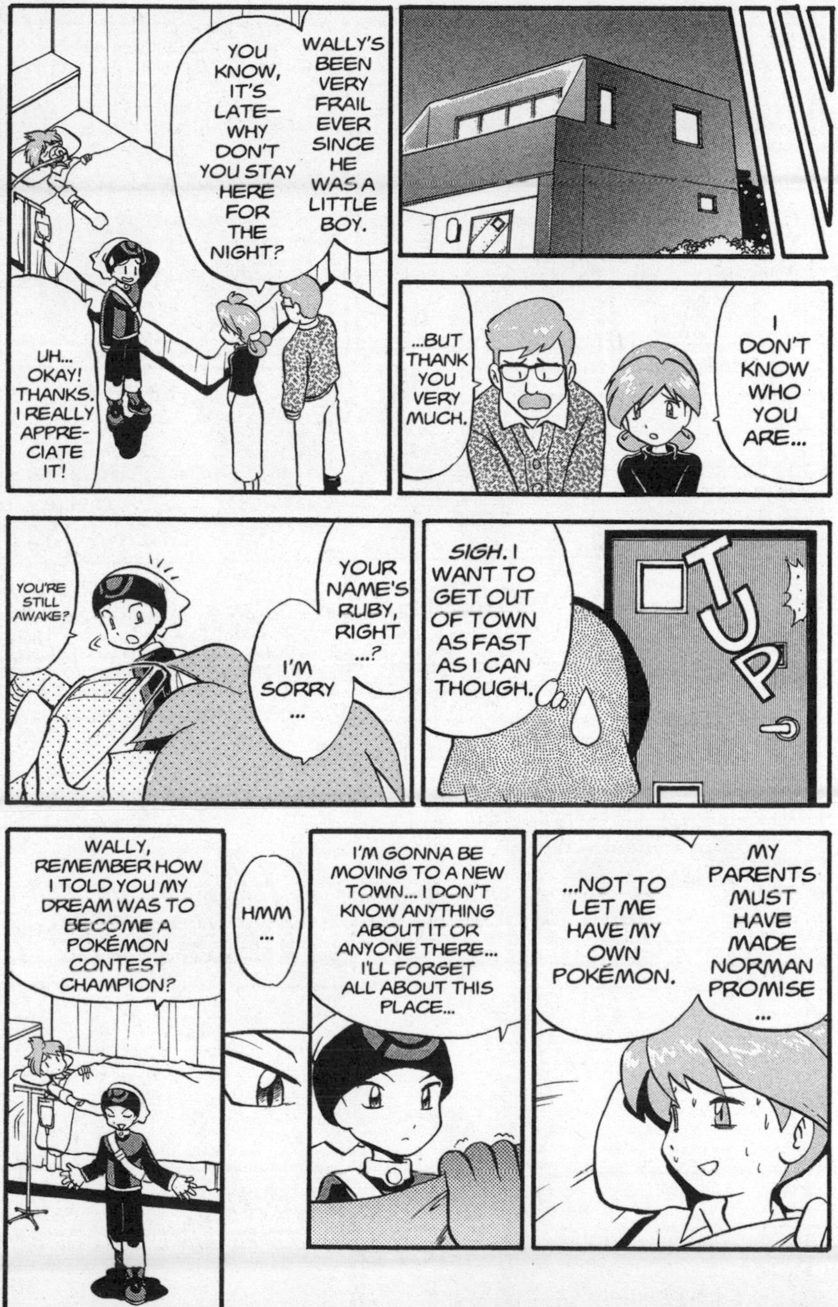
I DON'T KNOW WHO YOU ARE...
...BUT THANK YOU VERY MUCH.
WALLY'S BEEN VERY FRAIL EVER SINCE HE WAS A LITTLE BOY.
YOU KNOW, IT'S LATE—WHY DON'T YOU STAY HERE FOR THE NIGHT?
UH... OKAY! THANKS. I REALLY APPRECIATE IT!
TUP
SIGH. I WANT TO GET OUT OF TOWN AS FAST AS I CAN THOUGH.
YOUR NAME'S RUBY, RIGHT ...?
I'M SORRY ...
YOU'RE STILL AWAKE?
MY PARENTS MUST HAVE MADE NORMAN PROMISE ...
...NOT TO LET ME HAVE MY OWN POKÉMON.
I'M GONNA BE MOVING TO A NEW TOWN... I DON'T KNOW ANYTHING ABOUT IT OR ANYONE THERE... I'LL FORGET ALL ABOUT THIS PLACE...
HMM ...
WALLY, REMEMBER HOW I TOLD YOU MY DREAM WAS TO BECOME A POKÉMON CONTEST CHAMPION?

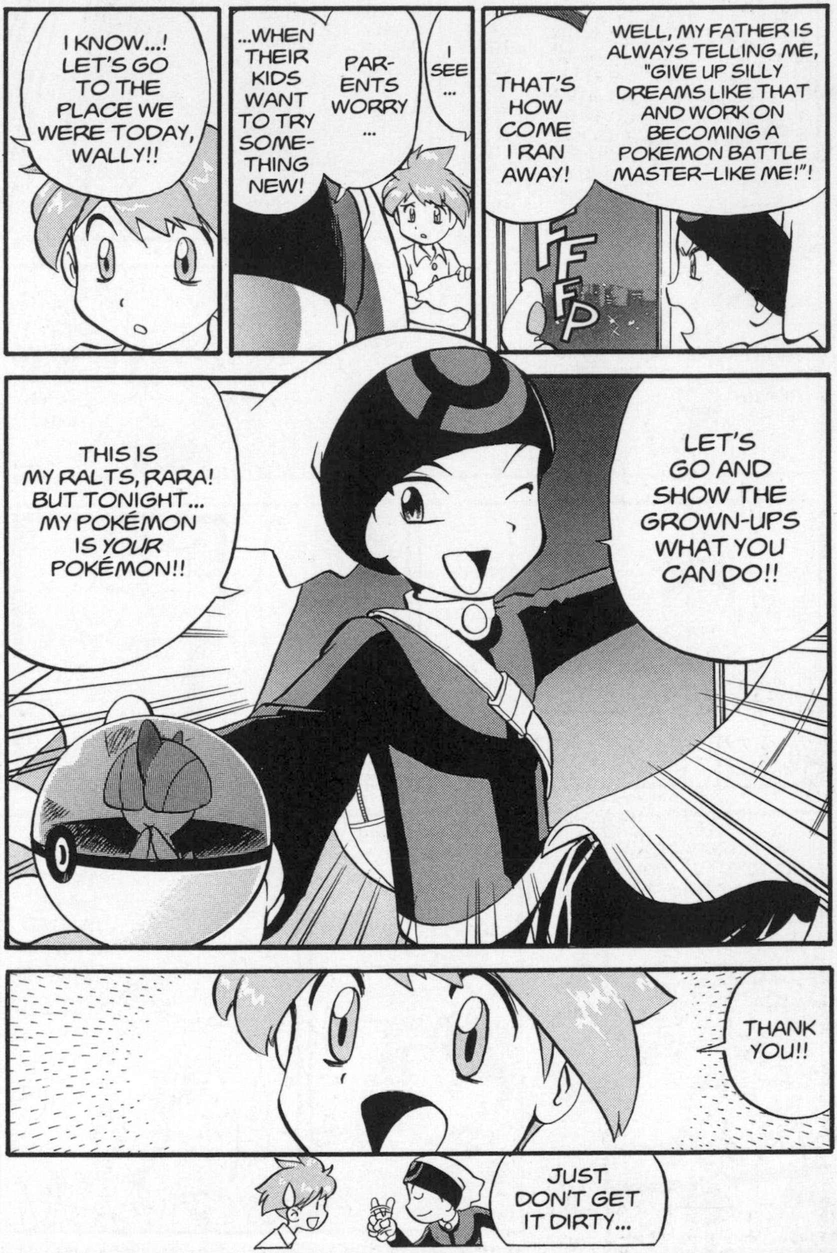
WELL, MY FATHER IS ALWAYS TELLING ME, "GIVE UP SILLY DREAMS LIKE THAT AND WORK ON BECOMING A POKEMON BATTLE MASTER–LIKE ME!"!
THAT'S HOW COME I RAN AWAY!
FFFP
I SEE...
PAR-ENTS WORRY...
...WHEN THEIR KIDS WANT TO TRY SOME-THING NEW!
I KNOW...! LET'S GO TO THE PLACE WE WERE TODAY, WALLY!!
LET'S GO AND SHOW THE GROWN-UPS WHAT YOU CAN DO!!
THIS IS MY RALTS, RARA! BUT TONIGHT... MY POKÉMON IS *YOUR* POKÉMON!!
THANK YOU!!
JUST DON'T GET IT DIRTY...

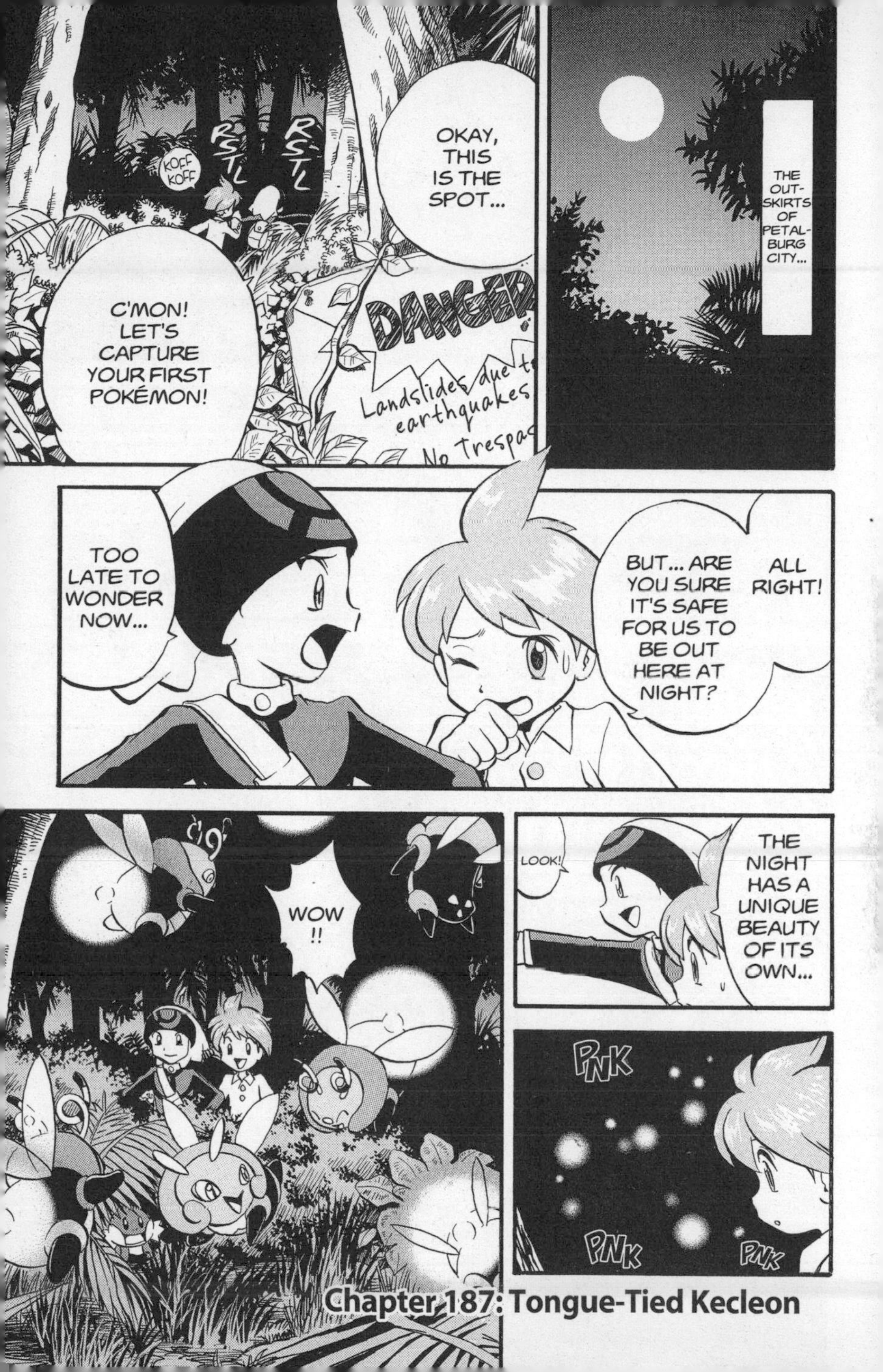
THE OUT-SKIRTS OF PETAL-BURG CITY...
OKAY, THIS IS THE SPOT...
RSTL
RSTL
KOFF KOFF
C'MON! LET'S CAPTURE YOUR FIRST POKÉMON!
Landslides due t
earthquakes
No Trespas
ALL RIGHT!
BUT... ARE YOU SURE IT'S SAFE FOR US TO BE OUT HERE AT NIGHT?
TOO LATE TO WONDER NOW...
THE NIGHT HAS A UNIQUE BEAUTY OF ITS OWN...
LOOK!
PNK
PNK
PNK
WOW !!

Chapter 187: Tongue-Tied Kecleon

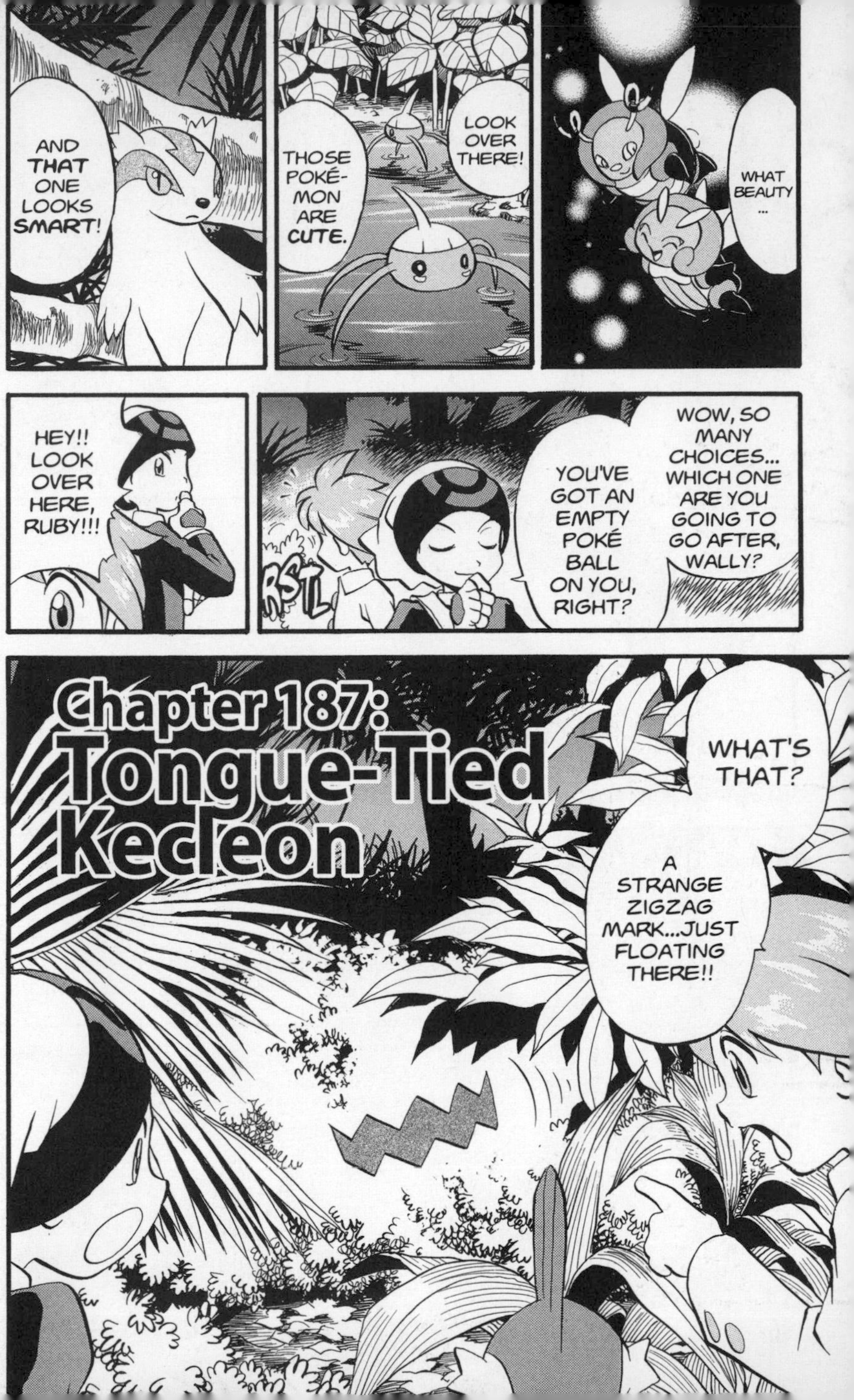
WHAT BEAUTY ...
LOOK OVER THERE!
THOSE POKÉMON ARE CUTE.
AND THAT ONE LOOKS SMART!
WOW, SO MANY CHOICES... WHICH ONE ARE YOU GOING TO GO AFTER, WALLY?
YOU'VE GOT AN EMPTY POKÉ BALL ON YOU, RIGHT?
RSTL
HEY!! LOOK OVER HERE, RUBY!!!
WHAT'S THAT?
A STRANGE ZIGZAG MARK...JUST FLOATING THERE!!
Chapter 187: Tongue-Tied Kecleon

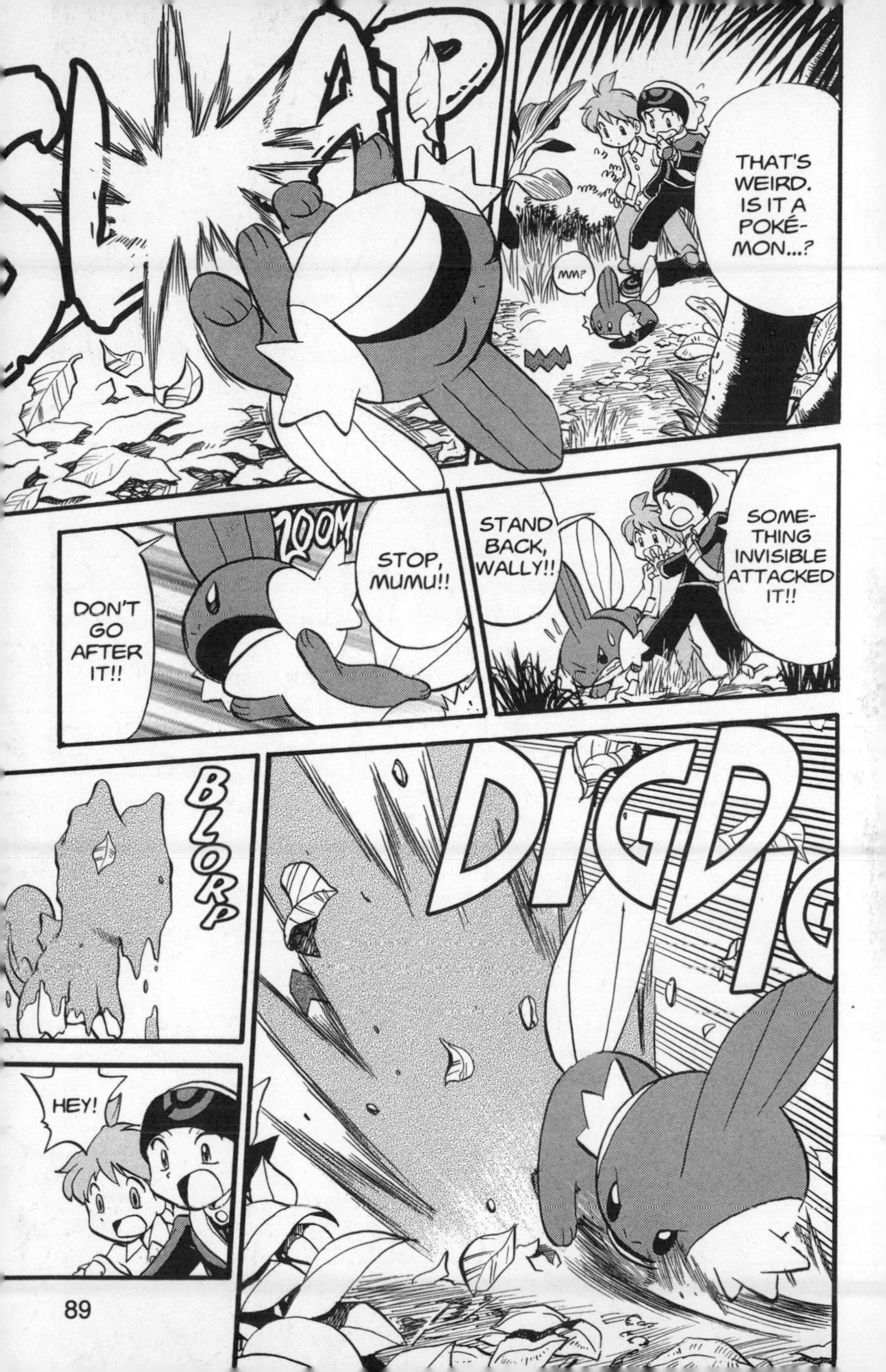
THAT'S WEIRD. IS IT A POKÉ-MON...?
MM?
SOME-THING INVISIBLE ATTACKED IT!!
STAND BACK, WALLY!!
STOP, MUMU!!
ZOOM
DON'T GO AFTER IT!!
DIGDIG
BLORP
HEY!

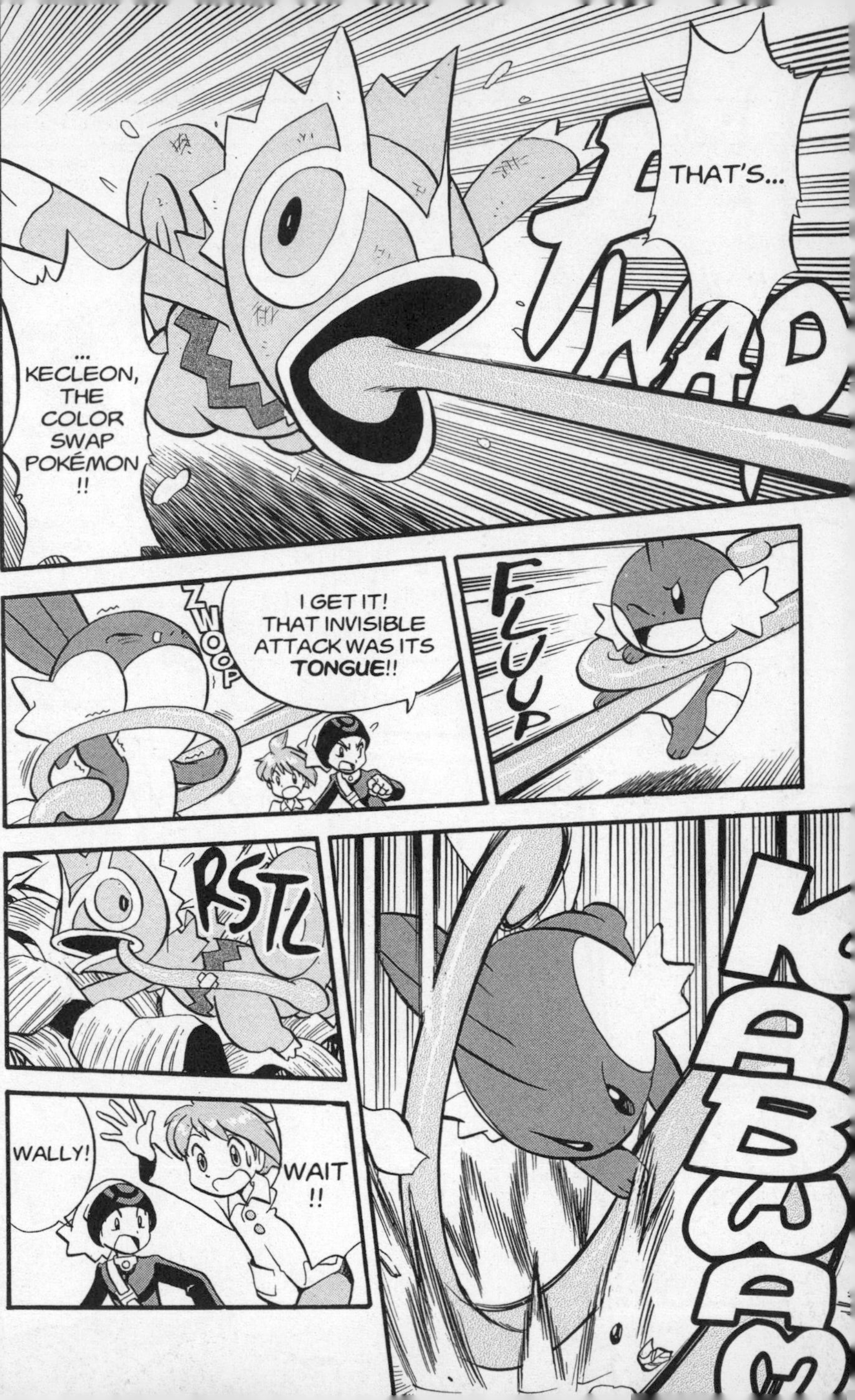
THAT'S...
TWAP
... KECLEON, THE COLOR SWAP POKÉMON !!
FLUUP
ZWOOP
I GET IT! THAT INVISIBLE ATTACK WAS ITS TONGUE!!
KABWAM
RSTL
WAIT !!
WALLY!

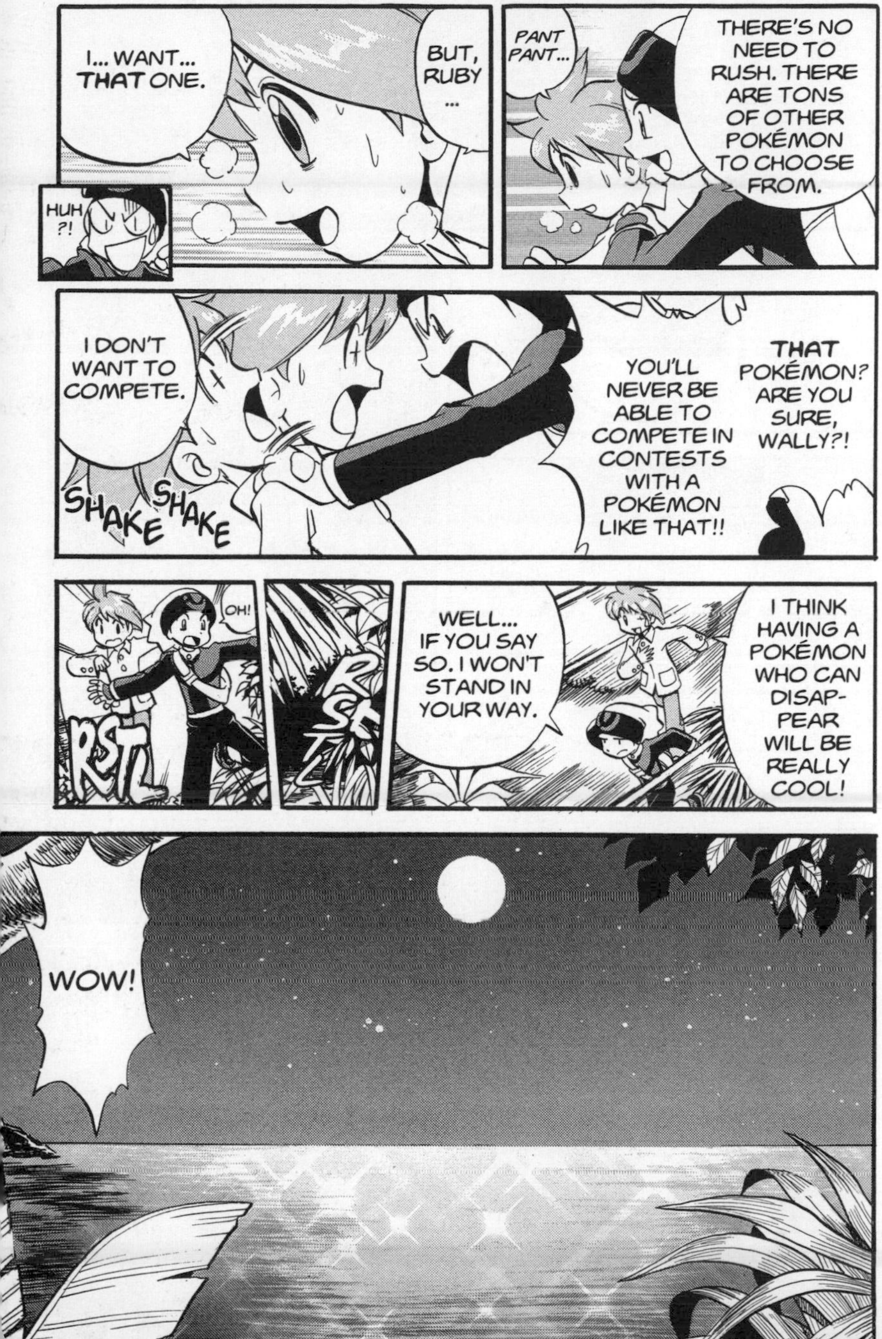
THERE'S NO NEED TO RUSH. THERE ARE TONS OF OTHER POKÉMON TO CHOOSE FROM.
PANT PANT...
BUT, RUBY ...
I... WANT... THAT ONE.
HUH ?!
THAT POKÉMON? ARE YOU SURE, WALLY?!
YOU'LL NEVER BE ABLE TO COMPETE IN CONTESTS WITH A POKÉMON LIKE THAT!!
I DON'T WANT TO COMPETE.
SHAKE SHAKE
I THINK HAVING A POKÉMON WHO CAN DISAP- PEAR WILL BE REALLY COOL!
WELL... IF YOU SAY SO. I WON'T STAND IN YOUR WAY.
RSTL
OH!
RSTL
WOW!

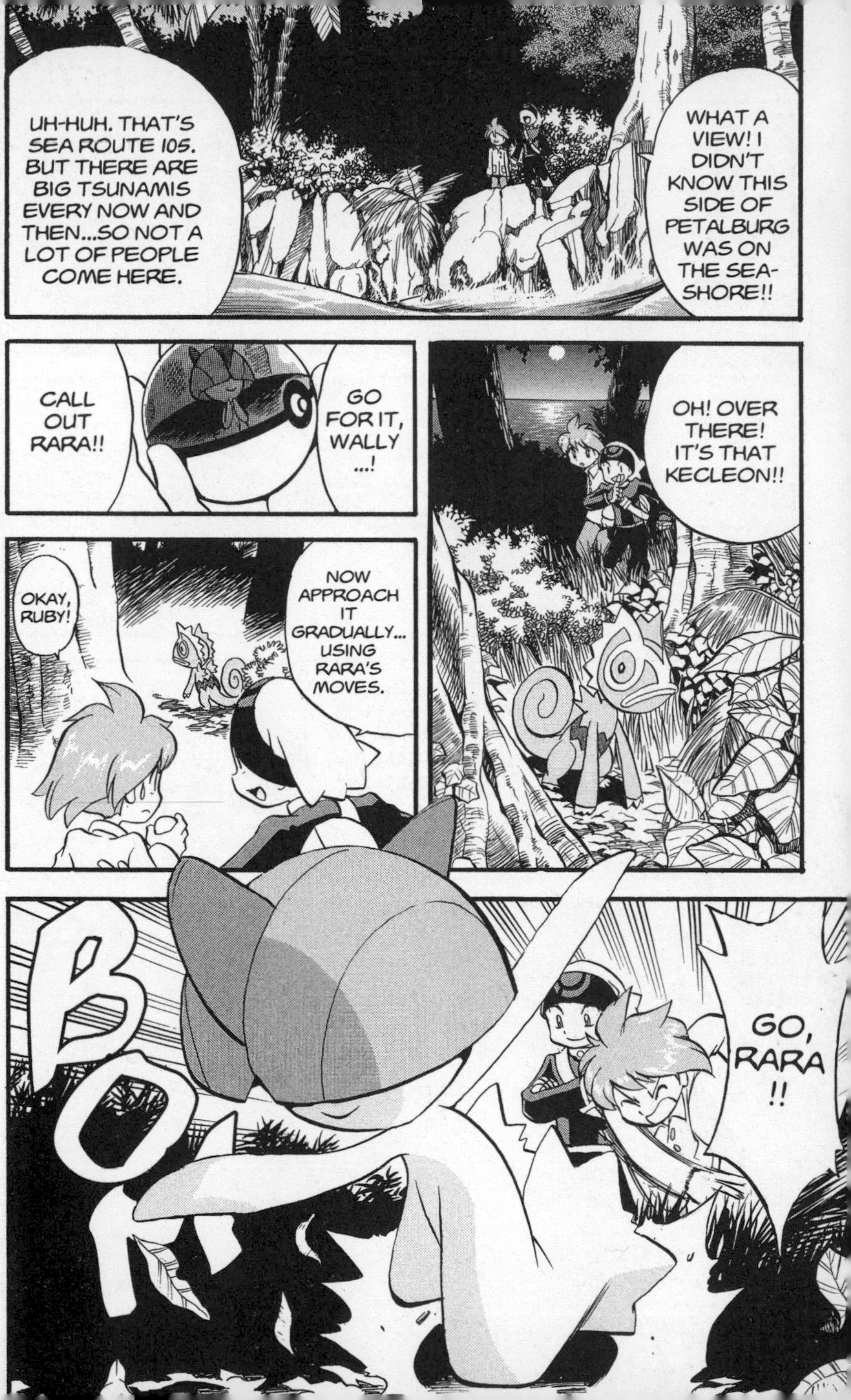
WHAT A VIEW! I DIDN'T KNOW THIS SIDE OF PETALBURG WAS ON THE SEA-SHORE!!
UH-HUH. THAT'S SEA ROUTE 105. BUT THERE ARE BIG TSUNAMIS EVERY NOW AND THEN...SO NOT A LOT OF PEOPLE COME HERE.
OH! OVER THERE! IT'S THAT KECLEON!!
GO FOR IT, WALLY ...!
CALL OUT RARA!!
NOW APPROACH IT GRADUALLY... USING RARA'S MOVES.
OKAY, RUBY!
GO, RARA !!
BO

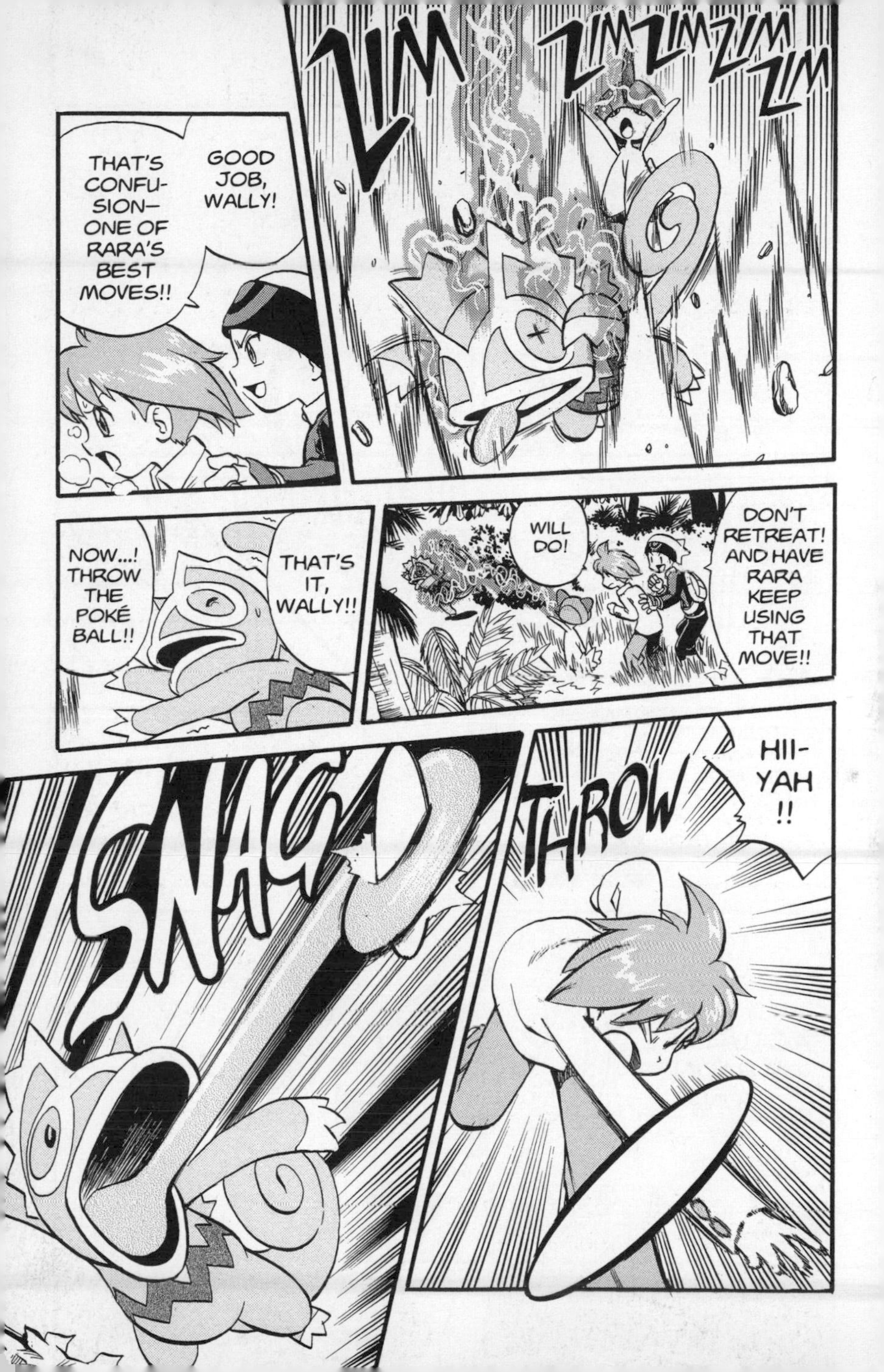
ZIM
ZIMZIMZIMZIM
ZIM
GOOD JOB, WALLY!
THAT'S CONFUSION—ONE OF RARA'S BEST MOVES!!
DON'T RETREAT! AND HAVE RARA KEEP USING THAT MOVE!!
WILL DO!
THAT'S IT, WALLY!!
NOW...! THROW THE POKÉ BALL!!
HII-YAH!!
THROW
SNAG

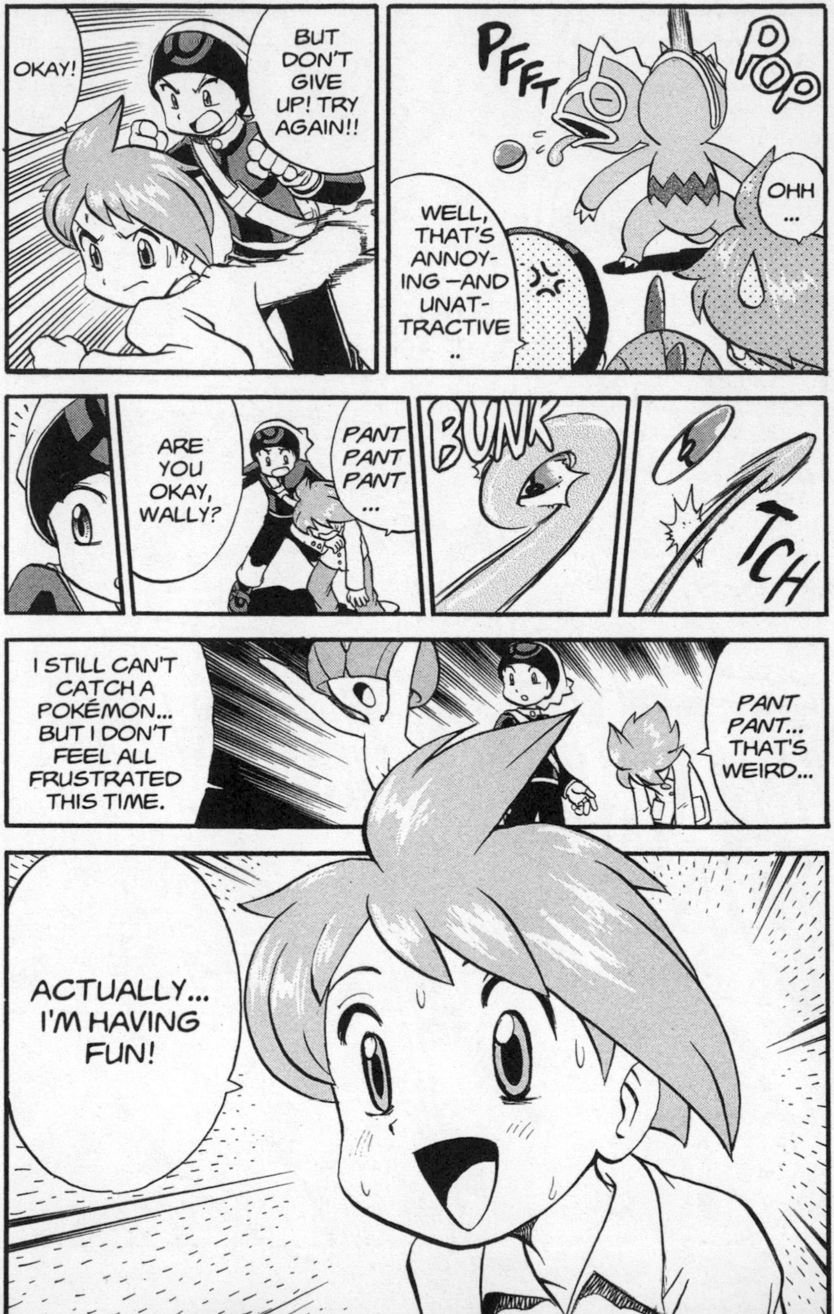
POP
PFFFT
OHH...
WELL, THAT'S ANNOYING—AND UNATTRACTIVE..
BUT DON'T GIVE UP! TRY AGAIN!!
OKAY!
TCH
BUNK
PANT PANT PANT...
ARE YOU OKAY, WALLY?
PANT PANT... THAT'S WEIRD...
I STILL CAN'T CATCH A POKÉMON... BUT I DON'T FEEL ALL FRUSTRATED THIS TIME.
ACTUALLY... I'M HAVING FUN!

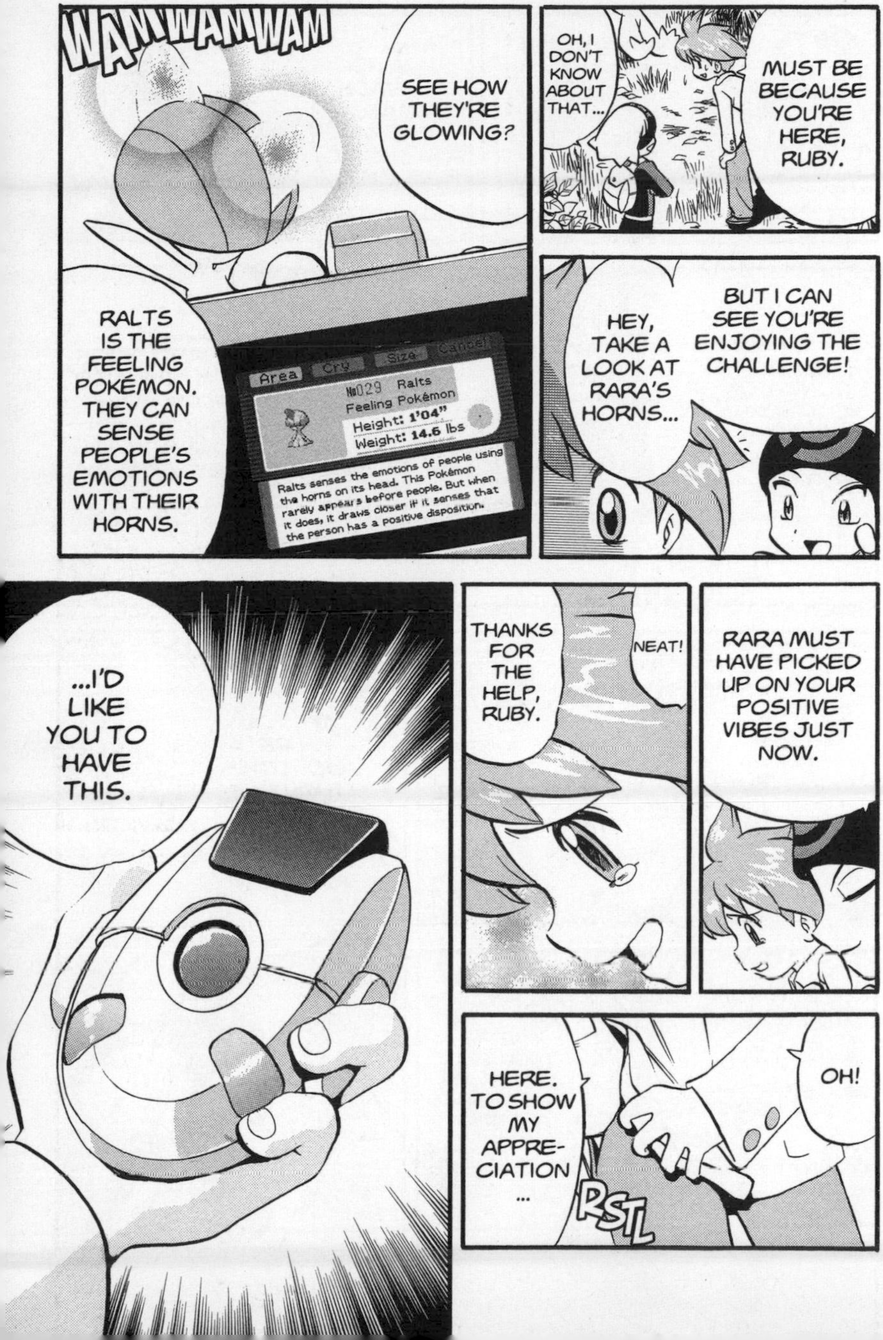
MUST BE BECAUSE YOU'RE HERE, RUBY.
OH, I DON'T KNOW ABOUT THAT...
BUT I CAN SEE YOU'RE ENJOYING THE CHALLENGE!
HEY, TAKE A LOOK AT RARA'S HORNS...
WAMWAMWAM
SEE HOW THEY'RE GLOWING?
RALTS IS THE FEELING POKÉMON. THEY CAN SENSE PEOPLE'S EMOTIONS WITH THEIR HORNS.
Area Cry Size Cancel
No029 Ralts
Feeling Pokémon
Height: 1'04"
Weight: 14.6 lbs
Ralts senses the emotions of people using the horns on its head. This Pokémon rarely appears before people. But when it does, it draws closer if it senses that the person has a positive disposition.
RARA MUST HAVE PICKED UP ON YOUR POSITIVE VIBES JUST NOW.
NEAT!
THANKS FOR THE HELP, RUBY.
OH!
HERE. TO SHOW MY APPRECIATION...
RSTL
...I'D LIKE YOU TO HAVE THIS.

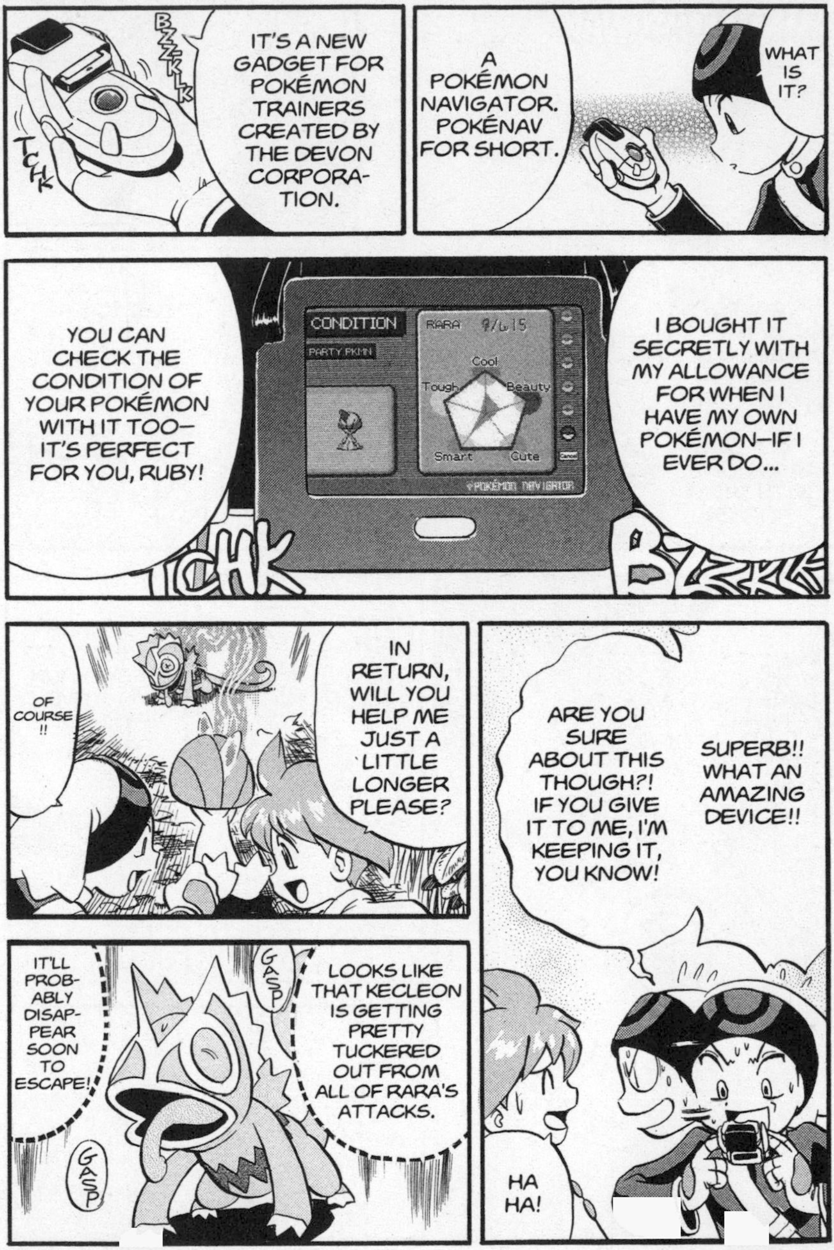
WHAT IS IT?
A POKÉMON NAVIGATOR. POKÉNAV FOR SHORT.
BZZKLK
IT'S A NEW GADGET FOR POKÉMON TRAINERS CREATED BY THE DEVON CORPORATION.
TCHK
I BOUGHT IT SECRETLY WITH MY ALLOWANCE FOR WHEN I HAVE MY OWN POKÉMON—IF I EVER DO...
CONDITION
PARTY PKMN
RARA
Cool
Tough
Beauty
Smart
Cute
POKÉMON NAVIGATOR
YOU CAN CHECK THE CONDITION OF YOUR POKÉMON WITH IT TOO—IT'S PERFECT FOR YOU, RUBY!
BZZKLK
TCHK
SUPERB!! WHAT AN AMAZING DEVICE!!
ARE YOU SURE ABOUT THIS THOUGH?! IF YOU GIVE IT TO ME, I'M KEEPING IT, YOU KNOW!
HA HA!
IN RETURN, WILL YOU HELP ME JUST A LITTLE LONGER PLEASE?
OF COURSE!!
LOOKS LIKE THAT KECLEON IS GETTING PRETTY TUCKERED OUT FROM ALL OF RARA'S ATTACKS.
GASP
IT'LL PROBABLY DISAPPEAR SOON TO ESCAPE!
GASP

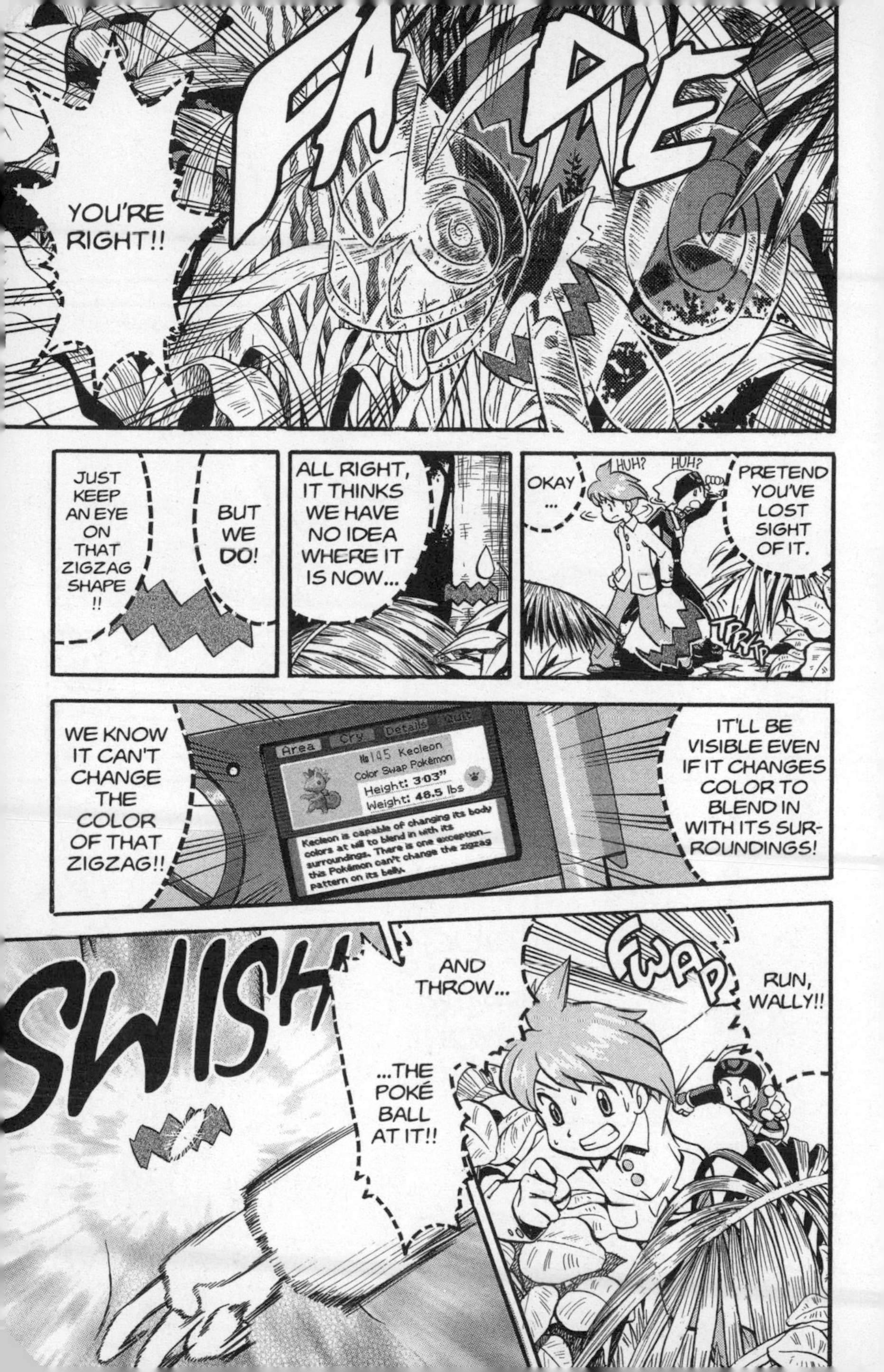
FADE
YOU'RE RIGHT!!
PRETEND YOU'VE LOST SIGHT OF IT.
HUH?
HUH?
OKAY ...
ALL RIGHT, IT THINKS WE HAVE NO IDEA WHERE IT IS NOW...
BUT WE DO!
JUST KEEP AN EYE ON THAT ZIGZAG SHAPE !!
IT'LL BE VISIBLE EVEN IF IT CHANGES COLOR TO BLEND IN WITH ITS SURROUNDINGS!
Area Cry Details Quit
No145 Kecleon
Color Swap Pokémon
Height: 3'03"
Weight: 48.5 lbs
Kecleon is capable of changing its body colors at will to blend in with its surroundings. There is one exception... this Pokémon can't change the zigzag pattern on its belly.
WE KNOW IT CAN'T CHANGE THE COLOR OF THAT ZIGZAG!!
RUN, WALLY!!
FWAP
AND THROW...
...THE POKÉ BALL AT IT!!
SWISH

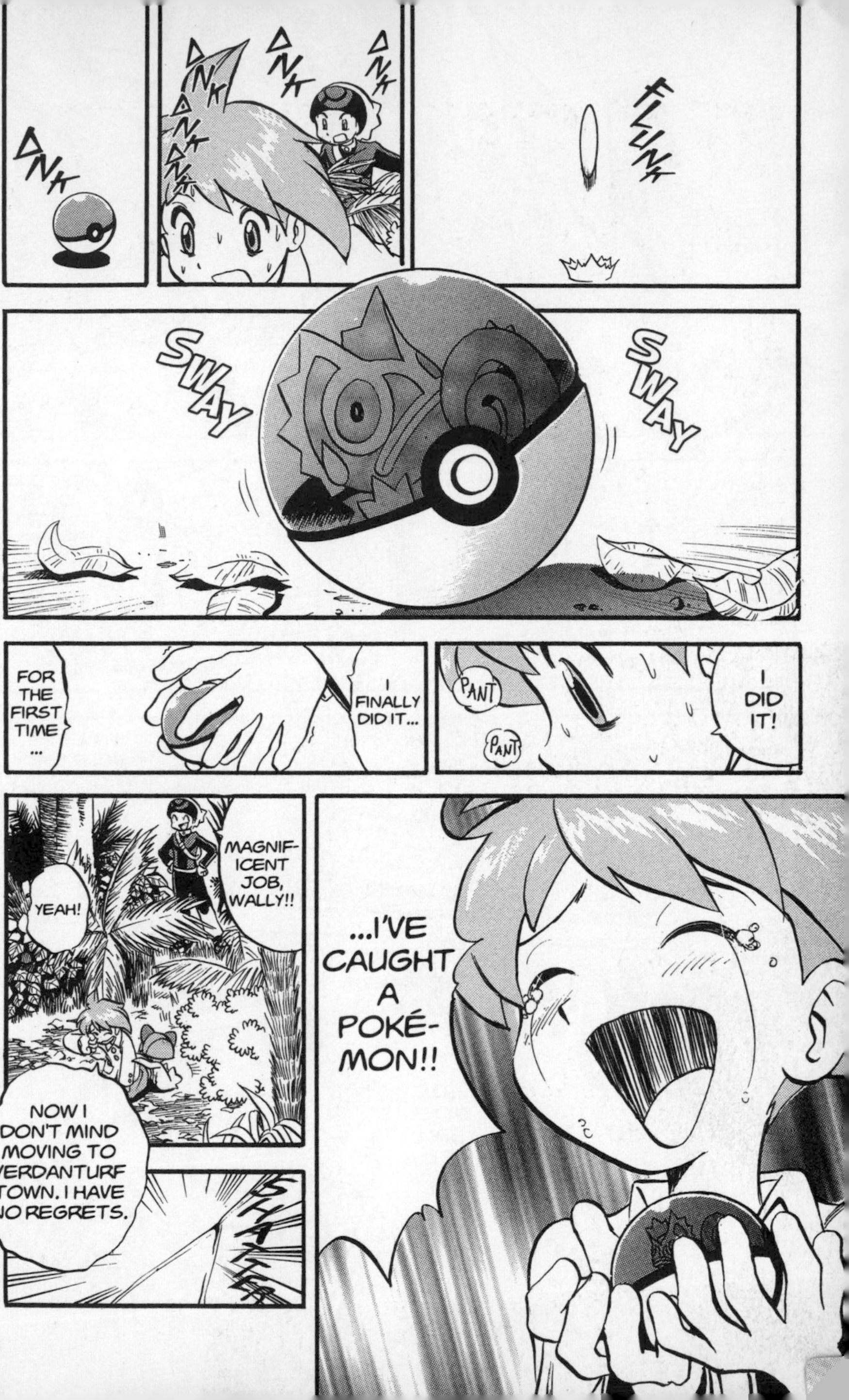

FLUNK
DNK
DNK
DNK DNK DNK
DNK
SWAY
SWAY
I DID IT!
PANT
PANT
I FINALLY DID IT...
FOR THE FIRST TIME ...
...I'VE CAUGHT A POKÉ-MON!!
MAGNIF-ICENT JOB, WALLY!!
YEAH!
NOW I DON'T MIND MOVING TO VERDANTURF TOWN. I HAVE NO REGRETS.

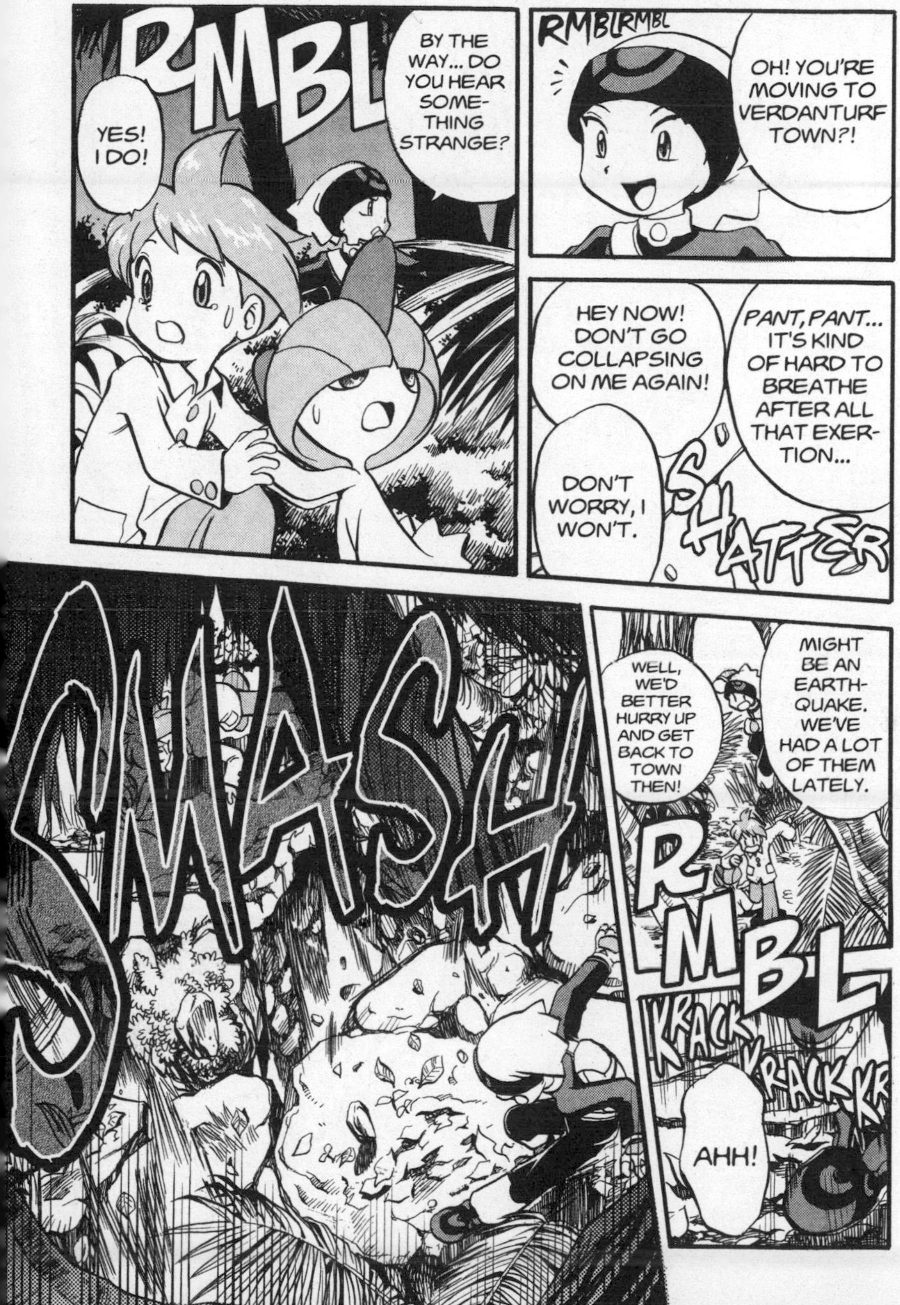
RMBLRMBL
OH! YOU'RE MOVING TO VERDANTURF TOWN?!
PANT, PANT... IT'S KIND OF HARD TO BREATHE AFTER ALL THAT EXER-TION...
HEY NOW! DON'T GO COLLAPSING ON ME AGAIN!
DON'T WORRY, I WON'T.
SHATTER
RMBL
BY THE WAY... DO YOU HEAR SOME-THING STRANGE?
YES! I DO!
MIGHT BE AN EARTH-QUAKE. WE'VE HAD A LOT OF THEM LATELY.
WELL, WE'D BETTER HURRY UP AND GET BACK TO TOWN THEN!
RMBL
KRACK KRACK KR
AHH!
SMASH

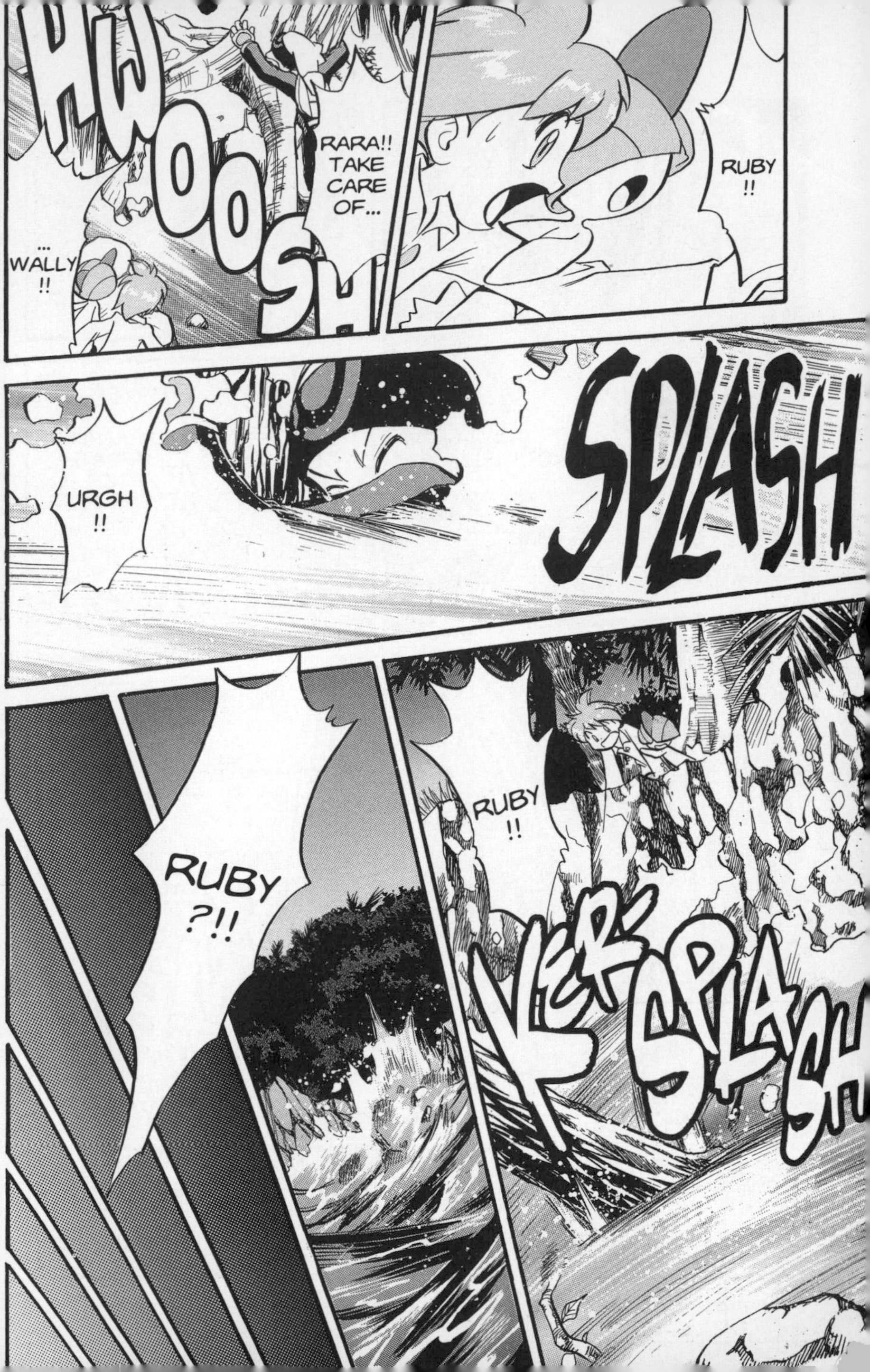
RUBY !!
RARA!! TAKE CARE OF...
HWOOOSH
... WALLY !!
SPLASH
URGH !!
RUBY !!
KER-SPLASH
RUBY ?!!

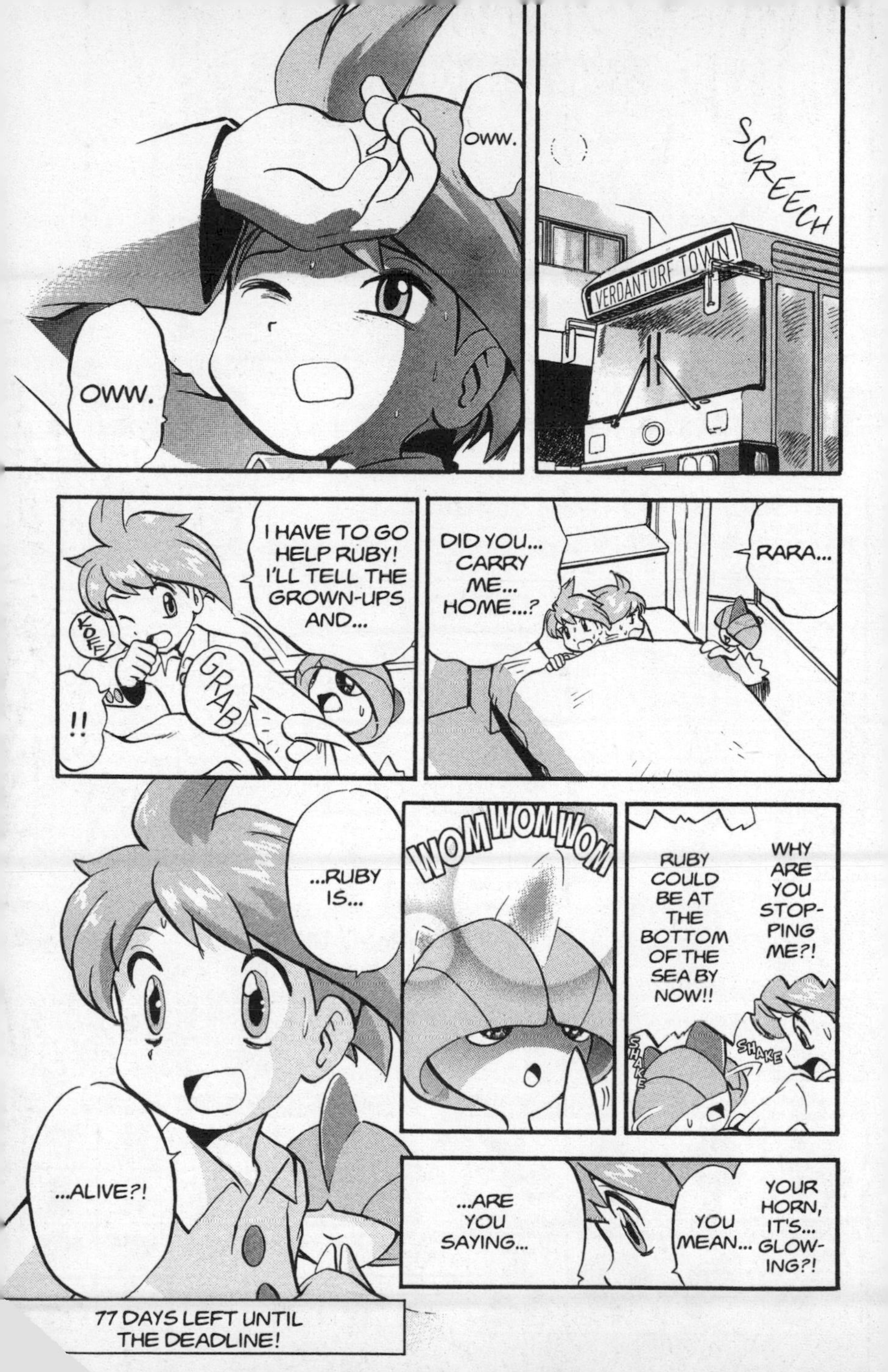
SCREECH
VERDANTURF TOWN
OWW.
OWW.
RARA...
DID YOU... CARRY ME... HOME...?
I HAVE TO GO HELP RUBY! I'LL TELL THE GROWN-UPS AND...
KOFF
GRAB
!!
WHY ARE YOU STOP-PING ME?!
RUBY COULD BE AT THE BOTTOM OF THE SEA BY NOW!!
SHAKE
SHAKE
WOMWOMWOM
YOUR HORN, IT'S... GLOW-ING?!
YOU MEAN...
...ARE YOU SAYING...
...RUBY IS...
...ALIVE?!
77 DAYS LEFT UNTIL THE DEADLINE!

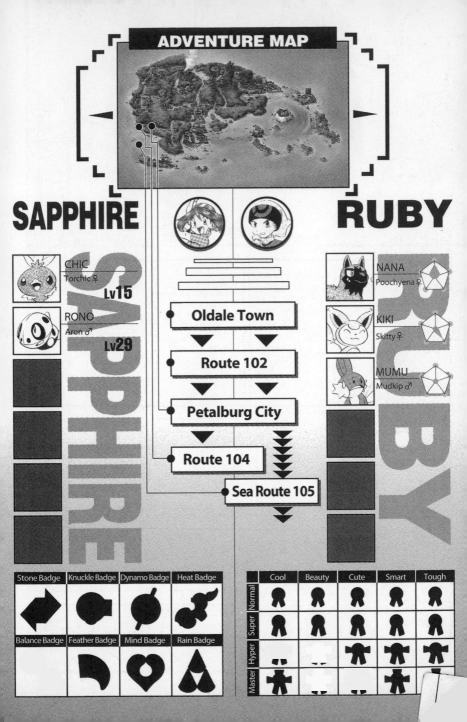

ADVENTURE MAP

SAPPHIRE

CHIC
Torchic ♀
Lv15

RONO
Aron ♂
Lv29

SAPPHIRE

RUBY

NANA
Poochyena ♀

KIKI
Skitty ♀

MUMU
Mudkip ♂

RUBY

Oldale Town
↓
Route 102
↓
Petalburg City
↓
Route 104
↓
Sea Route 105

Stone Badge	Knuckle Badge	Dynamo Badge	Heat Badge
Balance Badge	Feather Badge	Mind Badge	Rain Badge

		Cool	Beauty	Cute	Smart	Tough
Super	Normal					
Hyper						
Master						

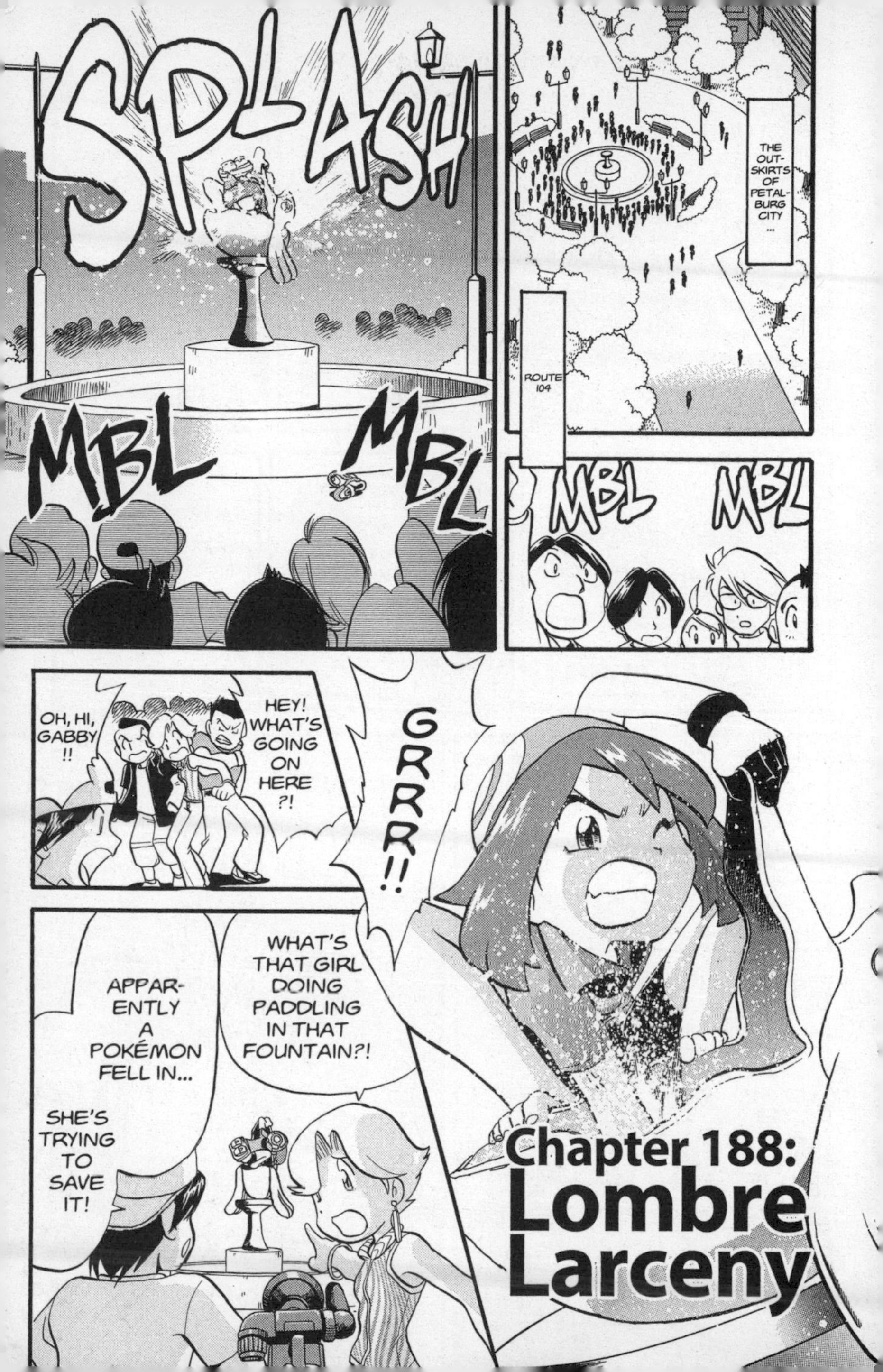
THE OUT-SKIRTS OF PETAL-BURG CITY ...
ROUTE 104
MBL MBL
SPLASH
MBL MBL
GRRR!!
HEY! WHAT'S GOING ON HERE?!
OH, HI, GABBY!!
WHAT'S THAT GIRL DOING PADDLING IN THAT FOUNTAIN?!
APPAR-ENTLY A POKÉMON FELL IN...
SHE'S TRYING TO SAVE IT!

Chapter 188: Lombre Larceny

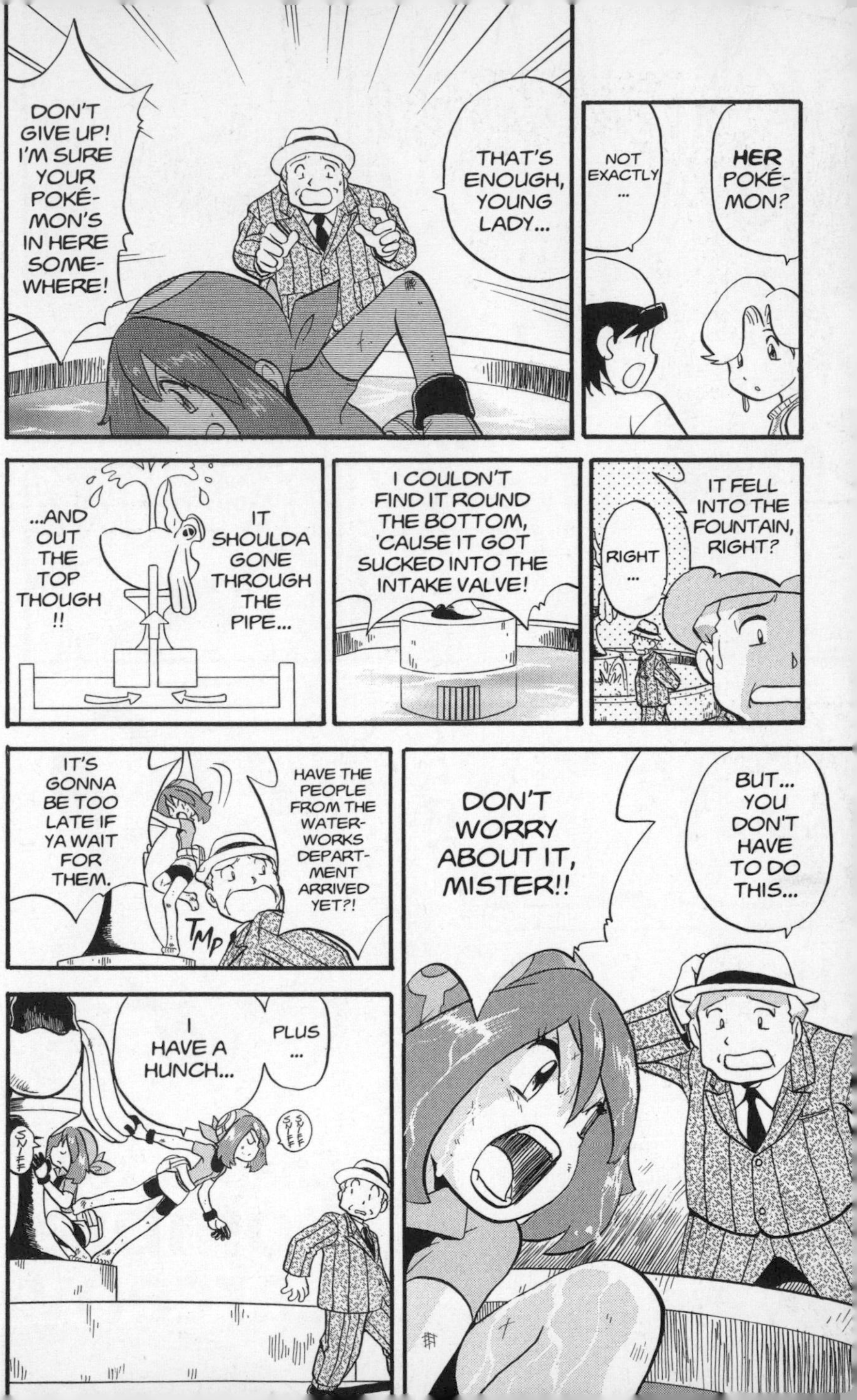
HER POKÉ-MON?
NOT EXACTLY...
THAT'S ENOUGH, YOUNG LADY...
DON'T GIVE UP! I'M SURE YOUR POKÉ-MON'S IN HERE SOME-WHERE!
IT FELL INTO THE FOUNTAIN, RIGHT?
RIGHT...
I COULDN'T FIND IT ROUND THE BOTTOM, 'CAUSE IT GOT SUCKED INTO THE INTAKE VALVE!
IT SHOULDA GONE THROUGH THE PIPE...
...AND OUT THE TOP THOUGH!!
BUT... YOU DON'T HAVE TO DO THIS...
DON'T WORRY ABOUT IT, MISTER!!
HAVE THE PEOPLE FROM THE WATER-WORKS DEPART-MENT ARRIVED YET?!
IT'S GONNA BE TOO LATE IF YA WAIT FOR THEM.
TMP
PLUS...
I HAVE A HUNCH...
SNIFF SNIFF
SNIFF

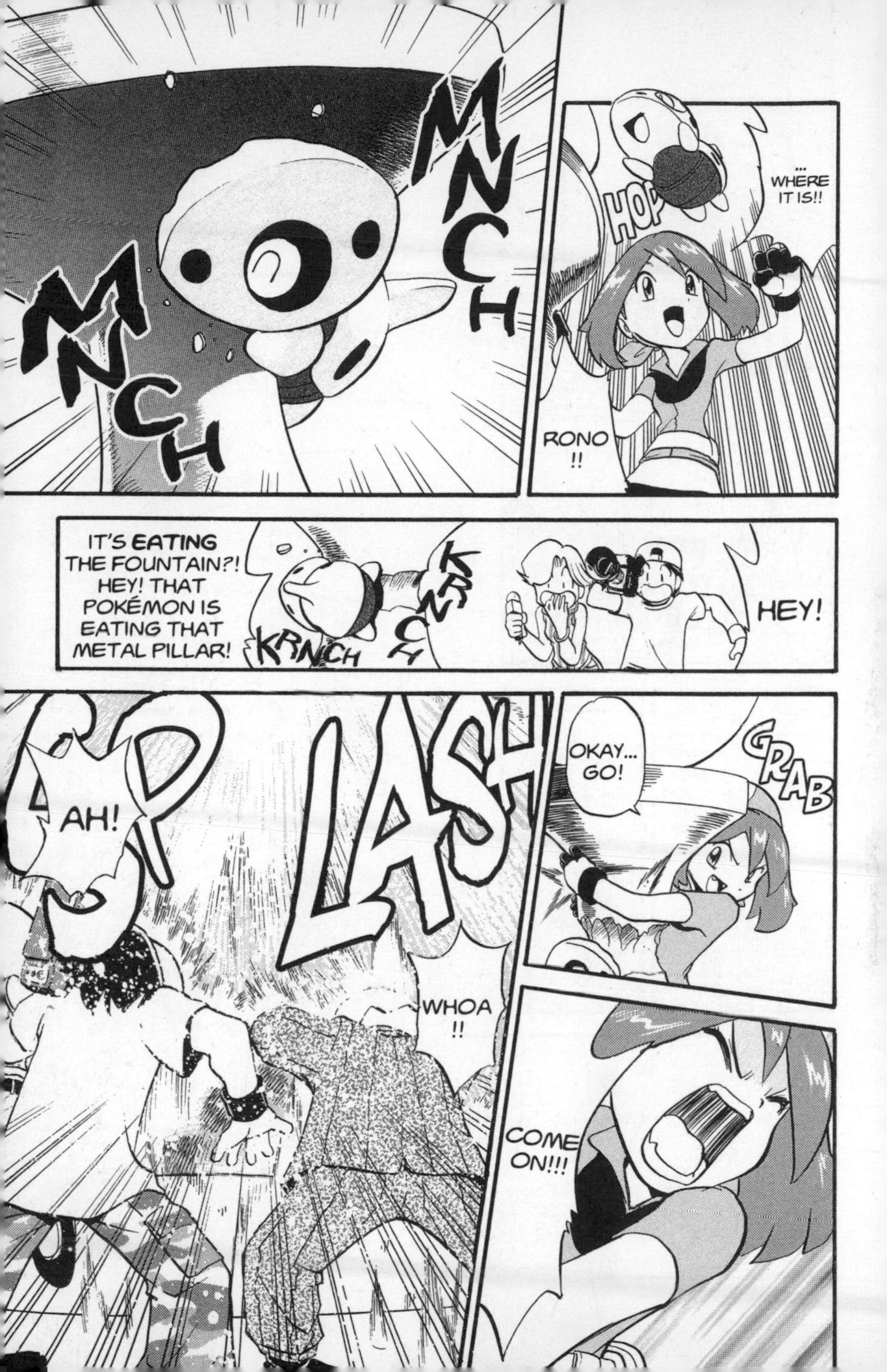
...WHERE IT IS!!
HOP
RONO !!
MNCH
MNCH
HEY!
KRNCH
KRNCH
IT'S EATING THE FOUNTAIN?! HEY! THAT POKÉMON IS EATING THAT METAL PILLAR!
GRAB
OKAY... GO!
COME ON!!!
LASH
AH!
WHOA !!

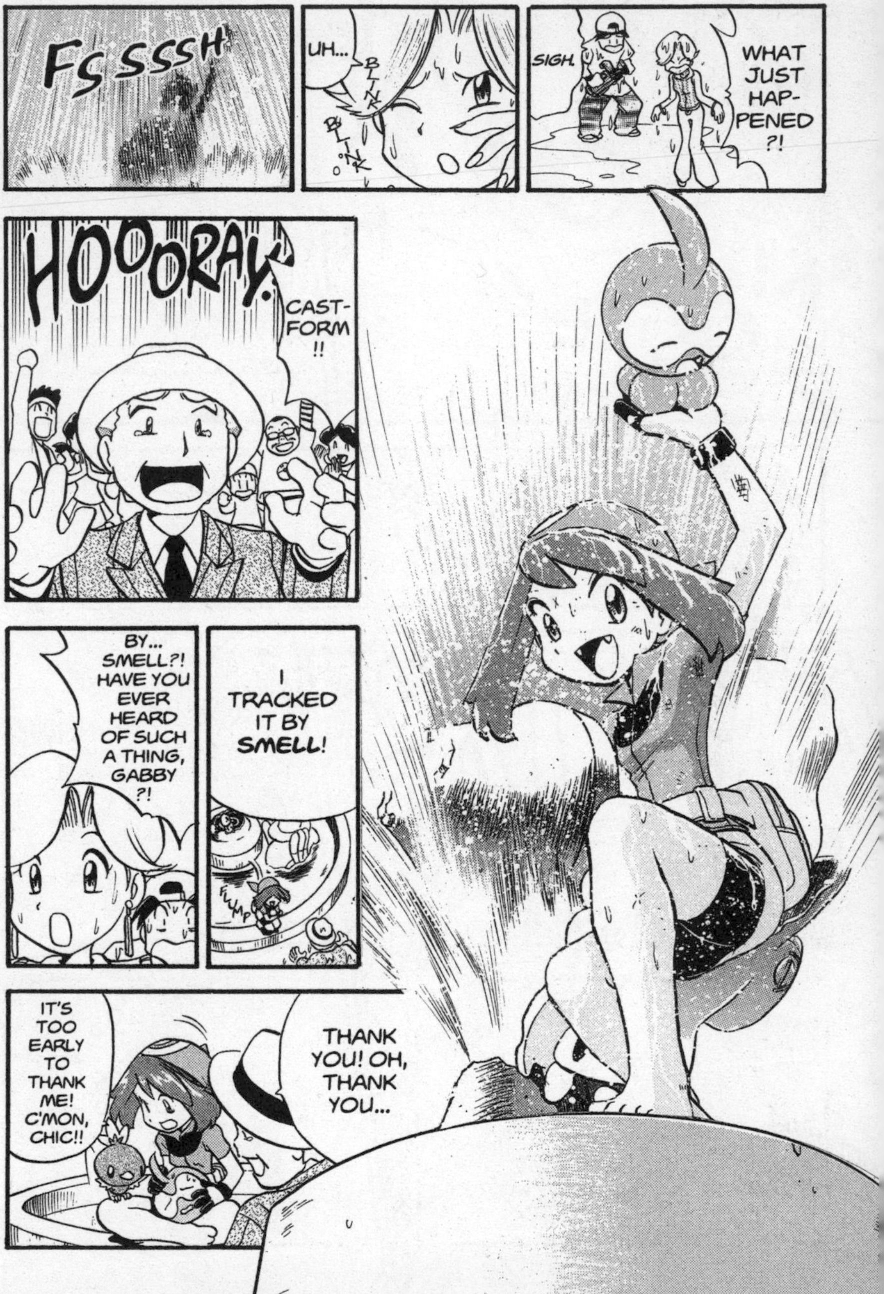
WHAT JUST HAPPENED?!
SIGH.
UH...
BLINK
BLINK
FSSSSH
HOOORAY!
CAST-FORM!!
I TRACKED IT BY SMELL!
FLUMP
BY... SMELL?! HAVE YOU EVER HEARD OF SUCH A THING, GABBY?!
THANK YOU! OH, THANK YOU...
IT'S TOO EARLY TO THANK ME! C'MON, CHIC!!

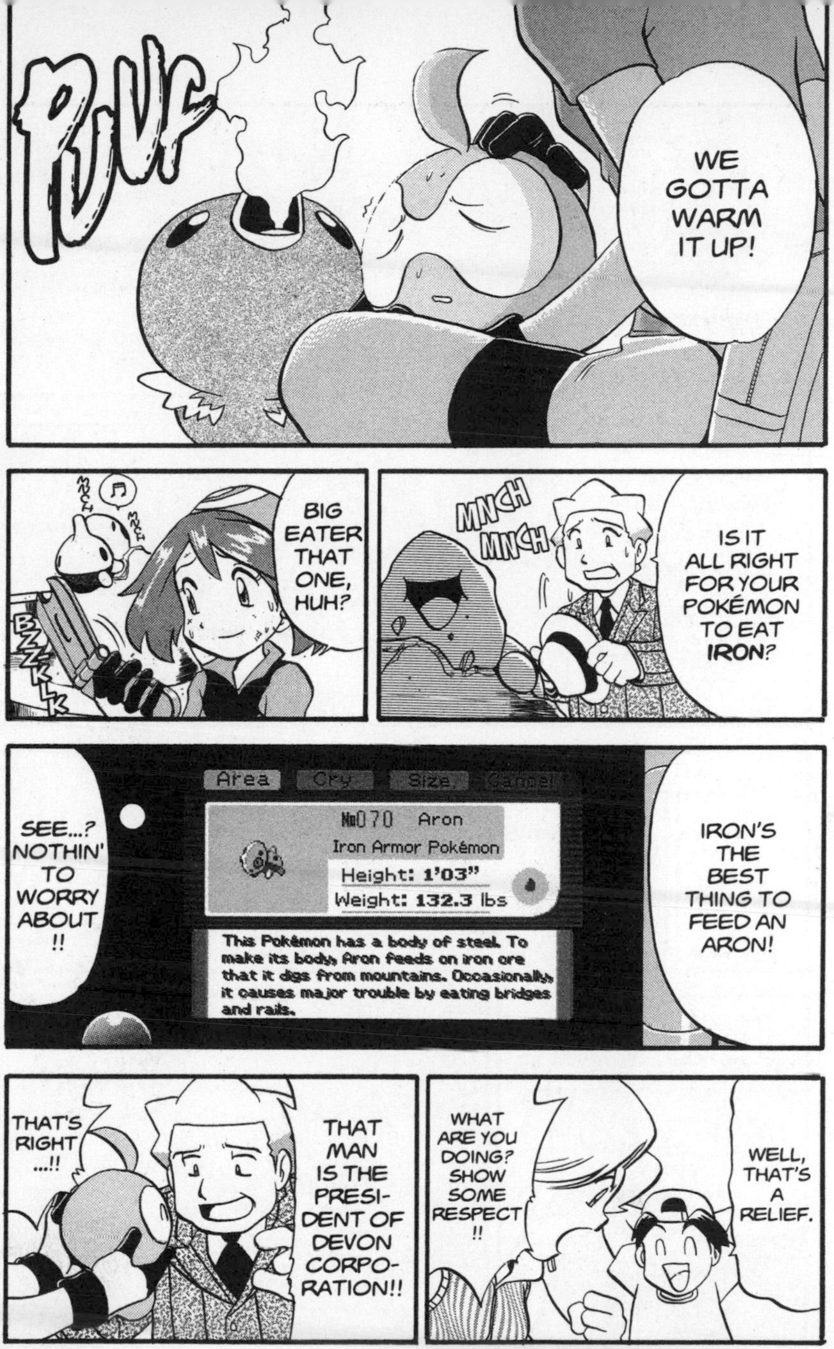
WE GOTTA WARM IT UP!
PUF
IS IT ALL RIGHT FOR YOUR POKÉMON TO EAT IRON?
MNCH MNCH
BIG EATER THAT ONE, HUH?
BZZKLK
IRON'S THE BEST THING TO FEED AN ARON!
Area Cry Size Cancel
No070 Aron
Iron Armor Pokémon
Height: 1'03"
Weight: 132.3 lbs
This Pokémon has a body of steel. To make its body, Aron feeds on iron ore that it digs from mountains. Occasionally, it causes major trouble by eating bridges and rails.
SEE...? NOTHIN' TO WORRY ABOUT !!
WELL, THAT'S A RELIEF.
WHAT ARE YOU DOING? SHOW SOME RESPECT !!
THAT MAN IS THE PRESI-DENT OF DEVON CORPO-RATION!!
THAT'S RIGHT ...!!

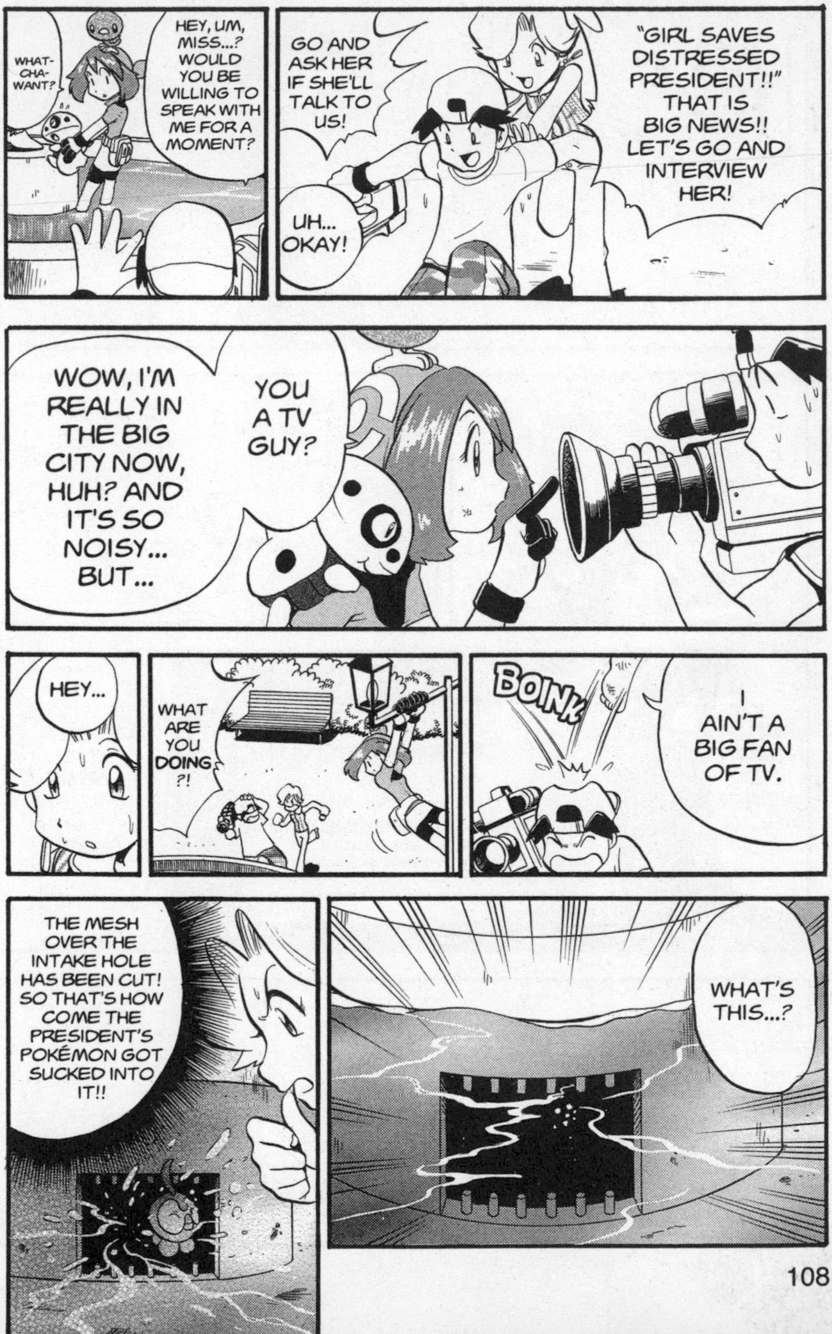
"GIRL SAVES DISTRESSED PRESIDENT!!" THAT IS BIG NEWS!! LET'S GO AND INTERVIEW HER!
GO AND ASK HER IF SHE'LL TALK TO US!
UH... OKAY!
HEY, UM, MISS...? WOULD YOU BE WILLING TO SPEAK WITH ME FOR A MOMENT?
WHAT-CHA-WANT?
YOU A TV GUY?
WOW, I'M REALLY IN THE BIG CITY NOW, HUH? AND IT'S SO NOISY... BUT...
I AIN'T A BIG FAN OF TV.
BOINK
WHAT ARE YOU **DOING**?!
HEY...
WHAT'S THIS...?
THE MESH OVER THE INTAKE HOLE HAS BEEN CUT! SO THAT'S HOW COME THE PRESIDENT'S POKÉMON GOT SUCKED INTO IT!!

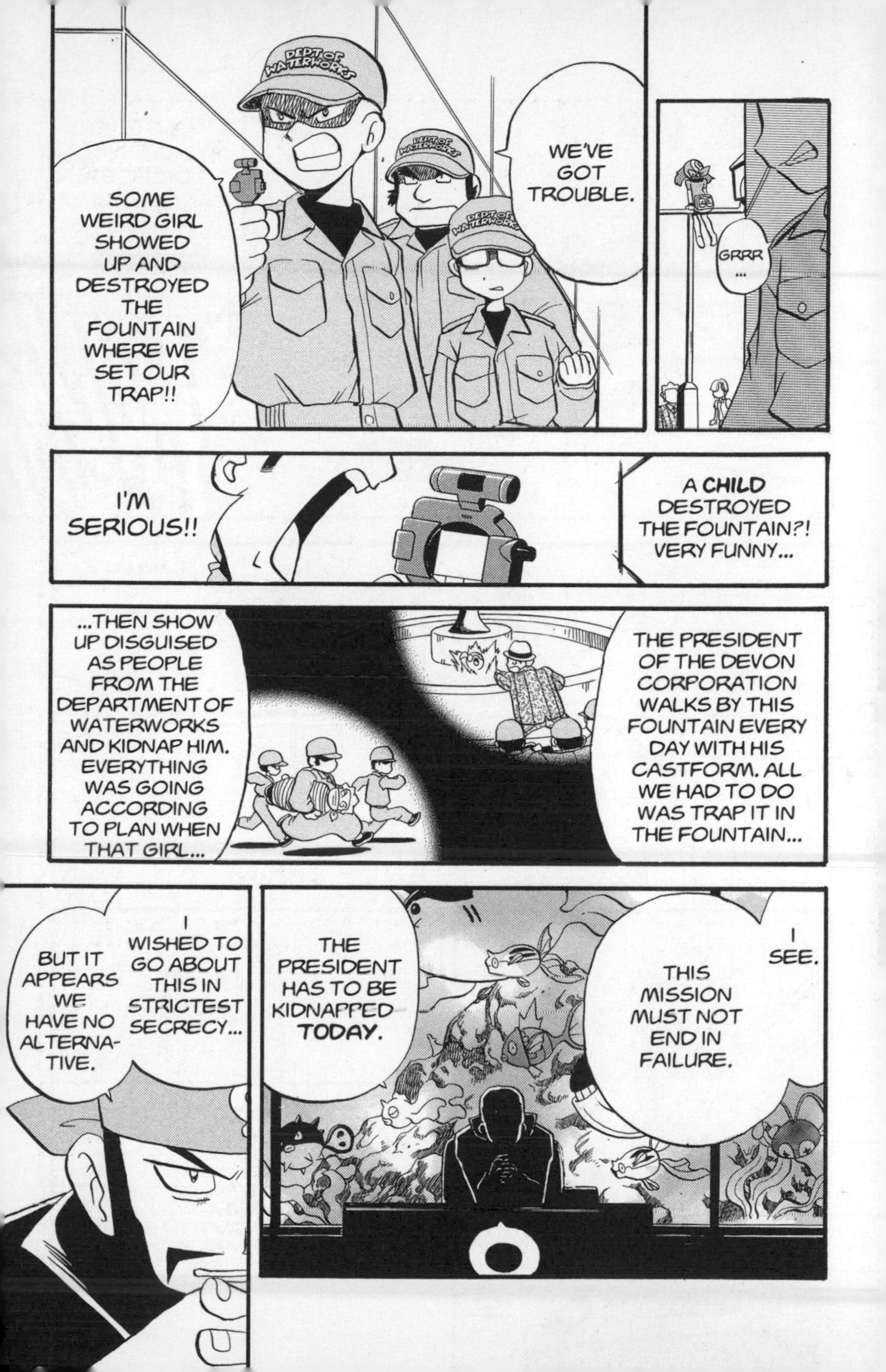
GRRR ...
WE'VE GOT TROUBLE.
DEPT OF WATERWORKS
SOME WEIRD GIRL SHOWED UP AND DESTROYED THE FOUNTAIN WHERE WE SET OUR TRAP!!
A **CHILD** DESTROYED THE FOUNTAIN?! VERY FUNNY...
I'M SERIOUS!!
THE PRESIDENT OF THE DEVON CORPORATION WALKS BY THIS FOUNTAIN EVERY DAY WITH HIS CASTFORM. ALL WE HAD TO DO WAS TRAP IT IN THE FOUNTAIN...
...THEN SHOW UP DISGUISED AS PEOPLE FROM THE DEPARTMENT OF WATERWORKS AND KIDNAP HIM. EVERYTHING WAS GOING ACCORDING TO PLAN WHEN THAT GIRL...
I SEE.
THIS MISSION MUST NOT END IN FAILURE.
THE PRESIDENT HAS TO BE KIDNAPPED **TODAY**.
I WISHED TO GO ABOUT THIS IN STRICTEST SECRECY...
BUT IT APPEARS WE HAVE NO ALTERNA-TIVE.

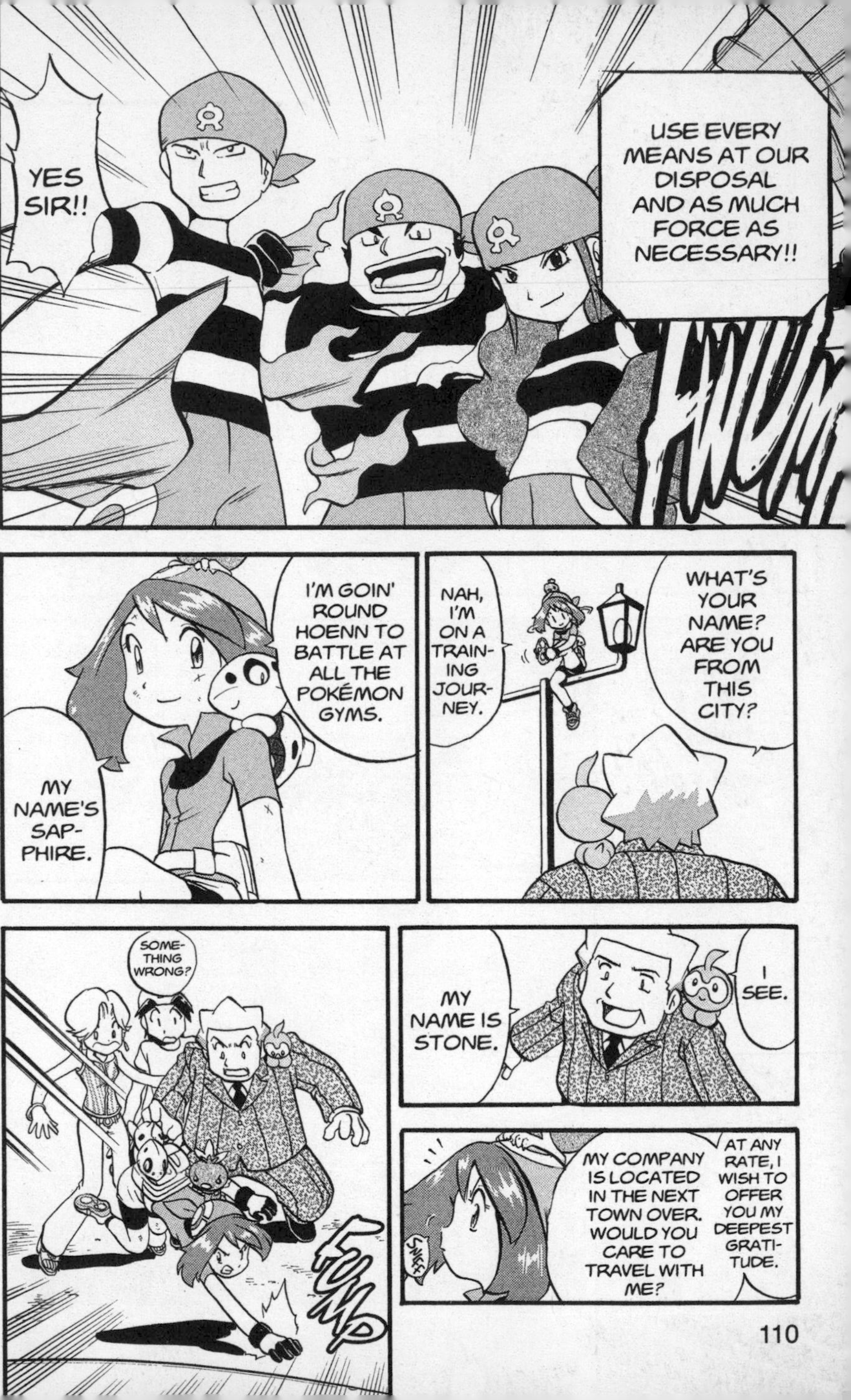
USE EVERY MEANS AT OUR DISPOSAL AND AS MUCH FORCE AS NECESSARY!!
YES SIR!!
WHAT'S YOUR NAME? ARE YOU FROM THIS CITY?
NAH, I'M ON A TRAINING JOURNEY.
I'M GOIN' ROUND HOENN TO BATTLE AT ALL THE POKÉMON GYMS.
MY NAME'S SAPPHIRE.
I SEE.
MY NAME IS STONE.
AT ANY RATE, I WISH TO OFFER YOU MY DEEPEST GRATITUDE.
MY COMPANY IS LOCATED IN THE NEXT TOWN OVER. WOULD YOU CARE TO TRAVEL WITH ME?
SOMETHING WRONG?

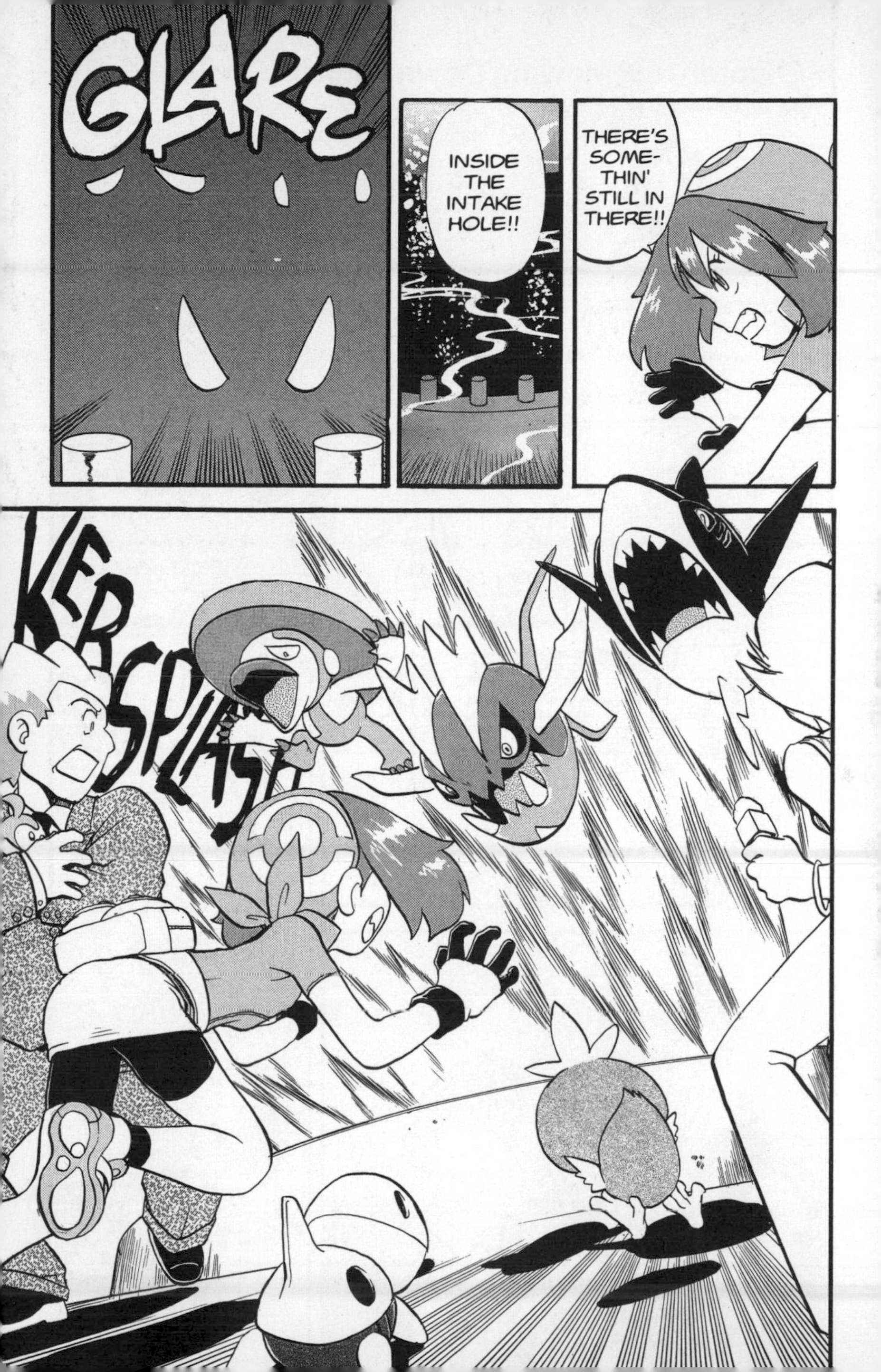
THERE'S SOME-THIN' STILL IN THERE!!
INSIDE THE INTAKE HOLE!!
GLARE
KER SPLASH

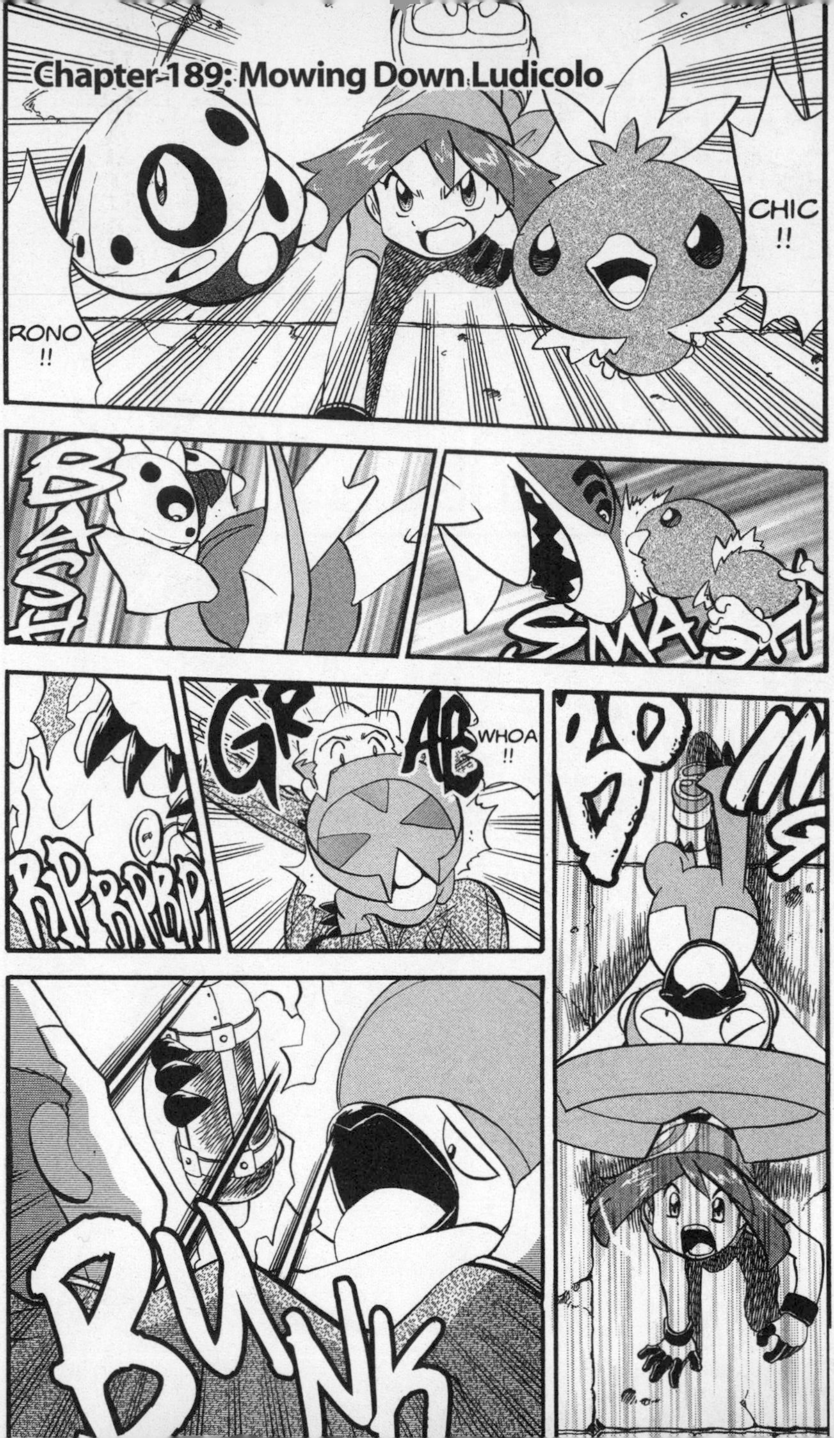
Chapter 189: Mowing Down Ludicolo
CHIC !!
RONO !!
SMASH
BASH
BOING
GRAB
WHOA !!
RIPRIPRIP
BUNK

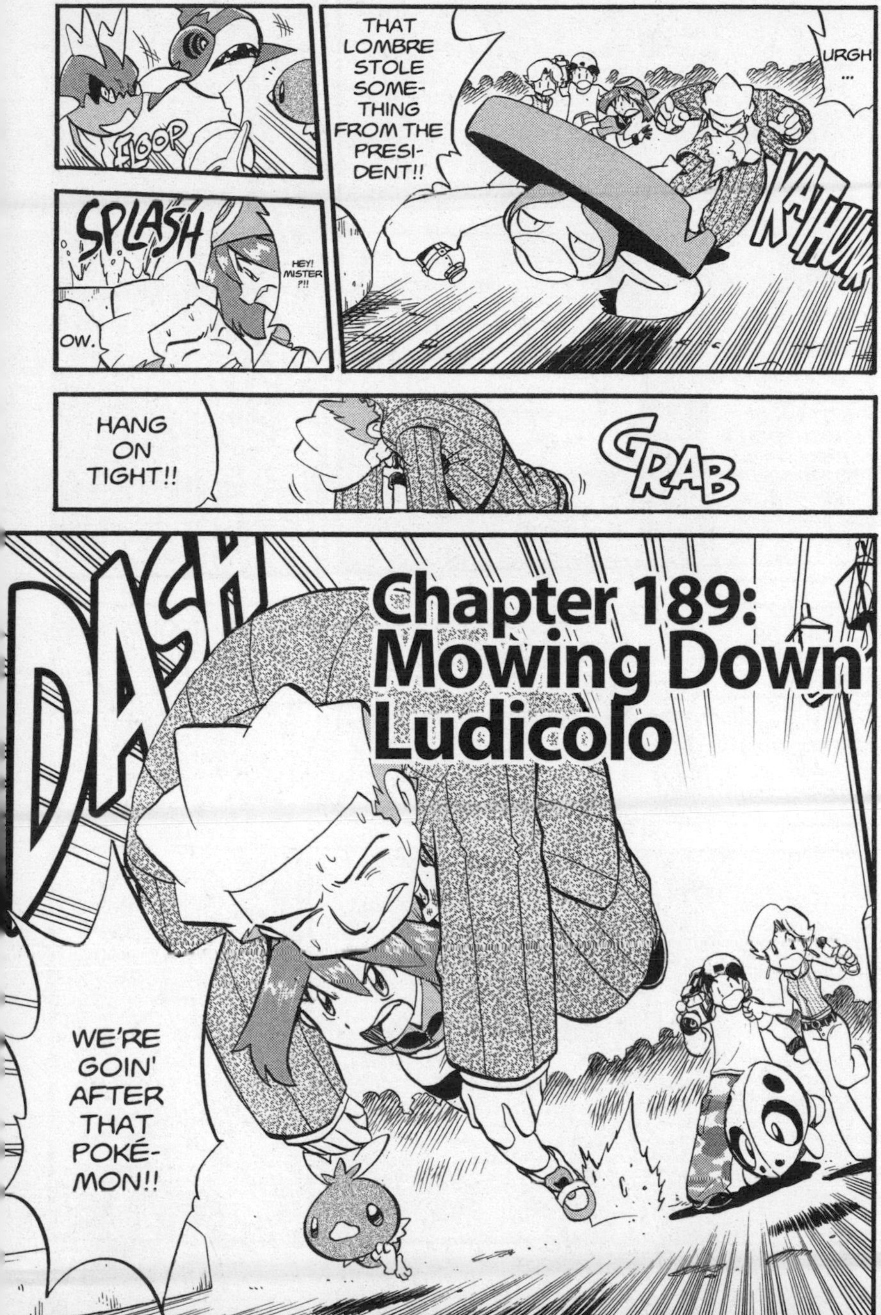
URGH ...
THAT LOMBRE STOLE SOME-THING FROM THE PRESI-DENT!!
KATHUNK
FLOOP
SPLASH
HEY! MISTER ?!!
OW.
GRAB
HANG ON TIGHT!!
Chapter 189: Mowing Down Ludicolo
DASH
WE'RE GOIN' AFTER THAT POKÉ-MON!!

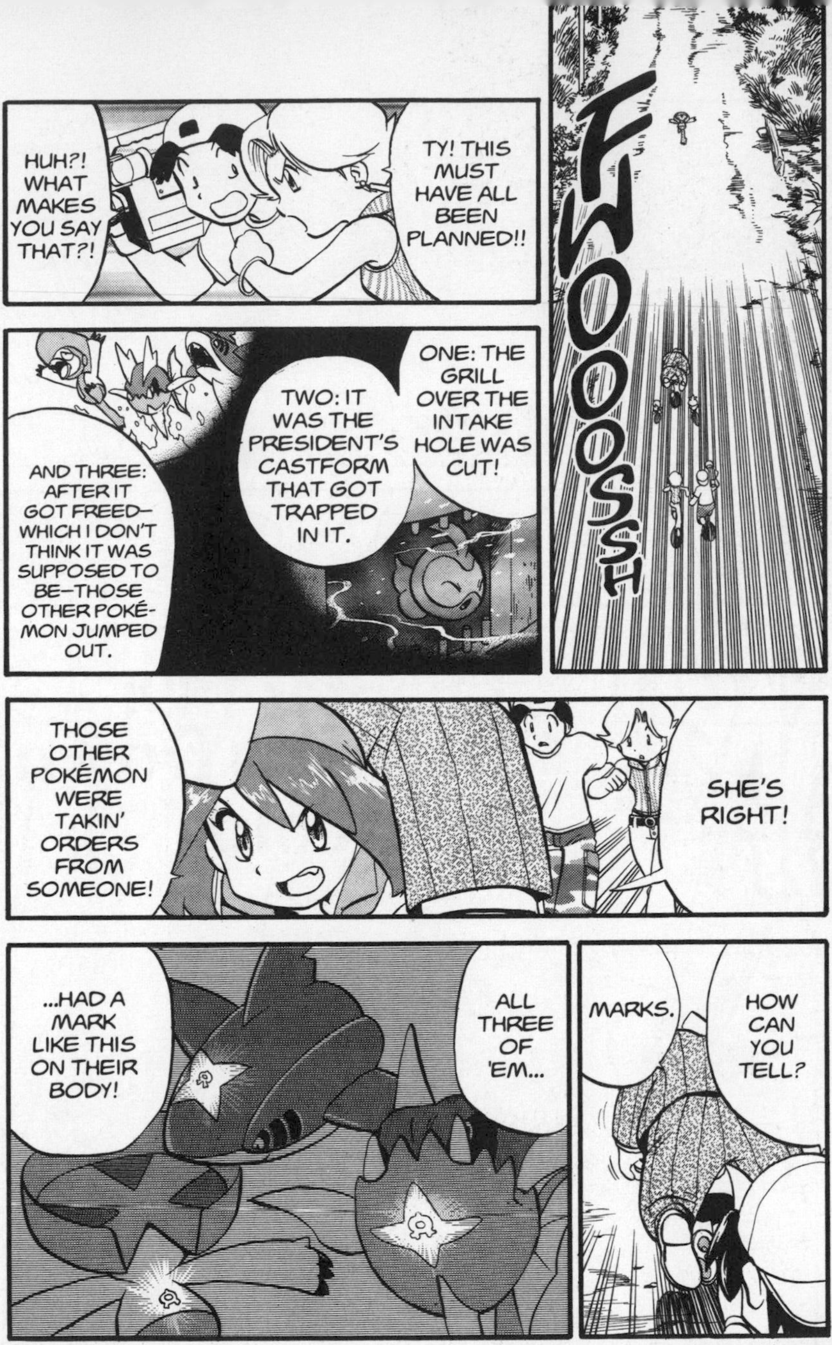
FWOOOOSSH
TY! THIS MUST HAVE ALL BEEN PLANNED!!
HUH?! WHAT MAKES YOU SAY THAT?!
ONE: THE GRILL OVER THE INTAKE HOLE WAS CUT!
TWO: IT WAS THE PRESIDENT'S CASTFORM THAT GOT TRAPPED IN IT.
AND THREE: AFTER IT GOT FREED—WHICH I DON'T THINK IT WAS SUPPOSED TO BE—THOSE OTHER POKÉMON JUMPED OUT.
THOSE OTHER POKÉMON WERE TAKIN' ORDERS FROM SOMEONE!
SHE'S RIGHT!
HOW CAN YOU TELL?
MARKS.
ALL THREE OF 'EM...
...HAD A MARK LIKE THIS ON THEIR BODY!

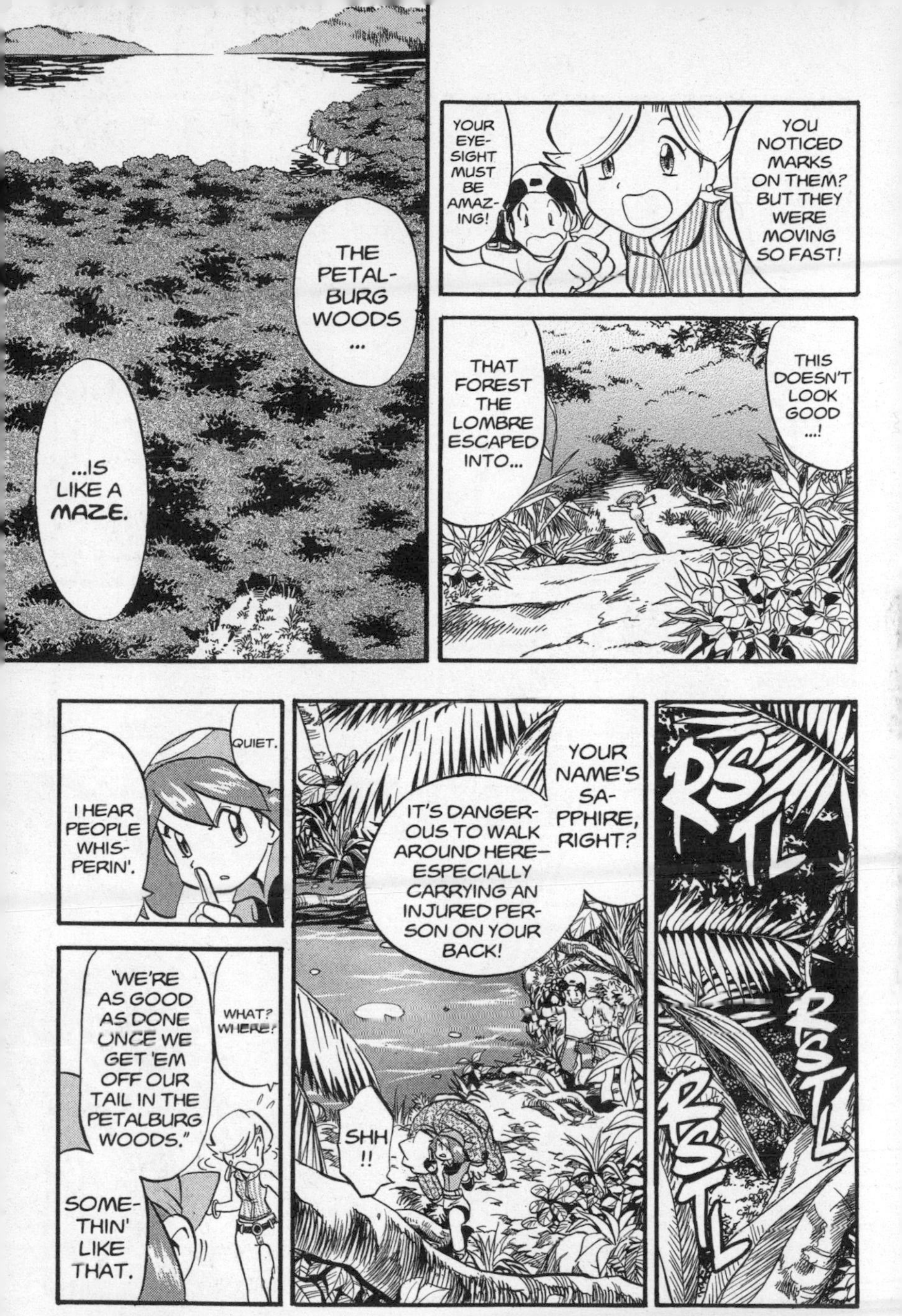
YOU NOTICED MARKS ON THEM? BUT THEY WERE MOVING SO FAST!
YOUR EYE-SIGHT MUST BE AMAZ-ING!
THIS DOESN'T LOOK GOOD ...!
THAT FOREST THE LOMBRE ESCAPED INTO...
THE PETAL-BURG WOODS ...
...IS LIKE A MAZE.
RSTL
RSTL
RSTL
RSTL
YOUR NAME'S SA-PPHIRE, RIGHT?
IT'S DANGER-OUS TO WALK AROUND HERE— ESPECIALLY CARRYING AN INJURED PER-SON ON YOUR BACK!
SHH !!
QUIET.
I HEAR PEOPLE WHIS-PERIN'.
WHAT? WHERE?
"WE'RE AS GOOD AS DONE ONCE WE GET 'EM OFF OUR TAIL IN THE PETALBURG WOODS."
SOME-THIN' LIKE THAT.

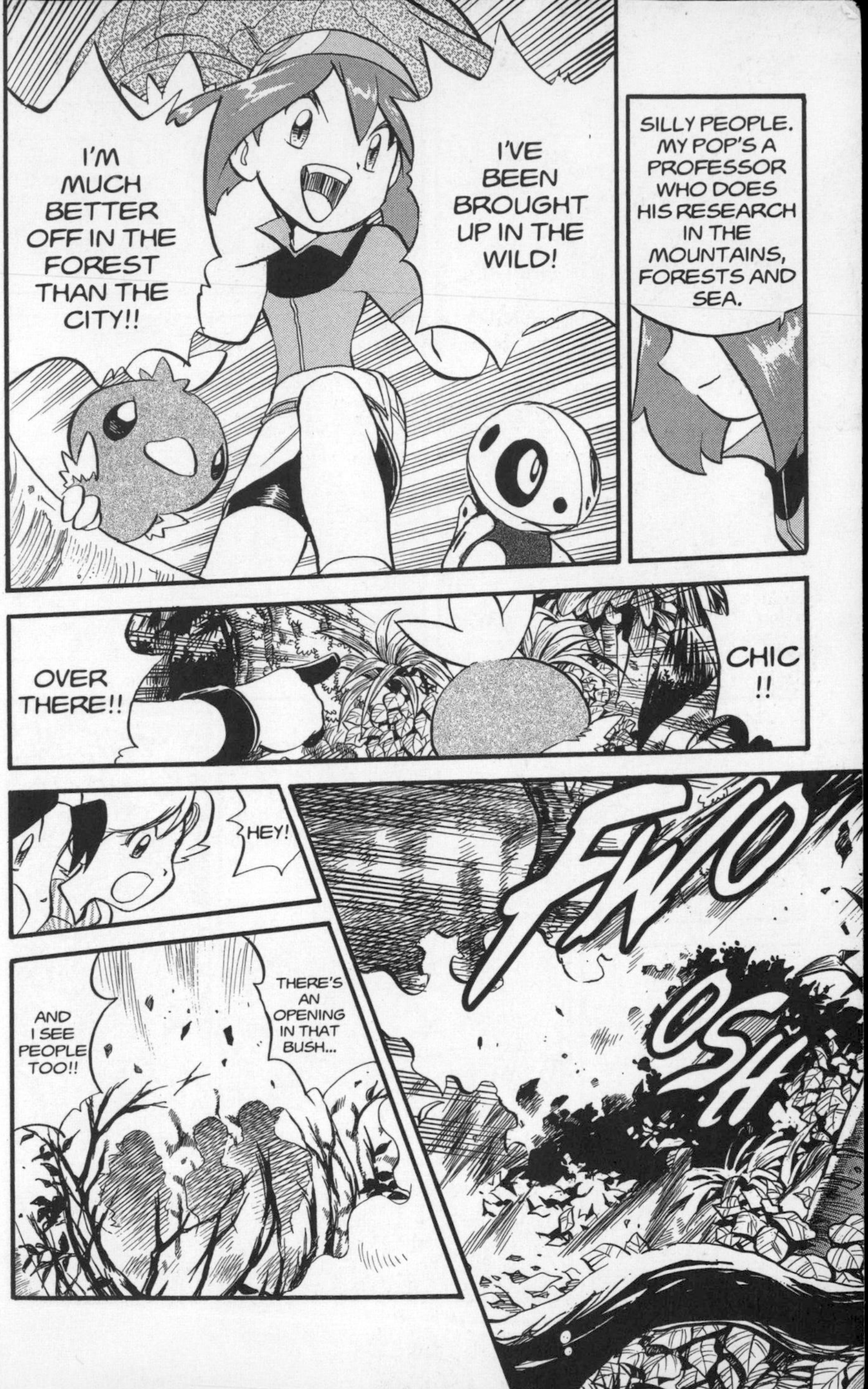
SILLY PEOPLE. MY POP'S A PROFESSOR WHO DOES HIS RESEARCH IN THE MOUNTAINS, FORESTS AND SEA.
I'VE BEEN BROUGHT UP IN THE WILD!
I'M MUCH BETTER OFF IN THE FOREST THAN THE CITY!!
CHIC !!
OVER THERE!!
FWOOSH
HEY!
THERE'S AN OPENING IN THAT BUSH...
AND I SEE PEOPLE TOO!!

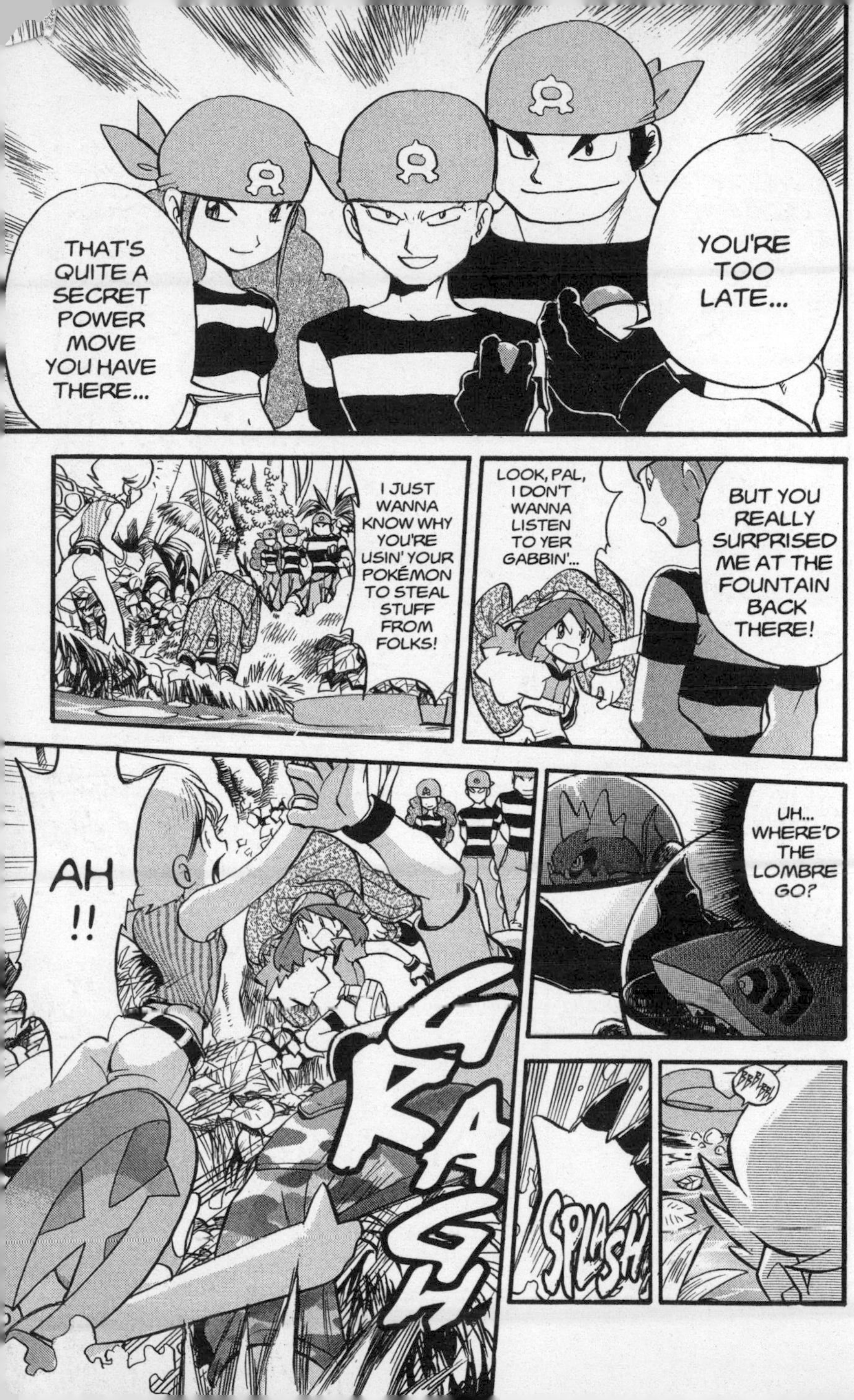
YOU'RE TOO LATE...
THAT'S QUITE A SECRET POWER MOVE YOU HAVE THERE...
BUT YOU REALLY SURPRISED ME AT THE FOUNTAIN BACK THERE!
LOOK, PAL, I DON'T WANNA LISTEN TO YER GABBIN'...
I JUST WANNA KNOW WHY YOU'RE USIN' YOUR POKÉMON TO STEAL STUFF FROM FOLKS!
UH... WHERE'D THE LOMBRE GO?
SPLASH
AH !!

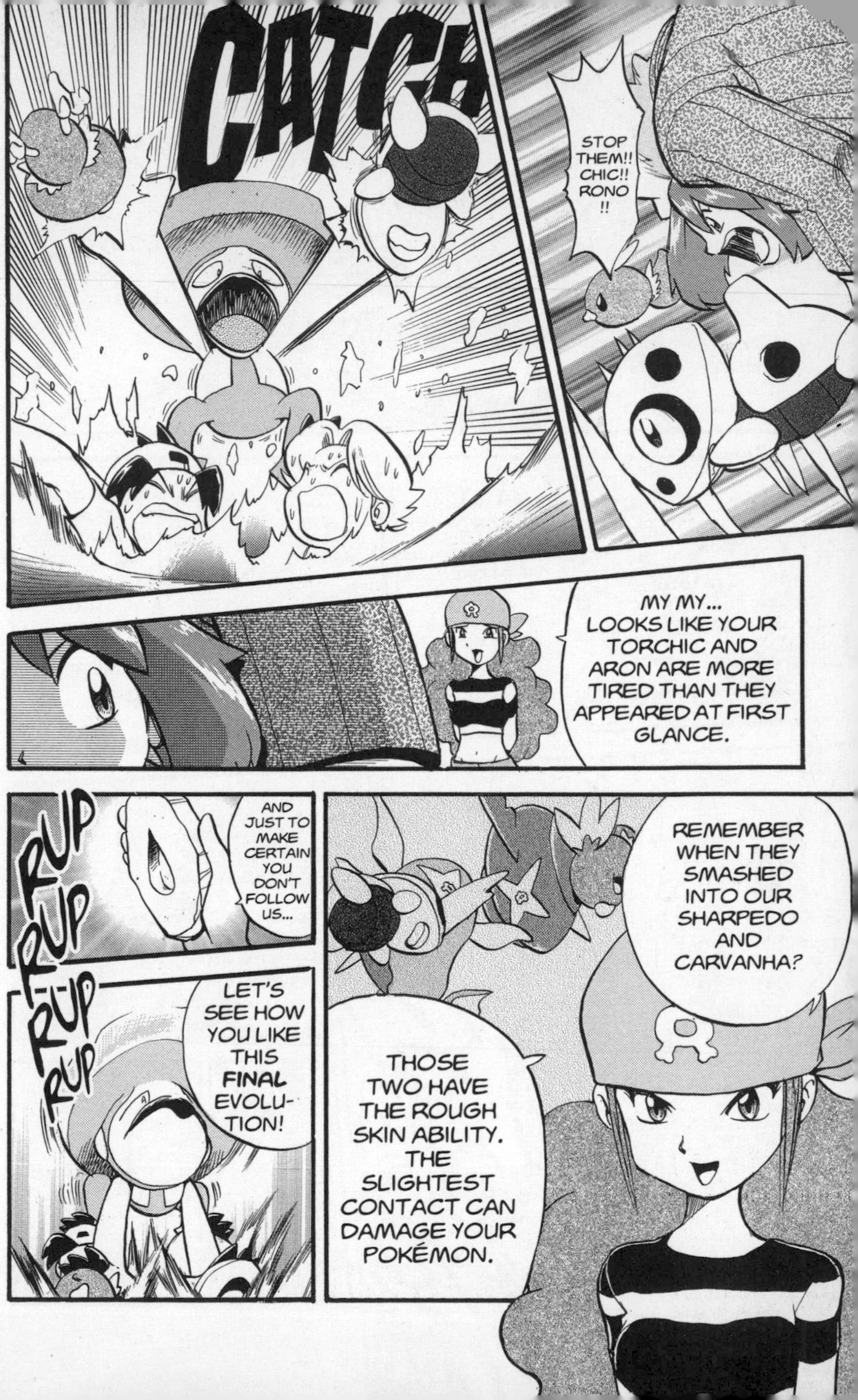
STOP THEM!! CHIC!! RONO !!
CATCH
MY MY... LOOKS LIKE YOUR TORCHIC AND ARON ARE MORE TIRED THAN THEY APPEARED AT FIRST GLANCE.
REMEMBER WHEN THEY SMASHED INTO OUR SHARPEDO AND CARVANHA?
THOSE TWO HAVE THE ROUGH SKIN ABILITY. THE SLIGHTEST CONTACT CAN DAMAGE YOUR POKÉMON.
AND JUST TO MAKE CERTAIN YOU DON'T FOLLOW US...
RUP RUP
RUP RUP RUP
LET'S SEE HOW YOU LIKE THIS FINAL EVOLUTION!

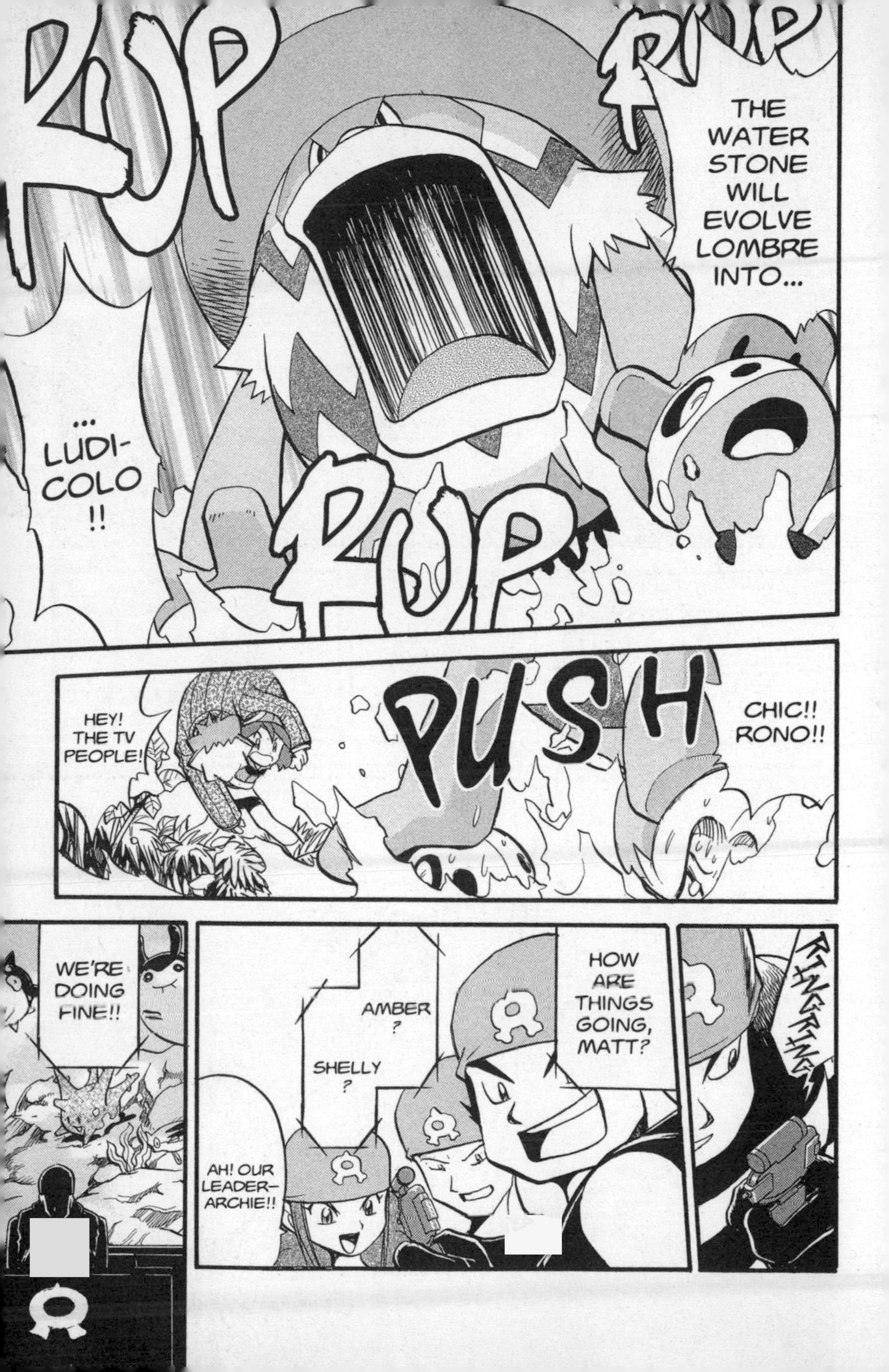
THE WATER STONE WILL EVOLVE LOMBRE INTO...
RIP
...LUDI-COLO!!
CHIC!! RONO!!
PUSH
HEY! THE TV PEOPLE!
HOW ARE THINGS GOING, MATT?
AMBER?
SHELLY?
AH! OUR LEADER—ARCHIE!!
WE'RE DOING FINE!!

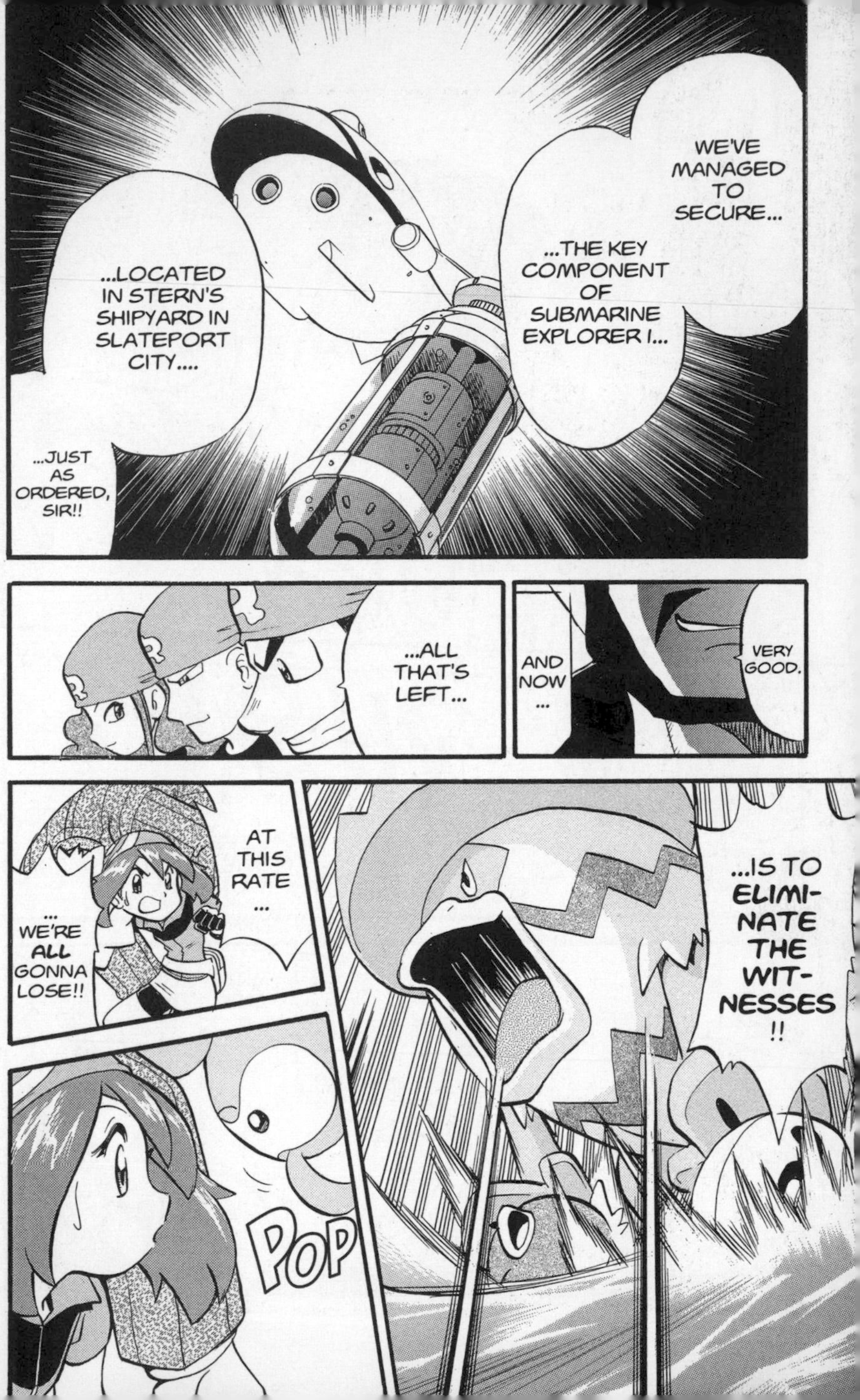
WE'VE MANAGED TO SECURE...
...THE KEY COMPONENT OF SUBMARINE EXPLORER I...
...LOCATED IN STERN'S SHIPYARD IN SLATEPORT CITY....
...JUST AS ORDERED, SIR!!
VERY GOOD.
AND NOW ...
...ALL THAT'S LEFT...
...IS TO ELIMINATE THE WITNESSES!!
AT THIS RATE ...
... WE'RE ALL GONNA LOSE!!
POP

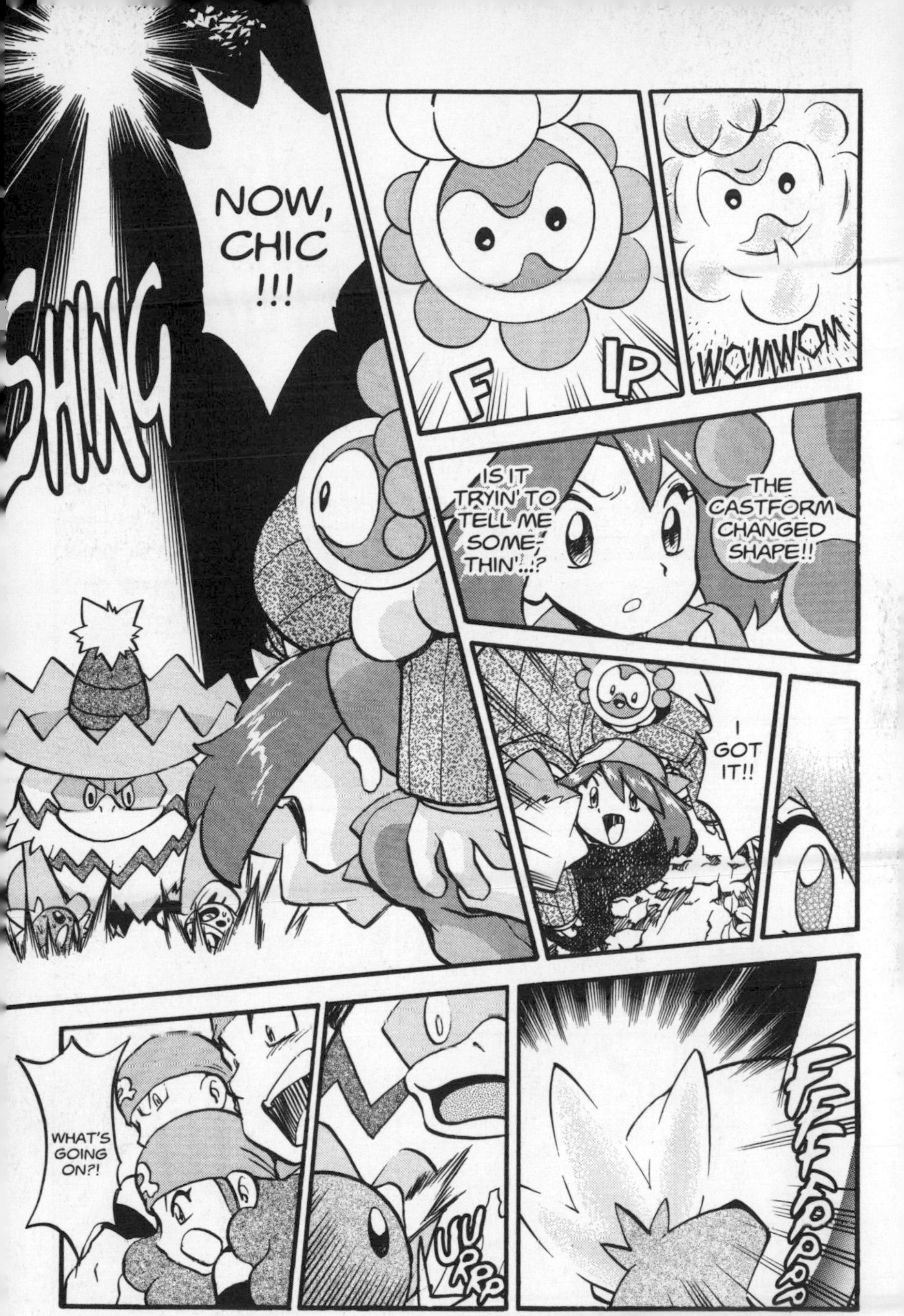
WOMWOM
F IP
THE CASTFORM CHANGED SHAPE!!
IS IT TRYIN' TO TELL ME SOME-THIN'...?
I GOT IT!!
SHING
NOW, CHIC !!!
WHAT'S GOING ON?!

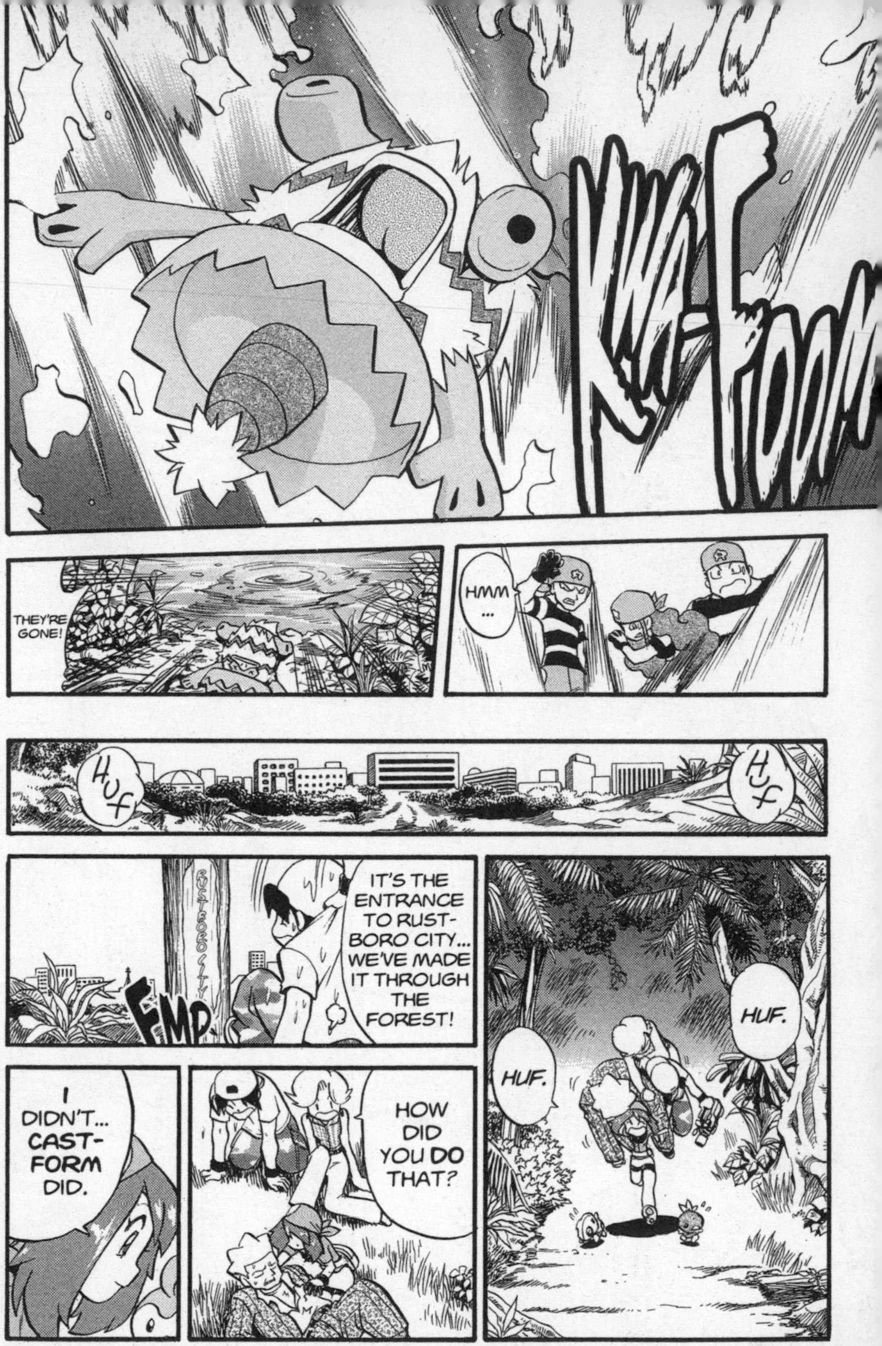
HMM ...
THEY'RE GONE!
HUF
HUF
HUF.
HUF.
IT'S THE ENTRANCE TO RUST-BORO CITY... WE'VE MADE IT THROUGH THE FOREST!
RUSTBORO CITY
FMP
HOW DID YOU DO THAT?
I DIDN'T... CAST-FORM DID.

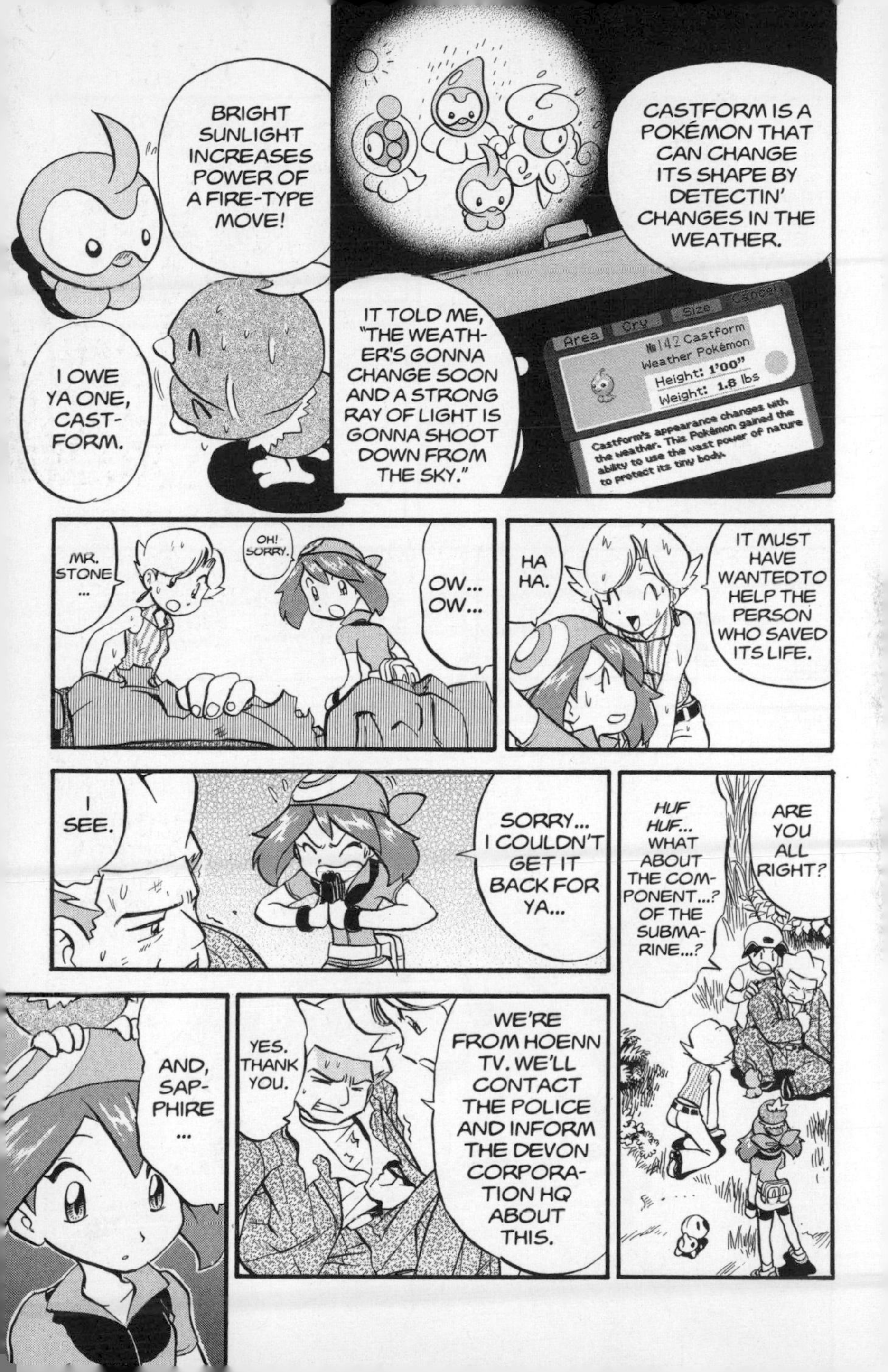
CASTFORM IS A POKÉMON THAT CAN CHANGE ITS SHAPE BY DETECTIN' CHANGES IN THE WEATHER.
Area
Cry
Size
Cancel
No142 Castform
Weather Pokémon
Height: 1'00"
Weight: 1.8 lbs
Castform's appearance changes with the weather. This Pokémon gained the ability to use the vast power of nature to protect its tiny body.
IT TOLD ME, "THE WEATHER'S GONNA CHANGE SOON AND A STRONG RAY OF LIGHT IS GONNA SHOOT DOWN FROM THE SKY."
BRIGHT SUNLIGHT INCREASES POWER OF A FIRE-TYPE MOVE!
I OWE YA ONE, CASTFORM.
IT MUST HAVE WANTED TO HELP THE PERSON WHO SAVED ITS LIFE.
HA HA.
OW... OW...
OH! SORRY.
MR. STONE ...
ARE YOU ALL RIGHT?
HUF HUF... WHAT ABOUT THE COMPONENT...? OF THE SUBMARINE...?
SORRY... I COULDN'T GET IT BACK FOR YA...
I SEE.
WE'RE FROM HOENN TV. WE'LL CONTACT THE POLICE AND INFORM THE DEVON CORPORATION HQ ABOUT THIS.
YES. THANK YOU.
AND, SAPPHIRE ...

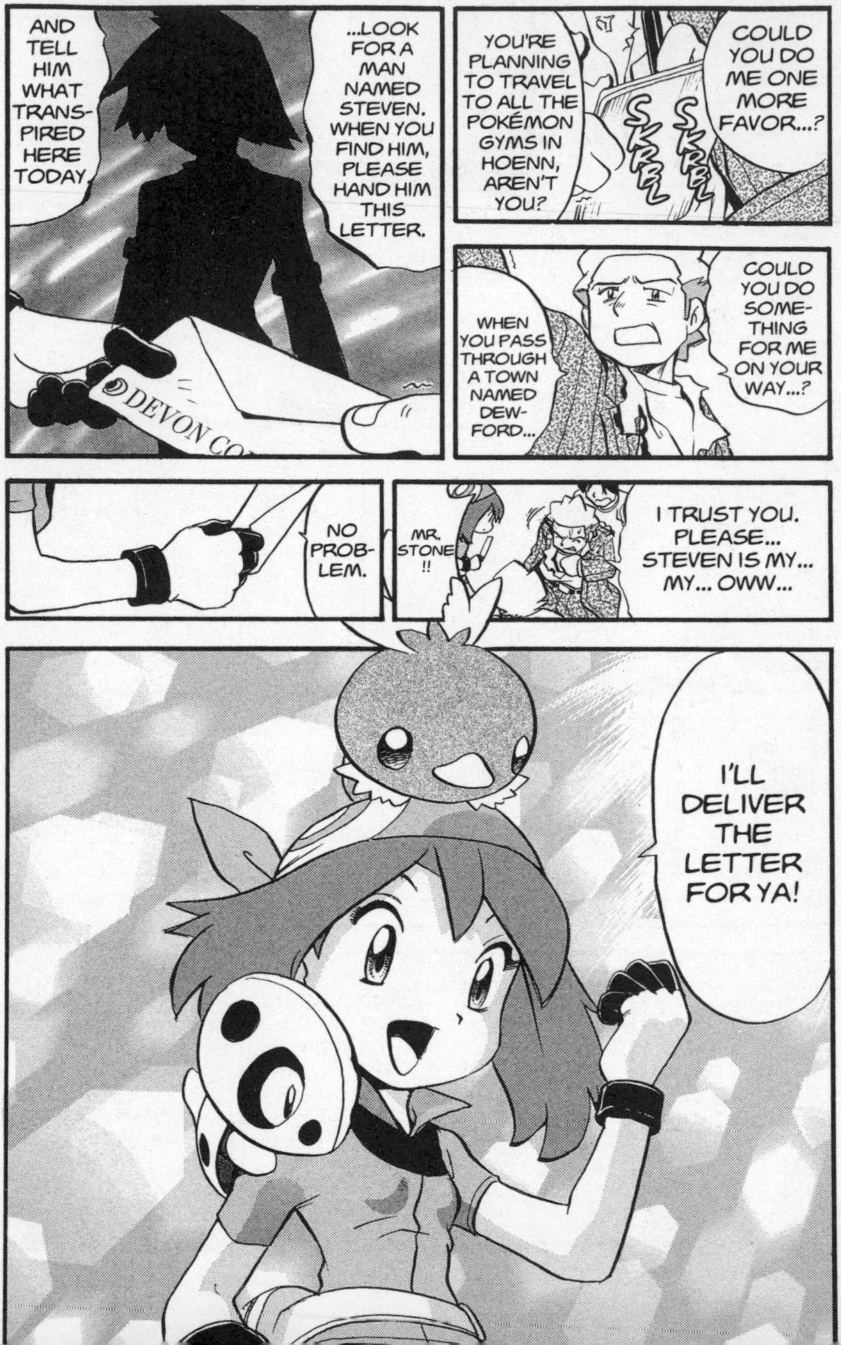
COULD YOU DO ME ONE MORE FAVOR...?
SKRBL
SKRBL
YOU'RE PLANNING TO TRAVEL TO ALL THE POKÉMON GYMS IN HOENN, AREN'T YOU?
COULD YOU DO SOME-THING FOR ME ON YOUR WAY...?
WHEN YOU PASS THROUGH A TOWN NAMED DEW-FORD...
...LOOK FOR A MAN NAMED STEVEN. WHEN YOU FIND HIM, PLEASE HAND HIM THIS LETTER.
AND TELL HIM WHAT TRANS-PIRED HERE TODAY.
DEVON CO
I TRUST YOU. PLEASE... STEVEN IS MY... MY... OWW...
MR. STONE !!
NO PROB-LEM.
I'LL DELIVER THE LETTER FOR YA!

Chapter 190: Blowing Past Nosepass 1

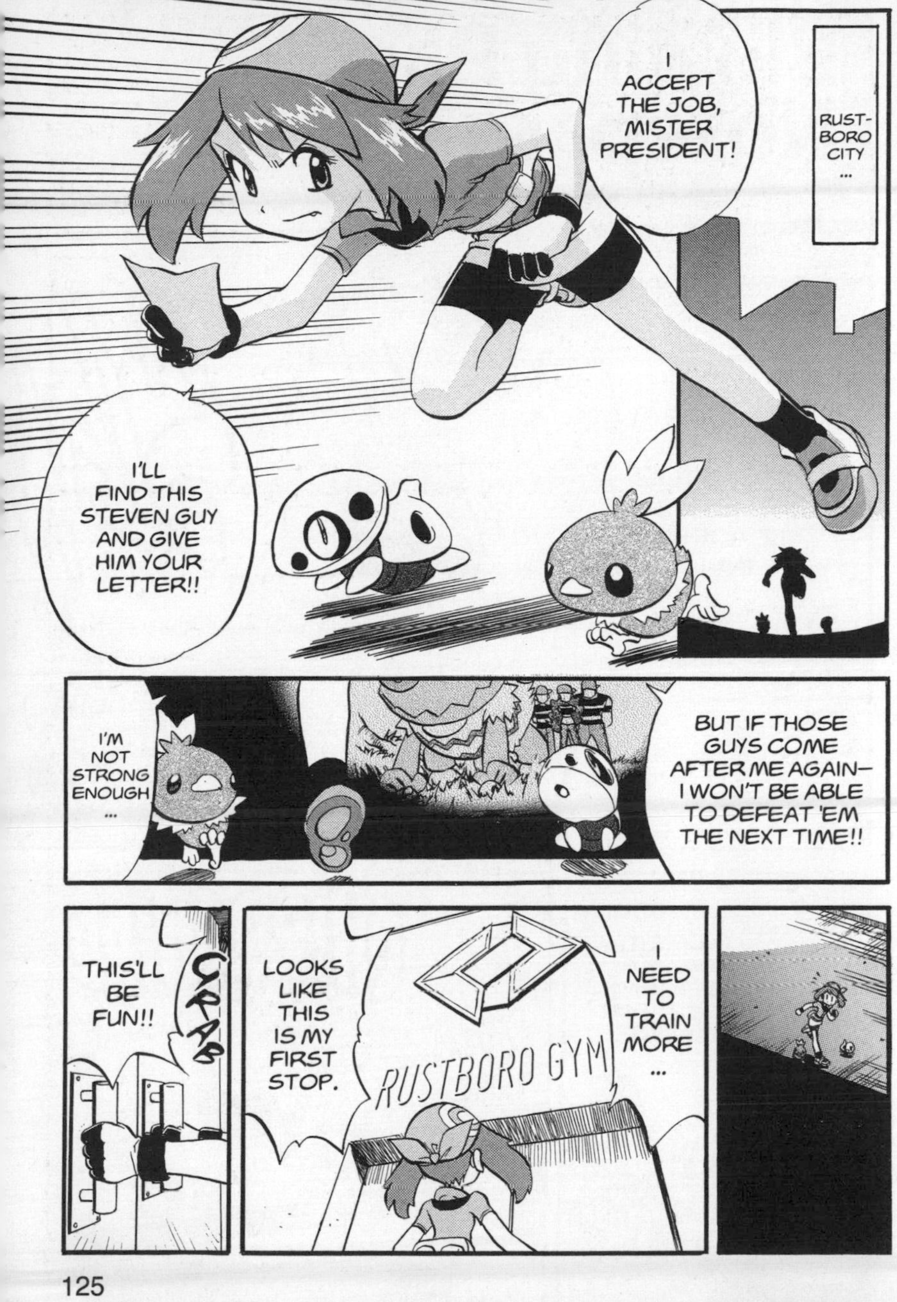
RUST-BORO CITY ...
I ACCEPT THE JOB, MISTER PRESIDENT!
I'LL FIND THIS STEVEN GUY AND GIVE HIM YOUR LETTER!!
BUT IF THOSE GUYS COME AFTER ME AGAIN— I WON'T BE ABLE TO DEFEAT 'EM THE NEXT TIME!!
I'M NOT STRONG ENOUGH ...
I NEED TO TRAIN MORE ...
LOOKS LIKE THIS IS MY FIRST STOP.
RUSTBORO GYM
GRAB
THIS'LL BE FUN!!

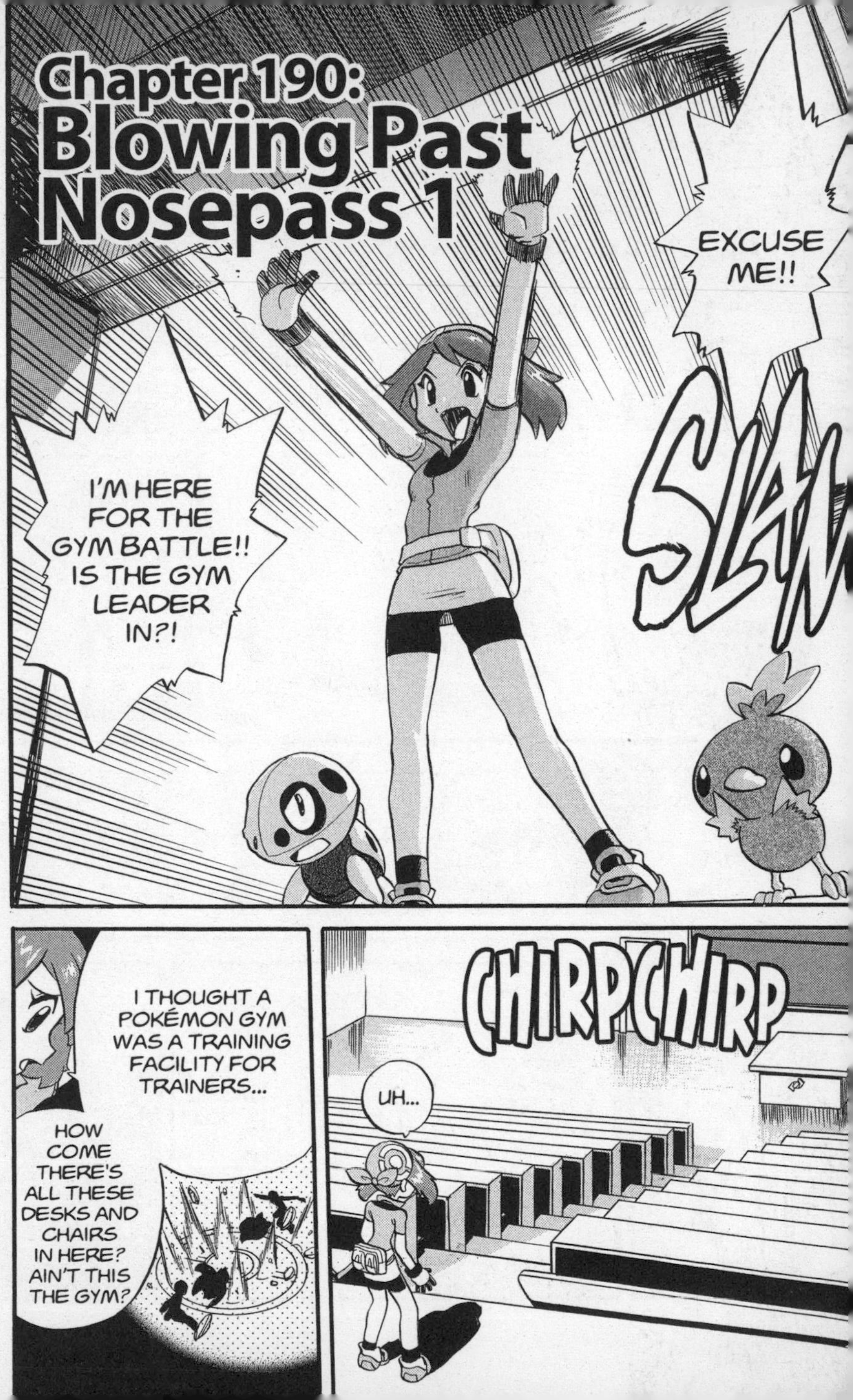
Chapter 190:
Blowing Past Nosepass 1
EXCUSE ME!!
I'M HERE FOR THE GYM BATTLE!! IS THE GYM LEADER IN?!
CHIRPCHIRP
UH...
I THOUGHT A POKÉMON GYM WAS A TRAINING FACILITY FOR TRAINERS...
HOW COME THERE'S ALL THESE DESKS AND CHAIRS IN HERE? AIN'T THIS THE GYM?

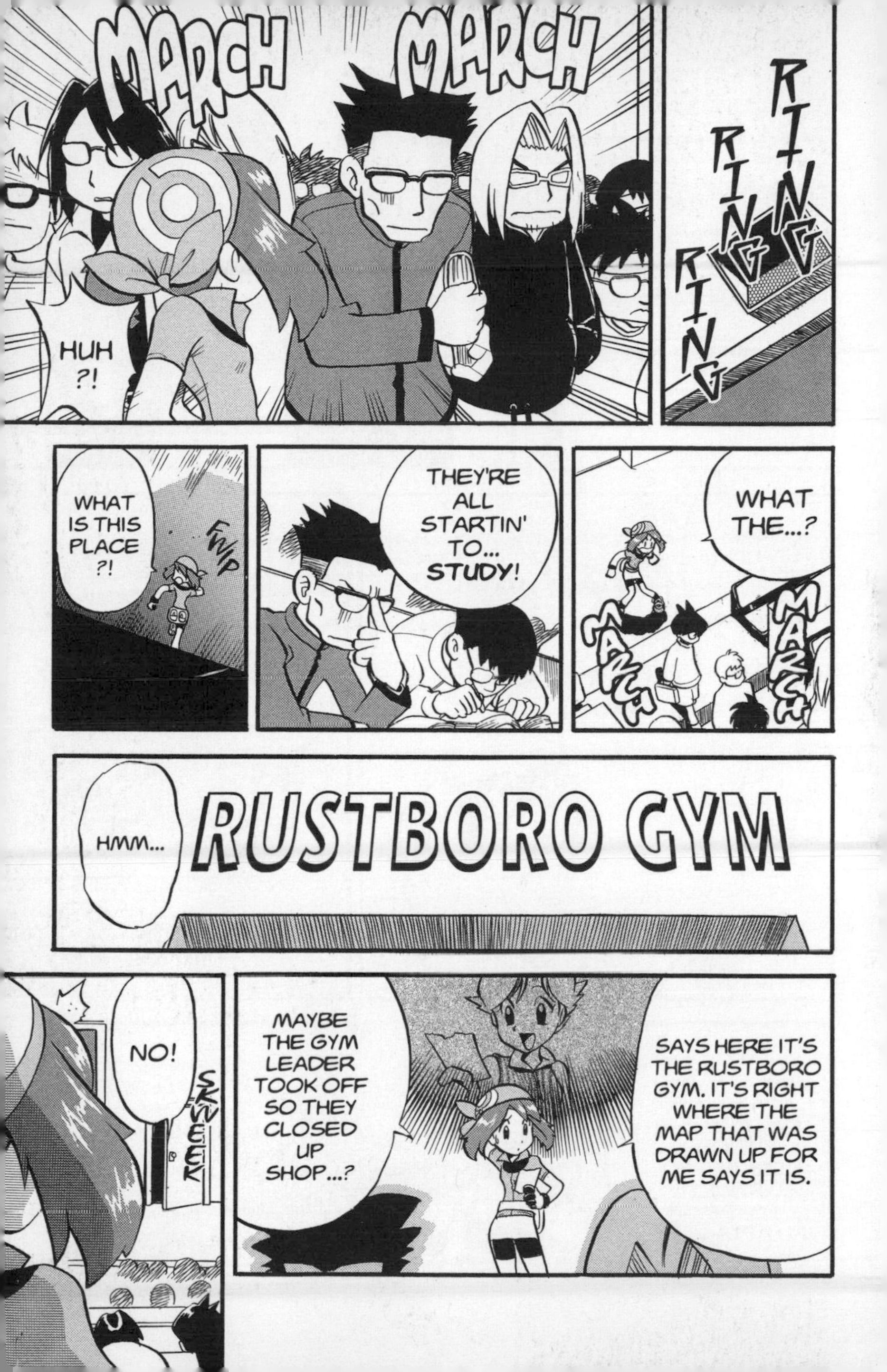
RING
RING
RING
MARCH
MARCH
HUH ?!
WHAT THE...?
MARCH
MARCH
THEY'RE ALL STARTIN' TO... STUDY!
WHAT IS THIS PLACE ?!
FWIP
HMM...
RUSTBORO GYM
SAYS HERE IT'S THE RUSTBORO GYM. IT'S RIGHT WHERE THE MAP THAT WAS DRAWN UP FOR ME SAYS IT IS.
MAYBE THE GYM LEADER TOOK OFF SO THEY CLOSED UP SHOP...?
NO!
SKWEEK

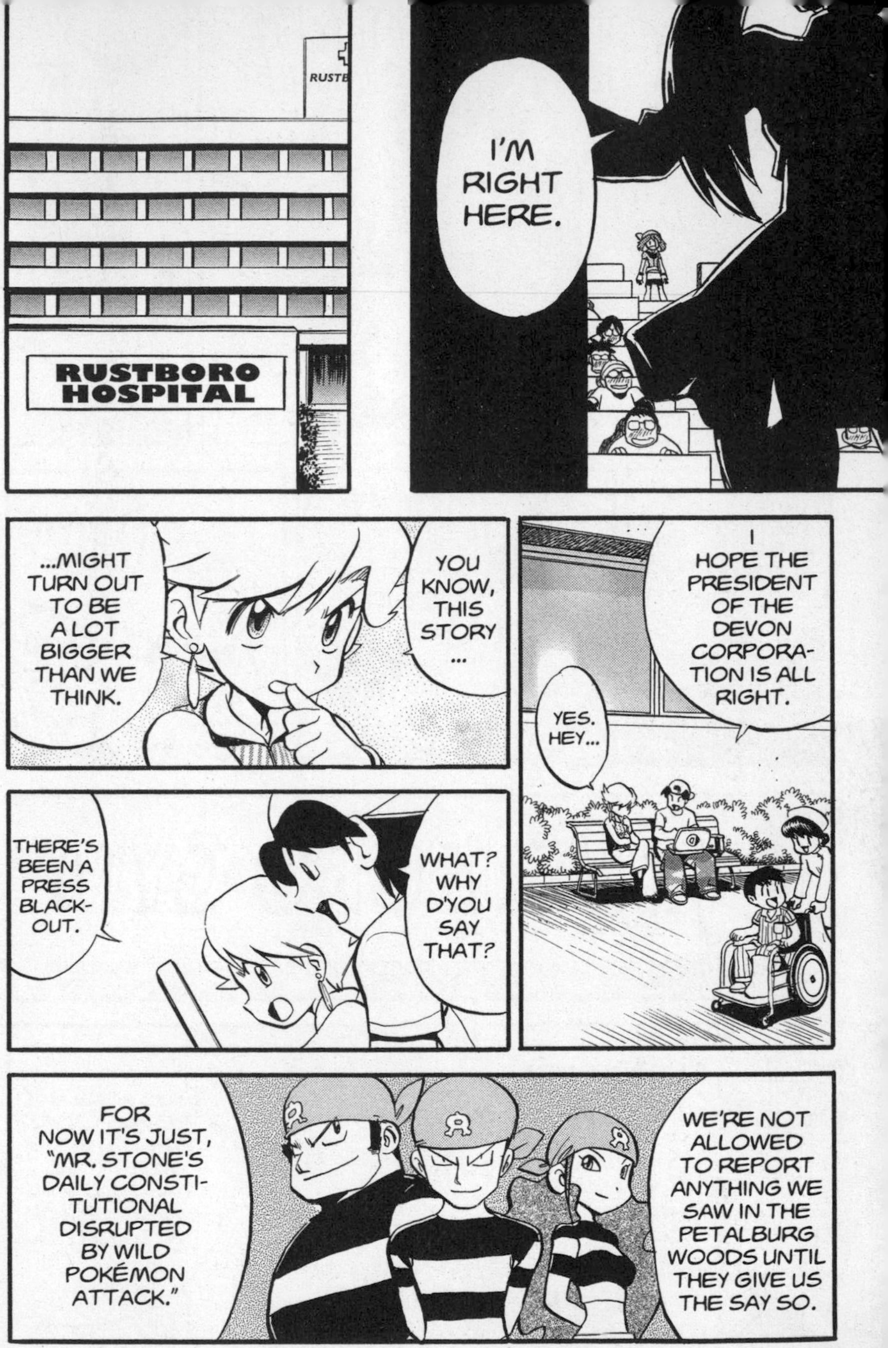
I'M RIGHT HERE.
RUSTB
RUSTBORO HOSPITAL
I HOPE THE PRESIDENT OF THE DEVON CORPORATION IS ALL RIGHT.
YES. HEY...
YOU KNOW, THIS STORY...
...MIGHT TURN OUT TO BE A LOT BIGGER THAN WE THINK.
WHAT? WHY D'YOU SAY THAT?
THERE'S BEEN A PRESS BLACK-OUT.
WE'RE NOT ALLOWED TO REPORT ANYTHING WE SAW IN THE PETALBURG WOODS UNTIL THEY GIVE US THE SAY SO.
FOR NOW IT'S JUST, "MR. STONE'S DAILY CONSTITUTIONAL DISRUPTED BY WILD POKÉMON ATTACK."

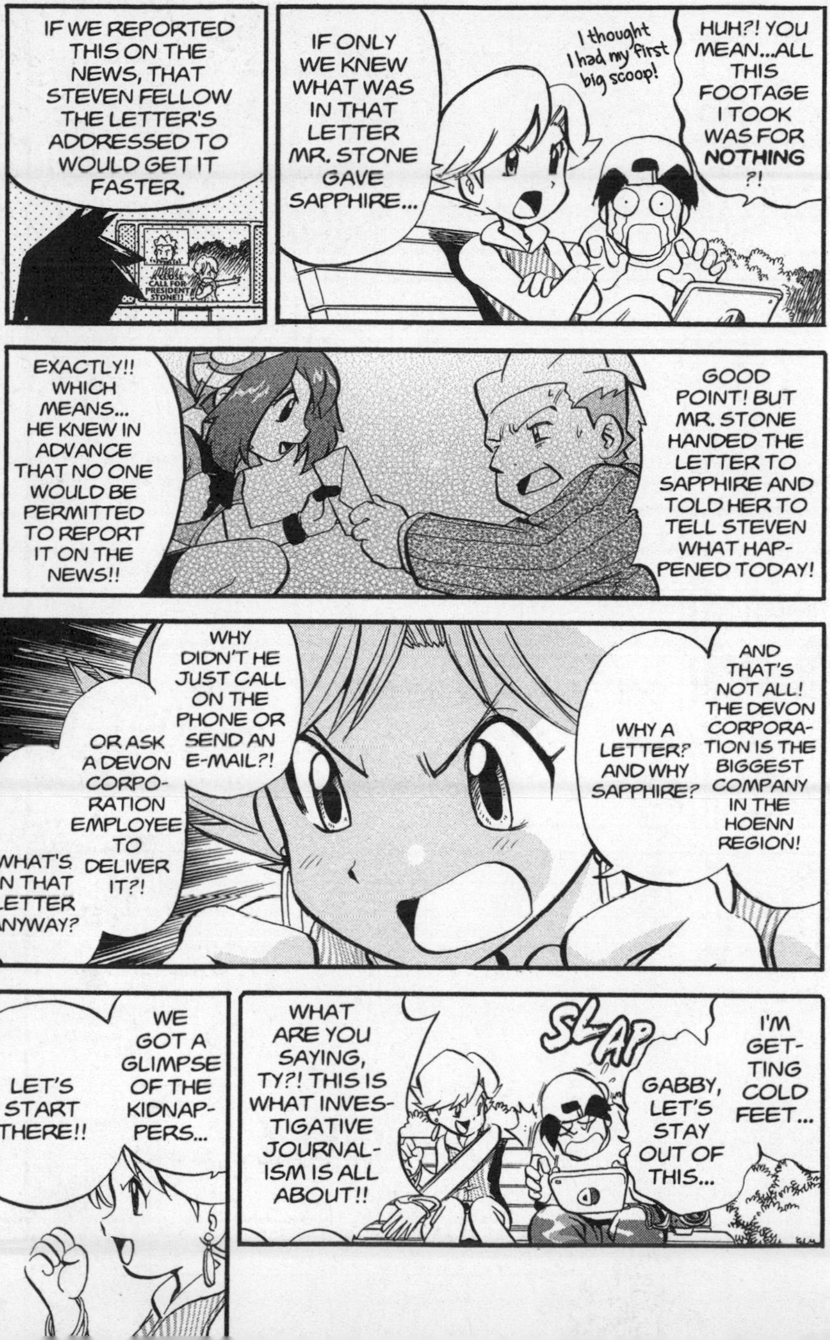

HUH?! YOU MEAN...ALL THIS FOOTAGE I TOOK WAS FOR **NOTHING**?!
I thought I had my first big scoop!
IF ONLY WE KNEW WHAT WAS IN THAT LETTER MR. STONE GAVE SAPPHIRE...
IF WE REPORTED THIS ON THE NEWS, THAT STEVEN FELLOW THE LETTER'S ADDRESSED TO WOULD GET IT FASTER.
CLOSE CALL FOR PRESIDENT STONE!!
GOOD POINT! BUT MR. STONE HANDED THE LETTER TO SAPPHIRE AND TOLD HER TO TELL STEVEN WHAT HAPPENED TODAY!
EXACTLY!! WHICH MEANS... HE KNEW IN ADVANCE THAT NO ONE WOULD BE PERMITTED TO REPORT IT ON THE NEWS!!
AND THAT'S NOT ALL! THE DEVON CORPORATION IS THE BIGGEST COMPANY IN THE HOENN REGION!
WHY A LETTER? AND WHY SAPPHIRE?
WHY DIDN'T HE JUST CALL ON THE PHONE OR SEND AN E-MAIL?!
OR ASK A DEVON CORPORATION EMPLOYEE TO DELIVER IT?!
WHAT'S IN THAT LETTER ANYWAY?
I'M GETTING COLD FEET...
GABBY, LET'S STAY OUT OF THIS...
SLAP
WHAT ARE YOU SAYING, TY?! THIS IS WHAT INVESTIGATIVE JOURNALISM IS ALL ABOUT!!
WE GOT A GLIMPSE OF THE KIDNAPPERS...
LET'S START THERE!!

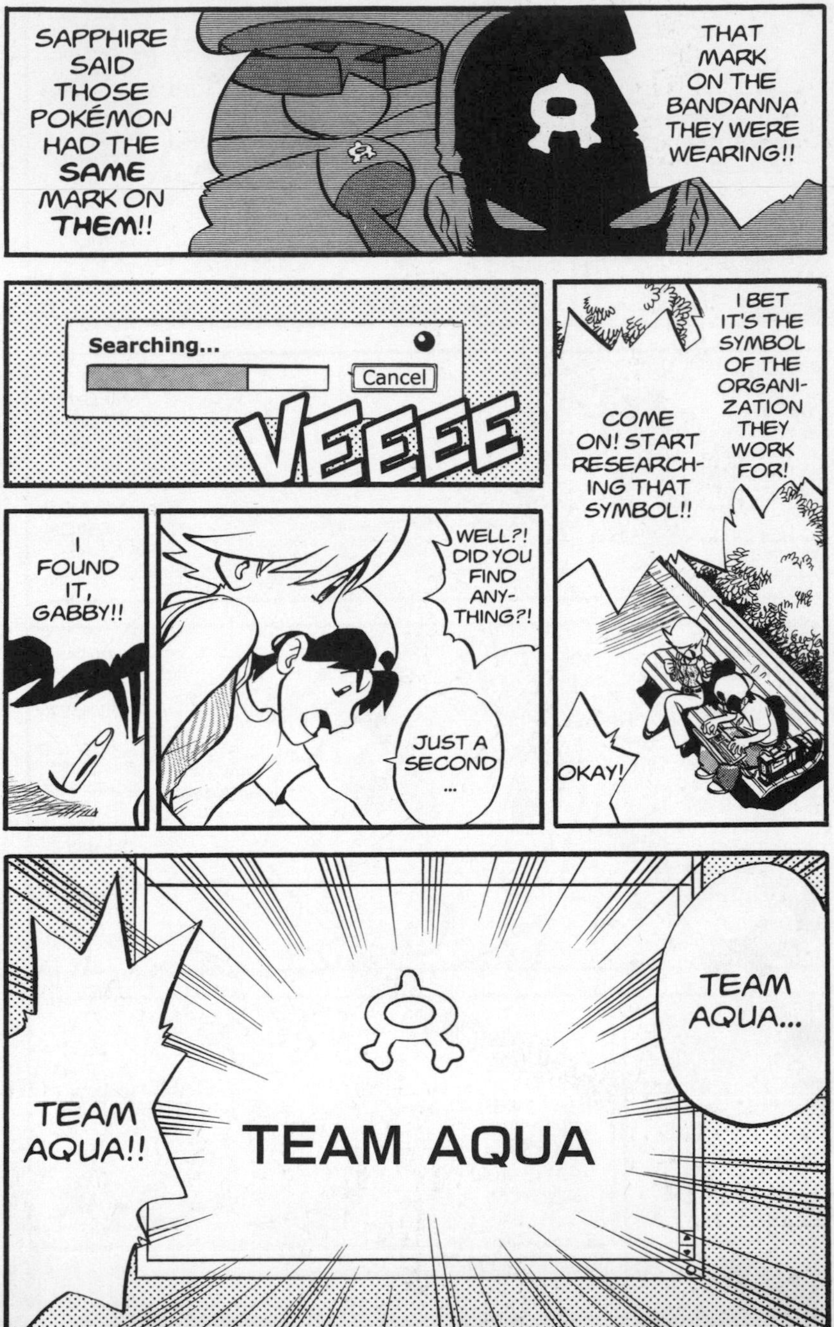
THAT MARK ON THE BANDANNA THEY WERE WEARING!!
SAPPHIRE SAID THOSE POKÉMON HAD THE **SAME** MARK ON **THEM**!!
I BET IT'S THE SYMBOL OF THE ORGANIZATION THEY WORK FOR!
COME ON! START RESEARCHING THAT SYMBOL!!
OKAY!
Searching...
Cancel
VEEEE
WELL?! DID YOU FIND ANYTHING?!
JUST A SECOND ...
I FOUND IT, GABBY!!
TEAM AQUA...
TEAM AQUA
TEAM AQUA!!

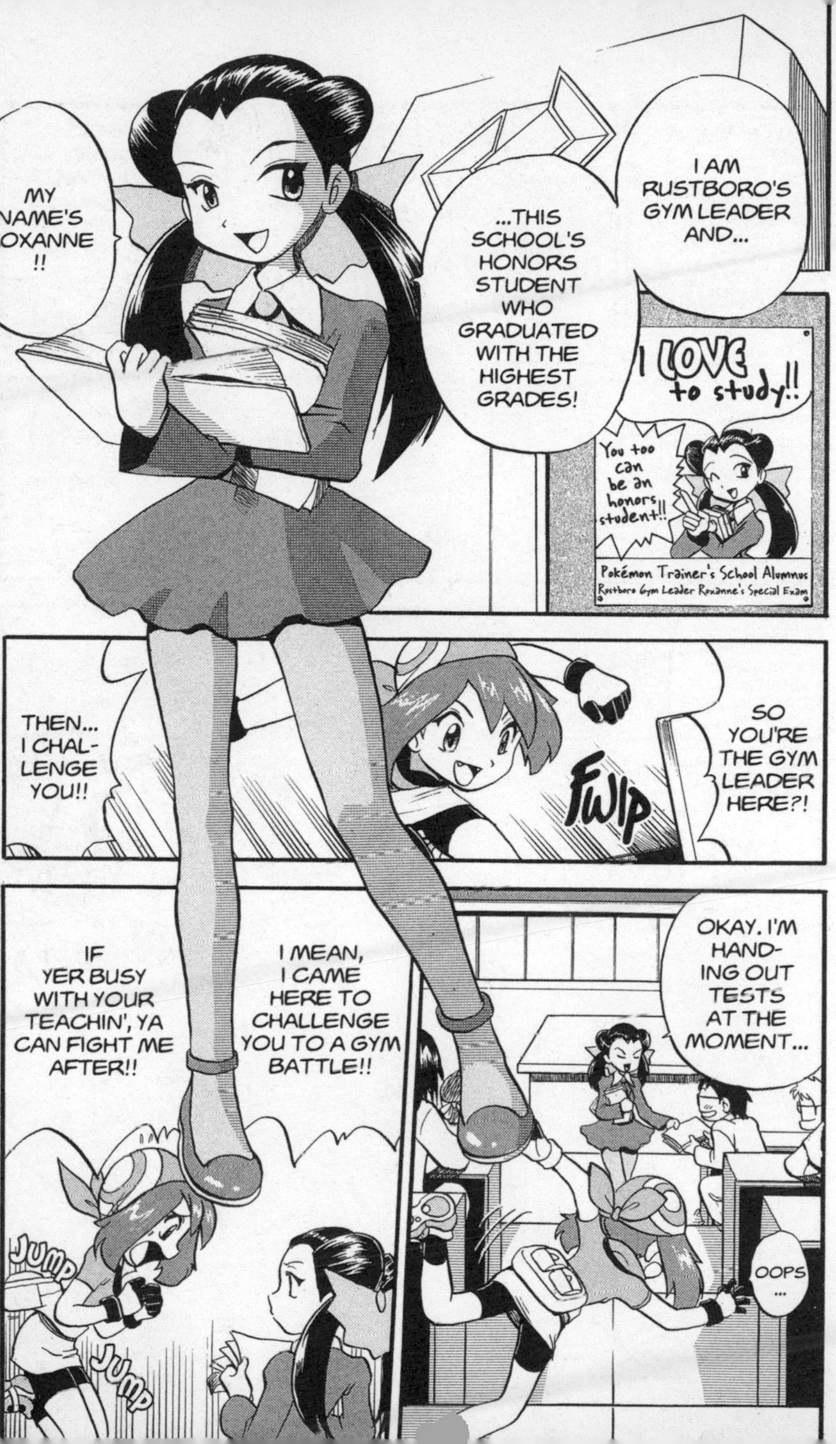
I AM RUSTBORO'S GYM LEADER AND...
...THIS SCHOOL'S HONORS STUDENT WHO GRADUATED WITH THE HIGHEST GRADES!
MY NAME'S ROXANNE!!
I LOVE to study!!
You too can be an honors student!!
Pokémon Trainer's School Alumnus
Rustboro Gym Leader Roxanne's Special Exam
SO YOU'RE THE GYM LEADER HERE?!
FWIP
THEN... I CHALLENGE YOU!!
OKAY. I'M HANDING OUT TESTS AT THE MOMENT...
OOPS...
I MEAN, I CAME HERE TO CHALLENGE YOU TO A GYM BATTLE!!
IF YER BUSY WITH YOUR TEACHIN', YA CAN FIGHT ME AFTER!!
JUMP
JUMP

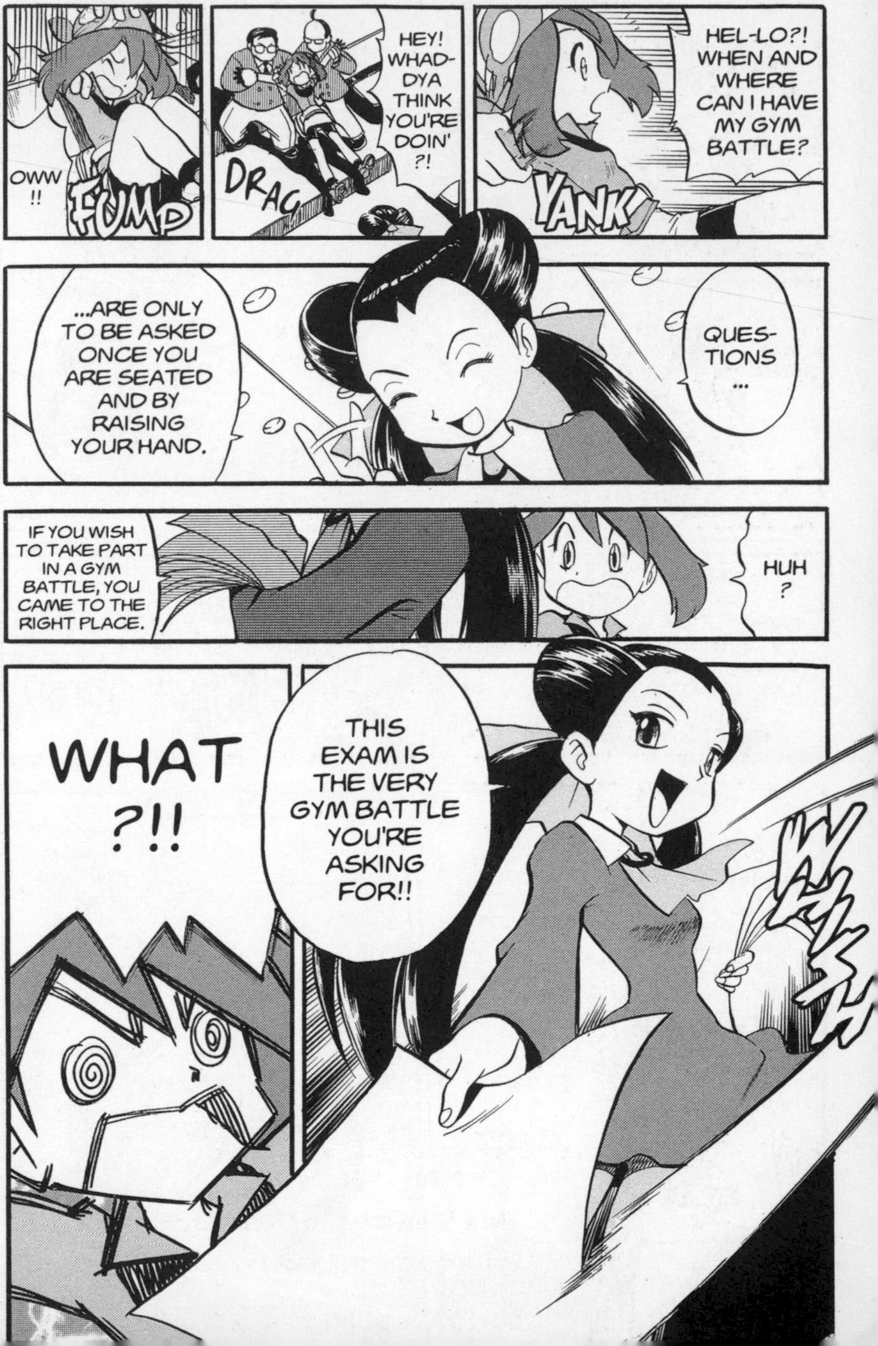
HEL-LO?! WHEN AND WHERE CAN I HAVE MY GYM BATTLE?
YANK
HEY! WHAD-DYA THINK YOU'RE DOIN' ?!
DRAG
OWW !!
FUMP
QUES-TIONS ...
...ARE ONLY TO BE ASKED ONCE YOU ARE SEATED AND BY RAISING YOUR HAND.
HUH ?
IF YOU WISH TO TAKE PART IN A GYM BATTLE, YOU CAME TO THE RIGHT PLACE.
THIS EXAM IS THE VERY GYM BATTLE YOU'RE ASKING FOR!!
WHAT ?!!

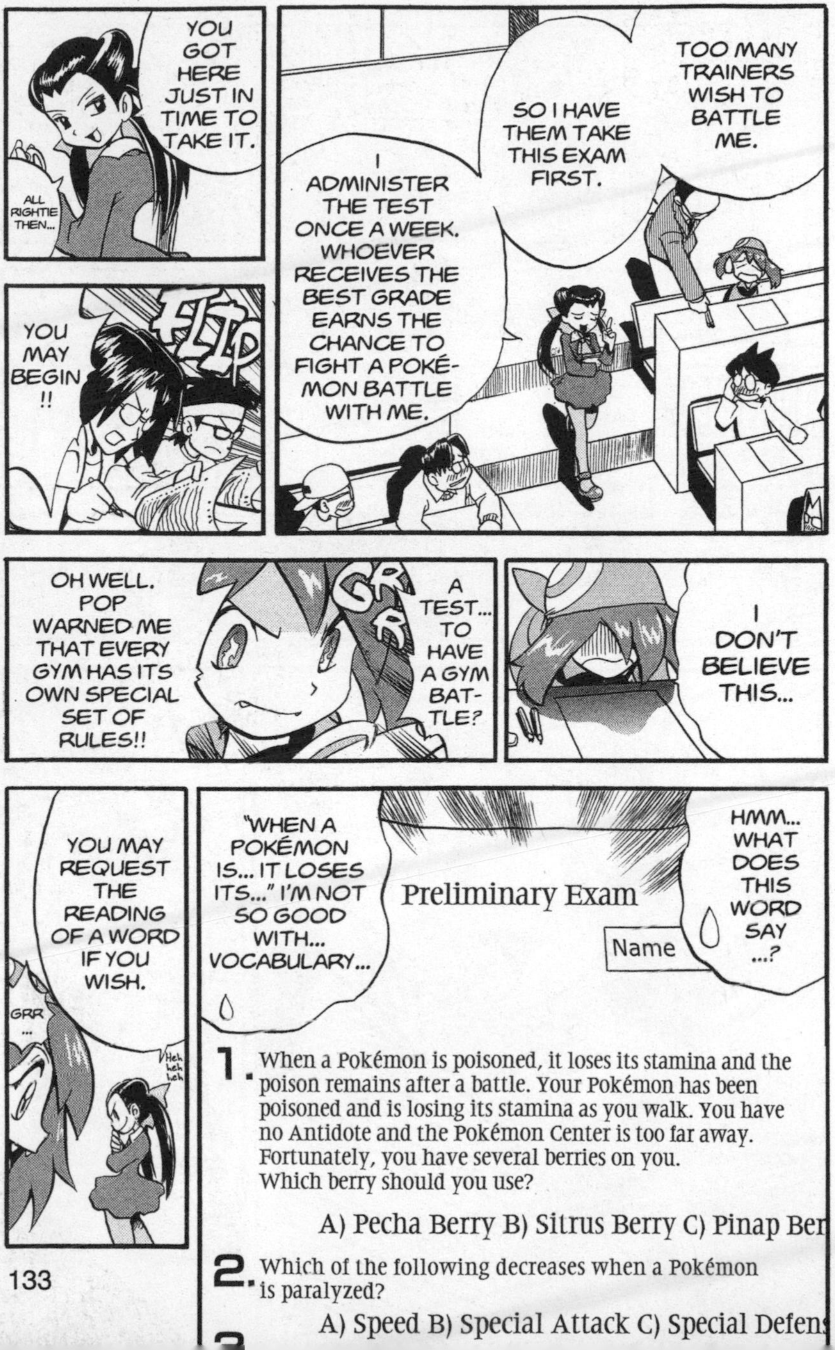
TOO MANY TRAINERS WISH TO BATTLE ME.
SO I HAVE THEM TAKE THIS EXAM FIRST.
I ADMINISTER THE TEST ONCE A WEEK. WHOEVER RECEIVES THE BEST GRADE EARNS THE CHANCE TO FIGHT A POKÉMON BATTLE WITH ME.
YOU GOT HERE JUST IN TIME TO TAKE IT.
ALL RIGHTIE THEN...
FLIP
YOU MAY BEGIN!!
I DON'T BELIEVE THIS...
A TEST... TO HAVE A GYM BATTLE?
GRR
OH WELL. POP WARNED ME THAT EVERY GYM HAS ITS OWN SPECIAL SET OF RULES!!
HMM... WHAT DOES THIS WORD SAY ...?
"WHEN A POKÉMON IS... IT LOSES ITS..." I'M NOT SO GOOD WITH... VOCABULARY...
Preliminary Exam
Name
1. When a Pokémon is poisoned, it loses its stamina and the poison remains after a battle. Your Pokémon has been poisoned and is losing its stamina as you walk. You have no Antidote and the Pokémon Center is too far away. Fortunately, you have several berries on you. Which berry should you use?
A) Pecha Berry B) Sitrus Berry C) Pinap Ber
2. Which of the following decreases when a Pokémon is paralyzed?
A) Speed B) Special Attack C) Special Defens
YOU MAY REQUEST THE READING OF A WORD IF YOU WISH.
GRR ...
Heh heh heh

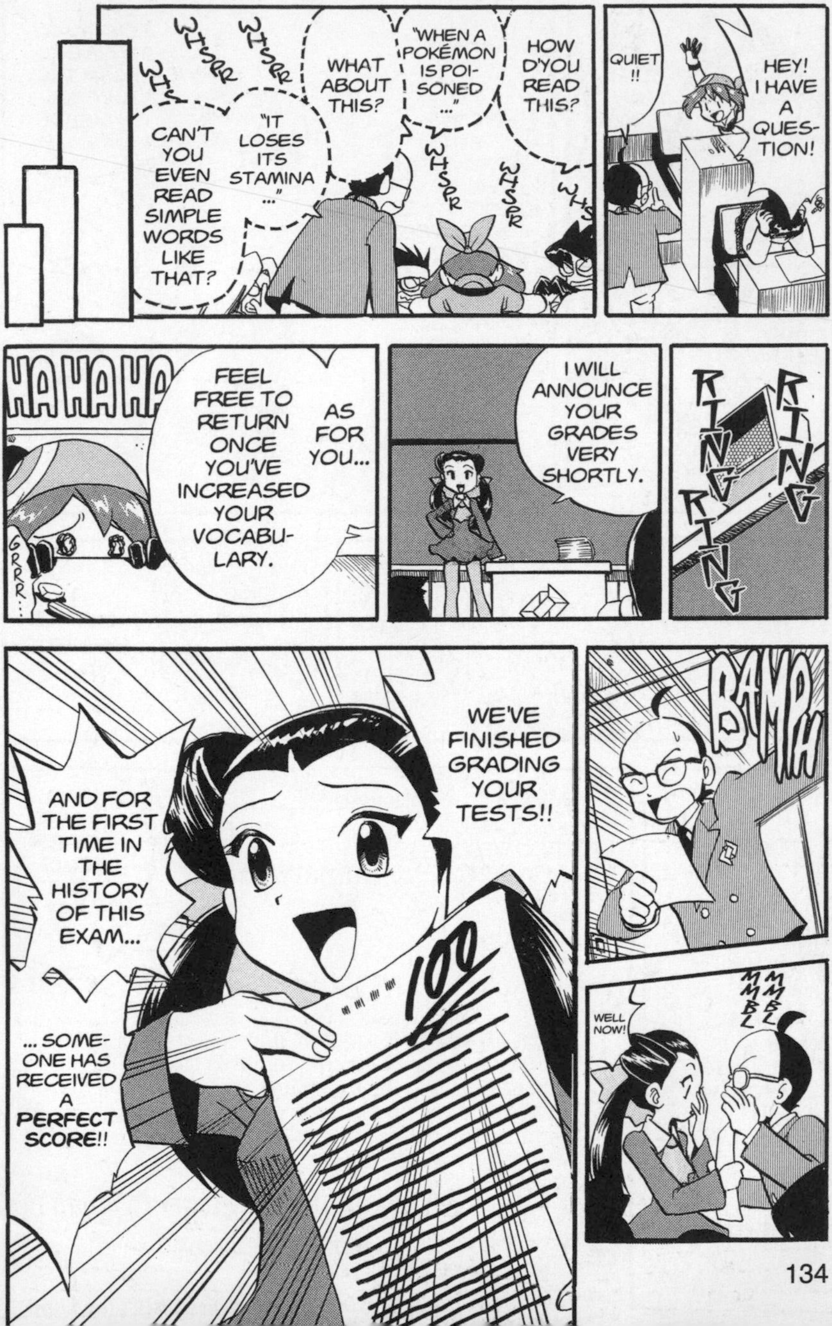
HEY! I HAVE A QUES-TION!
QUIET!!
WHS
HOW D'YOU READ THIS?
WHSPR
"WHEN A POKÉMON IS POI-SONED ..."
WHSPR
WHAT ABOUT THIS?
WHSPR
WHSPR
"IT LOSES ITS STAMINA ..."
WHS
CAN'T YOU EVEN READ SIMPLE WORDS LIKE THAT?
RING RING RING RING
I WILL ANNOUNCE YOUR GRADES VERY SHORTLY.
AS FOR YOU...
FEEL FREE TO RETURN ONCE YOU'VE INCREASED YOUR VOCABU-LARY.
HA HA HA HA
GRRR...
BAMPH
MMMBL MMMBL
WELL NOW!
WE'VE FINISHED GRADING YOUR TESTS!!
AND FOR THE FIRST TIME IN THE HISTORY OF THIS EXAM...
100
... SOME-ONE HAS RECEIVED A PERFECT SCORE!!

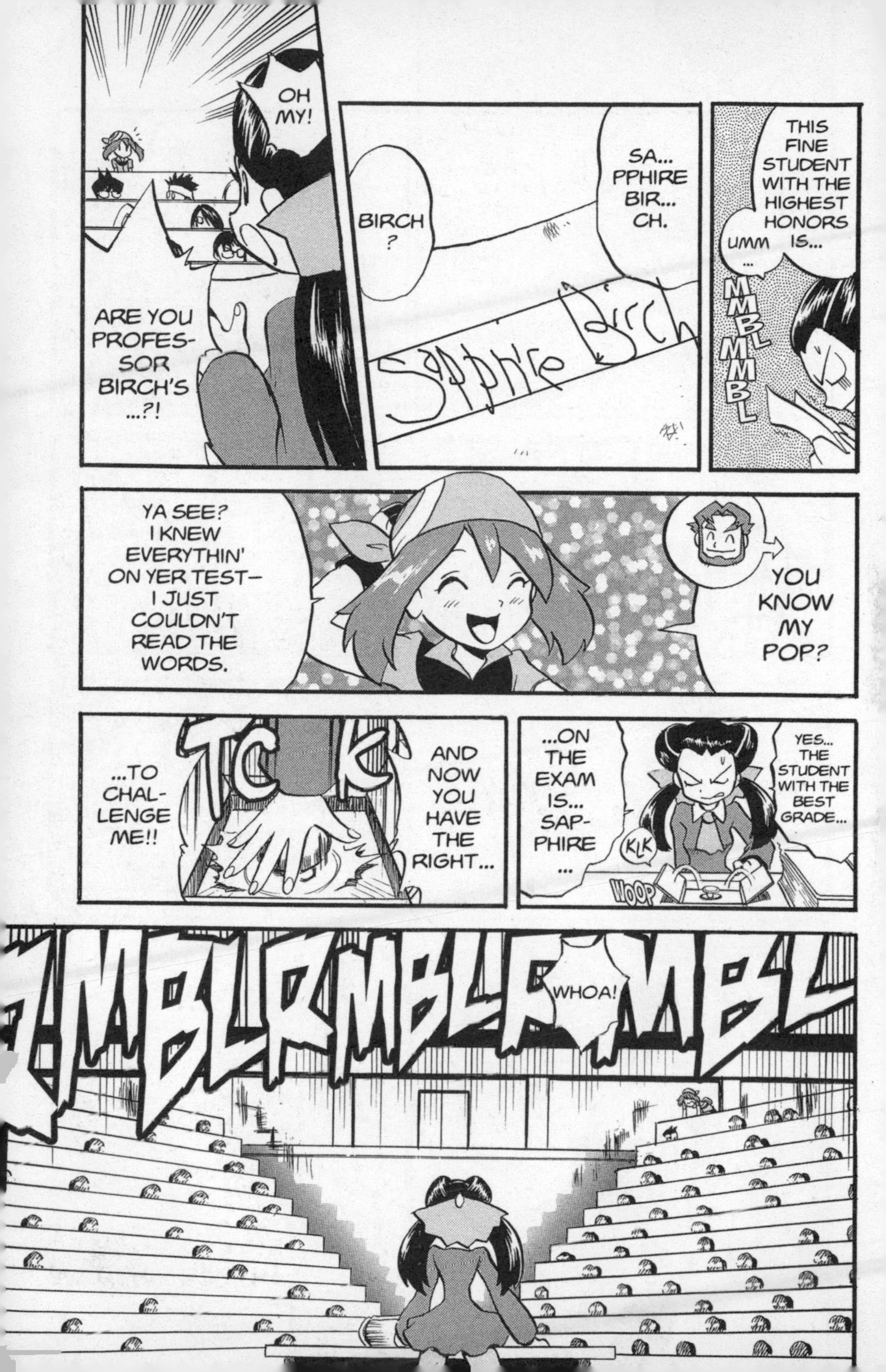
THIS FINE STUDENT WITH THE HIGHEST HONORS IS...
UMM ...
MMBL MMBL
SA... PPHIRE BIR... CH.
BIRCH ?
Sapphire Birch
OH MY!
ARE YOU PROFES-SOR BIRCH'S ...?!
YOU KNOW MY POP?
YA SEE? I KNEW EVERYTHIN' ON YER TEST— I JUST COULDN'T READ THE WORDS.
YES... THE STUDENT WITH THE BEST GRADE...
...ON THE EXAM IS... SAP-PHIRE ...
KLK
WOOP
TCK
AND NOW YOU HAVE THE RIGHT...
...TO CHAL-LENGE ME!!
WHOA!

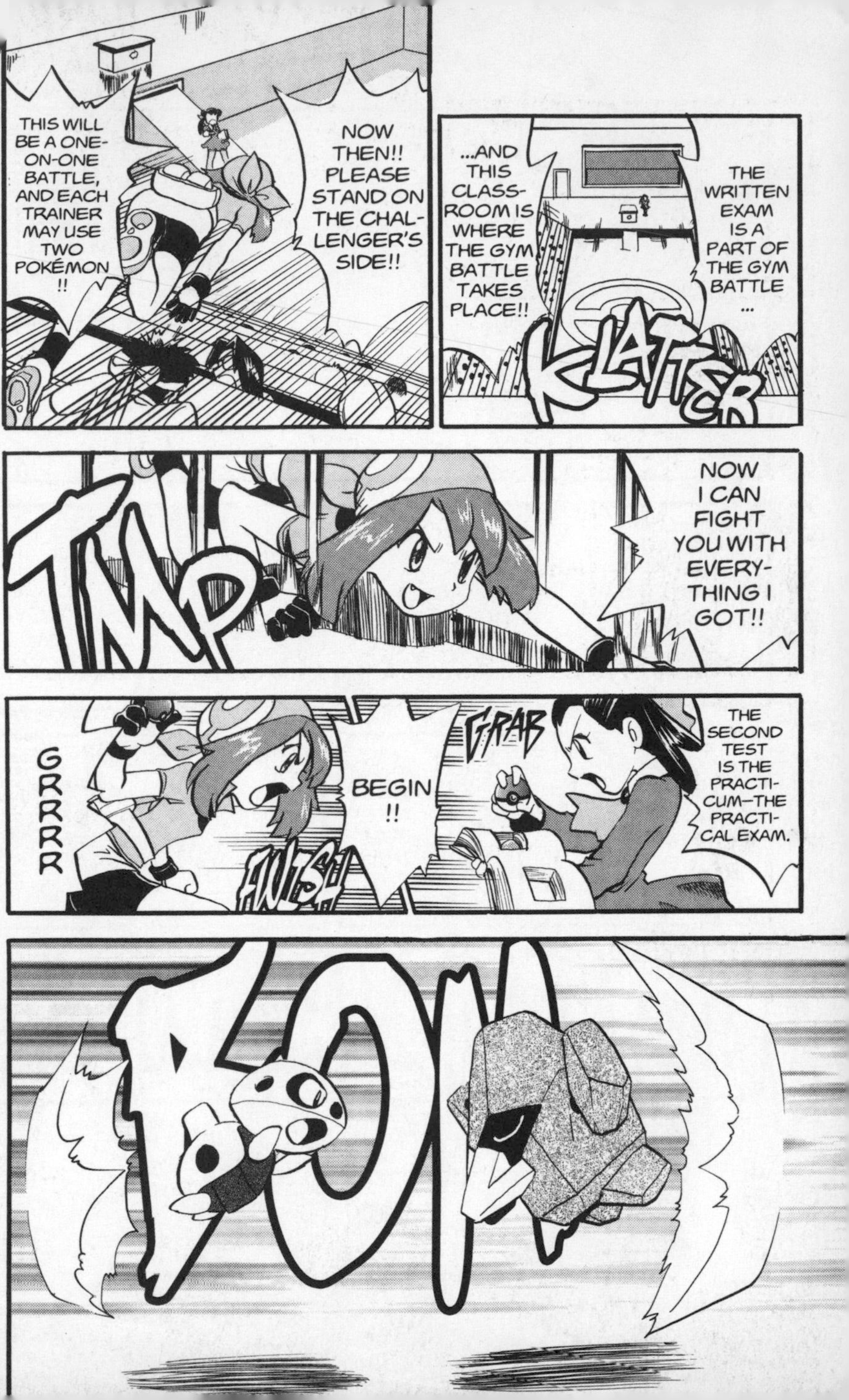
THE WRITTEN EXAM IS A PART OF THE GYM BATTLE ...
...AND THIS CLASSROOM IS WHERE THE GYM BATTLE TAKES PLACE!!
KLATTER
NOW THEN!! PLEASE STAND ON THE CHALLENGER'S SIDE!!
THIS WILL BE A ONE-ON-ONE BATTLE, AND EACH TRAINER MAY USE TWO POKÉMON !!
NOW I CAN FIGHT YOU WITH EVERYTHING I GOT!!
TMP
THE SECOND TEST IS THE PRACTICUM—THE PRACTICAL EXAM.
GRAB
BEGIN !!
FWISH
GRRRR
BOM

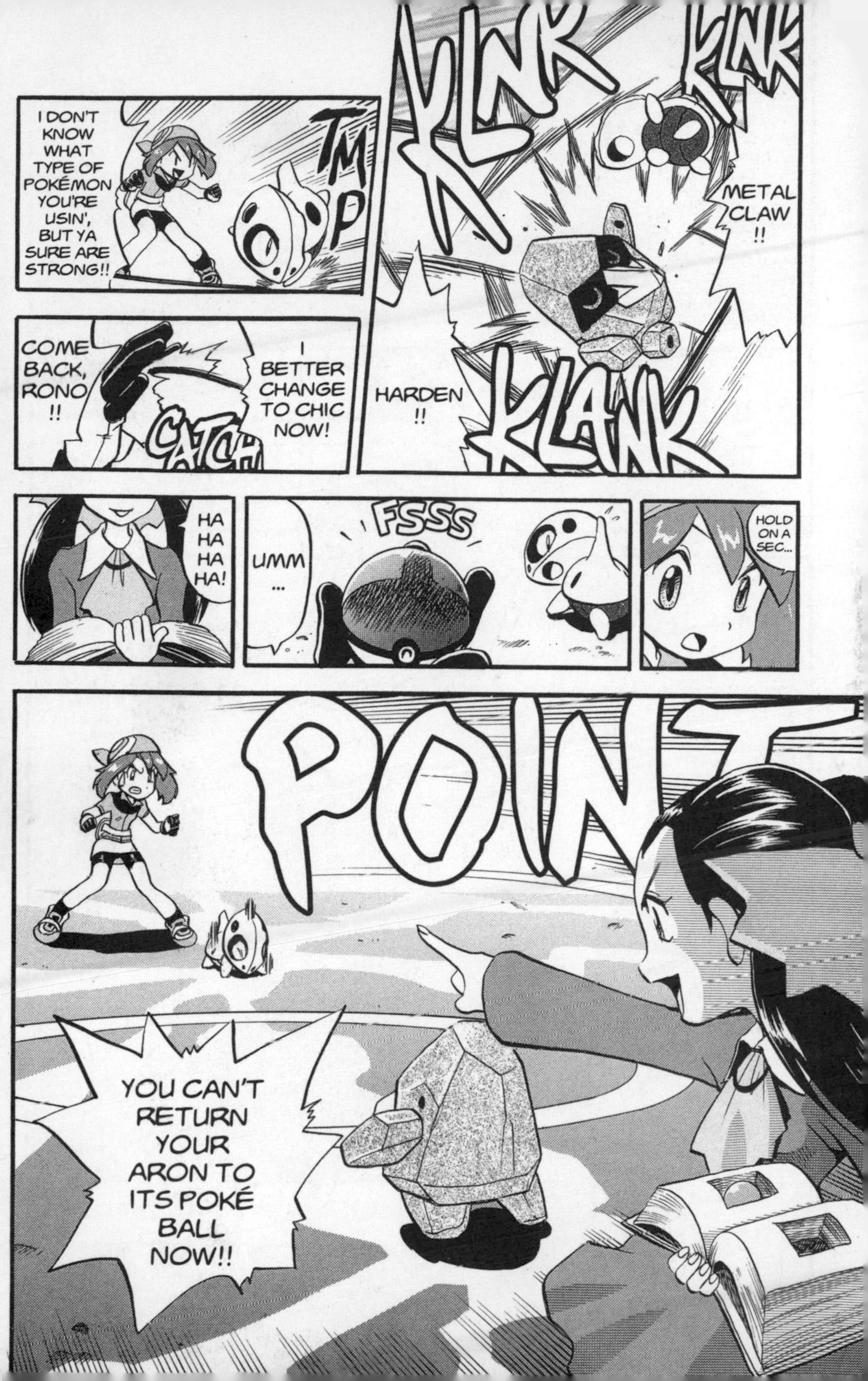
KLNK
KLNK
METAL CLAW!!
HARDEN!!
KLANK
I DON'T KNOW WHAT TYPE OF POKéMON YOU'RE USIN', BUT YA SURE ARE STRONG!!
TMP
I BETTER CHANGE TO CHIC NOW!
COME BACK, RONO!!
CATCH
HOLD ON A SEC...
FSSS
UMM...
HA HA HA HA!
POINT
YOU CAN'T RETURN YOUR ARON TO ITS POKé BALL NOW!!

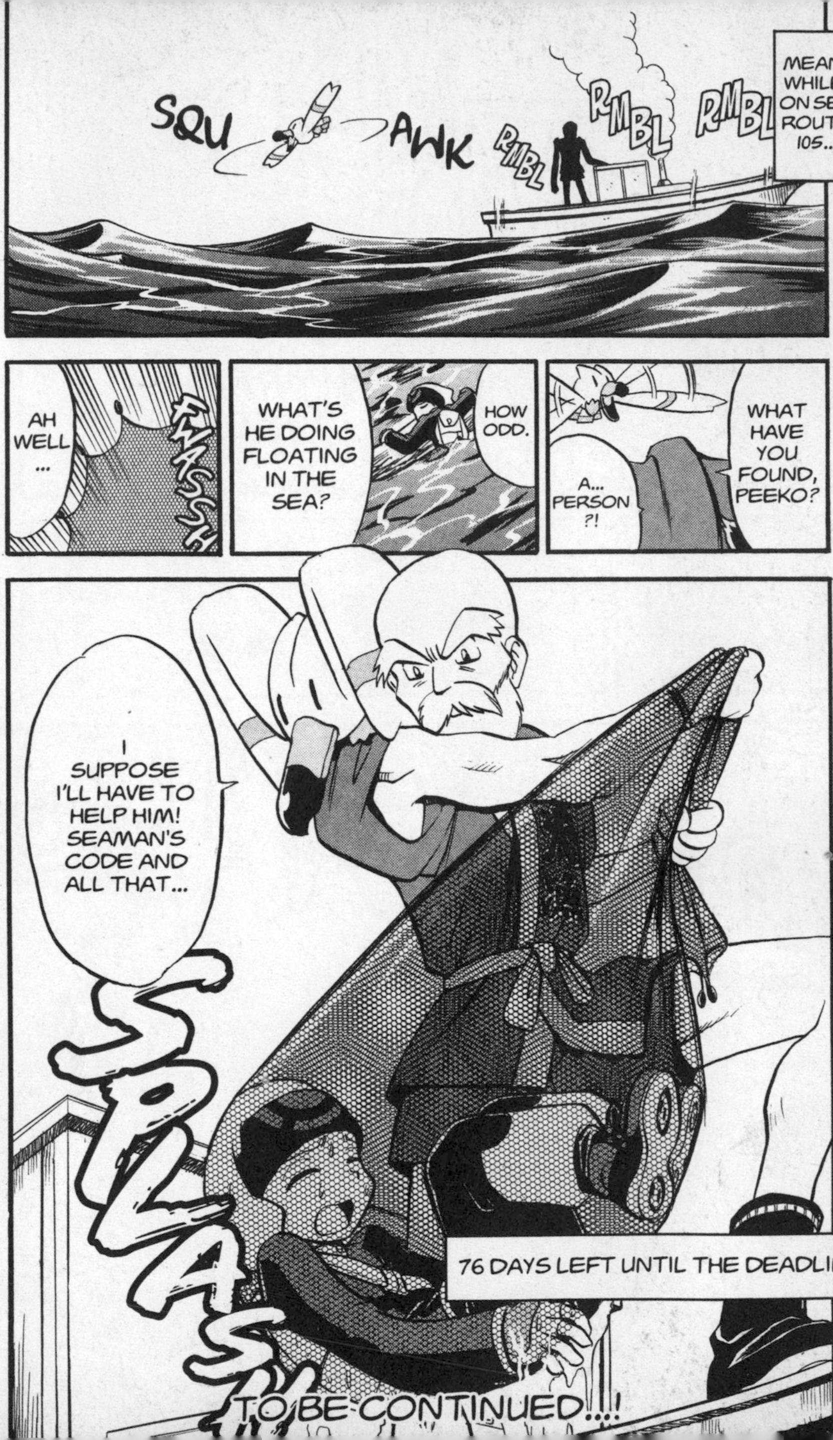
MEAN-WHILE, ON SEA ROUTE 105...
RMBL
RMBL
RMBL
SQU AWK
WHAT HAVE YOU FOUND, PEEKO?
A... PERSON ?!
HOW ODD.
WHAT'S HE DOING FLOATING IN THE SEA?
FWASSH
AH WELL...
I SUPPOSE I'LL HAVE TO HELP HIM! SEAMAN'S CODE AND ALL THAT...
SPLASH
76 DAYS LEFT UNTIL THE DEADLINE!
TO BE CONTINUED...!

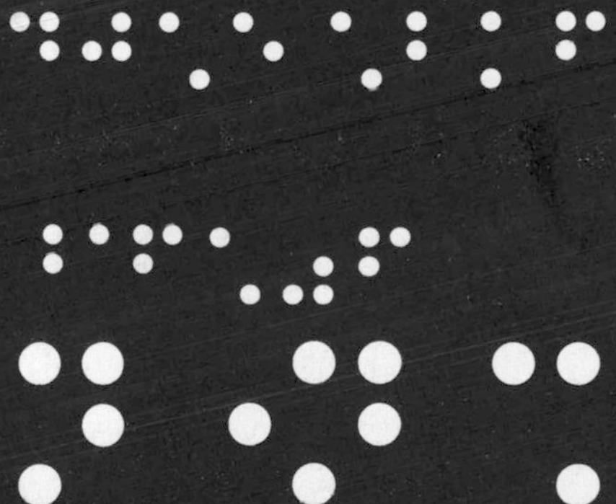

Message from
Hidenori Kusaka

The Hoenn Region is a land of natural wonders! And Ruby and Sapphire are about to spend eighty days in this gigantic area! This volume marks the start of their adventure. And for the first time ever, the two main characters are a boy and a girl. This is complicated and requires me to put a lot of creativity into the story arc. See them compete, grow and maybe fall in love... Enjoy!

Message from
Satoshi Yamamoto

The long Gold, Silver and Crystal story arc has come to a climactic end, and now the Ruby and Sapphire episodes begin! Also, I updated my image to a Swalot! From the very first moment I saw it, I thought its looks, Abilities and even type were just like me—so it's my favorite Pokémon.

READ THIS WAY !!

SWWING

THIS IS THE END OF THIS GRAPHIC NOVEL!

To properly enjoy this VIZ Media graphic novel, please turn it around and begin reading from right to left.

This book has been printed in the original Japanese format in order to preserve the orientation of the original artwork. Have fun with it!

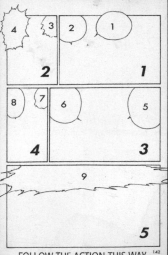

FOLLOW THE ACTION THIS WAY.